I0614919

# THE WHITE SANDS

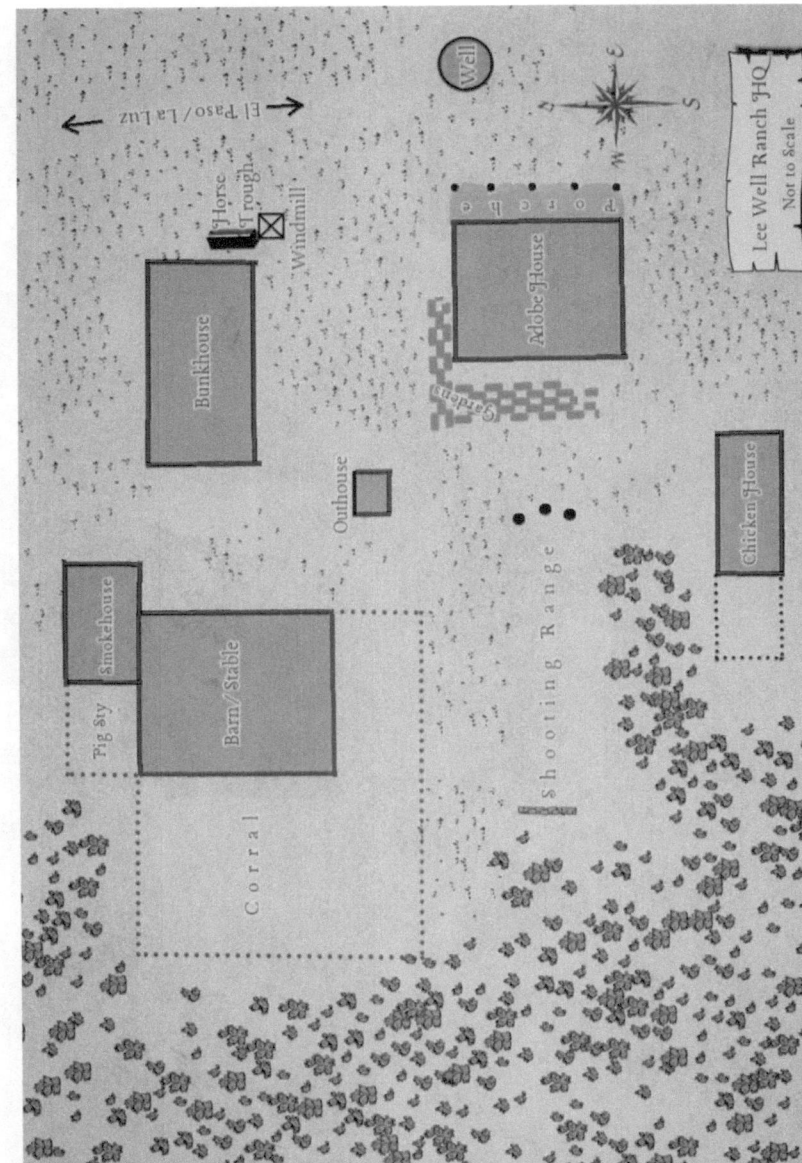

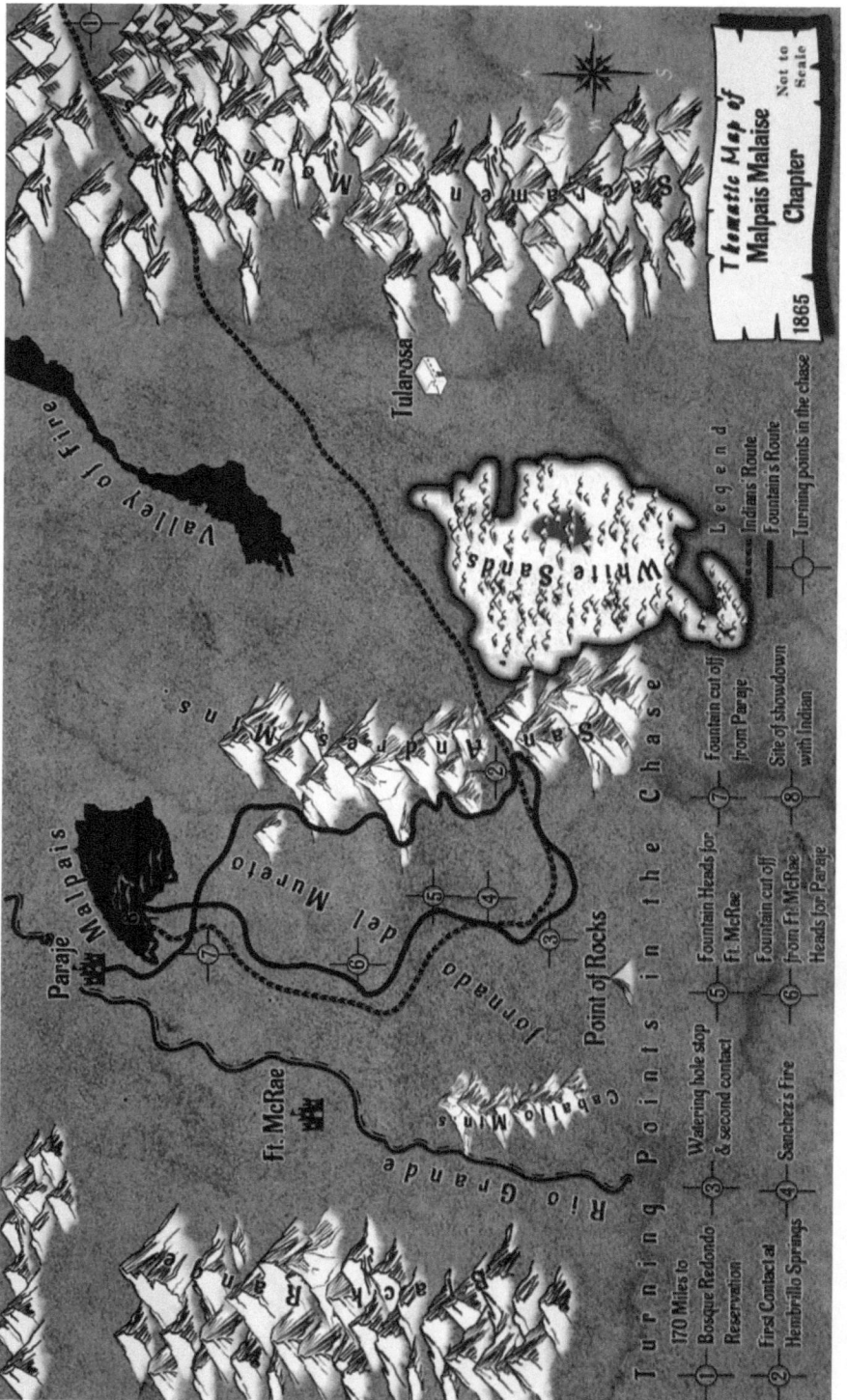

Thematic Map of
Malpais Malaise
Chapter

1865                                                              Not to Scale

**Legend**
Indians' Route
Fountain's Route
Turning points in the chase

**Turning Points in the Chase**

① 170 Miles to Bosque Redondo Reservation
② First Contact at Hembrillo Springs
③ Watering hole stop & second contact
④ Sanchez's Fire
⑤ Fountain Heads for Ft. McRae
⑥ Fountain cut off from Ft. McRae Heads for Paraje
⑦ Fountain cut off from Paraje
⑧ Site of showdown with Indian

Valley of Fire

Tularosa

White Sands

Sacramento Mtns.

San Andres Mtns.

Paraje Malpais

Jornado del Muerto

Point of Rocks

Caballo Mtns.

Ft. McRae

Rio Grande

Black Range

# THE WHITE SANDS

*The Two Valleys Saga: Book Three*

# Mary Armstrong

Enchanted Writing Company

Copyright © 2023

All rights reserved

No part of this book may be reproduced, or stored in a retrieval system, or transmitted in any form or by any means, electronic, mechanical, photocopying, recording, or otherwise, without express written permission of the publisher.

Text copyright © 2023 by Mary Armstrong - All rights reserved. The contents of this work may not be reproduced or transmitted in any way or by any means, whether electronic, mechanical, or otherwise, without the prior written consent of the author.

ISBN: 979-8-218-20792-2

Cover design by White Rabbit Arts at The Historical Fiction Company

Library of Congress Control Number: case #1-12536817451

Printed in the United States of America

*For the people of the Mesilla Valley and Tularosa Basin. We may never agree about what happened on February 1, 1896, but cooperation benefits us all.*

# Contents

# Author's Note

To my readers and the living families of the ancestors portrayed in this book:

The Two Valleys Saga is a fictional story interwoven with historical events that occurred over ten years. It is largely based on modern published accounts and historical newspaper reports. Characterizations of the historical figures and events are fictional and a product of my imagination. Some of my imagined historical characters concur with the known facts of their real lives and I have occasionally quoted from their works, letters, and other writings. I have done my best to use the information I could find to bring the people and times to life for you. However, they are just that, only my impressions. Some of you may not agree. Regardless, I hope you enjoy *The White Sands* and the other books in the series.

As with the first two books in *The Two Valleys Saga*, there are some words or dialogue that may disturb some readers. The decision to include them was difficult. Please understand they are there for authenticity's sake. In the final analysis, as a historical fiction writer, I feel it is my responsibility to convey life and times as they were and not as we might prefer them today.

Please read the first two books before diving into *The White Sands*. I assure you it will make this book more rewarding and enjoyable.

You might wonder how closely this book adheres to history. I depended heavily on historical local newspapers, official records, and scholarly accounts to carry the plot and subplots. There are a few instances where the precise chronology has been adjusted to produce a more entertaining read or where the actions leading to a historical event aren't known and I have had to project what I think happened. Still, I have tried to make all deviations within the spirit of the characters, times and events. If you find yourself questioning my events or characters, by all means, do your own research. That, in fact, is one of the reasons I have written this series — to encourage people to read scholarly accounts of history and to research the times for themselves.

There have been a few questions about Edward Fountain's nickname. When I first started writing the series, the references I used referred to him as "Larlo". Some people have suggested that they felt it was "Lalo". According to my research either is acceptable and I decided not to change.

If you need a further refresher on the primary characters or want to know whether names in this book are historic or fictional, refer to the "Character Refresher" and "Cast of Characters" sections at the back of the book. You will also find a list of "Selected References" there. The paperback version will not include the online reference links. Many of the references noted in the previous books apply to this one, as well.

Now, open your minds to the life and times of 1888 in the wild west New Mexico Territory, and enjoy!

# 1: Another World

**June 1, 1888**

*A shiny, dark stained oak railing and gate separated me and a crowd of glaring people. A young woman with fire in her eyes scowled at me. The judge raised his gavel ... the crowd leaned toward me, poised to leap from their seats and charge ... suddenly a buzzard swept down, hovered in front of me and pecked at my eyes.*

---

**July 1929**

For many years, I thought my nightmares and hallucinations resulted from my accident. However, as I write this memoir, I have discovered that I have had them much longer than that. Until February of 1896, my nightmares varied, but since that fateful day, I have a recurring terror that awakens me in a cold sweat.

My wife says I have them because I am too kind-hearted to have experienced the horrible things this series recounts. However, sometimes I think it results from never feeling that my father truly loved me and that my mother, respecting his feelings, couldn't give me the maternal love a mother should. When they sent me away to the Fountains in Las Cruces I found a life I could never have hoped for in Mexico, but my ill feelings toward my family lingered. We were never close when I lived with them. Even today, after my father has passed, we don't keep in touch.

Perhaps it's the longing for belonging that keeps us apart and draws me to others.

I have read some recently published books by noted psychologists to understand why I am plagued by these dreams. Sigmund Freud, a psychoanalyst of recent note, has suggested that dreams like mine result from repressed feelings. I suppose that makes sense.

Once again, I feel the need to tell you, dear reader, that my memories don't match well with the accounts I have in my hands — journals, diaries, historic newspaper clippings and so on. I mentioned this on the first page of the first book, but I am compelled to remind you that while my memories didn't match what I have written, the facts that I have discovered remind me that our memories can deceive us.

---

## June 1, 1888

I awakened, sweaty, and shaking. "It was only a dream," I whispered. There were footsteps on the roof. I blinked to focus and clear my mind. Pitch darkness — not event he moon's soft glow pierced the drawn curtain at the other end of the room. I gathered myself and rose to sit on the edge of my bed. Mary had smoored the cook stove the night before. Across the room, a glow hinted at the outline of the firebox door.

"Right. Mary … Mary and Nettie … and Oliver," I mumbled to myself.

In the several nights since I had come out of my coma, I often awakened befuddled by my surroundings. It could take me several minutes to realize my circumstances.

Hushed words disturbed the quiet of the early morning hour. "Must be Eph and Ed, the two negro brothers," I mumbled. *They will fetch the horses from the remuda. Nettie said they and some of the other cowboys slept on the adobe roof as the weather got hotter.* Yesterday had been scorching. The rest of the men slept in the bunkhouse.

When I had first awakened from the coma, two women said that a man had brought me to them. The older woman said the man was her son. He told them he had heard a gunshot and a horse's frantic whinny. As he rode up the trail toward the sounds on the San Augustin peak, a pinto horse galloped wildly out of the rocks, stirrups flying. At first, he tried to give chase, but the mare was frantic, and he soon realized he could not catch the riderless horse. He backtracked the pinto and found me, head bloodied and unconscious, laying in the trail. A mountain lion lay at the edge of the path, its hindquarters mangled and bleeding. As the man approached, it clawed at the ground with its front paws in a failed attempt to escape. They said the man's name was Oliver Lee, and that they were his mother Mary, and his niece, Nettie.

They encouraged me and offered suggestions about who I was and why I was on the San Augustin, but nothing helped. A letter in my coat breast pocket was cryptically addressed to '*Dearest I'll call you whatever you like*' and signed '*All my love, Me.*' The body of the letter stated one of the two referenced people was going to visit the other. I couldn't know which person I was, or if the letter had anything to do with me at all. On my third awakened evening, I wanted to record what I had done that day and I requested a pen and paper. After writing the date in the upper left-hand corner, I wrote a few paragraphs.

As I had every morning since I could walk, I sat on the porch after breakfast on an old broken Windsor chair. It lacked its spindled back, and so I leaned against the adobe wall and awaited the sun's glorious entry. As the sky brightened, the eastern stars faded while Mars and Jupiter lingered above the mountain horizon. Oliver passed with a tip of the hat and said, "I'm off to meet the Graham Ranch buyer. 'Spect I'll be back by noon. By the way, I think it's time for you to bunk with the the cowboys."

Negro Ed, Eph's older brother, followed Oliver as he trotted to the north.

I rehashed Mary and Nettie's telling of how Oliver rescued me against the backdrop of the rising sun. I finished before the first sliver of the sun to appeared. As I sipped my coffee, I parsed the women's story for a clue that could connect me to … something.

As the sun warmed the Sacramento peaks, a cool easterly breeze flooded the valley. Nettie emerged from the adobe, with a small Indian blanket and a couple of papers. "I had a thought," she said sweetly as she handed me the papers and spread the blanket over my lap. "You might find a clue if you compare the writin' between your journal and the letter."

My journal entry wasn't as steady as the writing in the letter, but when we compared the two, it was clear I wrote the letter. Nettie tittered as she pointed to the letter's closing: All my Love, Me; and said, "I suppose we could call you 'Me'."

She grinned and while I didn't find her mockery of the moniker 'Me' funny, I had no interest in diminishing her cheer and I smiled in return. Nettie had never been sour in her moods and today, she had a heightened demeanor, perhaps because the previous night, Oliver had told her that her betrothed, George McDonald, would visit the next morning.

Brows arched high, Nettie pointed to the letter. "You must have been wooing her."

From inside the adobe, Mary hollered, "Leave him alone Nettie and get to pickin' the last of those peas and whatever greens you might see."

Nettie paused, because I reasoned, she had changed from her chore clothes into her best dress and tied a pink ribbon in her glistening chestnut hair. She walked to the side of the adobe, where she stood peering to the north, hands on hips, as though she could will George's approach. When he didn't appear, she picked up a small oaken bucket and continued out of sight around the corner.

The blocky Sacramento Mountains western exposure made the view from the porch a favorite spot for the infrequent times a person could relax for a moment. Five Windsor chairs sat against the east wall of the adobe. When I first made it to the adobe doorway, I braced myself and sized up my options for a place to rest. Despite being without its spindled back, I was achy and tired, and the decision was easy. I didn't assume to claim it. That would be too bold for a stranger to assume, but since it was the only one without a back, I thought it the least desirable and continued to use it.

Nettie returned and proceeded to the well twenty feet east of the adobe. She pumped enough water into her bucket to cover the gift of God's grace. The desert spring had been cooler and wetter than usual, and the early kitchen garden crops were prolific. They complemented the usual wild spring herbs. After the severe winter with beans or rice nearly every day, the greens had improved the family's diet and with it their energy and spirits restored. Nettie returned to the porch. She told, didn't ask, me to shell the peas. Mary would blanch greens and peapods, then fry them in bacon grease. She would toss the peas into the stew pot for the noon meal.

A horse and rider loped in and stopped next to the bunkhouse, where the man looped his reins over one of the corral rails next to the watering trough. That must be George, I thought. During our dinner discussions, he told me he and Nettie would marry once he had a sufficiently large stake to make it a go of it. Back then, he worked for the Stuart brothers up toward Coyote Springs. George was thickset but quick and he covered the short distance to the open adobe door in short order. He tipped his hat, tipped it back off his forehead some, then paused and turned to me. "Mornin' Sunshine, ain't they gave you a proper name yet?" I glanced at him. His white banded forehead — never exposed to the sun — caught my eye, and I turned away, shrugged, and grinned. He almost ran into Nettie in the doorway as she recognized his voice and rushed out to meet him.

They were out of sight of Mary and stole a brief hug. Nettie pulled back and said, "I was expectin' ya. It was payday yesterd'y, wasn't it?" They were a handsome couple: she with her petite frame, tiny waist and dark brown hair; and him, stocky and strong, with sandy hair and blue eyes. I wondered which of them their children might favor.

George handed Nettie a small wad of money and said, "I hope you're not puttin' this in the picklin' jar. It's our future, and I'd hate to think it ain't secure." Mary called out from the bedroom, against the *whisk-whisk* of her broom across the plank floor, "Don't you worry George, we got last month's wages tucked away where even you can't find it." The hint of her playful cackle made it clear that George was well accepted by the family elder.

"Here's your fiver back. Are you sure that's enough for ya 'til July?" George tried to give her a peck on the cheek, but Nettie's hand flew up in time to block him. "George! You know that ain't proper." She whispered to him just loud enough for me to hear, "If Aunty Mary had seen that, she'd have taken the broom to ya."

George laughed and placed his hand on the small of her back. "Ain't bein' betrothed good for nothin'?"

Nettie slipped out of his tentative grasp and handed him a fresh biscuit. "You just behave yourself, Georgie." and she giggled with the prospect of their life together, which she had dreamed about over the years since Oliver brought George into the house along Little Elm Creek back in Texas.

George squinted at the five-dollar bill. "Could you give me some real cash? This paper money just ain't got enough heft to it. I'm always afeared that I've accidentally pulled it out of my pocket or somethin'."

From the bedroom doorway, Mary said, "Sorry George, we ain't got nothin' but greenbacks."

George leaned back from the doorway and looked left and right. "Is Oliver hereabouts?"

Mary had returned to her housework and yelled from the bedroom, "He'll be back directly. Had to run up to Grahams to meet a fella what wants to buy the place. Come on in and have a cup of coffee. Nettie, make your man some breakfast." The two of them smiled at the prospect of even this small sanction for them to play house.

After George and Nettie settled into their domestic make-believe, I resumed my assigned chore. I struggled a bit with the dexterity required to shell peas, but with each pea pod, my fingers became nimbler. I had to stop and flex my hands when they cramped, but I could tell that my facility and strength were returning.

The day after I awakened, Mary and Nettie got me out of bed. Step by step, we walked to the kitchen and back to my bed in a corner of the front room. We did that three times that day. It left me exhausted, but every day we did a bit more. Little by little, I grew stronger. Eventually, I could help with some chores around the house.

It occurred to me that no one had shown me how to shell peas … or write, for that matter … someone had taught me before my accident. It seemed logical that other things I knew could clue me into my identity.

When I had finished the peas, Nettie brought them and the rest of the greens into the adobe. I took a walk around the yard. As I circled the barn, I passed George as he left the bunkhouse. Something in the corral caught his eye, and he stopped and squinted. A post must have looked out of plumb because he walked over and leaned against it. It gave way a fraction of an inch. He called to me, "Hey you." I turned, and he motioned me to him. As I trotted toward him, he said, "Why can't Oliver come up with a name for you?" I could manage but a few steps before I slowed to a walk. Something struck me about what George had said.

"Say that again, George."

"What? You mean 'why can't Oliver ...'"

"No, before that."

George hesitated. It seemed he was unaware of anything he had said that was worth repeating. "You mean 'hey you'?"

"Yeah. Hey you, hey-YOU, HEY-you, hey-you."

George chuckled. "What the ... why —"

"That's what I want you ..." and I waved my right arm toward the house "all of you, to call me." It sounded ridiculous, I knew, but there was something about it. I broke it down into the two words and scratched my head. "I know it makes little sense to you, but somehow it does to me."

"Well, alright then, if that's what you want ... Hey-you."

# 2: John Good

George told me to fetch a pail of water while he got a shovel and iron rod. When he returned to the corral, he shoveled soil into the small opening between the ground and the loose post while I sloshed water into the crevice. When he had filled the gap with soil, George tamped the filled hole with the iron rod to compact it and we added more soil and water to finish the job.

As we reset loose posts around the corral, George called me Hey-you, but he made funny faces and snickered. He apologized twice, but I worried people would laugh at me when I told them my name. I almost stopped him, but Hey-you had something to do with me, somehow. I just didn't know what, and I figured it would come to me if I heard it a lot.

As we wrapped up the repairs to the corral, Oliver arrived. "Thanks boys, I was gonna have one of the hands do that tomorrow." Oliver turned his horse loose in the corral as the bell rang for the noon meal.

We settled in with our plate of stew and greens. Mary glanced around the table to make certain she hadn't forgotten something, then asked how it went at Graham's old ranch.

"The fool backed out," said Oliver.

Mary passed a platter of biscuits to Oliver. "Whatever for?"

"He wanted Charlie to hold 'the paper' on it. Charlie told me in no uncertain terms that he needed the full 'cash on the nail' right away 'cause he lost some of his stallions on the trip north and he needed to replace them."

"I'll write Charlie and Emma a letter and let 'em know," replied Nettie.

George rolled his eyes. "Should never have left without sellin' it."

Mary forked a potato, then examined a dark spot on it before holding it in front of her mouth. "It was Emma," she said. "That girl's as nervous as a long-tailed cat in a room full of rockin' chairs. I don't know where she gets it, but it was her that convinced Charlie to move them from Little Elm Creek. The farmers and their barbed wire were squeezin' us, but they didn't have that problem." She popped the hunk of potato in her mouth, followed by a tender morsel of meat.

Oliver shook his head. "Charlie and Emma did what they had to do. But their impatience cost 'em. 'Sides, they were too far from the good range. Told him that when he staked it out." Oliver sipped his buttermilk and took a bite of stew.

George glanced at Nettie. "The folks that have been here longer than us say that dune land they call the White Sands is movin' toward Charlie's place."

Oliver shifted in his chair. "Keep that talk to yerself, George." He finished his buttermilk. "I s'pose we'll need to put someone up there now and then to keep an eye on the place. Shouldn't be a problem for Ed."

We all focused on our meal for a moment. As George tore a biscuit in half, he said, "It's good they're gone now 'cause things are gettin' tighter than a bull's ass … rear end during fly season." Mary glared, while Oliver gave him a brief but stern look, and Nettie grimaced. "Pardon my impudence," George said, as he realized his cursing. "Forgot where I was."

Mary reached for what she called her Methodist Bible, which was never far away. "Nettie, you've got your work cut out for you when it comes to makin' this young man a child of God, but I hope you'll manage it."

George frowned, bent his head for another spoonful of stew, then renewed by a thought, changed the subject. "I think we have a name for the boy."

I focused on my plate as I wished I hadn't suggested it to George. 'Hey-you' wasn't a name anyone would aspire to be called.

"He wants to be called Hey-you." He accented the *you* and ended with a bit of a chuckle. What he said didn't resemble what had stricken me as familiar before, and I kept my focus on my plate.

With the slight tilt of my head, I saw Mary and Nettie's forlorn glances. Oliver forked a chunk of pork.

I kept my eyes on my plate. *What could I say? It just ... just sounded familiar. I don't know why, but I hoped it would help me remember ... something.*

Oliver pulled a piece of bread and pointed it toward George. "So what's happened on the range up your way now?"

"It's John Good ... again." Mary and Nettie groaned, but Oliver appeared unaffected. A short time after they had arrived from Texas, George and Oliver had found a small spring-fed pool on the open range near Coyote Springs. After they had dug it out and made it into a dependable watering hole for their cattle, Good tried to run them off, but he underestimated the two young men. Sometime later, the situation resolved in favor of George and to Good's indignation when Eli Reynolds offered a good trade of several breeding heifers for the watering hole.

Oliver swallowed a mouthful of bread, sopped with stew gravy, then said, "Tell me."

"I should have told you this last week, but I thought Good's shenanigans was over." George took a drink of his wine and wiped his mouth with his sleeve. "Last Saturd'y I was comin' out of Myer's Mercantile, and Good threatened me."

Nettie gasped and once again Mary reached for her Bible.

For the first time, I became involved with table talk. "Why? Did you do something to him since the watering hole situation?"

Oliver smirked, "Man like Good, it don't take no real provocation. It's all in his head."

George wiped his mouth with his napkin. "Well, for the roundup last month, Mr. Stuart told me not to let John hornswoggle any of our calves into his herd. Sure enough, I had a calf ready to brand Triangle T Cooper, and Jim Cooper was standin' right there behind me. John's son Walter stepped in and said his daddy told him that any calf that didn't have a brand was theirs. He tried to force me to brand him with their *Seven-H-el*. Well, Jim and I had seen that calf follow his Cooper branded mama. Walter grabbed his fired brand and made a move to push me out of the way. I whacked his iron with the next one in the fire and Walter's went flyin', sparks 'n all. Before he could do or say more, I branded the calf. Walter backed off and put his hand on his six-gun. None of Walter's men were at the brandin' site, and there were small ranchers behind me. I told him, 'Walter, I wouldn't do that if'n I was you. Every one of these men will fill you full of holes before you can get a second shot off.'"

Nettie gasped, while Oliver smiled and said, "You handled it well. Us small ranchers gotta stick together." Oliver stared at George for a moment. "That ain't all, is it."

George reached for his cup of water. "No, but I think it's run its course,"

Oliver said nothing. He just sat there, fork held chest high over his plate, and waited.

"Honest, Oliver. He ain't gonna bother me no more."

Oliver continued his stare. "Tell me."

"T'weren't nothin' as bad as it sounds, but when John stopped me in the street in La Luz, he said we needed to shake hands and calm things down. He said he heard I was workin' for the Stuarts and seein' how them and John were friends we should bury the hatchet. Well, you know me Oliver, I ain't gonna shake no man's hand just cause he says I gotta, and I told him so. As you might imagine, John took offense. He said, 'I could have you fired. Is that what you wanted?' I didn't give him much notion either way, but then he says, 'Well, goddam it' — sorry ladies — 'no so and so like you are gonna work for Stuart if I have to kill him to stop it.'"

Mary reached for her Bible again and Nettie put her hand over half her mouth in alarm. Oliver, his eyes locked on George, waited for the rest of the story.

George took a deep breath. "Well, he went for his six-shooter. As he pulled it out of his pants, I guess the trigger got stuck on his shirt and he lost his grip and the gun fell down his pants leg."

Such a scene amused me, but the room was solemn, and I restrained myself to a faint smile.

"So, I pulled my gun, and I stuck it in ol' John's gut and said, 'Well, by God, I think I'll just keell you.'" He put up his hands and took a couple of steps back and I kicked his gun toward him, but he motioned for one of his hands to fetch it. I guess he figured if'n he picked it up, I might just unload on him. I think the situation's resolved. Don't you?"

"Aren't you afrai … concerned that John might … might …." Nettie said, putting her hand over her mouth.

"Nah, John came to me to settle it and I think he knows he better just steer clear of me and mine." George smiled, but Nettie frowned.

"What about Walter? If he tells his daddy, won't that mean he has to do somethin'?" asked Nettie.

"I don't think Walter will say anythin' to his daddy. His pride won't let him. He stayed away from the brandin' site after that. I think he knows I'll embarrass him if he tries to tangle with me again." Nettie's question seemed to tinge George's confidence. His expression belied his words, and I could see that he wasn't cock-sure about the situation.

Nettie and Mary exchanged concerned looks while Oliver saluted George with a fresh cup of buttermilk. "You handled it well, my friend, but don't be too certain that this is the end of it."

Later, Nettie told me that a couple of weeks before they arrived in the Tularosa, they heard that John Good had gunned down his neighbor Charlie Dawson in the streets of La Luz. She murmured to herself, "I wonder what ever happened to his woman … what was her name?" She paused and turned to me and said, "Susan … no Sue … Sue Dawson … Don't know why, but I've heard some folks call her Bronco Sue."

Now that struck me. I knew that name — but why and from where?

It had been another cold, wet winter. A cowboy named Virgil — he never offered his last name — had come south from the Morley Ranch near Datil when spring finally broke. He said scores of bleached white antelope bones littered the Plains of St. Augustine where the previous summer they had competed with the Morley's steers for rangeland browse.

In his southern twang, Virgil said, "Mr. Ray, Ray Morley — I always called him Mr. Ray — anyways, he rode with me on his way to Magdalena and while his face showed otherwise, he said the demise of the antelope would mean a greater share of browse for his herd."

Later, I asked Virgil what brought him to the Tularosa. "I cain't handle the cold. So I headed south. If'n it's still too cold here next winter, I'ma gonna head for San Antone."

---

That afternoon, I watched over the grazing herd as I sat on Ol' Nasty with one hand planted on the saddlehorn. He was a pinto with a solid black head, and he felt familiar somehow. Eph, one of the Lee's negro cowboy brothers, sat a bay about twenty yards to my left. Virgil, to my right, trotted down the line a bit on his roan to discourage a steer that seemed intent on wandering toward the White Sands.

It was a hot, dry day. Summer was upon us and at lower elevations, the chewed-off browse barely poked through the gritty excuse for desert soil. Oliver decided to move the herd further up the canyon to fresh grass and water. Several others of Oliver's hands scattered to gather strays and any mavericks they might come across. My job was to stay where I was — an anchor behind the center of the herd, while Eph, Virgil and the other cowboys kept them from wandering away.

Ahead of Eph and Virgil were the flankers and then the swingmen. Oliver and two swingmen singled out some steers they knew were leaders. We did everything slow and easy. They gently waved their hats and got the leaders to move in the right direction. Oliver and then Eph and Virgil had cautioned me against frantic movements that could spook the herd, but once they moved in the right direction, they kicked up a dust cloud such that I doubted anyone would have noticed had I stood on my saddle and did somersaults. Still, I did as I was told and ate dust.

---

Rumors filtered south that millions of head of cattle starved or froze to death from Colorado to Montana the previous winter. The winter of '86-'87 might have been worse, but there were far fewer head of cattle up north then. Great herds continued to move north through the summer of '87 for open range with dependable water and grass. By the time word got to the ranchers about the herd die-offs in '86-'87, it was too late, and ranchers thought two such winters in a row were unlikely. Meanwhile, ranchers in the southern plains of west Texas, New Mexico and Arizona experienced better-than-average weather for grass production. But the die-offs in the north caused a shortage of beef and 'on the hoof' prices escalated, which led ranchers to add stock and that led to over-grazing of rangeland. A three-year drought was on the horizon, but nobody could forecast that.

The match was lit, and the tinder was the range itself.

# 3: George McDonald

**June 10, 1888**

I was never quite certain whether Oliver was shy or just secretive around strangers. At home amongst family, he was always eager to share his exploits and plans around the supper table. He would turn only twenty-two that month, but it was clear the family took their lead from him. After a week or so, they must have either forgotten I was there, decided I had become a part of the family, or just couldn't restrain their excitement over his recent accomplishments and plans.

One evening as we finished supper, with no cue, Mary pushed out her chest, raised her chin, turned to me, and said, "Before Perry came with his new wife in the spring last year, Oliver and his ranch hands had claimed this place, added the back rooms, repaired the adobe and barn and built a bunkhouse."

She paused. Before Nettie could continue, Mary said, "When he saw what a chore it was for us to haul water in from the canyon, he ferreted where it flowed under the ground and dug that well out front." She beamed and added, "It's the best water on the trail between La Luz and Ysleta, Texas."

Mary's pride for her youngest son's accomplishments was always clear, for even a glance toward him brightened her face. She must have wanted to enlighten me for several days because they just poured from her as Nettie smiled. Oliver, head down over his plate, continued to eat. "He built an acequia in the mountains and is growin' alfalfa with the water. Then he got control of the stock tanks at Grapevine Horse Camp." She turned to Oliver, who grimaced at her accolades. Unphased, Mary's eyes glistened. "How you ever got that rancher to let you take over those tanks, I do not know."

Oliver mumbled, "He made it hard. He didn't have to."

After several suppers, I became confused about a family member named Emma. She seemed to be married to both Perry and Charlie Graham. One evening, when Nettie joined me on the porch after she finished her chores, I asked her about it.

Nettie snickered. "No, no, no. But I can see that could be a might confusin'." She shifted in her chair and began, "We've got two Emmas. One's a blood relative and the other ain't."

I must have still looked confused, because her brow wrinkled. "You know Charlie Graham?"

I nodded. "Just by name."

"Well, Charlie's married to Emma Altman, Aunt Mary's oldest daughter."

"Oh, so, Perry's sister?"

"Yep, and Perry married the other Emma who comes from the Wooten's of Abilene. They got married a little before we moved out here."

"So, how do you know which one you're talking about?"

"We've mostly called our Emma, Em, but now with the other Emma comin' we are tryin' to make sure we *always* call Mary's daughter Em and when we talk about Perry's Emma, we always call her Emma. Got it?"

I scratched the back of my neck. "I think so, but how do you fit into this family? You call her aunt, but where's your folks?"

"My folks? I never knew 'em. Aunt Mary raised me from when I was a baby."

"It's none of my business, I suppose, but do you know what happened to them?"

Nettie looked away and squinted at the orangish tinted Sacramento escarpment. "I honestly don't know. When I was old enough, Aunt Mary told me she wasn't my mother, but when I asked her where my mother was, she just said, 'it's too awful to tell, darlin'. You're best off not knowin'." Nettie turned back to me and half-whispered, "My last name's Fry. that was my daddy's name."

---

The cowboys had completed hard work of the spring and early summer, and they had herded the cattle and horses from spring to summer range in the canyons. There, the terrain and plentiful browse secured the herds. While I was with Oliver, he often pointed out that other ranchers had overgrazed the range north of Lee Well. Not long after I arrived, he shifted expansion of his ranch to the south and he established The Sacramento Cattle Company with that in mind. In 1887, he and his El Paso investors established satellite ranches and line camps manned by one or two cowboys. They focused their acquisitions in the southern part of the Tularosa between the Sacramento and Jarilla Mountains beyond Culp Mountain.

Meanwhile, Virgil, Eph, and his brother Ed, and a couple other hands, and I rode into the San Andres Canyon every day, where Oliver kept most of his northern herd. The Hackberry and Cottonwood springs were steer magnets. Therefore, we rarely had to chase strays into the brushy canyon side slopes. As a rule, we just watched for the odd cow and calf that should have been with the cow-calf herd. Occasionally, we would come across cows that hadn't calved, an animal that was in distress or a maverick that we could note for the next round up. Sometimes, I would visit the herd in San Andres Canyon and the other hands rode to Lead and Muleshoe Canyons to check the smaller herds there.

When they first settled in the Tularosa, half-brother Perry Altman chose his ranch site west of La Luz, while Oliver seemed drawn to the open range further south. Earlier settlers had tied up just about everything from La Luz north and up the Tularosa Creek Canyon to the Mescalero Reservation. Oliver, Eph, and Ed scouted the canyons for weeks that gouged east into the Sacramento range from La Luz to Grapevine Canyon. Dog, Escondido, and Grapevine, which was over ten miles south of Lee Well, offered the best conditions for grazing. Beyond those front range canyons lay plentiful water in the Sacramento River.

Dog Canyon was the 'king' of the front canyons because the water was the best. There was little browse in the narrow canyon, but the spring-fed creek was as dependable as any water on the east side of the Tularosa. There was one problem — a squatter by the name of Frank Rochas had set up right at the mouth of the canyon. He kept a small herd of cattle, but his gardens and orchard were testimony to the water quality and quantity, and Oliver wanted it.

At supper that evening, Oliver, ever the enterpriser, and always shrewd, suggested that he wanted control of Dog Canyon. He hoped to befriend the old man. He reasoned that Frenchy, as he was known, was content to be alone, and alone, he could only use a fraction of the water that Dog Canyon provided. Another rancher might have got rid of Frenchy, but Oliver knew the law and time were on his side. Old timer Frenchy hadn't filed a land claim.

Oliver bided his time during those first several years. He'd stop by Frenchy Rochas' place on his way back from his southern holdings. A relationship developed that eventually paid off. Oliver's ranching empire would stretch all the way to the Texas state line.

Oliver would mention that he had stopped in to see Mr. Rochas when he reviewed his day's activities at the supper table. On the surface, it seemed neighborly enough. Years later, I remembered the size of the rocks that Frenchy had positioned for corrals and sheds. I decided Frenchy must have had some help and Oliver would have offered it without condition.

---

My journal said Tuesday, June twelfth, but it was much like any other Tularosa late spring day. The morning was clear and comfortable, and the afternoon sprouted puffy clouds that engendered thoughts of an evening thunderstorm, but when supper was done, the sunset painted sky left us without even the sweet scent of a shower that dried out before it hit the ground.

George and Perry had come by the previous Sunday for the family's traditional midafternoon dinner. Beef roast with root vegetable aromas wafted through the room. The talk around the table began when George asked no one in particular, "How's that new Altman child doin'?"

"Oh, she's doin' real good," replied Perry.

"Perry's goin' to El Paso to pick up the baby and Emma Saturday," interjected Nettie.

Oliver cut the roast into wide slices and George forked one, but paused with a confused look on his face as the hunk of meat dripped onto his plate. "Why'd she have to go back to Buffalo Gap to have the baby? Ain't they got no birthers here 'bouts?" George dropped the roast beef onto his plate with a thunk. The meat juices splattered onto the table, and he wiped them with a quick swipe of his shirt sleeve, much to Nettie's chagrin.

Mary passed the biscuits to Nettie. "Emma's mother insisted that she didn't want no daughter of hers havin' a baby in the wilderness. She said it nearly kilt her when Emma was born. When we told her folks we were leavin' the area, they insisted she come back to them when we was sure she was pregnant."

Oliver, knife and fork in either hand, said, "She's been gone so long, the kids probably walkin' and got teeth by now."

He and George laughed, while Nettie and Mary frowned. Mary said, "The child's just two months old. Emma held out here as long as she could afore her mama threatened to come git her herself. I think she's been gone about five months now."

The room quieted for a bit until Nettie turned to Mary. "I'd like to go with Perry to do some shoppin' for the weddin' and to help Emma out with the youngin'."

George nodded, and the conversation swung to the subject of rising beef prices and with it the men's enthusiasm for Oliver's long-range plans for a new ranch headquarters at the mouth of Dog Canyon.

"What about the old hermit?" asked George.

"Mr. Rochas?" said Oliver. "He's harmless."

"I heard that after that kid Morrison shot him a couple years ago, he armed-up."

Oliver shook his head. "Just a 12-gauge. That kid was an idiot."

George shrugged. "What say we take a ride down there before I head back to Coyote Springs?"

Oliver nodded.

Nettie wanted to talk with George about her growing wedding plans. "George, you'll come with me to El Paso, won't you?"

"Why?" he asked, "I can't do nothin for Perry's youngin'."

"Well, just because it's *your* weddin', too. You'll be needin' a new suit of clothes, won't you?"

"What's wrong with what I've got on? I wore my Sunday best."

"Oh, George. Please? We can spend some time with Perry and stay in that nice hotel ..." Mary gave her a stern look. "... separate rooms, mind you." A flustered Nettie realized he wouldn't go. She gave up with a frown and an aggressive fork to the potato she had on her plate.

But George persisted, "Why? I ain't got no money for a room — you got it all. 'Sides, there ain't nothin' you want to do there that needs me. You'll do just fine. Mr. Stuart probably wouldn't give me two days in a row off anywhoo."

This seemed like a good chance for me to make my request. "I'd like to go with you. It would be a long ride for me, but you'll take the wagon, won't you? I only have this one set of winter clothes. It's hot out on the range and a hat would be nice." Mary frowned. "I didn't have much money when you found me, but I could work off whatever the clothes cost." I wasn't sure whether to address my request to Mary or Oliver, and I glanced back and forth between them.

For whatever reason, Mary took the lead. "I 'spect you've done worked off whatever a set of range clothes will cost us. You can go, but Perry will carry the money and," she turned to Nettie, "you make certain that he gets good quality work clothes that will wear, understand? These clothes you wore when Oliver found you look like they're for city folk."

We both nodded, and I wondered if that was another clue to my identity. Perhaps I was from El Paso or Las Cruces.

Tuesday evening, as I sat in my broken Windsor chair, a rider came out of Muleshoe Canyon on a dead run as a dust cloud kicked up behind him. I wondered if I should alert someone. Before I could rise, Eph stood next to me "Ah, yes", he said. "That's Mr. Stuart's man, Benito Montoya, on their prized buckskin. Smells like trouble. I'd better git Mr. Oliver."

Benito didn't slow his horse until the last second when he yanked on the reins and the horse reared back, throwing stones and dirt as the horse stumbled and struggled to stay upright. Before

Benito had swung his leg around to dismount, he asked for Mr. Lee. Montoya's horse, a mare, was 'wind-broke'. She was lathered up in a full sweat and blood spurted from her nostrils as she wheezed, and her flanks heaved with exhaustion.

"Eph went to fetch him." *Had he ridden that horse hard all the way from Coyote Springs?*

Mary and Nettie appeared at the doorway as they wiped their hands on their aprons.

Oliver and Eph ran from the barn, and Benito hurried to meet them halfway.

*He doesn't want the women to hear. Something's happened.*

# 4: The Beginning of the End

Everything stopped while they talked for what seemed like hours. The birds didn't chirp, and Shorty stopped pounding on an iron part that needed repaired. A cloud swept in and obscured the ever-present sun. The landscape assumed an ominous cast. Oliver asked questions, while Eph shook his head with despair. Benito apologized over and over for his poor English, but in the end his meaning was clear. Mary and Nettie asked me who that Mexican was and why he had ridden that horse so hard. All I could do was shake my head and say that I didn't know. After a few moments, the three men approached us. Oliver signaled he wanted to speak with Mary and Nettie alone. Eph, Benito, and I moved a few yards away, while Oliver took off his hat and stood before Mary and Nettie on the porch.

Oliver patted his hat against his side a few times. He started to say something, but his voice cracked. When the words came, they came in a high-pitched whine of a man who held back tears, "He's gone Nettie, they done got him."

Nettie's knees buckled and her arms went limp as she swooned, but Mary and Oliver caught her as she fell backward. Mary stared at Oliver, wide-eyed and mouth wide open. Oliver could only shake his head, for he also bore the loss of his longest and best friend.

Nettie came around enough that she and Mary could turn and stumble into the house. I thought I heard a sob from Oliver, but maybe it was just the sound of his boots against the gritty dirt as he shifted between his feet. He wiped his mouth and bit his lip. Benito and Eph watched him as they awaited his direction.

With the sun nearly down and his position in the shadows of the porch, it was difficult to see, but when he turned, I thought his eyes glistened with tears before he put on his hat and pulled it down low on his forehead.

He crept toward us with his head bowed. It was quiet except for the distant howl of an awakened wolf and the crunch of Oliver's boots against the barren desert dirt. A rare east breeze brought the scents of the Sacramentos flooding down the canyons. When he stopped in front of us and looked up, his despair and indecisiveness had turned to anger and resolve.

"Who did this Benito?"

Benito shrugged, put up his hands and shook his head. "Not know, señor."

"Did you find George?"

"Sí."

As best he could in his broken English, Benito told how George didn't come back to the bunkhouse for supper and so some of the cowboys went to look for him. He said he knew George had a special place where he liked to relax near a spring under an overhanging ledge. Benito said when he got to the spring, George looked like he was asleep from a distance. His hat was in his lap, his legs crossed, and his head pitched against the rock behind him.

Benito swallowed hard. "When I got close ... señor," Benito sighed, and he switched to Spanish as he pointed to his forehead. "*Había sangre y un agujero de bala ... aquí.*"

Eph looked away, and Oliver scowled. I wasn't sure they understood, and so I translated, "There was blood from the bullet hole in his ..."

Before I could finish, Oliver held out his hand to stop me. "I understood well enough."

"I leave heem there señor and go to tell señor Stuart. He tell me come here. One of the *vaqueros* there weeth heem. Weeth George, I mean."

Oliver, hand still over his mouth, turned to look at the porch, but Mary and Nettie were inside. He looked west, where a fragment of the sun had illuminated a dying day a few moments before.

When he turned back, he was decisive. "Well, I guess with no moon we won't see nothin'. 'Sides, we know who dunit and they might just come here next. Benito, I think you had better stay here for the night. It's gonna be too dark for ridin' back."

Eph's brow wrinkled. "But, Mr. Oliver," said Eph, "we ain't done nothin' to the Goods. Why would they come here?"

"Eph, you don't know that man like I do, and George got him and his son Walter plenty riled up. They all know George is like a brother to me and engaged to Nettie. I don't want to be caught unawares if they come, and so we will be ready. Eph, you go get the boys from the bunkhouse and tell 'em to load up on ammunition and bring every piece of iron they got. I want everybody on the roof of the adobe where they can have the parapet for cover."

"Hey-you, can you handle a shotgun?" I nodded I could, although I wasn't sure how I knew that.

"Follow me."

We went inside. He sat me at the supper table while he went into the backroom. When he returned, he put a 12-gauge double-barreled shotgun on the table in front of me, along with a dozen shells. "Load-up."

Again, I didn't know how I knew what to do, but I broke the gun down, slid a shell into each chamber and snapped it back together. I checked the safety, and it was on.

Oliver nodded his approval. "Now, I want you to sit there, ready to fire, unless you hear the password before the door opens."

"What is the password?"

Without a second thought, he said, "Loyalty. I'll let the boys on the roof know before I head out."

"If you don't mind me asking, where are you going … in case I need you for something?"

"I'll be in a place where I can see if anyone comes our way, although I'll probably hear 'em first. When I do, I'll come down to give y'all fair warnin' so we can be ready."

A worn-down Mary appeared at the adobe doorway. She took a couple of steps onto the porch, and Oliver turned to see her. "What're you doin' son?"

"It's too dark to go up to Coyote Springs tonight, Ma, but I think we should be prepared for an attack." He explained how he had positioned everyone. "You take that four-ten with those special loaded shells I made and wait there in the bedroom with Nettie. If they get past Hey-you, you can unload on 'em with all you got. How's Nettie takin' it?"

Mary shook her head and looked at the floor, then looked out toward the mountains. "Poor thing just cried herself asleep. She'll be alright. You know yerself just how tough she is, but it'll take a while."

She turned on her heel to fetch the shotgun and shells Oliver mentioned, but stopped after a couple of steps, and spun to face Oliver. "But we can't let this stand, Oliver. You know we can't, not after what happened on Little Elm Creek … we just can't."

Oliver nodded. "I know ma, I know."

It was a long night. Coyotes howled, and desert breezes rose and fell. The earthy scent of the desert was as constant as the mountainous backdrop to the Tularosa Basin. But that night, it was strong and I could smell it even inside the adobe.

When you wait for something that might happen, time crawls, and it felt like I passed a week's worth of night-times. I might have dropped off asleep a time or two but became instantly alert when Mary came from the bedroom or Oliver shouted, "Loyalty" before he opened the front door to check on me.

Mary came out along about three-thirty in the morning and fired up the cookstove for breakfast. By sunrise, Mary and Nettie had fed everyone, and Oliver had laid out how the day would go. He reasoned that if John Good wanted to scatter one of his herds, there was little he could do about that and if he stampeded them, most wouldn't wander far anyway with the sparse water situation. He figured that if Good wanted to do him real harm, he burn down their barn or some such thing. Therefore, he kept most of his hands in the ranch yard for the day. The bulk of them worked to expand the pig sty while others did some neglected repairs. He sent his best marksmen to strategic locations to wait and sent the rest to the various canyons to check on his widespread herd.

"Hey-you," Oliver called out to me. "I know you ain't no artist, but I noticed you're handy with a pen. I want you to come with me and draw a likeness of George and the way things are before we bury him. You can also write down what we see in case it's needed for the law, if they come. I s'pose they've got a grand jury of sorts in 'Cruces."

*Grand jury?*

There was something about that. It seemed familiar. I stored it away for future consideration while Eph and Ed saddled our horses. The ride to Coyote Springs would be a long ride for me. At a lope, the trip would take close to three hours to get to the Stuart Ranch headquarters. We didn't know how far it was from the there to the hidden spring where George lay. Oliver had a pick and shovel strapped to his horse and he insisted I carry a pistol, which he provided with a gun belt. "You don't have to use it, but just havin' it in sight'll discourage most."

We stopped at Jim Cooper's place a few miles east of Tularosa and traded horses. Jim hadn't heard about George. When Oliver told him what had happened, Jim looked at us in disbelief. "Are you sure it's George?"

When we assured him it was, Jim insisted on coming with us. "George stood up for my brand against them Goods. It probably got him kilt and, well, I figure I owe him a decent burial."

Oliver couldn't disagree with that and Jim came along. When we arrived at the Stuart's ranch, old man Stuart stood on his porch with his hands his pockets. His Winchester was slung under his armpit and against his wrist.

"I'm right sorry about George, Oliver. One of my men's been up there all night makin' sure the varmints couldn't get to his body. Do you need a hand gettin' him home?"

Oliver just stared at him. "Why do you think I brought these men along with me?"

"Just tryin' to be neighborly Oliver, ain't no sense in startin' somethin' now. John tells me they had a bit of a tussle over at La Luz a couple of weeks ago. Now, I want you to know John, nor Walter, nor any of his men have been here for the last several days, so…"

"So, what ol' man.? So you want to clear that no good … . Never mind. Just have your negro boy there show us the way." The old man waved both hands in dismissal of Oliver and then waved to his negro boy to show us the way to the hidden spring. The spot was further up the mountain and the wash narrowed to where we needed to walk our horses. When we got within hearing distance someone shouted, "who goes there?"

We stopped, and Oliver replied we had come to claim George's body. The man must have been weary from spending the night next to a dead body because, without a word, he passed us before we got within fifty feet of George. As he passed, he said, "I ain't touched him.". The negro boy followed him as the man scrambled down the mountainside.

It was a peaceful spot. A much stronger musky smell supplanted the desert dirt scents, with hints of moisture-loving plants that would relax someone that had been breathing caliche dust all day. While the water gurgled from the spring, several birds chirped and sang while they flitted through the shady mesquite trees. It was an ideal place for a nap or just to settle oneself after a full day's work.

The temperatures had fallen in the canyon overnight and the body hadn't stiffened, but with the rising sun, the corpse would soon go into rigor mortis. I sat down on a rock and took out my pencils and pens and the wide board I had brought to use as a portable desk.

I had never seen a corpse before and had thought myself lucky. Lucky I was. The scene was haunting. But it was also oddly peaceful when I could focus on anything but the bullet hole in the middle of his forehead, the now dried blood across his right eye and the scatter of bone fragments and flesh across the rocks. Oliver and Jim looked around the area for any clues they could find while I did my crude sketches. They found some hoof prints and talked about whether they should try to track the killer. I showed them my sketches and descriptions, and they nodded their approval.

I pointed to Ol' Nasty. "Shall I bring my horse around so we can put him on behind the saddle to take him back?"

Oliver, still focused on whether to track the person who killed George, looked up. "What? Oh, no, I think we'll bury him here."

Jim and I were both shocked at that. I could see we were thinking alike. Jim spoke up first. "Don't you think Nettie will want to …."

Oliver shook his head. "No, I don't think so. By the time we get him back home, with the heat of the day … and I don't think seeing him with a bullet hole in his forehead will be good for her. Better she remembers him from other times."

"You don't think she'll want to visit his grave?" I asked.

"No, she will, and she still can. George loved this place. He mentioned it a few times to me. I think she can come here, and it will remind her of George and it's a private, peaceful place; so much better than somewhere out in the desert behind the house." He paused and wiped his mouth. "'Sides, she needs to move on with her life."

The area was rocky. We tried a few spots before we found a place where the stones were small enough that we could dig them out. At one point we had a narrow trench dug, and we considered burying him on his side, but Oliver refused. "He's goin' to heaven, and I want him facin' that uh-way."

By the time we finished the burial and had placed additional stones over the fresh grave, the sun had sunk close to the San Andreas Mountains horizon. We returned to Cooper's Ranch for the night, where we ate a thrown together supper. Jim couldn't escape his regret. "If I hadn't backed George up about brandin' that calf at spring roundup, we probably wouldn't be here today."

Oliver shook his head. "George was never one to swallow his words. He always spoke up when he thought someone had been wronged. No, Jim, I don't think you had anything to do with what happened." Jim frowned and tapped his fork on his plate. "Anyways," Oliver said, "I'll take a whack at trackin' the culprit. We won't catch him, but we might get a line on who he is."

Late the next morning, we trotted into Lee Well. Mary was at the door and Ed and Eph stood at either corner of the adobe on guard. Mary said that Nettie hadn't left her room, but as she spoke, Nettie pushed her way past Mary and asked to see her betroths body.

Oliver put his hands on Nettie's shoulders and looked down at the ground to gather his thoughts. "No Nettie, I want you to remember him as he was at the supper table last Sunday. Seeing him the way he was when we found him ... well, you don't want to remember him like that. I know you are hurtin', and we can go up to his grave anytime, but please accept that I know what's best for you now. We buried him there. It was a place he loved, and I think you will love visiting him there."

Jim Cooper came by the next day. "Oliver, I followed the hoof prints for about three hundred yards up the canyon before the murderer's horse stumbled and fell. He must have held onto the reins though because he continued into Salado Canyon and then into Tularosa Creek, where I lost him. There weren't nothin' odd about the tracks other than they were deeper than mine, so the shooter and his horse were heavier."

Oliver nodded. "About what I figured. Unlike his daddy, Walter's much taller and stockier than you. I knew it was probably John or him, so now we know it's Walter."

"How can you be so sure?" asked Cooper.

"Cause I know George and I know where he's been and what he's done and the only people that he's had a problem with are the Goods. The Goods branded themselves as sinners from the first time they confronted me and George over the watering hole."

Cooper kicked at the caliche dust. "Well, 'spect we orta report this to the deputy sheriff in La Luz."

Oliver snickered. "Rucker? Why? That makes no sense. He's John Good's foreman, for one. Second, those dang Republicans over in 'Cruces that carry water for Thomas Catron and the Santa Fe Ring appointed Rucker. No point in gittin him involved 'cause he'll just take his orders from John."

Cooper put his hands on his hips and nodded. "Folks say John don't own none of those cattle. He's just managin' the herd for Catron."

Oliver nodded. "They don't like it when folk stand up for themselves. They ain't gonna run us out like they did that Dawson fella and his woman."

"But John and his son shot him down; they didn't run him out," said Cooper.

"Well, better yet, I'd gladly meet either one of 'em on the street in a fair fight."

Rumors were as varied as they were rampant throughout the Tularosa over the next several weeks, and tensions remained high throughout.

# 5: Fountains Forlorn

**May 25, 1888**

Neither the uplifting scent of the gobernadoras after an early monsoon shower nor the glorious emergence of yucca blossoms dotting the desert could lift the spirits of the Fountain family. A week turned into a month, with nary a trace since Jesús's disappearance. Oh sure, there were plenty of false reports as there always are when someone offers a reward; and Colonel Fountain's offer was substantial. In a couple of instances, they exhumed impromptu graves to prove the identity of the corpse. About the time things settled down, a Navajo wandered into town and reported an emaciated body in the White Sands. The spring winds shifted the dunes the next day and no one thought they could find the body again. Sheriff Santiago Ascarate, who now wanted to be called by his anglicized name of James, begged off the mission and former sheriff Eugene Van Patten came along with Colonel Fountain instead. Miraculously, the Indian led them to the exact spot. By then, the drifting sands left only a boot exposed. They dug the pure white grains for another half-hour or so. The loose sands caved on themselves with each shovel full. At last, they revealed enough of the corpse that they could determine it wasn't Jesús. Later, Van Patten confided in Colonel Fountain that he wondered if it might have been better if it was Jesús, just to gain some conclusion to the case, because the prospects for his survival were dim.

The week after Colonel Fountain and Van Patten returned from their search, Larlo came home to help, but his father told him there was nothing he could do, and sent him back to his job with the mining company near Pinos Altos.

Colonel Fountain's hyper-political interests waned, and he told Wil Rynerson that he was no longer interested in the Territorial Legislature seat. The election was just six months away. Rynerson hoped the Colonel would change his mind, but there wasn't much time.

Visitors to the Fountain's adobe sensed a somber aura. It began with Rosa's subdued greeting at the door, and Colonel Fountain's clients reported none of the usual banter. He took care of business, but nothing more, and sometimes clients complained to mutual friends that he bordered on a terseness that left them sad as well. The family no longer entertained guests and canceled their thespian activities. Tommy didn't relish his return to his Papa's office, but he asked for and received leave from his militia duty to do so. Once again, Colonel Fountain tasked him with the mundane jobs of copying contracts and composing wills. They removed the typewriter from the office that Jesús had used. There was no talk of the territorial politics and Colonel Fountain neglected to read the weekly paper to the family when they gathered at the breakfast table on Saturday mornings, and the story-hearth begged even the shortest poem or tale.

Soon after Colonel Fountain and Van Patten returned from their initial search for Jesús, Father Lassaigne conducted a prayer vigil where he and many of the church's parishioners prayed to St. Anthony, the Patron Saint of the lost. Even Colonel Fountain attended and when groups from the church would visit the Fountain adobe and offer prayers, he bowed his head with them.

In the early 1870s, Colonel Fountain joined a movement that had taken hold across the nation when he organized his former California Column veterans with a Decoration Day celebration. The first occasion featured a memorial service, a banquet, and a ball. Attendees danced from dusk 'til dawn. It was such a success that Colonel Fountain and Wil Rynerson organized a permanent association. Memorial Day, or as it was sometimes called back then, Decoration Day, grew locally until we treasured it over the Fourth of July.

Before Jesús's disappearance, Wil Rynerson and Colonel Fountain had planned an extra-large celebration for 1888. The National Guard and other militias had encamped near Las Cruces in April and the Decoration Day celebration would coincide with their decampment. They marched in the streets and organized a dusk to dawn dance. As he had in the past, Colonel Fountain hosted a full-dress reception for the men of his regiment, but everyone could see that his worries took him far away. Colonel Fountain gave a brief speech and toast, and while he remained standing, Wil Rynerson rose and called the veterans to attention. He verbalized what all the men thought when he said, "To a man, we vow to do our best to find Jesús." Colonel Fountain was visibly touched as they saluted until he sat.

Tommy, as one might expect, cracked the malaise that wafted through the Fountain adobe when he planned a prospecting trip to one of the Colonel's several mine claims. Tommy convinced his brothers, even Albert Jr., when he mentioned that his father and Colonel Van Patten hadn't searched for Jesús in that area. Larlo had returned home for a baseball game, and Jack got Wil Rynerson to give him a few days off. Their destination was an abandoned mine their father had acquired the previous winter near Fillmore Pass in the Organ Mountains.

The four of them didn't coordinate well and when they reached the claim, Albert Jr. realized that they hadn't brought what they needed. The next morning, he headed back to Las Cruces, about fifteen miles to the west, to get the required items. Not long after he left, Jack and Larlo decided there were things they wanted as well and so they left Tommy alone.

When they returned that afternoon, the three young men decided this was their chance to get back at Tommy for all the practical jokes he had foisted on them. They spread out and hid at a distance from the campsite. As the horizon swallowed the sun, a flaming campfire revealed a nervous Tommy and the three of them made Indian whoops and ululates. In an unexpected response, a spooked Tommy got his rifle and fired toward the yells. He continued to spray bullets around them as the pranksters shouted for him to stop. At last, he heard their frantic apologies, and put away his rifle.

Otherwise, there was little to excite them during their prospecting and the next Tuesday they returned home tired, broke, with nary a nugget of ore. They spoke to everyone they saw, but the lone sign of Jesús was the guilt they felt when they used him as an excuse for a self-indulgent expedition.

---

**June 4**

When Rosa returned to work at the Fountains on Monday, she had decided that she could no longer stay with the family in the face of Jesús's disappearance and the death threats against Colonel Fountain. She knocked on the Colonel's office door. Before he could respond, she entered.

Colonel Fountain sensed something was amiss and said, "What's wrong? Do you need to go to Lohman's?"

"No sir, it is nothing like that." She couldn't look him in the eye, and instead stared out the high window at the cloudless sky. She glanced at him, then looked back at the sky and blurted, "I can't work for you anymore."

"What do you mean 'you can't work for me, anymore?' Don't we pay you enough? Do you need some time off?"

Rosa wagged her head 'no' once.

"Oh, I think I know what it is." He stood up and came to the front of his desk and sat in one of the facing chairs. "It's the death threats … and now Jesús is … missing." He motioned for Rosa to sit opposite him.

Rosa sat and stared at her hands in her lap before she looked up at Colonel Fountain. A tear escaped her dark eyes and she held back a sob. She composed herself enough to say, "Don't you worry that they … they took Jesús to … to …."

"No, no, that's not what this is." He pulled his handkerchief from his pocket and handed it to her. "There have been no threats since the one that came through your family." He licked his lips and then wiped them with his hand. "Have I thought that one of these malefactors might have … taken Jesús?" He wiped his hand across his mouth. "Of course, I have. But if I, and others that have similar responsibilities, didn't hold criminals culpable … well, we might as well leave because New Mexico would become unlivable for law-abiding people like ourselves. We would have to go armed, and our women would have to remain home."

"But I cannot take the worry. When you had the accident on your way back from Lincoln in March, I thought they had …"

"Killed me?" he asked. "This old campaigner has been shot up and knocked down more times than you can count. If I'm still standing here in front of you, it's because I must be invincible. I have a duty to perform, and I won't let anyone sway me from my office."

"*You* might think you are invincible, but what about your family? I can't bear it when you go on your trips." A muted sob escaped her mouth before she said, "I must go."

Colonel Fountain shook his head. "No, please don't. Mariana and the girls will have my hide. I'll double your pay and I'll have Maggie take over Little Henry's care. Please, Rosa. What can I do?

She stood motionless before him for a moment and then turned to leave.

"Wait, what if I told you I could protect you from your bad ... notions?"

Rosa stopped just short of the door. With her hand on the latch, she said, "And how could you do that?"

"I don't know, but I'll think of something. If I can't, what will you tell Mariana and the girls?"

Rosa stood speechless for a moment and then said, "I won't say anything. It will be up to you to tell them. I'm sorry, but unless you can reassure me by the end of the week, I must go."

When she left, Colonel Fountain went to his desk, but couldn't think of a way to comfort Rosa without letting the family in on the threats. His conversation with Rosa haunted him all week.

He looked at the paper on his desk. It was a letter from the United States attorney for New Mexico, Thomas Smith. He, not for the first time, reminded Colonel Fountain that his title was Special United States District Attorney and not simply Assistant District Attorney. He ended the brief letter with a request that Colonel Fountain identify himself properly to the newspapers and at hearings.

*Right. That would certainly reduce the death threats*, thought Colonel Fountain sarcastically

He scribbled a sarcastic response, but then tore it up and threw it in the wastebasket. He scanned his desk without a hint of where to start with the day's work. His eye caught a twice-folded *Chicago Tribune* at the corner of his desk. The article from early April announced the introduction of the Omnibus bill, H.R. 8466, which would "enable the people of Dakota, Montana, Washington and New Mexico to form constitutions and state governments".

At the time it had excited, but bewildered him, because New Mexico had not pushed for admittance. Still, his thoughts reexamined the benefits of getting elected to the Territorial House. He had long relished the thought that he might help prepare the required state constitution. As he had scanned the article, he realized that the author of the bill, William Springer, a southern Illinois Democrat, probably thought New Mexico was the sole territory being considered for statehood that could elect Democrats to the U.S. Congress.

This reminded him of the resounding defeat he and the rest of the GOP had suffered in the '86 election when the Democrats swept them out of their local offices. In part, it resulted from the flood of Texans and other southern Democrats into southern New Mexico, beginning in 1884. The spirit of the confederacy hadn't died with their Civil War defeat. Reconstruction failed to reunite the country and instead brought radical ideas about Republican intentions. Many Democrats accused Republicans of policies that would wipe away their southern customs and culture. The former rebels might have given up on slavery, but they would fight to the death to keep their way of life.

The Dakota territory had satisfied all the requirements of statehood, but it was Republican. Democrats controlled the House of Representatives, and they weren't about to go along with the single admittance of a decidedly Republican territory. The burgeoning Republican populations of Minnesota and Washington also pressured a Congress that hadn't admitted a state since Colorado in 1876.

Since the Democrats controlled the U.S. House while the Republicans held the Senate, there was little chance that only GOP aligned territories could gain passage. Springer and his fellow Democrats realized this and so they offered their votes in exchange for including New Mexico, where it mistakenly appeared to them that Democrats were in power.

With Jesús's disappearance, Colonel Fountain had lost his fire for politics, but when he received a copy of the final bill a week or two later through the Republican party's network, he saw Springer proposed Montezuma replace New Mexico as the name for the new state. For a moment Colonel Fountain considered whether statehood would be worth a name that had nothing to do with the place, as well as the ill will much of the Spanish colonial families had for Montezuma over his massacre of Spaniards centuries before. It angered him that a congressman that hadn't set foot in the territory would presume to rename it, but he wasn't ready to recommit to the November election, just yet.

As the end of the week neared, Colonel Fountain couldn't get Rosa's threat to quit out of his mind. He tried to nudge the thoughts aside, but he couldn't escape her look and tone. Even the most captivating texts and conversations didn't hold his attention. He had to do something. He also knew his family would learn of the veiled and not-so-veiled threats someday, but he felt his silence protected them.

Colonel Fountain considered who was best to approach Rosa. I imagined how he arrived on the right person as he thought: *Tommy? ... no, Tommy is too high-strung. Perhaps Jack? No, Jack hadn't shown any sign of a genuine connection with Rosa. Maybe Maggie? Yes!*

That evening, Colonel Fountain asked Maggie to walk with him. It was something they did after the evening meal sometimes. She expected her father wanted to ask her to help with one civic project or another.

As they turned toward Main Street and passed the new cemetery, Colonel Fountain said, "Rosa is leaving us."

"What? Why?" Maggie replied.

"It's her nerves. She worries when I am away from home and now with Jesús missing, I suppose it's just too much for her."

Maggie walked a few steps in silence before saying, "Well, we must do something."

"I tried," replied her father. "I talked to her Monday morning, and she said that unless I can convince her I am ...," He paused. He didn't want Maggie to know about the threats to him.

"Safe?"

Colonel Fountain stopped mid-stride and turned to her. "You know?"

"About the threats, you mean?"

Colonel Fountain removed his hat and wiped his brow. The sun sat on the western horizon, but the heat of June had lingered long past sunset as it would for the rest of the summer. "How did you know?"

She shrugged and said, "I just knew. People we know love you and they all will say everyone thinks the world of you, but it seems to me that a highly respected person will find that there are those that despise him just as deeply — it's in people's nature, I guess. Besides, you are a prosecutor. You don't suppose that I believe the people you send away to prison forgive you, do you?"

Colonel Fountain gave a faint nod, brought his hands to his hips, and said, "I always thought you were the wisest of all my children. So, what can we do to keep Rosa?"

They walked for a spell and as they turned to head north on Main Street, Maggie said, "I wonder if it will help if she realizes I know about the threats? Another person to share the burden might help."

"I have my doubts. She had Jesús to share with …"

"Maybe that is the difference now. With Jesús gone, she has no one to steady her. I think it will work."

Her father looked skyward and said, "I hope you are right."

Maggie flipped a lock of her black hair from her eyes and said, "Let's walk past her parent's adobe and I'll stop and talk with her."

―――――――――――――――――――――――――――

Colonel Fountain lay wide awake next to Mariana, awaiting the sounds of Maggie's return. He hadn't expected that it might take hours for Maggie to convince her. His thoughts raced.

At last, there was the click of the latch, and he rose to discover whether Maggie had succeeded. He met her in the parlor, and they returned to the *porche* where they could talk without disturbing the rest of the sleeping family.

"What did she say?" he asked.

"It's not that simple. We talked for quite a long time. It's not like when you and Wil Rynerson make a decision. Women don't do it that way."

He looked bewildered. "I don't understand, but I don't need to. What did she say?"

"She said a lot of things. She's worried that Jesús' disappearance is connected to the threats against you. I think she may have had feelings for Jesús. I didn't pressure her, and I never asked her if she would stay."

"What? Well, what did you ask her?"

"We just talked. It's better this way. I think she will stay with us, but she needs time to rehash our talk."

Colonel Fountain ran his fingers through his pillow-mussed hair and stared into the darkness. He conceded to his confusion and said, "OK."

The next morning, Rosa arrived on time. At breakfast, it was all Colonel Fountain could do to keep his eyes on his food as he tried to discern her intentions. Maggie gave him a brief glare. Tommy noticed Maggie's expression and said, "What the devil is going on between you and Papa?"

"Oh, nothing. It's just that he told me he planned to give Rosa a raise and I wondered why he hadn't told her and all of us."

Colonel Fountain swallowed his *mollete* hard as he gawked at Maggie, then rose from his chair. He wiped his mouth with his napkin and then realized that Maggie had set him up. He shifted from one foot to the other and said, "Why yes, I uh … I guess it slipped my mind and I couldn't get your meaning from your expression, my dear. Of course, yes, that is what I told her, Maggie, that is, last night. I want to give Rosa a raise. Uh, let's see now, my memory is a little hazy," he mumbled. "Was it ten per … no, no, that's not … fifteen …" his voice lilted with the hint of a question as he tried to judge Maggie's expression out of the corner of his eye. "No, no, it was … uh, twenty percent and it will begin with today's pay." He grinned, but everyone knew something was up.

Rosa rushed over and gave Colonel Fountain a brief hug at his seat and said, "Oh, señor Fountain, thank you very much. I hope I can stay with this family for a long time."

Maggie pursed her lips with a faint smile. Colonel Fountain recognized her smug expression, snickered, and said to Rosa, "Just as long as you want, my dear. We love having you."

## June 12

Colonel Fountain was the busiest man I ever met. People often came to his doorstep to ask him to help them achieve a worthy community cause. He was generous with his cash and time, but for all of his life, he was denied the achievement of his greatest conviction — good public schools for New Mexicans.

The Colonel's public-school goals got a boost with Hiram Hadley's arrival. Hadley was an accomplished educator, and he was the perfect asset for the Colonel's strong local voice. The Colonel was still in the throes of despair over Jesús's disappearance when Hadley approached him about their joint desire to see a college in Las Cruces. Hadley was sympathetic to the Colonel's anguish over Jesús' disappearance and agreed to take charge of the effort. Despite his worry for Jesús, Colonel Fountain's civic pride led him to join the committee that met at Hadley's Mesilla Park real estate office in early May.

Numa Reymond, George Bowman, Wil Rynerson, and Eugene Van Patten also attended that first meeting. Their primary objectives were incorporation and fund raising. They voted for Hadley to chair the organization. Colonel Fountain agreed to take a post on the Ways and Means Committee.

At the second meeting, Colonel Fountain suggested a target of twenty-five thousand dollars sold at twenty-five dollars per share. They discussed where the college should be located, and it was quickly agreed that the Mesilla Park area would provide the best location since three of the committee members could donate contiguous lands there. However, their donated holdings weren't enough. Numa Reymond suggested that Martin Lohman's father-in-law, Jacob Schaublin, owned an abutting parcel of substantial size. Reymond volunteered to approach Mr. Schaublin, but he suggested some enticement might sweeten the deal. The committee agreed that if Schaublin donated his property, it would be the location of the first buildings for the new campus.

Jacob Schaublin donated the needed land, and the committee felt they had the basis for selling the Las Cruces College to the community. Their goal was to establish it as a land grant agricultural college. They didn't have the funds to build on the assembled properties, but they had the fiscal capability to rent a two-room building from Numa Reymond on the southern outskirts of town, which they remodeled into classrooms and an administrative office.

On September 15, the school opened. Eventually sixty-four students and three teachers, including Hadley, used the facility. In the end, since there were so few previously educated students, they reorganized 'college' into classes at three levels — elementary, college preparation, and business. This required additional facilities, so the committee secured the South Ward property and the DeMiers Building. Hadley agreed to a salary of whatever was left after expenses. That first year, he made only $23.69.

# 6: El Paso

**June 15, 1888**

Oliver's half-brother Perry Altman looked forward to the reunion with his wife Emma and their newborn baby girl. He was to meet them at the Texas and Pacific Railroad Depot in El Paso on Saturday the sixteenth. Perry had sent Emma 'home' to Abilene to be with her family for the final part of her pregnancy, and now he would finally meet his little daughter, whom they had named Rena. He had hoped for a son, of course, and cared little when Emma suggested Rena, if it was a girl.

Nettie was to come along to buy wedding clothes. A few days earlier, Perry had ridden into La Luz and paid for round-trip stagecoach tickets for himself and Nettie, which assured they could sit inside the coach. He also arranged for the driver to stop at Lee Well to pick them up on that morning, Friday the fifteenth.

While ranchers tried to maintain a 'claim' on rangeland, herds intermingled occasionally and therefore cowboys had the opportunity to pass along news and information. As a result, rumors spread like wildfire. Before Perry put a foot in the stirrup to return to his ranch seven miles west of La Luz, a cowboy came up to him and said, "Hey, ain't you Oliver Lee's brother?"

Perry nodded, and the man told him that George McDonald was found dead over near the Stuart's Ranch. The man rattled off some tale about how it happened, but Perry knew that whatever the cowboy said, it wouldn't resemble the facts. Perry doubted

George was dead. Ordinarily, he would ride right over to Lee Well to get the truth, but since he would meet the stagecoach there Saturday morning, he decided to wait. As the evening passed and his own cowboys came in from the range, the stories grew ever more outlandish. Perry couldn't be sure that George was involved at all.

Nettie wanted to buy wedding clothes, but if George was dead or maimed, she might not want to go. No matter, he reasoned, even if the stories were true, they could use the ticket some other time. Besides, Oliver made frequent trips to El Paso to wangle the bankers and investors and he could use it.

When Perry rode into Lee Well on the morning of June the sixteenth, he didn't know what to expect. I sat in my usual spot, on the old backless Windsor chair on the porch. When I saw someone approach in a carriage, I called for Oliver, who met Perry at the hitching post in front of the adobe. They spoke in half-whispers until Perry slapped his hat on his thigh and said, "You can't be sure!"

Oliver pushed his hat back. "I'm as sure as I need to be."

Nettie appeared in the doorway, and Mary stood behind her. Nettie wore a plain, drab brown denim dress. She said, "I got no black to wear. I need to go with you for my mournin' clothes, and Hey-you is comin' for some things he needs as well."

While Oliver explained my name to Perry, we sat at the table and sipped coffee.

"By the way, Perry, the man that wanted to buy Charlie's place didn't have the cash."

Perry twisted his mouth. "That's too bad. What shall we do now?"

"Well, I think we need to keep an eye on the place. I was thinkin' about sendin' Ed over there. Thing is, he don't need to be there all the time, and it's a long way from there and back. He'd waste most of a day ridin' back and forth."

Perry licked his lips. "We can use a good hand I can trust. He can work for me and check in over at Charlie's now and then."

Oliver tipped his hat back. "I like that idea."

They continued to chat about the Graham's place until we heard the stagecoach rattle over the hard-baked and yet dusty trail.

---

The coach wasn't crowded, and Nettie paid the driver for a ticket for me. In fact, it was only the three of us. As the stagecoach gathered speed, the grinding sounds of steel against stones made it necessary to shout to the person next to you. Perry glanced at Nettie as though he wanted to share his excitement for his coming reunion, but then he noticed Nettie's tear reddened cheeks and he settled back against the straight-backed wooden bench. When he saw I had noticed, he shrugged as if to say, 'I can't help feeling eager.'

I settled in as best I could and tried to keep my eyes closed against the dust. My mind wandered, as it often did, to who I was and where I belonged. I wondered if there were people that worried about me. Perhaps they had given up and believed I was dead? I decided to take stock of what I *did* know. My name 'Hey-you' somehow reminded me of something. Was it my first name … my last name … my father's or mother's name? My other clue was from Mary's observation that when Oliver had found me, I had worn clothes city-folk would wear.

*I must be from a city — could it be El Paso? Maybe I should walk around and see if anything jogs my memory.*

The seventy-mile route sloped slightly downhill toward El Paso, which enabled our stagecoach driver to stop just twice to change horses.

Our late-afternoon arrival left us dust-caked, parched of the throat, and ready to stretch our legs. The driver deposited us in front of the modern and sophisticated Grand Central Hotel. It sat on a corner across from San Jacinto Plaza, where the prettiest little park you ever saw bloomed out of the surrounding dusty streets. Nettie and I wacked each other with my hat a few times, which generated billowing clouds of fine Tularosa dust, to the dismay of some well-dressed dandies chatting in front of the hotel. Nettie said she would like to get some air, and Perry suggested I walk with her while he made our room arrangements and took Nettie's bag to her room. Everything I had; I wore.

As I peered up and down the busy St. Louis Street, Nettie could not take her eyes off the well-kept grounds of San Jacinto Plaza. The gardens there seemed to pull Nettie out of her pall, and so we walked across Oregon Street and paused at the corner to admire the beautiful landscape. The block square park featured well-groomed paths that radiated from a round central flowerbed with the grandest blooming yellow tickseed, pink evening primrose, and white poppies surrounding a large central bed of Indian Blanket in full bloom. When taken as a whole, it resembled a flamboyant tapestry. Nettie marveled at how many trips to a central well the caretaker would have to make to keep the beds so lush and vibrant.

We walked to the center of the plaza and around the circular central bed, admiring the bee-covered blooms up close. When we arrived back where we started, we turned down another radiating path back to St. Louis Street and then up Utah. I was glad it was still broad daylight because taverns, saloons, and casinos lined the southwest side of the street. Even though it was still daylight, there were cowboys coming and going, laughing, and playfully poking their friends. Cowboys and vagrants lay passed out here and there in the alleys between the buildings. About halfway down the block, on the opposite side of the street, the steepled bell tower of a church rose above the other single story adobe structures.

Nettie shook her head. "How odd that a pastor — an Episcopal one, at that, would erect a church in such a den of iniquity."

"Perhaps it was here before the other ...," I paused because beyond the church was a stately, Victorian-style wooden house surrounded by a brilliant white picket fence. It seemed familiar, and I expected that its unique appearance amongst all those adobe buildings was the reason. As I admired the structure, my gaze fell upon the veranda where 'painted women' sat with bare legs and shoulders. The disturbing image didn't diminish the familiarity. If anything, the familiarity swelled.

I felt my mouth drop and glanced at Nettie to see if she noticed my reaction to the scene. "I ... I ... am sorry ... perhaps we should return, it's nearing supper time and I'm sure you want to freshen-up before we eat."

We rushed back to the hotel as I puzzled over why half-dressed women were familiar. When we reached St. Louis Street, I realized Nettie had returned to her inward gloom.

Later, when I slipped away for a moment, the concierge confirmed my suspicions. He told me the place I described was Tillie's Parlor House, a well-respected house of ill repute. I couldn't accept that it was familiar. *Why would I have been to such a place?* And yet there was a definite connection. The image of a young woman, just a girl, came to me in a foggy vision. *Her frilly underthings came into greater focus. The girl leaned against a post as she sat at the top of the veranda stairs. Her long legs, smooth and creamy, and thighs that glistened ... .* I shook my head to stop my carnal thoughts.

*I know her. But why? Was the real me someone that frequented these places?*

Perry and I shared a room while Nettie had the one next door. As I entered the room, he lay on the bed nearest the door in his drawers, short-sleeved undervest, and stockings. He had both hands behind his head.

Perry raised his head and pointed with one of his hands. "I washed up already. After you're done, put your shirt and pants over the chair there and when the young man returns my clothes, you can have him brush yours for you," he said.

*Had I experienced such care before? Was I accustomed to this kind of treatment? Did my 'city clothes' translate to wealth and status?*

I washed best I could, but I still wore my long johns. I looked forward to something cooler. When the boy arrived, he brushed my tattered shirt and pants with a puzzled look. Then I realized it was my raggedy city clothes. They belied the work that would damage them like that. I smiled and explained that I had rousted calves out of the brush. He nodded and when he handed my clothes back; they had a woody scent. I must have had an inquisitive look, for he said, "It's sandalwood. We soak our brushes in a sandalwood scent."

It was funny how just that slight bit of scent made me relax as I entered the ornate dining room with Nettie and Perry. Still, I walked behind them to avoid stares my poor clothes might bring. I rushed, without deference to Nettie, to sit as soon as Perry moved toward a table. Besides the state of my clothing, I had not combed or washed for over a week and my beard was scraggly. I must have been a sight.

Our waiter, back straight, nose in the air, with a towel over one forearm and the other behind his back, arrived at our table and gave us menus. He introduced himself to Perry. "Good evening, sir. My name is George and I'll be taking your orders and will serve your every need this evening."

Perry glanced at Nettie. I was concerned that the mention of the name George might disturb her, and I thought it worried Perry, as well, but she had focused on the menu.

As we perused the fanciful names for common dishes, we overheard a woman's complaint to her friend about a man at an adjacent table. It seemed he had begun to trim his fingernails onto his plate.

The man, who wore fine clothing and a bowler hat, fit with the other dandies in the dining room. When he heard the woman's complaint, he said, "Name's Dankworth milady, and I need to trim ma nails on this day — it 'tis Friday, is it not? You see, milady, I have sent for a young gentlewoman whom I will fetch from the depot on the 'morrow and I must be certain she will be partial to me." A belch erupted from his mouth, followed by a yellowed, snaggle-toothed smile.

I didn't think the man could attract anyone that could afford a train ticket. After Dankworth's impropriety, the well-dressed woman slammed down her fork, glared at him as she stood. Her male friend pulled at her arm, but she wasn't to be deterred. She wrested her arm from her companion's grasp, pointed at the man. "I don't care if trimming your nails will bring you a thousand dollars. It's gauche and disgusting and I don't want my dinner spoiled."

Perry ignored the ruckus, but Nettie said, "Jessie, back on Little Elm Creek, used to repeat this sayin' about cuttin' your nails: 'Cut them on Monday, you cut them for news; cut them on Tuesday, a new pair of shoes; cut them on Wednesday, you cut them for health; cut them on Thursday you cut them for wealth; cut them on Friday, a sweetheart you'll know; cut them on Saturday, a-journey you'll go; cut them on Sunday, you cut them for evil; for all the next week, you'll be ruled by the devil.' "

As the maître d' approached, the woman overheard Nettie. Still indignant, she half-turned toward us and said, "Nothing more than a children's song and superstition. It's loathsome and … and," she threw up her arms with repulsion and surrender. "Come Horace, we can get better service down the street."

The maître d' arrived as the couple rushed past him. He gave Dankworth a stern look and pulled his soiled dinner plate from the table, held it at arm's length, and removed it from the dining room.

"I do not know why anyone would want to live in a city," said Perry.

Nettie nodded and acknowledged George as he moved our plated meals from the tray he had placed on a small table behind me. He kept one arm behind his back, and I pondered whether he wanted to show-off or if this was the service wealthy folks expected.

Nettie noticed the peculiar way the waiter approached us each time he came to our table. Whether he brought a dish or removed one, he always had his right hand behind his back and leaned in from our left side to complete his task.

When Nettie had finished her meal and the waiter removed her plate, she shook her head. "Such airs."

I wondered why Perry selected what must have been the most expensive hotel in town. A few moments later, when we had finished our meal, I found out why. A man from across the room approached us as Perry ordered a cigar and whisky. As the man's pace increased, his jacket flew open, revealing suspenders that strained over a prosperous belly. He bowed to Nettie and me, then turned to Perry. "Excuse me sir, Aren't you Oliver Lee's brother?"

Perry nodded. "Perry Altman, at your service, sir. I am Oliver's older half-brother."

"I see. Joshua Jefferson's the name — President of the El Paso First National Bank. Word is, Oliver has requested a line of credit from some lenders here in town for his beef operation."

"Wouldn't know about that. I deal in fine horses."

"Well, would your wife and son excuse us to the bar so we can talk some business?"

Just then, George, our waiter, showed up with Perry's order and Mr. Jefferson said, "Put that on my account, George. Mr. Altman and I have some business to tend to at the bar." It seemed Oliver had made quite a name for himself in El Paso.

This time, the mention of the name George disturbed Nettie. She looked away and pulled her handkerchief from her sleeve. When Perry turned to introduce us, Nettie smiled and extended her hand as a woman with her southern heritage should.

"This is my niece, Nettie Fry and ... uh ... Hey-you."

Mr. Jefferson took her hand with a slight bow. He gave a cursory nod my way, while his eyes never left Nettie.

Perry gave me the 'you take care of her' look and rose to follow Mr. Jefferson into the other room. The waiter fell in step behind Jefferson as he held Perry's whiskey and cigar perched shoulder high on a tray.

I never heard Perry enter our room that night. Mr. Jefferson must have wanted Oliver's business badly.

# 7: City Life is No Life

**June 17, 1888**

The next morning, we rose at our usual early hour. When I lit the room's gas light, Perry squinted, groaned and said, "We don't need that. Ain't got it at home and don't need it here."

We arrived downstairs to find no one in the dining room and nary a maitre d'hotel or waiter. After Perry inquired at the desk, the night clerk brought us a pot of coffee, cups, sugar, and fresh cream.

Perry said nothing of the evening he spent with Mr. Jefferson, and neither Nettie nor I asked about it. He seemed under the weather, and I thought Mr. Jefferson must be keen for Oliver's business. Two hours later, we finished our breakfasts and Perry seemed revived. We were ready to find a store that would provide the clothes we needed.

Perry introduced us and told the concierge what we needed. The concierge checked his pocket watch. "I can certainly direct you, sir, but it's barely seven and I don't believe our stores will be open yet."

Perry snickered. "My lord son how do you folks get anything done with gettin' such a late start?".

"Well sir, many will make it up in the evening I suppose. Let me write down some places where you will find exactly what you want. Now, the work clothes for the young man will be no problem, but would it be dresses you want for the young lady?"

"My niece here is in mourning. Do you know of any ready-made shops that would have mournin' dresses?"

The concierge sized up an oblivious Nettie. He apologized when he noticed Perry's frown. Nettie understood his examination of her dimensions and said, "They don't make ready-made clothes for women Perry, didn't Em teach you nothin'?"

Perry shrugged, and the concierge said, "This is true, however," his finger went into the air, "we have a couple of consignment shops where you can buy used clothing. Now, the reason I … uh … examined Miss Nettie's uh … person," the young man shifted his weight and bit his lip, "or I'm sorry, I suppose you were married?" He turned back to Perry. "It's just that she looks so young."

Perry didn't care for what he considered the concierge's needless prying. "Engaged."

"Still, I'm so sorry for your loss ma'am, however, as I was saying, we have a couple of consignment shops, but it would be rather unusual that a woman with your youth and … well, yes youth, to lose a husband and then die herself and therefore have her dress find its way to a consignment shop … even in El Paso." He paused in thought as he wrote something on the sheet of paper. "Still, it's your best chance to get something right away. I have included those and some dress shops that make the dresses you require. They will send them to you as well."

---

As we happened upon the first consignment store, the proprietor was moving a sign onto the boardwalk. We startled her when she turned back toward us.

"My, my you folks are awake with the chickens this mornin'. I usually don't get no one into my store for another hour or so.

Now, what can I help you with … for the young lady I imagine … come right in. I've got some pretty dresses that will fit her well." The proprietor was a small, middle-aged woman, but with the wrinkles and graying hair of a hard life. She fashioned her gray streaked chestnut hair into a neat bun at the back of her head.

I looked at the sign she had placed. It read:

**Widow Christiansen's Ladies Wear**

**Used, Consigned or Made-to-order**

**Alterations included with each sale**

I gave Perry a little nudge and motioned to the sign.

Perry wrung his hands for a moment, then followed the woman inside. He pointed to Nettie. "Uh, she needs mournin' dresses, ma'am."

The woman spun, which put her face to face with Perry, and he took a step back. Unaffected by their closeness, she said, "Mournin' clothes?" She glanced at Nettie. "Excuse me, but mournin' clothes for such a young thing as you? My goodness darlin' you can't be no older than fourteen years."

Nettie spoke up, "Fifteen, I'm fifteen years old, and I was engaged to the man who … was … murdered." Her voice trailed as she realized she would have to talk about George.

"Well, you just come right on in here." She pushed Perry aside. "Now, I know we can find you something here and if'n I has'ta take it in a smidge, then it won't take no time at all."

Perry turned to follow them, but the woman half turned and extended her hand into Perry's midsection. "You boys just stay out here." She spun back to Nettie, then reconsidered her order. "Better yet, go on about your business. She'll be ready in an hour or so."

Perry and I proceeded down St. Louis Street until we found the establishment the concierge had noted. In the matter of half an hour, Perry selected a pair of denim pants, two light blue chambray shirts, two under-vests and two pair of drawers, a tan Stetson hat — Perry wouldn't allow a sombrero — a new pair of boots, two pair of stockings, a leather vest with lots of pockets, a dark blue bandana, and pairs of chaps and gloves. Perry paid for all this with the money Mary had given him.

I changed into one set of my new clothes in the back storeroom, while the storekeeper bundled my old and new clothes into separate packages. Perry asked, and the storekeeper agreed to hold them until we returned.

As we walked out of the mercantile, Perry spotted Jim Cooper across Pioneer Square and we dodged horses, freight wagons, and carriages before a raucous herd of goats driven by an old Mexican stopped us in the middle of the street. As we waited for the goats to pass, Jim saw us, and we met at the corner of San Francisco and Santa Fe.

Jim shook our hands and said, "What brings you all to town, Perry?"

"I'm pickin' up my wife, Em, and our new baby girl off the eleven o'clock train."

"So, what d'ya think about the story John Good's cowboys told?"

"What story Jim? We left Lee Well yesterd'y mornin'."

"I stopped by y'all's place yesterd'y afternoon, and Oliver was saddlin' up his horse. Seems a couple of Good's hands had come by earlier. One of 'em told Oliver that he heard Walter Good brag about the revenge he got on George McDonald. The other one said he saw a broken Spanish dagger spike at the site of George's murder that he thought it matched a scabbed-over wound on Walter's paint horse. Oliver was fixin' to go find that horse and match it up to the broken spike."

After looking at Jim with weary eyes, Perry kicked at the dusty street. "I hope he knows what he's gettin' into. Them boys is certain to see the wrath of John Good."

"He said he hired Good's hands on the spot and told 'em they were under his protection."

Perry waved with a dismissive flick of his wrists. "Well, Oliver's his own man now. Unless he comes to me for help, he's on his own. Brother-in-law Charlie Graham's already moved his family north." Perry took a big breath. "I'll be damned if I'll see my new family get involved in another range war. I suppose I'll have to have a talk with Oliver."

"Well, you better make it quick. He wasn't faunchin' at the bit, but he had that look in his eyes like t'weren't nothin' gonna stop him from his goal."

Perry gazed to the north, toward the Tularosa. "Assumin' the train's on time, we'll be on the noon stage."

The train wasn't on time, but the stage company delayed until folks got to their station. Nettie and I stayed back at the hotel while Perry waited on the train platform for his young family.

Perry had told me he would tell Em about George before they got to the hotel, so there would be no uncomfortable moments. Nettie was relieved that they didn't mention George when they came to our room.

I arranged for the hotel to prepare something for us to eat on the road, and it was a welcome treat as we headed northeast from El Paso. Perry beamed as he held his little daughter, Rena, while the driver helped Em into the coach.

We arrived with the setting sun to see Oliver seated on one of the Windsor chairs, reading a newspaper. Mary came to the door and called out for Ed to hitch Perry's horse to their buggy and bring it out front of the adobe.

While Mary and Nettie talked about her dress and the materials she bought to make others, I took my wrapped packages to the bunkhouse. I returned to the adobe and ladled a bowl of stew from the cookstove and grabbed a spoon. I went back onto the porch to eat. Oliver and Perry were in an intense discussion while Em and the baby waited in the carriage.

I heard Oliver say, "Yes, last evening I found Walter's paint, and the gash on the horse's chest is the same height as that broken spike on the Spanish dagger. After I proved out their story, I turned the paint back into the pasture with the rest of Good's remuda."

Perry frowned. "So, what will you do now?"

"It's either fight fire with fire or run scared like you had us do from Little Elm Creek."

"You were just a kid, Oliver — you and George. Me and Charlie couldn't stand up to those folks. You know that. I got a family now," he glanced over at Em and the baby, "and I ain't gonna put them through some kind of range war. My place is the first one they'll come to if you go after Walter. They'll hit me before they come to you. If you're gonna go off half-cocked and start somethin', just you remember it ain't just you that'll have to answer for it."

"They already started it. George was as good as a part of this family. What would you have me do, Perry?"

"We gotta try the law agin. They wouldn't do anything back in Texas, but this ain't Texas. I know Good and the Santa Fe Ring has the La Luz deputy under their thumb. That's why you gotta go direct to 'Cruces and file a complaint on George's murder. I hear you've got two of Good's hands that say they know what happened. Take 'em along and see if you can get heard by the grand jury. I'd go with ya if'n I hadn't just brought Em and little Rena home. I need to stick around the ranch for a while."

Oliver gazed out to the north toward the Good Ranch. "Alright Perry, I'll go to 'Cruces, but I know it won't do no good. We'll leave in the mornin'."

Oliver came to the house, head down, deep in thought. I wasn't sure I should disturb him, but I didn't know how to break in my new boots. Mary saw me. "Don't bother Oliver with that. Go out to the bunkhouse and Ed, Eph, and the boys will help you."

Sure enough, Ed and Eph knew what to do. In unison, they said, "We gotta put 'em in the horse trough." At first, I thought they were teasing, but I couldn't detect a hint of a practical joke at play. Half the cowboys in the bunkhouse followed us to the horse trough. Ed said to put a hand in each boot and hold the boots under the water with just the top of them exposed.

"Now, y'all hold it there 'til ya feel water startin' to seep into the bottom of the boot," said Virgil. Fitting new boots must have been quite an occasion because several cowboys gathered round. Since they had my hands occupied, I expected something was up. Instead, Virgil introduced the two cowboys that had joined them from John Good's ranch. I nodded to them, and they asked if I was going with them to Las Cruces the next morning. I replied I didn't know and a few moments later I could feel the moisture ooze into the bottom of the boot and so I brought them out.

Ed took the boots from me. "Now, sit on the side of the trough, and we'll help you put 'em on." Virgil struggled to pull them on while I put my arms around Eph and Ed's shoulders for support. Eph said, "Now, you gotta leave 'em on all night. By mornin', they'll form perfect to your foot and leg."

I figured it would be an uncomfortable night's rest, but when the boots felt as though they had molded to my feet, I relaxed and fell fast asleep.

I dreamed I was on a trail with the girl from El Paso. She rode a burro that I led. She was naked, while I wore what she had on when I saw her in El Paso. We were heading down a mountainside with a green valley below us. A man on a white horse appeared, but I couldn't see his face.

*The man on the horse said, "Hey-you, that girl is no good for you. She is tainted and will sicken you. You mustn't be with her. If I had my gun ...." And then he disappeared — poof, gone. The dream continued as my hand went to my waist where it rubbed against something hard. I looked down. It was Oliver's six-gun. I took the gun from the scabbard and aimed it at the girl ... .*

# 8: Life Goes On

**June 15, 1888**

The desert willow Colonel Fountain had transplanted seven years before had grown to where it cast its morning shade nearly across the settled soil that had heaped over the small grave. The dappled shade danced with the wind as a young grackle chased some unseen insect across the disturbed ground of the final resting place of Fanny Fountain.

Colonel Fountain rode back to Mesilla every year on Fanny's birthday to tell her his regrets and dream of what might have been. Her brief life was so wrought with painful memories down to the miserable end. Reverend Salpointe had laid her down in Mesilla's little Basilica St. Albino graveyard at the end of Calle de Guadalupe. As the Padre prayed, an unusual morning cloudburst drenched all the attendees, but no one moved until the word, "Amen" was heard. The storm soaked them to the bone, and they must have appeared as somber as anyone had at that small cemetery.

Mariana and the rest of the family visited her modest grave on the anniversary of her death, but the Colonel couldn't bear the memory. Instead, after a year or two, he came alone on her birthday and had every year since. He had collected a small bouquet of wildflowers on his ride from Las Cruces. The Colonel kneeled to them next to Fanny's modest headstone.

"I'm sorry, little one," he whispered to the small marker. "We were so distraught when you died. Father Salpointe handled the arrangements, and I suppose he thought such a brief life didn't warrant a larger marker." He scanned to the right, as he laid out the ten grave sites in his mind that he had later purchased next to Fanny's. It was a guess that eleven would suffice.

Behind him, two young men laughed as they horsed around in the dirt street. The Colonel overheard one of them say, "Jesús, you'll never be as good at mumblety-peg as me."

Jesús said something in return. Colonel Fountain ignored the words, but not the name. It was the voice … the voice … was it him?

The Colonel turned and cried out, "Jesús."

The young man turned, and Colonel Fountain saw he was mistaken — his desire for it to be his long-lost nephew had overcome his usual fine voice recognition. It wasn't the first time it had happened since Jesús disappeared and it wouldn't be the last. Colonel Fountain fluttered his hand in dismissal and turn back to the little grave.

Would a marker for Jesús comfort him? He wondered. Mourning someone that isn't in a grave isn't mourning. It's more like a longing and yet, he needed a place where he could long for the young man, a private place where his sensitivity wouldn't affect his reputation should he decide to resume his territorial legislature campaign.

Wil Rynerson and the others would soon come to cajole him into running for the Territorial House of Representatives. It reminded him of the federal election statute, which he knew word for word, "the Tuesday next after the first Monday in the month of November." November sixth would arrive sooner than he wanted to think about.

It was almost noon when he returned home. A trio of influential Republicans greeted him in the parlor. Wil Rynerson turned from his seat on the Récamier. "Oh, there you are A.J." He was one that called him by his initials, as the Colonel's fellow soldiers had during the war.

Messrs. J.H. Riley and McFie flanked him in the side chairs and Riley added with a smirk, "We thought perhaps you had crashed in a snowbank in the mountains again." They all laughed at Riley's joke, the Colonel somewhat less than the others, which harkened to the Colonel's mishap the previous March.

Colonel Fountain wagged his finger. "Oh, no. I had some business to attend to in Mesilla. I believe I know why you are here. Come into my office where we can talk in private."

There, Riley sat on the leather Chesterfield sofa while Wil and McFie occupied the chairs that faced Colonel Fountain's desk. The Colonel offered them a cigar, which they refused. "Now, tell me, to what do I owe this momentous visit?"

Wil chuckled. "You were right A.J.; you know why we are here. But the situation has changed. All our party members grieve the … uh … I mean worry with you and your family about, uh … Jesús's disappearance, but … well, I'm afraid this can't wait any longer. A few weeks ago, you told us you might withdraw, but things have changed. The Democrats have convinced a man to run that they believe will woo the Mexican vote."

"Who?"

The three men looked at each other. "Albert Fall, new fella from Kentucky." said Riley.

Colonel Fountain turned to Wil. "How does he intend to do that?"

McFie spoke up, "Well, it seems he spent a considerable time mining in Mexico, and he speaks the language well."

"Has he ever been elected to office?" asked the Colonel.

Wil shook his head. "Irrigation Commissioner, but nothing else that we can discover."

Colonel Fountain rocked back in his chair and frowned. "I suppose we can't be too insouciant. Not after what happened in '86."

"Our thoughts, as well, A.J." Wil put up his hands. "I know what you're thinking, but I can't run this year because I've got too many businesses to attend to."

The Colonel stared down at Wil. "I don't have many appointments available myself."

The room was quiet, and Colonel Fountain knew they were waiting him out. "Alright, I'll run, but only to see this college business through and have a hand in drafting the state constitution."

The three men shook hands and smiled. McFie mimed flicking cigar ashes. "We'll have those cigars now, legislator." he said.

The Fountain household seemed to fall back into an uneasy routine, as each family member harbored personal haunts as to the fate of Jesús. The Colonel handled some minor land claim cases, while Tommy returned home to assist his father as he had before Jesús arrived. Mariana threw herself into her church work and Maggie produced more sketches, paintings, and other art works than she had for the previous Southern New Mexico Fair. Jack bunked with his cowboy pals at Wil Rynerson's Ranch. He came by the adobe whenever he was in town, but rarely slept at the Fountains. Katie could now sit on the old Sears and Roebuck catalogs at the table, and Little Henry had taken over the highchair.

---

Tommy had left the El Paso lawyer clerk position only a few months earlier and was therefore still proficient in every task his father would assign him. However, the boredom he experienced in his El Paso job returned. His mind wandered and when

Tommy's mind was unoccupied, a calamitous caper was usually on the horizon.

His initial plan was to print handbills that read "Fireworks Extravaganza". The caper would play out at the fairgrounds on the Fourth of July. He would pay an innocent boy to light long fuses to fake explosives, and then, when everyone had left in disappointment explode a real stick of dynamite as the finale. No, he thought, he'd gone down the explosives road before. That hadn't ended well.

His next idea for some fun was to take a pickaxe onto Main Street and dig. When people asked what he was doing, he would say a geologist told his father a gold motherlode was a foot or two under Las Cruces. He would offer to split the profits with anyone that would help reveal the treasure. When he created enough ruckus, he would walk away. As he considered the possibilities, he realized that his reputation as a trickster would mean certain failure.

A couple of days later, as he did his usual post and telegraph office errands, he noticed an old man slumped against a trash can in the alley behind The Commercial Saloon. His likeness struck him as familiar, but he couldn't place it. As he walked along the boardwalks on the west side of Main Street, it hit him — the man looked like President Grover Cleveland.

When he got to the telegraph office, Miles was busy with a customer, so he trotted to the Democrat's side of the street. There, every business had a picture of their beloved Democratic president. He stared at the photo in the gunsmith's shop until the storekeeper recognized Tommy as a Fountain. The man shooed him into the street where Tommy pondered how to parlay his prank with the tools at hand.

Excitement overwhelmed him. He needed to tell someone. Tommy started back across the street to the telegraph office, when a team of horses and wagon nearly ran over him. The driver screamed, "Watch where you're goin' kid." When he reached the telegraph office, Miles was busy with another customer. He waited until the man left, then went in, closed the door, turned the "open" sign to "closed" and pulled the door's window shade.

Miles sat at his desk with his back to the door. When he heard the shade move, he turned to see Tommy. "What in tarnation are you uh-doin', Tommy?" asked Miles.

"Just listen, Miles. I've got a prank that will out do all my other ones together." He was so excited that he bobbed up and down as he spoke.

Miles scratched the back of his neck and grinned at a memorable one. He took a deep breath. "Well, you can't involve me in this. It could cost me my job."

"Yes, I know. I just need someone to help me get a piece of Democratic Party mail."

Miles shook his head and started to say something, but Tommy interrupted. "I'm not asking you to do anything."

Miles put his hands on his hips. "Well, what then? I got a business to run here, and I don't see how I can …. Whoa, wait a minute. Wait one single, solitary minute. I've got it. You could probably go in the back of those lawyers' offices — say Newcomb or one of them — and fish a letter out of their trash can. That wouldn't be against any laws … I think."

Tommy fidgeted with excitement. "Oh boy, Miles, oh boy." He turned and opened the door. "Just you wait. This one's …" And the door closed. After a moment, Tommy opened it again, pulled up the shade and returned the open sign to face the street. As he turned to leave, he smiled and waved to Miles.

Miles returned to his desk and mumbled, "Sure am glad I know nothing about whatever that boy has in mind … at least I'm tryin' not to," followed by a huffed chuckle.

# 9: Visions or Nightmares

**June 27, 1888**

I awakened from my torment drenched in sweat. I tried to decide who was in my horrible dream as I swung my feet over the side of my bunk. The dream had repeated itself several times in the last couple of weeks. *The girl was the El Paso prostitute, but who was the man on the white horse and why did I have Oliver's pistol?* I looked around and spotted my new boots scattered on the floor in front of me. *Did I take them off?* Through the window, a sliver of the dawn sky over the Sacramento Mountains caught my eye. The door opened and Oliver entered the bunkhouse.

"Oh good, you're awake," he half-whispered. "Gather your things. Oh, and don't forget the likeness you made … of George. We'll be gone for a few days." Then, in an afterthought, "maybe you'll see someone there that will know you."

We would probably go to Las Cruces to report George's murder. I dressed and wondered what to do with my new boots. They and my stockings were still damp. I looked around to ask someone what I should do, but they were still groggy in their bunks. The previous night they had said I should wear them all night, and I didn't know when I had taken them off, so I decided I should continue to wear them since they were still damp. It wasn't easy putting them on, but I succeeded just as one of the other cowboys came to my aid. I hung the damp stockings over the headboard of my bunk and grabbed the rest of my new clothes, still in the storekeeper's bundle, and took them outside. John

Good's former cowboys were there along with Oliver behind them. As I fastened my bedroll and clothes to the saddle, I noticed Oliver was on a huge white horse. The recent nightmare hit me. He noticed my attention wasn't just a casual glance. I refocused on my task and swallowed hard. "Forgot something."

I didn't make eye contact with Oliver. "Make it quick," he said. "We need to get to 'Cruces in time to make a report."

Without looking at him, I nodded and trotted back to the door. Nettie stood in the doorway. She turned to let me pass. "Isn't Oliver's horse a beauty? It's his goin' to town horse."

I grinned and went to my old bed in the corner of the front room. I turned to see if Nettie watched me. She was talking to Oliver. I took my knife from my pocket and held it up as I walked back outside. "Forgot my pocketknife," I said as innocently.

Oliver turned his horse and led us away. I waved goodbye to Nettie, and we set off across the desert. Oliver was in a hurry to get to Las Cruces, and he led us through cactus laced gobernadora patches to save an hour or two. I soon realized that I should have worn my chaps. I had them strapped to the saddle, and so I dismounted and put them on as Oliver and John Good's cowboys moved ahead at an easy pace.

After a few hours, we joined the La Luz to Mesilla trail that would take us to the spur into Las Cruces. Oliver brought his white stallion into a slow lope. As we rode along, my thoughts returned to my dream and the man on the white horse. I could sense a connection to a vague memory, but that was all. As I watched Oliver riding high in the saddle ahead of me, I hoped the man in my dream wasn't him. But I didn't know what my dreams were like before my accident and maybe I had had odd dreams that included people in my life then, as well.

A short time later, we stopped at Pellman's Well to water our horses and take off our chaps. As we turned off the main trail, Pellman's dogs sprinted from his porch, barking. When they reached our horses, they nipped at their fetlocks until Fred

Pellman called them off. Fred and Oliver talked while the other cowboys and I got acquainted. They introduced themselves as Jackson and Fritz and they didn't so much as flinch when I told them my name was Hey-you. I wanted to tell them about my accident, but Oliver was back on his horse and on the trail before I could swing our conversation back to myself.

Even at an easy lope, conversation isn't easy with more than two riders. Oliver seemed to push us a little harder as we left Pellman's Well. My thoughts went back to my visit to El Paso and the girl in front of the parlor house. Memories surfaced. My current experiences always triggered them, but whatever memories I had were only glimpses and my efforts to connect with them always left me frustrated.

I sat on Ol' Nasty as we loped along next to Fritz in a consistent rhythm; I fell into a sort of trance. We crested a small hill where the trail had cut into the sandy soil.

Suddenly, a buckboard wagon appeared in front of me. The man driving it wore a military officer's uniform. A little boy sat next to him. The man snapped the reins as he urged his team to go faster. He had a trimmed mustache, and despite the warm day he wore a military overcoat and the boy had an Indian blanket pulled over his head. When the boy tried to turn to see who chased them, his father pulled him back and pushed him onto the floor of the wagon under the seat. The man turned the buckboard hard to the left off the trail when a shot rang out from my right, and the man fell from the wagon as the little boy threw up his arms.

I blinked and the vivid images were gone and instead, the back of Oliver, his white stallion, and Jackson on his bay were all that was there. Fritz must have noticed my look of confusion and terror. All at once, my feet and ankles itched something terrible, and I reached down and tried to dig through the stiff leather.

That distracted Fritz as well, and he said, "Shouldn't have worn those boots, your stockings are probably soaked."

"I didn't wear any stockings."

Fritz just shook his head and said, "You're in fer pure hell, then."

I swallowed hard and hoped Fritz was exaggerating how bad it might get. To distract myself, I checked the sun, and I wondered if we would make Las Cruces in time to see whoever we needed to see. We gained some refreshing cooler air as we turned past Mineral Hill and climbed toward San Augustin Pass. I wanted to stop and claw at my ankles, but two riders several hundred yards ahead of us distracted me. They rode slower than us and when we caught up to them, I could see that one rode a white horse like Oliver's. *Maybe it wasn't Oliver in my dream.* Oliver whistled and the two men waited for us.

Oliver introduced the man on the roan as Tom Tucker. He was stout, and at first I thought his face was ruddy and weather-worn, but on further consideration it seemed full of scars. When he turned to say something to the other man, I noticed he lacked the top half of his left ear. I later learned it resulted from one of the many fracases Tucker got into. He had left Arizona with the law on his heels after his latest bloody scrape. As I watched him, he reached for his six-gun over and over as though he thought it had fallen out of its scabbard. When Oliver introduced me as Hey-you, Tucker gave me a once over as I tried to claw through my new boots. The entire scene made me uncomfortable.

Tucker introduced his friend, a bearded, eye-patched hombre by the name of Bill Carr. Carr said, "My friends call me 'Good-Eye' and my Mexican friends 'Tuerto'." Neither Tuerto nor Tucker looked like someone you would want to have on your tail.

After exchanges of destination and the like, Oliver asked Carr where he got his white horse.

"I didn't steal 'em, if that's what you mean."

"No, no. I was wonderin' if you got him from old man Stearns back in Taylor County. That's where I got … well, it was my Pa what got Baron for me."

"My Pa got Pearl from some old man in Texas, but I don't know where 'zactly. She's just a filly. It's the first time I've rode her this far, that's why we are takin' it easy."

Tucker looked me over, then turned to Oliver. "Hey-you? What kind of beef-headed name is that? Your mama must'a dropped her reins when she named you."

As I opened my mouth, another episode of itchy feet and ankles overwhelmed me, and Oliver stepped in. "Found him up on the San Augustin in April. Lost his mind. Don't know who he is or where he belongs, but he's right smart otherwise. Says Hey-you reminds him of somethin' and asked that we use it ... so we do."

Tucker and Carr chuckled. "Do tell," said Carr. He slapped his thigh with a guffaw. "I heard everythin' now."

Oliver scratched his two-day beard. "So, what's your business in 'Cruces?"

Tucker cocked his head. "My business is right, and it's gonna stay that way."

"No offense. I respect your right to keep your business to yourself. I was jus' thinkin' that if we all rode into 'Cruces, we would make quite a sight with our two whites leadin' the way."

Tucker smiled. "Folks'll surely take note. You can bet on that."

Scratch ... scratch ... scratch. Switch sides and dig ... dig ... dig.

"Why not?" said Carr, as he ignored my frantic gesticulations. "Any particular place you want us to follow you to?"

"I ain't quite decided ... "Oliver paused and looked at me. "Hey-you, what in the devil is wrong with you?"

"I'm not quite sure, but my feet are about to itch me off this horse."

Jackson pointed to my feet. "It's them new boots. They soaked 'em last night, and he's been wearin' 'em all day with no socks in this hot sun. Probably got foot rot."

Oliver stood in his stirrups. "Well, one of ya git 'em off him. Anybody got any bakin' soda with 'em?"

Carr rummaged in his saddlebag as he said, "I got some." He pulled out a new box of Arm & Hammer and tossed it to Fritz. He and Jackson got off their horses, pulled off my boots, and sprinkled a good bit of baking soda into them. Jackson brought a long leather thong, which they used to finagle a way to attach the boots and throw them over the back of my horse. Fritz said, "Ya don't want that stink out in front of ya."

I rubbed baking soda into my feet and between my toes, as Oliver continued, "Like I said, I ain't quite decided whether we should go to the courthouse or the sheriff's office. I want to report the murder of my friend."

"George McDonald? I heared he shot himself," said Tucker as he struggled to ignore the clamor to tend to my feet.

"Ain't so," said Oliver. "And I got these two men that will testify to the fact that Walter Good executed him."

"Them Goods is a cantankerous bunch," said Carr. "You know what you're gettin' yerself into?"

"I do," said Oliver.

"Well," began Tucker, "I ain't too eager to get any closer to the sheriff's office than the nearest saloon."

"Fine then," replied Oliver. "If we're gonna walk our horses and I'm to make it in time, we best get started."

We rode into the north end of Las Cruces' wide main street after supper time with just enough speed to raise the dust on the wide caliche street. The courthouse and sheriff's office were at the south end, so we had to ride all the way through town. There weren't near as many people on the street as Oliver would have liked, but enough folks noted four rough looking cowboys led by two serious looking men on white horses that word got around.

The town was a little bigger than La Luz. I studied both sides of the street. I hoped something would be familiar. As we approached the plaza, on the right was a storefront with a prominent sign that read "Las Cruces Telegraph Office" and a little further down the street, in the middle of the plaza was a church — St. Genevieve's Church, the sign read. It seemed like I had seen both places before.

Unlike La Luz, boardwalks fronted most of the Main Street stores, but it was the church that sparked a memory. The magnificent building had two tall bell towers, crowned with crosses, which flanked a double door entry. A short staircase was wide at the bottom and narrowed to the width of the main entry doors. A memory flashed of me next to a girl with others lined up along the edges of the stairway and a photographer's tripod set up in the street. *Was I from Las Cruces? Was the girl my wife? Had we just been married?* Before I could dwell on these questions for which there were no answers, we came upon the sheriff's office.

Just as it came into view, Tucker turned into the Alhambra Saloon hitching post and the rest of us followed. Oliver said, "We're too late for the courthouse, so I'll have a nice glass of buttermilk with you boys."

Carr snickered, "Buttermilk?"

"Yep boys, I don't drink."

"You sure are strange bunch," said Tucker.

The Alhambra Saloon was not just the closest drinking establishment to the sheriff's office, it was also the nearest to the courts and therefore attracted lawyers and clerks. A rough and dusty bunch of cowboys walking through the batwing doors was sure to be noticed — along with me in my bare feet. A large round table in the center of the room was open, despite the crowded bar.

So, we sat there. After we placed our order with the waitress — no saloon girls here — a middle-aged man came to the table and introduced himself as Charles Metcalfe, editor, and publisher of the Rio Grande Republican newspaper. "You boys made quite an entrance. Is there some special reason for coming into town today?"

Tucker took a small step forward. "We've come to be heard by the grand jury about a murder," said Tucker.

Oliver's stare would have iced-over a pot of hot coffee on a southern New Mexico July day. He never revealed his purpose without a good reason.

"Are you talking about the George McDonald murder? I reported on that in last Saturday's paper."

Oliver realized the cat was out of the bag. "How did you find out about it?"

"Fella by the name of Cooper, Jim Cooper, came by the newspaper office last Friday, and I interviewed him." Metcalfe removed the newspaper from under his arm and handed it to Oliver.

While Oliver read it, Metcalfe asked, "Were you boys subpoenaed?"

The two cowboy witnesses, as well as Tucker and Carr looked at each other and shrugged.

"Will Deputy Rucker from La Luz accompany you to court?" asked Metcalfe.

Oliver looked up from the paper and said, "He's as worthless as a sidesaddle on a sow. The man works for the people that did the deed."

"Well then, will you go to the sheriff or Colonel Fountain to ask them to investigate?"

The mention of the name Fountain distracted me, but my mouth opened and words tumbled out, "No sir, Mr. Lee is here as an affiant to swear out a private criminal complaint against the man that murdered George, and we have these two cowboys to testify before the grand jury."

Everyone at the table, Mr. Metcalfe included, stared at me in disbelief. Even I was aghast at my use of the word affiant. *How did I know that?*

Oliver had scanned the article and threw the newspaper into the middle of the table. "Seems like a fair account to me. I'll read it to you boys later."

"Uh," I couldn't believe I was about to speak about the law again. "No sir, I don't think you should do that because there are lots of lawyers in here that will testify that you tainted the evidence brought by these men when you read them an account that might differ from their own initial observations."

Again, the stares.

Everyone had stopped their own conversations to listen in when Metcalfe approached us and now murmurs swept through the saloon about the ragtag boy with legal knowledge.

Oliver blinked several times. "How do you know this and why didn't you tell me before?" asked Oliver.

"I ... I don't know. It might be something about this place. I feel like I have been here before. And it now comes to me that a federal court may not allow a private citizen to make a criminal complaint because it would encourage revenge filings."

I couldn't believe the words that came out of my mouth. I had my back to most of the room and so I couldn't see their reactions. They couldn't have been surprised as much as I was.

Oliver drank the last of his buttermilk while the waiter brought another round of drinks. "Ain't no sense in goin' to the sheriff here. The man's a Republican and tied in with the Santa Fe Ring."

Metcalfe wagged his head, "Oh no, sir, you are positively mistaken on that. Santiago Ascarate is a Democrat. In fact, nearly all our county officials are Democrats. They swept the elections in '86."

Oliver squinted at the man. "A Democrat here ain't a Democrat in Texas."

"Well, no, I imagine not, but we are in New Mexico." Metcalfe saluted Oliver with his whiskey shot. "I think you'll get a fair shake from Santiago if you can catch him in his office. Dona Ana is a mighty big county and you'll do well to find him here."

# 10: The Puzzle Grows

We stayed in the Commercial Hotel for the night. The Good ranch hands and Tucker and Carr must have 'painted the town' because the next morning they were slow to rise despite Oliver's insistent knocks on their door.

The Commercial Hotel was cheerless, bordering on dismal. After the elegant Grand Central in El Paso a couple of nights earlier, I felt like I had awakened from a dream and found myself in a stable. The beds didn't have straw on them, but the mattresses seemed filled with it. I reasoned perhaps Oliver thought we might have to stay longer than a couple of days and therefore, frugality was in order.

It wasn't unusual for me to lie awake as I tried to solve the puzzle of my identity. Images of the telegraph office and church spun in my mind. The difference on this night was that I had to pause every few minutes to scratch my itchy feet. Then there was the previous night's dream about a man on a white horse — I wrongly assumed it was Oliver. Still the man's direction to shoot the girl from the parlor house who rode the burro disturbed me. But the familiar and astounding events of the afternoon made me wonder how I was linked to Las Cruces. But nothing connected, and the frustration resulted in a restless night.

I could hear Oliver tossing and turning as well. It was likely because of his propensity to weigh the ramifications of every decision. When we arose the next morning, I felt inside my boots, and they had dried. My feet were better, although still itchy now and then. I patted baking soda on them and added more to the boots, then joined Oliver in the hotel dining room. As we waited for our breakfast and sipped coffee, Oliver caught my attention. "I don't know how you know about the law, but let me ask you somethin'."

I hesitated because I did not know how I knew those things myself. Without a hint of how I might answer him, I frowned and nodded my consent.

"I know Metcalfe said I would have to report the murder to the sheriff first, but since the sheriff won't be here for a while, if I take it straight to the district court and they won't hear us, will that prevent me from goin' to the sheriff later?"

As he spoke, my mind somehow churned up all the information I needed to answer. It was such an odd sensation — like I had no control of my mind. I wanted to walk away to stop it, but I couldn't do that to Oliver. He, Mary, and Nettie had been so good to me. If I could help him now, I felt I should, regardless of how unsettled it made me feel. I clenched my teeth and closed my eyes, and the words just came out: "I would say no. The court will just refer you to the sheriff. They can't make any judgements about your case unless the sheriff notifies them."

"Well then," I opened my eyes to see him rise from the table, "we'll check at the sheriff's office first and if he ain't there we'll head back over to the court and try our luck anyhow."

"How about Colonel Fountain? Metcalfe said ..."

Straight off, Oliver held his hand up for me to stop. "We ain't goin' to Fountain for nothin'. Cooper tells me the man can't be trusted to cinch yer saddle."

I nodded. The Fountain name was familiar. His reputation may have been the reason. Still, it seemed Oliver had more faith in my legal advice than I did.

As Metcalfe had predicted, Sheriff Ascarate wasn't in his office. A deputy sat at the sheriff's desk. Well, I suppose that's what you call what he was doing. He sat in the chair, but he had crossed his feet on the desk while his chair wobbled back and forth on the back legs. I guess he thought it was a test of his skill.

To Oliver's request about when the sheriff would return, the deputy shrugged. "He said Wednesday, but he hardly ever arrives when he says he will. He could return any time between now and a week from now."

Oliver frowned. "Well, where'd he go? Maybe we can catch up to him."

The deputy took his feet off the desk and spun to point to a county map tacked on the wall above him. "Well, he was doin' the east half of the county. Next month he'll do the west half. He said he was gonna start up north at Rincon then over to Engle and then through Mockingbird Pass and over around Three Rivers. He said he needed to check into a murder of some fella name McDonald. And … ".

I thought Oliver would throw his hat on the floor and jump on it. He held his temper, but his volume grew. "That's what I'm here for. I have two witnesses I want to testify before the grand jury."

I took a small sidestep closer to Oliver, hoping that would calm him.

The deputy said, "Gosh, too bad you didn't …." then stopped when he realized it would have upset Oliver further.

"Can you put my men on the grand jury witness stand?" Oliver asked.

The deputy stood and took off his hat. "I'm real sorry Mr. uh, …."

"Lee, Oliver Milton Lee and this here is my loyer Hey, ahem, uh … Mr. You."

I looked at my itchy feet.

"Well, I'm sorry, Mr. Lee, but deputy Rucker in La Luz sent us a message. He said there weren't no witnesses, but that is why the sheriff has gone over there 'cause we got word there was a feud goin' on and McDonald got caught up in it."

Oliver took off his hat and twirled it around on his finger. I'd seen him do that before when he was thinking something through. The deputy sat back down and raised his feet to the desk, but before he could place them there, Oliver said, "You didn't answer my question, sonny. What's a man supposed to do to get justice in this god forsaken county?"

"I can have your men write out what they saw — they witnessed it in person — right?"

Oliver put his hat back on. "No, but they have firsthand knowledge of what the man said to another man and there's scars on Walter's horse that match a broken Spanish dagger at the murder site."

"That ain't gonna do it, sir."

Oliver frowned and put his hands on his waist. The deputy sensed this was not acceptable and his words came fast and furious as he hoped to avoid a confrontation. "What you're describin' ain't what they call ad-missible ev-i-dence." Oliver tipped his hat up so the deputy could see his glare. "But I'll write down whatever it is you want to tell me and if the sheriff decides — and maybe he'll find out somethin' better over there — then he could go to the grand jury with the ev-i-dence he's got … and yourn; and then get an order to investigate further. But if'n he don't agree with y'all or the grand jury, don't see fit …."

Oliver groaned and looked at me. I turned to him and said,. "There's no sense going to the courthouse if we don't have the sheriff's support."

The deputy reestablished his teetering act with his feet back up on the desk, and I reached down to dig through the boot at an itch in my right ankle. "'Course, even if the sheriff agrees and gets an indictment it might take a couple years to convict the fella … if'n he's guilty, that is."

I wished the deputy hadn't said that and I think he was sorry he couldn't take it back. I sensed it was a good time to move the conversation in a different direction. "Shall I go get Jackson and …." I couldn't think of the other man's name.

"Fritz," said Oliver, as he glared at the deputy. He took off his hat and twirled it around a finger again.

The deputy took out his pocketknife and trimmed his fingernails while he rocked back and forth. It felt like a stare down without the stares. Behind us, each tick-tock of the pendulum clock elevated the tension in the room.

"Yep." Oliver put his hat back on. "You fetch 'em, but wait, neither one can write, and I want my loyer here to write down what they say and you both can sign it along with whoever is tellin' it."

The deputy paused his personal care and with his knife, pointed it toward Oliver. "That's fine sir, but I why would you doubt I would record what they say just as they said it?" I paused at the door, and thought, this could still go terribly wrong.

"Let's just say I've been down this road before." Oliver turned to me. "Yes, please fetch Jackson and Fritz."

It took some time, as they weren't in their room. My next best guess was correct and after no luck at a couple of places, I found them 'entertaining' a saloon girl in Jerrell's Saloon a few buildings down the street past the Commercial Hotel.

Oliver was waiting for us in front of the sheriff's office when I returned with Jackson and Fritz. "Hey-you, take care of this, please. I have some other business to tend to."

We recorded the boys' accounts for the rest of the morning and a good portion of the afternoon. Jackson scrawled his first name and said, "It's the only thing I know how to write." Fritz signed with an 'X'. I dated each document and my drawings with the time and place of the event and had the deputy countersign. When we finished, I told the boys they could go back to the saloon. I stayed and made copies, which I had them sign in the suitable place before they left.

At supper in the hotel that night, I asked Oliver why he called me his lawyer and how he knew I was smart. "You talk like a loyer. As for how I knew you are smart, you keep your mouth shut until you've let everyone else show how stupid they are." I thought about what he said for a minute or two while I chewed on a bite of tough steak, but it just seemed to get bigger and bigger. Finally, I gave up and forced it down followed by a long drink of beer.

As I wiped my mouth and rearranged the silver, Oliver also said, "And you've got good table manners. Fritz would have put that hunk of gristly steak on the table. I don't know where or how, but somehow you got exposed to some proper schoolin' and your writin' shows you did a lot."

It seemed like a good time to tell Oliver about the things that seemed familiar — all except the dream that might have included him. I told him I got frustrated because I couldn't make sense of how it all fit together. He replied, "Well, I think we know you weren't no cowhand, no-how. I mean, you're earnin' your keep alright, but that ain't nothin' you were doin' before I found you. "

We waited for the sheriff to return for several days. Tucker and Carr didn't stay in town for long, but Oliver liked their guns and hired them on as hands. He promised they would have little cowboying to do and that sold them on the job.

A full day without wearing my boots combined with some new cotton stockings made my feet feel much better. Nevertheless, I stocked up on baking soda from a mercantile on the east side of Main Street. No one recognized me.

Oliver grew impatient, unusual for him, and announced we would leave the next morning. That evening, after we finished our supper, I strolled up and down Main Street hoping someone would recognize me or that another clue to my identity would reveal itself. While I was gone, the deputy found Oliver in the hotel dining room and told him the sheriff wanted to talk to him.

When I returned, Oliver lay on his bed with his six-gun next to his hand. His boots stood beside the bed with his legs crossed at the ankles. When I opened the door, he opened one eye and, fast as lightning, his hand went to his gun. When he saw it was me, he closed his eyes and put his hand on his stomach. I removed my boots and mimicked his pose. Oliver turned to me and opened one eye. "Sheriff's back."

He filled me in on the ten-minute meeting with the sheriff. He ended with, "So, the deputy didn't put the sheriff in a bad spot. They must've practiced, because what he had to say was about word for word what the deputy tol' us."

I sat up in my bed. "Maybe it was because what the deputy told us is the truth?"

Oliver looked at me like I was a traitor for such a suggestion. "I mean, I imagine the court has some guidelines for the sheriff for referring cases to them."

"He won't recommend the case to the grand jury. I knew it was a wasted trip. So now, we have to decide how to handle Walter Good ourselves."

That sounded ominous to me. He didn't come right out and say it, but his mother was fond of quoting word-for-word Leviticus 24:19-21.

"Don't worry, we'll let things calm down. If we wait a while, it won't be obvious, but ol' John'll get the message."

As Fritz and Jackson packed their meager gear on their horses, I stood next door and looked at a small window display in a mercantile. My gaze picked up my reflection in the window and it surprised me. My hair and beard were so long and scraggly. I mumbled, "No one could possibly recognize me." Oliver overheard. "What? Somebody recognized you?"

"No," I pointed to the store window, "I saw my reflection in this glass, and realized that my face wouldn't be familiar to anyone with all this hair."

Oliver nodded. "When we get back home, you can use my razor and Ma will cut your hair."

# 11: Caper Capper

**June 26, 1888**

Tommy thought about his fourth of July caper during every spare moment. He even poured his own money into what he considered his grand finale prank on the town. Best of all, Democrats would suffer the greatest humiliation.

He found the man in the same spot he saw him the day before. He must have sat on the ground with his back against the wall of The Commercial Saloon, but at some point, he had slumped over. When Tommy saw him, he lay with his legs extended and his side against some trash piled next to a full garbage can. Tommy picked up the garbage can lid from the ground and clanged it back onto the can. The man stirred and Tommy helped him sit up. The smell of whiskey and something else wafted into the air. Tommy waved his hand in front of his nose to disperse what he then recognized as the putrid combination of urine and whiskey. When the man was alert ... well, at least awake, Tommy pulled a pint bottle of wine from his pocket and offered it to him.

Tommy didn't want to fully reveal himself. "My name is Tom."

"Thank you, kind sir. My name is Gruffydd." He paused for a moment and opened the bottle. "But my friends call me Gruff ... my enemies too, come to think on it, but I think you have just put ye-self into the friend category." He saluted Tommy with the bottle, "Lechyd da." Tommy expected that was some type of salutation, but even aside from that, the man's heavy accent was so odd that Tommy had to listen hard through the sing-song lilt to understand him. Gruff took a long draw on the bottle, draining over half. "Ahh, that's a tidy drink. As my friend, ye will thank me for knowing I prefer whiskey … and any brand or quality will do … but in a pinch, I've drunk much worse than this stuff." He finished the bottle and tossed it into the trash heap beside him.

During their casual conversation, Gruff revealed he was from Wales, while Tommy judged whether Gruff could manage the part of Grover Cleveland. Gruff was just happy to have someone to talk with that wasn't trying to shoo him away. Tommy would need Gruff to stay sober enough that he could step out onto a caboose platform and address Independence Day revelers.

He thought about Gruff as he walked back to his contracts and wills. By the time he reached the Fountain office, he had decided that Gruff was well-suited. He resembled Cleveland and his Welsh-English accent was so garbled that Tommy struggled to understand him, even when Gruff was sober. Tommy liked that because he didn't want the prank to incite people to do anything. He doubted anyone could understand him unless they had associated with drunken Welshmen before. He decided that was a remote possibility. The more Tommy thought about Gruff as his Cleveland the more he liked it.

Tommy needed to secure Gruff's services. The Welshman didn't comment when Tommy told him his basic plan, which included Gruff taking the train to El Paso after his 'speech' and a five-dollar payment. But Gruff was lukewarm to the idea. He licked his lips and Tommy took that as an overt clue about what might sweeten the deal.

Tommy smiled. "The fiver should be enough for a return ticket here and when you return, there will be three bottles of whisky for you at The Commercial Saloon."

"I'll need something to keep my spirits up on the train," prompted Gruff.

"Alright, I'll provide a bottle for the train as well. The morning before, I will take you to the station to the north and there will be someone to help you get on board. You'll need other clothes, and I will provide them when I pick you up on the morning of the third — that will be next Tuesday."

"Seems you have thought this out fairly well, sonny."

Tommy nodded. "Now, if you can't walk on your own to the back of the caboose to deliver the speech, our deal is off as far as any further whisky or payment. If you fulfill your end of the deal, I'll provide a bottle of whisky for the rest of the ride and when you return the next day from El Paso, there will be the three additional bottles." With the reward of whiskey established, Gruff only half listened to Tommy until he mentioned the speech.

"Speech?"

"Don't worry, it won't matter what you say because the people that will gather to hear you will have had something to drink as well. Besides, I can barely understand you now and you're sober."

Gruff laughed, dug around in the trash, and found a bottle with a cigar butt swilling in a spot of whisky. He expertly drank the whisky without ingesting the cigar butt.

As the moon popped in and out of some rare clouds one night, Tommy fished a Democratic Party letter out of Newcomb and McFie's trash. The next day, he cajoled a leery Maggie into making three copies of the letterhead. Tommy composed a notice on one that said the President was to travel incognito on the train and that the conductor and engineer were to cooperate with his security detail so that the president could make a brief speech at the Las Cruces stop. He held it up for a close examination. All he could do was hope it passed muster.

The railway schedule indicated the train would arrive about twelve-thirty on the fourth. That would be soon after the community picnic had begun, which was at the fairgrounds, a short distance from the depot. With any luck, people would time their picnic lunches around the train's arrival. If it was late, it would be even better because they would be a little more affected by their drinks.

Tommy wrote a second letter on the Democratic National Party letterhead. In it, he requested the local newspapers announce the President's arrival on the fourth of July afternoon train, when he would speak to his supporters. The letter also demanded the editors withhold the news until Monday, July second. He justified this hint of secrecy by writing:

> *This slight inconvenience is required considering the extreme Republican leaning community. This short notice will minimize the time that riffraff would have to plan an assassination attempt. The Garfield assassination is still fresh on the President's security detail's minds, and we cannot be too careful.*

He signed the letter, William B. Snogglebush, Director of Security.

Mr. Snogglebush did not exist.

The biggest problem he faced was making certain Gruff got onto the train at one of the stations to the north of Las Cruces. He wasn't sure why, but Dona Ana seemed too close. The next station to the north of Dona Ana was Selden, where the fort, ringed with its massive adobe walls, still held its ground with a minimum of one company of 'Buffalo soldiers'. At first, Tommy discounted Selden station because the fort had been on the decline since the army had recaptured Geronimo.

But then, as he considered his options, he remembered the army mustered out soldiers at Selden and many left without a smidgen of love for the experience. Still, he would have to be careful not to enlist actual soldiers to escort his fake president because of his own militia experience and status. Although he worked for his father, he still was an on-leave member of the militia. He didn't think a turn in the guardhouse would endear him to his father.

That afternoon, Tommy became bored with his work and a thought occurred to him. If he could find a couple of soldiers that would muster out soon, they could wear their uniforms as they left. The prospect excited Tommy so much that he disregarded his fears.

Soldiers often took their leaves in Dona Ana, or Las Cruces, and it wasn't uncommon to see them about. Tommy reasoned the serious drinkers wouldn't travel any further than they had to get liquored-up and so he rode up to Dona Ana one afternoon. The De La O Saloon appeared to be a favorite of the soldiers and he bought drinks for a few, which always led to some conversation. He would begin with his status with the militia. The soldier would reply with his own situation and Tommy could decide whether to continue or move on with a smile and a wish of good luck. On his third attempt, he found what he thought was a reliable candidate.

Corporal James Murphy, a white soldier, told Tommy that the army would muster him out on July third. In an Irish accent, he said, "Yep, I enlisted on Independence Day in 1883. Me time is up, and I cannot wait to rid me-self of these damnable wool uniforms."

Tommy took a sip of his beer. "Well, might you wear it for just one more day if you could make a few dollars?"

Murphy rubbed his rusty colored, well-trimmed beard and took a long draw on his beer. "Don't know. Wha' d' ye offer?"

Tommy's little scheme was costing him some real money. He hadn't decided what this part of his caper was worth because he wasn't sure he would even find a soldier that mustered out at the right time. "Well, how does two dollars sound ... in hard cash, no paper?" he asked Murphy.

Murphy grimaced. "I might be Irish, me, but I know two dollars ain't a few. No, I cannot don these miserable wool sacks any longer. If I must wear wool, ye can make it tweed, if ye please."

Tommy shook his head, drank the last of his beer, and got up to leave.

"Wait, for wha' is ye purpose?"

Tommy paused. If he told this man his plan and the man chose not to take part, then it was certain the prank would spread like wildfire. "It's for a … uh, kind of joke I want to play on … some friends."

"Well, why didn't ye say so, laddie? I adore jokes. Tell me about your prank."

Tommy gave Murphy some details, but stuck to the specific role Murphy would play. He didn't want to mention President Cleveland's name.

"I don't catch your meanin'. Where is the joke in that?"

Tommy frowned. "If I tell you …." He stopped because he didn't know this man and Tommy was sure, based upon his experience in the militia, that Murphy would tell someone and then it would be all over the fort.

Murphy's face brightened. "So, it seems this might not be just a simple joke. Am I right?" Tommy's face told Murphy all he needed to know. "So, then laddie, when I was but a pup, me brother and me would play jokes in the streets to make a wee bit of spendin' money. In Ireland, we called it 'taking the piss.' Ye have come to the right man for the job. Now tell me how it is … all of it and I won't peep a word to nobody."

Tommy laid out his plan in full, and when he mentioned President Cleveland, Mr. Murphy grinned in delight. "The man should be hanged." At which point, Tommy realized they should find a private place to finish their discussion. A half-hour later,

Murphy had told Tommy that he despised the President for some obscure reason related to the Army.

"Keep ye pennies me boy. I'd nearly pay ye to do this."

Murphy said he had a friend that would help. He vouched for the man, also a corporal, that would muster out the day before Murphy. Tommy had solved his biggest problem. They reviewed how it would go several times and agreed to meet the morning of the third at a location along the Rio Grande. Once they had settled Gruff, and they had rehashed the plans, Tommy would return to Las Cruces. The morning of the fourth, the two 'soldiers' would take Gruff north to the next station at Randall. As near as he could tell, the prank was legal, but Tommy didn't want them to buy Gruff's ticket in person. After a back and forth about it, Murphy said he knew a Mexican girl that would buy the tickets for them, and that was that.

Tommy had been selecting presidential garb — including fresh under clothes — from the several used and consignment stores on the Democrat side of Main Street, but he couldn't find a top hat. He knew no other hat would do. At last, one in good condition was available and Tommy made the purchase the Monday morning before the fourth.

On the evening of the second of July, he went over his plan as he lay in his bed. The post office had delivered his handwritten notice to Mr. Metcalfe at the *Rio Grande Republican,* and he had tucked the letter the soldiers would show the conductor into his jacket. The next morning, he would stash a backup copy in his saddlebags. He hoped his penmanship, which wasn't the best — certainly not what one might expect from the party's director of security — was good enough to fool the conductor. He wished he had typed it on the Remington typewriter, which reminded him of Jesús.

How insensitive he was to his cousin's plight. Animals could have emaciated and stripped Jesús' body to the bone. He might have wandered pell mell or decided, for some unknown reason, to leave the Fountains. *Had he said something mean to Jesús without realizing it?* Tommy glanced at the window where moonbeams cast through a slit between the curtains. *I should never have started this prank. It's an offense to Jesús' memory.* A tear dribbled down Tommy's cheek and onto his pillow. He realized his prank was his selfish need to distract himself from Jesús' plight. *Come home to us cousin, we need you.*

The next morning, his father objected to Tommy's lame excuse for not working yet another day. After a quarter of an hour of heated discussion, he convinced his father that he would finish all the documents that needed copying by their due dates.

Mateo had the two-seater buggy ready for Tommy and he drove the several blocks to the alley alongside The Commercial Saloon. No Gruff. Tommy looked all around the building and finally found him down the street alongside another saloon. At least he was awake.

Gruff tucked one leg under himself and smiled at the sight of Tommy. "Why, Tom, I've been awaitin' for ye." he said.

"Why are you here and not back at the place I last found you? Never mind, you can tell me on the trail."

Gruff explained that the bartender at The Commercial Saloon had thrown him into the street over some minor disagreement over payment.

"Surely, you've brought me a tidy bottle to shorten the trip?" Gruff prompted.

Tommy handed him a pint of whiskey and suggested he make it last.

When they reached the location agreed upon, Corporal Murphy and a negro man in uniform stood next to a tent they had erected. The campsite was army neat.

Murphy approached the buggy and shook hands with Tommy. "I would like you to meet my friend, Corporal July Jones. He mustered out yesterday." Tom shook his hand and introduced Gruff. Jones picked up Gruff's sack of clothes from the back of the buggy and took them to the tent.

Gruff stepped out of the buggy and nearly fell on his nose. Murphy and Tommy helped him to his feet. The poor man's foot was twisted at an awkward angle.

Tommy grimaced. "Oh no, Gruff, have you broken your foot?"

"Oh, no, it's me lameness. 'Tis nothin' truly. I came to America to work the mines, but not long after I started in the Bennett Mine above Organ City, this happened to me. They said it was an accident, but the boys didn't like me, and I have often wondered …"

Murphy cringed at the sight of the twisted limb. "It's obvious you broke it some time ago. Couldn't the doctor reset it?"

Gruff shrugged. "The surgeon came and shook his head and said there was nothing he could do. But do not bother yourselves with it, boys. I've made my way and such as it 'tis, it is what I must accept. Which reminds me, is there another bottle about? This leg is painin' me somethin' dreadful."

Tommy was aghast. "Oh Gruff, I did not know."

"Aye, you thought I was just a hangin' waste of a man."

The men had probably seen worse, and yet their eyes darted back and forth between Gruff and Tommy. Gruff's face scrunched up in pain as he limped away from the buggy.

"The bottle man. I'm about to be a screamin' with the pain."

Jones ran to the tent and brought out a half-full whiskey bottle.

"Is that all there is? Lordy, just cut me leg off then. I mightn't make it otherwise."

While Gruff established himself on the sandy river beach under a young cottonwood, Tommy and the soldiers discussed how they might get Gruff the liquor he required to ease his pain. They realized the closest source would be the local senorita's place where the soldiers went to 'relax with the girls.' Tommy gave Jones the money and he and Murphy departed. Before he left, Murphy assured Tommy he could stay with Gruff until noon, when his duty-shift began.

Expenses mounted and between Tommy's second thoughts and Gruff's revelation, his resolve for the prank lessened. He gave the last of his money for Gruff's return ticket to Murphy to hold. Had the Corporals not volunteered to do their part free of charge, he wasn't sure he would have gone through with it. The buggy hit a pothole, and he realized it was too late for second thoughts. He snapped the reins, and the pinto his father had bought to replace Sinsin pranced down the trail to Las Cruces.

# 12: The Fourth

Independence Day brought cowboys into saloons and onto the Las Cruces streets. At midnight, they fired their weapons into the air. Tommy thrashed in his bed all night with the cacophony of discharged guns and worry over his caper. Toward dawn he fell asleep but dreamed that Gruff had pointed him out in the crowd. In perfect American English, he told the throng how Tommy had schemed to make fools of them all. Gruff then pulled him aside and lashed him to a pole while Murphy and Jones formed a firing squad. He awakened when he saw their eyes at the end of their rifle barrels.

Soon, Jack, Maggie, and Katie were ready to go to town to watch the parade on the wide Las Cruces Main Street. Tommy joined them; his angst masked by his drowsiness. Colonel Fountain had asked Rosa's family to join them for the community meal at noon and so Mariana and Rosa stayed behind to prepare their picnic lunch.

With Jesús still missing, Colonel Fountain wasn't as enthusiastic as usual, but no one noticed because the celebration was tip top. The Colonel's militia completed their rifle salutes at eight a.m., then gathered at the south end of town where they led the parade. Their cavalry, infantry units, and Forts Bliss and Selden's fife and bugle corps followed. La Mesa's fife and bugle corps and the Fort Selden band split smart marchers from Fort Bliss and Selden's military units. The Las Cruces band brought up the rear.

Each band played a patriotic selection at the four corners of Main and Acequia., always facing the Republican side of Main Street. The Mesilla Band led with "The Star-Spangled Banner" and everyone sang along with hats or hands over hearts. "Battle Hymn of the Republic" by the La Mesa Band primed the crowd for the finale. The Las Cruces Band, accompanied by the Fort Selden drum and bugle corps performed their rendition of "Battle Cry of Freedom", which brought the house down. There hadn't been rain for weeks and the dust billowed from the marchers and their horses, but it didn't faze a soul. Every person on both sides of the street knew the lyrics and sang their hearts out. At first, the two partisan sides tried to out-sing the other. Before long, prideful tears flowed throughout the parade route. As the music ended, people threw firecrackers into the street and fired six-guns into the air.

As the dust settled and the revelers dispersed, many noticed the handbills that Charles Metcalfe had scattered up and down Main Street. Tommy had expected the Democrats to meet the train. The excitement on their side of Main Street bore that out, but Republicans had interest, as well.

"Oh, God," mumbled Tommy, "what have I done?"

"What's that?" asked Maggie.

"Oh, nothing. It's nothing." Tommy picked at some imagined spot on his pants.

Maggie knew Tommy too well, and she was skeptical. She scanned the area for what might have disturbed him. Her eye caught the bold flyer on a nearby hitching post.

### President Cleveland to speak

### from the Atchison, Topeka, and Santa Fe caboose

### on the afternoon train on Independence Day

"Hmph!" Maggie turned to Tommy. "Do you know anything about this?"

A couple of people near Maggie looked as she pointed to the handbill. Tommy jerked his head in the other direction. He shrugged and tried to move away, but several onlookers pinned him as they moved closer to read the notice.

Maggie pulled Tommy away and whispered, "Does this have to do with the Democratic Party letterheads I made?"

Tommy shook his head and looked past her at some unseen object down the street.

Maggie's voice rose. "Tomás Fountain. If you have gotten me involved in one of your … your…." She threw up her arms and turned her back on Tommy.

About that time, Colonel Fountain joined them as the crowd moved down Depot Street on their way to the fairgrounds. He motioned Tommy and Maggie into an alley where Maggie told her father she had copied the Democratic Party's letterhead. The Colonel turned to Tommy. "Charles Metcalfe asked me this morning before the parade if I knew anything about this because no one had notified the local Democrats."

Tommy glanced up and down the alley where their father had taken them. He didn't want to look the Colonel in the eye. His remorse over Jesús's disappearance and the revelation that Gruff wasn't just your run of the mill drunk, had eclipsed his passion for the prank. There was nothing to do but tell Maggie and his father the whole story. Throughout his tale, Maggie wrung her hands and squinted at him in disbelief. At first his son's creativity amused his father, but when he heard why Gruff drank heavily, he grimaced and put his hands on his hips, then gazed into the sky and rubbed his chin.

Maggie threw up her arms, again. "We must stop this."

Tommy frowned. He couldn't object, but he couldn't figure out a way to stop it without revealing himself.

Colonel Fountain scratched at his sideburn and peered west toward the train station. "You've done it this time, Tommy, although I have to admit that it would be nice to watch the Democrats made fools of."

"Papa. You can't be serious." screamed Maggie.

Colonel Fountain looked to see if anyone had heard. "Control yourself my dear ..."

"It's him that should control himself, Father," Maggie half-whispered. "If this gets out ..."

"Now Maggie," Colonel Fountain responded, "It seems perfectly harmless to me ... well, perhaps not perfectly harmless, but what can we do? The telegraph station at Randall isn't open today and if we sent a message to the Selden station, I doubt they would attempt to find Gruff and his escorts before they left for Randall. I'm afraid we'll just have to ride this one out." The Colonel glanced around. "Now Maggie, where's Jack and Katie — weren't you supposed to watch Katie?"

Maggie frowned. "They are with Jack." She put her hands on her hips. "I guess I just don't understand you ... *you men.*" She charged-off toward the anvil firing contest at the fairgrounds while Colonel Fountain and Tommy trailed behind. Before they could reach the Depot, a speck dotted the sky followed by the deafening "boom" of the explosion that propelled the anvil into the air. As they passed the depot, the stationmaster waved from his perch on a stepladder while he pulled this way and that at red, white and blue bunting that flanked a series of flags. Colonel Fountain waved back, but Tommy's eyes didn't stray from his path. Another anvil flew into the sky with a thunderous boom.

Amidst the powerful odor of spent gunpowder, the thud of the iron blacksmithing piece seemed to shake the ground as frantic cries of spectators caused Colonel Fountain and Tommy to rush to the arena. When they arrived, a young girl was on the ground. Doctor Huber and his wife Etta, Colonel Fountain, and Tommy arrived at the same time. The men that had gathered round devised a litter from the fair's tent remnants and carried the girl to a wagon.

"What happened?" asked Colonel Fountain.

Wil Rynerson, who marshaled the event, pointed to the roped off arena, "We aren't sure, but it seems the girl's parents called for her and instead of going around the roped off area, she charged across as the gunpowder was lit."

"Oh my," cried Maggie as several of the other women that had gathered round voiced their dismay as well.

The Colonel watched the girl with the Doctor and Etta aboard the wagon head toward the sanitarium. "Well, she is in excellent hands with Doctor Huber," replied Colonel Fountain. "Will the contest continue?"

The next man up called from the center of the arena, "I'm next. Clear the way."

He prepared the gunpowder propellant, placed his own anvil over the stationary one, and lit the fuse. Since we were much closer this time, the boom was simultaneous with the anvil's launch into the sky faster than we could follow it. The weighty block of iron returned to earth with a heavy clunk about where the previous anvil had struck the girl. A few men whooped, but most remembered the injured girl and stayed silent.

"Alright," said Wil. "I think we've seen enough. I think we've lost our lust for this bit of fun. I do believe I will give the blue ribbon to the poor girl." He paused, gazed at the accident site, then said, "Although she may well not want it. On second thought. I'll leave it here for anyone that wants it." He placed it on the table where he kept track of the entrants and how well their entries performed.

Maggie grimaced. "I think I've had enough celebrating. I'm going back home to help madre and Rosa with the picnic." Colonel

Fountain asked her to take Katie with her and to bring the two cigars he left on the table, and Maggie headed east.

Colonel Fountain briefly spoke with Wil and some of the other men. Although Cleveland was a Democrat, they were excited to see a sitting president. Colonel Fountain smiled and agreed with a nod while Tommy wandered off to help some men set up temporary picnic tables.

As the noon hour approached, families streamed across the tracks with their picnic baskets and odds and ends they would need for a relaxing afternoon. As the throng gathered, the stationmaster crossed the tracks waving a slip of paper and yelling that the president's stop would not happen.

Colonel Fountain and Tommy looked at each other as their eyes widened and broad grins appeared.

The paper the stationmaster held was a telegram from Rincon. The telegram read, "Train derailed stop no service for two days stop".

It was a glorious picnic. As the day wound down and the fireworks display lit up the sky in front of the majestic Organ spires, Colonel Fountain caught Tommy alone. "Son, that would have been quite a spectacle, but I hope you learned your lesson … at last."

He and Tommy had a brief father-son hug. "Papa, I wonder if I'll ever see those fellas again."

A couple of days later, the train came through, late, as usual. The stationmaster still hadn't removed all the bunting.

John McFie and his wife, Mary, had celebrated their holiday with friends in Santa Fe. When John stepped off the train in Las Cruces, he said to Mary, "We must have missed some dignitary. I wonder who it was?"

That day, Tommy stopped at the Telegraph Office. Miles turned from his desk and said, "Word is a worker left a switch open. Derailed half the train, but no one was hurt."

Tommy smiled and asked Miles for his father's telegrams.

"Ain't uh one today, Tommy. It was you, weren't it? I mean the president prank?"

Tommy smirked, walked to the door, turned back to Miles, and murmured, "Thank goodness for mistakes."

Tommy sat at his desk and thought about what the last couple of weeks as he copied Mrs. Bracegirdle's last will and testament. He worked from dawn to dusk over the next few days to finish the work he had promised his father. A few days later, a letter came from Gruff. He had scrawled these words on a scrap of paper.

> *Ain't coming back to Las Cruces. It's too hot there.*

# 13: Ranching Tularosa Style

**July 8, 1888**

The fourth of July passed with little more notice than the effort to cross off the day on the calendar. The Altmans and Lees were of the confederacy. Celebrating the enemy's independence was tantamount to treason.

As Oliver had promised, when we returned to Lee Well, Mary had trimmed my hair. I imagined I had shaved before, but it wasn't one of those memories that had stuck with me.

Oliver loaned me his father's razor, which he had kept, but couldn't bear to use. I prepared to take the first swipe with the straight razor, but Oliver intervened. He must have feared the worst because he took the razor from me and demonstrated the correct technique. Still, I felt I would take a hunk from my throat and bleed out. In the end, I came out of it whole, albeit with several nicks and cuts.

Since we had returned from Las Cruces, things had calmed down in the Tularosa. While Oliver and his kin hadn't forgotten George — not by a long shot — the rest of the valley had put their tension aside.

Unlike the previous Tularosa winters, the winter of '87 - '88 provided lots of moisture. With the addition of a spring shower or two, the herds had enough browse in the flats until late May. As a result, there wasn't much to fight about between ranches that summer if the various herds stuck together, and nobody tried to swoop in and steal a watering hole or another's 'claimed' range. Barbed wire had made its way into southern New Mexico, and some of the larger ranchers used it to keep the smaller operations away from watering holes and prime pasture.

---

## July 14

Summers and winters on a ranch are a bit lower activity times, but that isn't to say there was nothing to do. The longer the summer went without significant rain, the further up the canyons the herd drifted for water. If the monsoon rains arrived, they would herd them back down to the flats when the browse regrew. We herded plenty that summer. There were the usual (I was told) strays, cows missing calves, and calves missing cows, cows that calved late, steers that needed doctoring and on and on. A crew stayed around the headquarters to handle the occasional emergency repairs to corrals, windmills, tack, leaky tanks and so on. They also helped the hands that were expert with horses as they broke and trained them for different purposes.

With all the work, I soon regained my strength and as the summer progressed, I worked harder and became stronger still. Physically, I felt wonderful.

Oliver was among the first ranchers to grow alfalfa on the flats. His first fields were at the foot of Dog and Grapevine Canyons where he could easily convey the needed water. We cut and sheaved his alfalfa hay several times through the summer. Most hands preferred the dawn to dusk roundups rather than the hot dusty summers when the herds were difficult to move.

One evening over supper, the bunkhouse cowboys discussed Oliver's new Hereford bull. Whether it was people or cattle, Virgil always wanted to talk about breeding. "The longhorn cows seem to be takin' a shine to that new Hereford bull y'all got from Chicago. It'll be entertainin' to see what the calves are like."

Eph said, "I ain't too sure what Oliver's thinkin', but if this bull is like the rest of the breed, they better foragers, even in bad weather, and they surely do put on the pounds quicker than the longhorns. We just might be on the road to a full herd of Hereford longhorn crosses. Might even start a new breed."

One cowboy I hadn't met wrinkled his brow and said, "Them Herefords ain't nearly as purdy as the longhorns, though."

Virgil scooped up a spoonful of stew. "Well, I ain't never met a rancher that would put winnin' a beauty contest ahead of a hunnert dollars."

Greenhorn that I was, I asked, "Why not just start over with the Herefords?"

Whether it was because the rest of the cowboys knew I was a tenderfoot or they themselves didn't know the answer, a few laughed and soon my innocent question amused most of them. Eph was among those that didn't laugh. None of the other negroes, of which there were several, laughed either, although they smiled at my innocence. After supper, Eph asked me to come along with him while he checked the livestock that he kept close to headquarters.

Before Ed went to the Altmans, he and Eph occasionally had supper in the house with Mary, Nettie, and Oliver. They weren't foremen, but every hand knew that when they spoke, whatever they said carried the weight of an order from Oliver.

When we entered the barn, Eph turned over two milking buckets and motioned for me to sit. The intermingled smell of fresh straw, leather, and animal waste wafted over us. "Don't pay the cowpokes no never mind," he started. Eph wasn't as tall as Oliver, but he had the same wiry build. The whites of his eyes in the dim light of the barn kept me focused on him. "Don't get me wrong, they's the best ranch hands around, but every one of 'em would be as poor as Job's turkey if they had their own ranches." When he sat on that upside down milk pail, his legs were so long that it looked as though his knees could poke him in his chin. The way he was folded up reminded me of someone from the past, but a name didn't come, and I didn't have time to dwell on it. He paused and wiped his hand across his mouth. "They don't remember that they had to learn once upon a time demselves. Folks are quick to forget when dey was young and curious."

"I don't mind. It seems like I don't know much these days. I get bits and pieces of who I am and what I know, but that's all."

"Don't you worry. I know dat's hard but my pappy tol' me about a fella slave that got kicked in the head by a horse once. He was lucky that the massa — Oliver's gran pappy — was a good 'un, and he let him stay on the plantation. Some would've jus' kilt him. As I recall, pappy said it took the better part of a year afore the slave man knew who he was."

"A year?" I didn't think I could stand the purgatory of living half in and half out of my true self for that long.

"Afraid so. I hope you gets back to your true self sooner, but I have faith in the Lord almighty dat he will bring you through dis." Eph turned and peered at the crescent moon over the Sacramentos through the gap between the barn doors he had left open. The moon's soft glow washed over him and the intensity of his eyes dimmed for a moment as I adjusted to the new light. Eph paused in thought. "What I'm about to tell you is only for you. Understan'?"

I nodded.

"Oliver don't like his bidnez to be spread all around. He seems to think you are right smart and I guess he trusts you. And so, he wanted me to 'splain the cattle bidnez to you so you can think on it for a while."

I worried that Oliver's flattery might suggest he would want me to stay with them even after I found out who I was.

Eph rubbed his hand across his mouth. "I ain't quite sure how much he wants me to tell you." He scratched his temple, then his brow. "I 'spose we should start with the simple facts of things. You know a baby is called a calf, right?"

I rolled my eyes.

He nodded. "Well then, did you know that a female calf is called a heifer until she bears a calf — usually about a year? And male calves is bulls right from the beginnin', but most o' the time we make 'em steers by castratin' 'em in d'spring cause a castrated male puts on the weight quicker."

"Why not have more bulls, so all the cows get bred closer to the same time?"

Eph grinned. "Too many bulls in the herd causes lots of problems. They'll fight over d' cows and there can be lots of ... well damage, to both bulls and cows. Steers are easier to handle when it comes time to herd 'em to market. We often call 'em all steers, but they's not all castrated males cause some heifers get culled from the breeding stock, too.

"The importantest thing to understand' is the calving cycle. You missed the calving period when the cows birthed their babies and spring roundup when we brand and castrate 'em. Sometimes we have to separate the cows that's got calves from the rest of the herd an' you probably missed most of dat, too. There will be a roundup in the fall for cutting' out the longhorn steers and heifers that will go to market. Da' browse hereabouts ain't as good as what we had back on the Little Elm Creek in Texas an' we found out the hard way that the market buyers discount the price they'll pay for the herd if'n too many of d'em are poorly. That only happened a couple uh times and so we chose more careful-like when we cut d'em out at the roundup. So, we hold some of the late spring calves for another entire year.

"Used to be, when old John Chisum was trailin' big herds up to Abilene and Dodge, he could set the price on the hoof hisself, but now the buyers set d' price. T'ings is getting' a lot tighter in the ranchin' bidnez and Oliver says somebody is gettin' a cut. He ain't sure how it's uh workin' yet, but it's gettin' harder and harder to turn a profit on a small spread like we's got."

It surprised me they thought Oliver's ranch was small. It seemed huge to me.

"Oliver says it wouldn't be no problem for a buyer at the rail yards to take our steers, fatten 'em up somewhere where d' grass and water is plentiful and then resell 'em for better quality and heavier weight. Oliver says they's takin' money from our pockets, but we cain't feed 'em out here because we need all the browse we got for the bulls, bred cows and heifers. That's one reason Oliver is growin' alfalfa — that and in case of drought or deep snow."

Once again, Oliver proved to be forward-thinking and analytical.

"Oliver gets newspapers and such from the beef folks in Chicago. They's got a contest ever' year to see what breeds put on the weight the quickest. Deeze here Herefords — dey been winnin' every year now. Dey put on pounds way faster and the meat is better. A year ago, or so, a two-year-old Hereford won the contest. He weighed more dan our four-year-old longhorn steers. If the Herefords do well here, we'll get better prices per pound and more total weight. Oliver paid good money for 'dis Hereford bull 'dis spring. Shipped him in from Chicago."

"So, why didn't he sell out and start a new herd of Herefords?"

Eph stretched one of his legs as he sat and wiggled around a bit. "Oliver's got over a thousand head. Their ain't no Herefords around these parts and shippin' all from Chicago would break the bank. 'Sides, we ain't quite sure Herefords can handle the Tularosa. People say dey can, but 'dis ain't nothin' like Illinois or even western Kansas. Oliver's cautious that a way. 'Sides, a Hereford — longhorn cross might be better here, but I'm gettin' ahead of m'self."

He gazed in thought at the crescent moon through the barn door. He turned back to me. "You're gonna know more about ranchin' than you ever figured."

He told me that the cows went into heat about a month and a half after they delivered, and the bulls became busy doing their job. "Every cowboy can tell when a cow is ready for breedin.' Lots o' times they gather and roam lookin' for a bull. Sometimes, they'll lick other cows or fight with them. Between the calves bawlin' for their mama's teat and the cows bawlin' for a bull it gets plenty noisy. Durin' breedin' season, there's mountin' everywhere, bulls on cows, cows on cows; shoot, a couple uh times I even seen cows on bulls."

He told me a good hand could also tell a bred cow from an unbred one. "You'll reco'nize it when ya see it, but that won't happen agin 'til nex' year."

Eph picked up his right leg and crossed it over his left while he pushed his left foot out so he could cross his legs with ease. He leaned forward on his forearms and said, "A good hand can judge all 'dis. He'll know when 'dere's too few bulls and when 'dere's too many. If that ain't reco'nized you've got big problems that can mean cows and bulls get beat up pertty bad. A cowboy that can judge em problems afore they happen and keep the bulls and cows happy is a valuable man indeed. It takes experience and a sharp eye.

Eph stared toward the bunkhouse. "Our hands gotta judge the maturity of calves for the market roundup. A good cowboy could tell you within twenty-five pounds the weight of any steer or cow and much closer den dat with yearlin's and younger."

Eph uncrossed his legs and arms, stood up and wiggled his long legs to get the blood circulating again. I rose as well and shifted from foot to foot, expecting my lesson was complete. But Eph put a finger to his forehead. "Uh, couple other quick things. We use sulpha' to doctor our steers. Mostly, it's for cuts and such. Each cowboy carries the powder in a pouch and they wet the hide around the wound and make a paste over it. If a steer is sick, most the time we shoot 'em so's the herd don't catch whatever he got. Lastly, I think, but I'll probably think uh somethin' else later, but anyhow, durin' roundups our hands cut out however many healthy heifers and bulls to stay with the herd to offset the losses to wolves and such for the year."

He kicked at the strawy dust of the barn floor. "Well, I guess that's about it. You got questions, jus' come to me. In a few days, Oliver'll find you and'll wanna hear your thoughts."

# 14: Shootin' Basics

**July 26, 1888**

On a Thursday, a fella drifted through while I helped Virgil plug a leak in the dam of one of Oliver's dug-out watering holes. He stopped to water his horse and said he had ridden down from Missouri as soon as the snow melted. He pronounced Missouri like it ended with an "uh" sound instead of a long "e" sound. After the usual getting acquainted talk, he said, "Dang it's hot here 'bouts. If'n I didn't know better, I'd swear New Mexico must be closer to the sun."

Virgil asked him where he was going. The man shrugged. Virgil then asked, "What are you lookin' for?"

The man shrugged again. "I'll know it when I see it."

As the man rode away, Virgil yelled, "You can fill your canteen at the well in front of the adobe ranch house."

As fate would have it, the next day, a man leading a burro loaded with boxes and equipment stopped as we finished our patch job. The man had a funny accent. He sounded a little like the Germans do when they speak English. He said he was a surveyor and wanted to find Oliver Lee. I still had what the Missourian said on my mind, and I thought he might know about such things.

After introductions, I said, "A fella from Missouri came by here yesterday. He said he thought the sun must be closer to us here than in Missouri because it felt much stronger. Could that be?"

The surveyor didn't hesitate. "He's right, by about three thousand feet. We are about that much closer to the sun than they are in Kansas City."

Virgil slapped his hand against his thigh. "Well, how 'bout that?"

That reminded me of Icarus from Greek mythology that I had read somewhere — but where?

---

That evening, Oliver invited Eph and me to have supper with him, his Ma, and Nettie. When we finished and the women were cleaning up, Oliver said to me, "Eph said he told you about how we run the ranch. Do you have any thoughts?" As usual, Oliver got straight to the point.

I nodded and Eph, who sat next to Oliver joined him with expectant expressions. "I've had little time to think about what Eph told me," I said. "But what do you expect to learn by putting the Hereford bull in with the longhorns?"

Oliver seemed surprised by my question at first. He grinned. "Why, whether a Hereford—longhorn cross does better than the straight longhorns, of course."

"Can you also tell if Herefords will do better than the cross or the longhorns?"

He must have thought of that before, because he answered right away. "No, I can't, but I also couldn't get enough Hereford cows to get a good call on that. Once I see how the bull does here, I'll buy some cows and keep them in a place where I know how the longhorns did."

"So you can rule out the browse quality as a factor?"

Oliver smiled at me and said, "I knew you were smart."

Our discussion went throughout the evening. By the time yawns interrupted our words, Oliver had developed and written a sound plan that would put his ranch on a prosperous path.

As Eph and I walked back to the bunkhouse under a sparkling sky, he told me I learned about ranching at a gallop. I replied I had an excellent teacher that made me want to observe and learn. "Sometimes, we are too close to our problems, and we only think about things in a certain way. Besides, questions are the prudent path to a mutual goal." Once again, I had imparted a tidbit of wisdom that didn't seem to come from me, but from whom did it come?

I was thankful that Eph, Virgil, Jackson, and Fritz treated me well in the bunkhouse. Oh, I got my share of practical jokes played on me, but it didn't seem that I was a primary target. Everyone got their share.

When Oliver signed-on Tom Tucker, it was pretty clear Tucker wouldn't be there for his roping and cutting skills. In fact, I don't think I ever saw a lasso tied to his saddle. He wore two pistols on his gun belt, and he always kept the belt filled with extra rounds.

One day, Oliver rode up into the canyon with Tucker and Bill Carr. Virgil searched through the brush for a calf while the mother mooed without end.

"I guess she lost him," I said.

"Virgil'll get him out if he's to be found," said Oliver.

Carr pointed to a large bird perched on a dead tree. "Might be dead already. Looks like that chickenhawk's got a bead on him."

Tucker pulled his rifle out of its scabbard and aimed at the chickenhawk, but Oliver reached over and pulled the barrel down with his arm. "Ain't no reason to kill that bird, Tom. 'Sides, it's a buzzard and you don't need a rifle for that shot and if you shot from here, you'd spook the herd." He paused as another thought came to him. "I need to show Hey-you here how to shoot. Why don't y'all come down behind the house this Sunday evenin' and we'll have ourselves a little shootin' contest?"

---

The Altmans came for the Sunday mid-afternoon meal, and this time, they didn't invite any of the hands. Eph and I fended for ourselves — well, Eph cooked, and I cleaned up.

Oliver had asked me to meet him behind the house after the meal where I had seen him shoot. Perry Altman came with him. I had never seen Perry carry a gun, and I later learned that was his custom. His wife once half-joked that Perry didn't own so much as a rifle, but we all knew that wasn't so. At a minimum, anyone in that country needed a rifle to protect stock from varmints.

When we got to Oliver's shooting range, there were three large log chunks, each about a foot in diameter and maybe eighteen inches high, where the people sat and watched. In front of the middle one was an old spindle-legged table. The business end of a rifle projected out from the table toward a section of split-rail fence that had a shelf perched on top of two rough cut posts about forty feet distant. Perry sat on a log-stool to the side and watched.

When we got close enough, I reached for the rifle, but Oliver snatched it away. "First lesson, always assume a gun is loaded, and the safety is off." He pulled the trigger, and I jumped as the round went off with a loud "BANG".

"Second, never pick up another person's gun without them tellin' you how it handles. See here," he pulled out his six-shooter. "I have my Winchester and Colt fixed such that the pull on the trigger is real light. If you didn't know that and your finger brushed the guard, you might graze the trigger, which could discharge the gun. There's other thing's folk'll do to their guns to suit their own ways, so even if you find a gun out in the desert, handle it real careful-like."

Oliver pulled the old Mexican blanket away from the table and revealed the rest of the Winchester 1877 and a Colt revolver nestled into a holster on a leather belt.

"What do you think you should do with this?" he asked.

My first thought was to grab the belt and put it on around my waist. Instead, I gripped the six-shooter by the hard rubber grip, careful to keep my fingers away from the trigger while pointing it away from us and the adobe.

"Right, now, good. Open the loadin' gate. Now, you can see there's a round already there, but what we don't know is how many other rounds are in the cylinder.

I tried to spin the cylinder, but it wouldn't budge.

"No, don't do that. It ain't gonna move cause the hammer stops it. This gun is a double action revolver and to check the cylinder or load or unload you need to half cock it. Pull it back easy. That's right. Now if you pulled it back too far, and it slipped off your thumb, the hammer might hit the firin' pin and discharge the bullet. So, unless you are expectin' trouble and 'when we are out on the range, carry it with the loadin' chamber open. That way, if the hammer would get caught on your lasso or somethin' the action would turn the cylinder to the open chamber and nothin' would happen. Otherwise, you might blow your foot off or kill your horse."

The subject excited Oliver because he barely took a breath as he described how to handle the gun. He explained other 'rules' that would keep me and others around me safe. When he finished, he handed me the gun belt, but when I tried to put it on, my waist was too small, and he had to use his pocketknife to make a new hole where it would fit me. He helped adjust it so that the bottom of the belt sat against my hips.

"Now, let's try a little target practice. You pick out a target and tell me what it is. Don't make it too small."

I looked around. There wasn't much to aim at other than a few tin cans on the board between the two posts. "Alright, I'm gonna aim at that tin can."

"Which one?" he asked.

I described it — it was an old coffee can that already had several holes in it.

"No," and he moved closer to me. "Point to it."

I pointed and before I could say, "That one," Oliver leaned over to sight down my finger.

"Perfect. And that's all you need to do with your Colt." Oliver noticed my quizzical look. "You didn't take a deep breath; you didn't hold your breath and didn't think about linin' up your eye with your finger and the coffee can. Did you?"

"Why, no, but I only wanted to show you … I don't understand."

"Pointin' your finger was automatic. You didn't have to think about it and your aim was perfect. If you could have shot with your finger, you would have hit it and you could have done that over and over."

"But how …"

"How do you aim the six-gun that way?" Oliver shifted his weight in thought. "It's simple." He moved me to his right and drew his Colt from its holster and, without pause, he put three shots into the coffee can. The first one knocked the can off the board; the second knocked the can further into the air and the third still further into the air.

"How …?"

Oliver stood there with his arm extended but relaxed. "Look at my hand on the revolver. I extend my first finger above the trigger and below the cylinder along the body of the gun just as you would when you are pointin' at somethin' without a gun. My second finger is my trigger finger. The handle is restin' hard against the base of my thumb in the palm of my hand. It is Just as important to have a solid stance. I have found that havin' my feet spread to just outside of my shoulders with my knees flexed a little, works best for me, but somethin' else might work for you. Give it a try. Shoot the can to the right of the coffee can."

I mimicked Oliver's stance and drew my Colt, pointed it with my finger and pulled the trigger. The gun went off, but I missed, and the desert dust kicked up about thirty yards past the cans.

"You shot low. Your line was excellent, but it went under the can by a couple of inches or so."

I lowered the gun. It seemed heavy, and Oliver noticed. "There ain't much difference between the three models. This here 38 caliber is the lightest Colt they make, but the important thing is balance. With a shorter barrel, the balance point moves closer to the grip. So your aim will tend to come up. This one is a five-inch barrel." He pointed to it. "You might get used to it with practice, but we could also trade it for a four or four-and-a-half-inch barrel that would balance better for you."

As Oliver explained his method with the Winchester rifle, Tucker and Carr arrived.

Did they put on a shooting show! Off to one side of the shelf was a barrel filled with tin cans. It was a perfect arrangement for setting up cans on the shelf. Tucker and Carr were good, but Oliver was out of this world. Even as I understood his technique, it was still uncanny the way he picked-off cans from the shelf and out of the air. He was like an automaton. It impressed me enough that I would have let him shoot a can out of my hand.

Tin can lids littered the ground around the barrel. Oliver holstered his Colt and told me to collect a dozen or so and go another ten paces further into the desert. When I turned for further directions, he called for me to throw the lids up one at a time so that they faced him. I threw the first one up, he drew his six-gun and shot. The lid flittered up and away. I threw another and another. He never missed.

About the time I ran out of lids, Sixto appeared with one of Oliver's range horses. He had saddled the shiny black, and it was ready for Oliver to ride. Oliver told me to pick up several can lids. He mounted his horse and said he was going to have the horse spin to his right, while I walked around him to his left and threw up lids as our paths crossed. Out of six, he missed one. ONE! As I threw a lid up, a familiarity struck once again. I thought I had done it before, but once again, my mind went blank. I had no connection to anything else and no recognition of where or when it might have happened.

*If he and I had met before, wouldn't he have told me by now?*

# 15: Might it be Me?

The jigsaw pieces of information that could reveal my identity didn't fit together. It made me think I needed to move on with my life — accept things as they were and push the omnipresent puzzle to the back of my mind, if not completely away. On occasion, Nettie and I had talked about these things after supper while we sat on the porch and watched the Sacramentos turn colors.

Water is the supreme commodity in the desert and yet I never met anyone that wanted paid for it. The desert humbles us all. Withholding or charging for water went against the code of the west. One of Oliver's hands, Sixto Garcia put it this way, "I would never stop no one from geettin' water from my well but eef he made a move for hees seex-gun after feeling hees canteen, I would feel heem full of holes."

Travelers often stopped at Lee Well, a fact that sometimes annoyed Oliver and the family. They shared their water with thirsty travelers without exception, but the family's congeniality, if ever they had it, must have remained in Texas. Or, perhaps their experiences in Texas spoiled their amiability. Whatever the reason, they had a guarded projection intended to discourage 'hanging about' by strangers.

One evening, a woman, accompanied by two men rode up to the well. They looked familiar and so I got up from my broken Windsor chair and walked out to say my hellos. The woman rode a palomino while the men were on roans — one a strawberry and the other a black. The combination made for such a striking appearance that I wondered if it was the horses I remembered and not the people. I froze when the woman looked me over. I hoped that would allow enough time for her to recognize me, and greet me by name. However, 'Hey there Juan or Alberto,' wasn't what she uttered. Instead, as she turned back to fill her canteen from the well bucket, she said, "Thank y'all for the water. It's a hot one today."

I nodded, "Sure is, thank goodness its cooled down some. This is a good well. Take all the water you need."

"Wish we had another canteen each. Where's the next well?"

I turned to motion toward the north. "If you're headin' north, it'll be in La Luz — 'bout twenty-mile on this trail. But y'all," I paused because I realized I had picked up the cowboy's twang, which felt wrong for me. "I doubt you'll make it that far before sunset. There's a good place to camp over yond ... on the other side of the barn."

The two men walked to either side of the woman. They supported her with their hands at the small of her back. I thought I remembered them. One man said, "Say sonny, you look familiar to me, don't he to you Elizabeth?"

"I thought so at first, but we ain't never traveled on this side of the Basin afore. Up to now, we've always took the trail along the eastern slopes of the Organs and Franklins."

That was the closest I had gotten to someone knowing who I was and so I tried to help them. "Well, I hoped you would recognize me because ... uh, I fell and hit my head a couple of months ago and I don't remember a thing before awakening at the Lees."

She turned to the second man. "What do you think, Horace?"

"Well, we might've seen him over yonder afore. I'm right sorry to hear of your misfortune, sonny."

A tinge of hope.

She looked at the other man, "Hubert, couple uh years ago when we'eze goin' to El Paso for that bull, seems to me … "

Hubert put his foot in his stirrup. "Nah, that boy was a foot shorter than this un here. Same color hair and eyes, I do believe, but shoot, all them Mexicans got jet black hair and dark eyes."

That dashed my hopes, but I wasn't ready to give up. "Was this person by himself?"

Elizabeth mounted her palomino. "There was somethin' about the older man that was with the boy. I had the feelin' that he was a soldier, except he wasn't wearin' army clothes. Oh yes, and there was a squaw. She got right upset when one of us asked the man if she was his squaw and she rode off. But you ain't that boy we saw … nah, ain't no way you could be him. 'Sides, I don't know his name … don't think we exchanged names."

So that did it. I took a deep breath and nodded to them.

Horace glanced around the ranch yard. "Ya say the place to camp is over behind the barn?"

"Yes, I'll show you."

I led them to the campsite. As I trudged back to the porch, tears filled the corners of my eyes. I vowed I wouldn't allow myself to be hopeful like that again.

## August 1

The summer dragged on and those monsoon rains never arrived on the Tularosa flats. George's death seemed forgotten. Still, on the days that George would have appeared at Nettie's door ready to contribute it to their future with his month's salary, she and I would ride up to his serene sepulcher next to the bubbling spring. The niche was always cool, moist, and smelled of fresh seedlings. I'm not sure if the irony of the vitality of the place occurred to her. She and I would sit on the rocks for the afternoon without saying much; her with her thoughts of what might have been and me with ruminations about who I was and where I belonged. Each time, I promised myself I would stop obsessing about it.

With the lack of rain, the browse dried and withered to nothing in the lower canyons, and the herds became restless. Most of the larger canyons had at least one dependable spring that was refreshed with elevation induced rains. The herds wandered up the main canyons and sometimes ranged into spring fed branches.

In the southwest, where there's water, there's brush. I was often thankful for my chaps and gloves. Still, I needed to pull thorns out of my shirtsleeves and wherever the chaps didn't cover, including my rear end.

Whenever I had a chance, I stole away and practiced with my Colt revolver. At first, Oliver didn't give me bullets and said to practice handling the gun and aiming. When he could see I had improved, he gave me a few rounds so I could see some results. As he suggested, the more I practiced, the better I got, but I never quick-drew, even when I got more confident. I knew he wouldn't approve. He always said, "Ain't nobody foolish enough to give ya an even chance if their lookin' to kill ya." Anyway, whether my hand and forearm got stronger, or I just got accustomed to balancing the revolver, I improved.

The heat of July dwindled. Tom Tucker, Bill Carr, and Jim Cooper increased their time at the ranch yard. One day I went to shoot before supper, and they were there. As I approached, I could hear Oliver's lament over Nettie's continued deep mourning of George. I didn't want to hear, so I returned to the bunkhouse.

The cowboys played cards while the cook prepared ham and beans for supper ... again.

# 16: Land Grant Woes

**August 1, 1888**

While Maggie and Marianita shopped in town, they overheard a well-dressed woman complain to the storekeeper. "Is there a hotel in this town away from a saloon? It's impossible to sleep in our hotel until well after midnight with the racket that comes out of those places."

The storekeeper apologized, but the woman wasn't a regular customer and so she gazed past her at Marianita, who walked to the woman's side and said, "Excuse me, aren't you Eloisa Otero?"

When the woman turned to Marianita, she revealed a young girl between herself and the shop counter. The woman smiled and said, "Marianita Fountain. I hoped we might happen upon each other here. You are from Mesilla, am I right? Oh, and yes, or I mean no ... I mean yes, I am that person, but Mr. Otero died five years ago — not long after we met at the Women's Suffrage meeting in Santa Fe. I have since remarried."

"Oh, I am so sorry Eloisa." Marianita smiled faintly with respect for her loss. After an appropriate pause, she said, "And who is this sweet girl?"

"Nina, say hello to Miss Fountain. We call her Nina, but her name is Maria."

The little girl — she looked to be six or seven curtsied with perfection. "It is my pleasure to meet you ma'am."

Maggie and Marianita returned the curtsy as they giggled over how cute Nina was.

When everyone had composed themselves, Marianita said, "I have married as well. My last name is now Clausen. My husband is a painter." Eloisa congratulated Marianita.

Maggie said, "Our family has room."

"Why yes," said Marianita. "Papa will remember you."

Eloisa chuckled. "I remember how shocked the women were when your father entered the meeting with you. He was the only man there."

"Yes, it was my first introduction to political groups and papa suggested I go, and he accompanied me since I was just thirteen."

"I'll look forward to seeing him again." Eloisa turned to Maggie. "Thank you for the invitation. We would love to visit, but we couldn't impose by staying with you."

Marianita smiled and cocked her head. "Oh, it wouldn't be an imposition. Albert Jr. and I have married, and Larlo works in Pinos Altos. They have plenty of room."

"My husband and two sons are here."

Maggie took the little girl's hand. "The more the merrier."

---

That evening when Eloisa and Maggie had settled Nina into the girl's room and Eloisa's youngest son, Manuel Jr. into a bed in the boys' room the rest of the two families gathered in the parlor. Eloisa's husband, Alfred Bergère, began a checker game with his oldest stepson, Eduardo, while the others gathered around the game table. When the conversation lagged, Alfred said, "Eloisa dear, you should tell the Colonel what happened to Manuel. As difficult as it is for you, I know you want to spare others the same fate."

Eloisa bowed her head for a moment, forced a smile, "Yes, you are right, husband dear. I shall when you have finished your game and we can settle Eduardo in his bed."

Despite himself, Colonel Fountain was happy to see the story-hearth reoccupied. While Eloisa and her husband took their son into the boys' room, Mia Tia and Maggie brought out a tray of snacks and wine. When Marianita and Carl arrived, Maggie returned to the kitchen for another bottle of wine and additional goblets.

At first, Eloisa refused to step onto the hearth in front of all of us, but Colonel Fountain's promise that he would tell a story when she had finished was encouragement enough. She began with her eyes on the ceiling and her hands at her sides. "I imagine you have heard or read about that mid-August day and perhaps you know that the Otero and Luna ancestors came to this area with the Conquistadors. The King of Spain himself granted us our land."

We all nodded, and Colonel Fountain said, "Yes, we know the basic story, but often the truth of an event gets lost in its passage from person to person. As you may know, the Territorial Attorney General has entrusted me with the preventing the transfer of legitimate landowners' property by fraudulent claims here in the third judicial district. I don't limit our prosecutions to Homestead law abuses. We have also indicted violations of other land ownership laws and I have been aggressive about protecting Spanish and Mexican land grant holders as well."

Eloisa nodded. "We have heard of your successes." She cleared her throat, and her hands became as active as her words as she told her horrendous tale.

"It was a difficult time for my family. The railroad wanted to route their tracks *exactamente* through our original Luna homestead, which we called *La Constancia*. At first my father, Antonio Luna, refused them, but they offered to build a mansion to his specifications if he would allow their preferred route. He never got to see the mansion finished." She paused with the unpleasant memory.

"My brother Tranquilino became the Luna family *patron*. A year later, not long after I married into the Otero family, Manuel Anotonio Otero died and my husband, Manuel Basilio, took charge of the Otero family estate." She hesitated again and then explained she didn't want to bore the Fountains with her heritage. Mariana smiled and encouraged her by saying that it was good to know how the Lunas and Oteros came together. Eloisa held her hand over her mouth as she licked her lips.

"Both families had large *rancheros* and the respect of our neighbors. We were a good match. Our wedding was the grandest of our time." She gazed over our heads, deep in thought. "For our honeymoon, we sailed up and down the Rio Grande in a gondola filled with flowers for a week." Eloisa smiled as the image in her mind took her back to that time.

Eloisa apologized for losing her train of thought and said, "Eduardo and then Nina were born just over a year apart. In 1882, our harvests were plentiful. The two families combined controlled over 700,000 acres. Our vineyards produced more wine than ever and the wool from our 150,000 head of sheep sold at a premium.

"Once again, I was with child. Anglos tried to homestead on our land often with the suggestion that the railroad had conveyed rights to them. Manuel, my husband, knew the courts would not support us and so he managed the squatters the best he could. It took up much of his time. I don't know how he did it, but either their claims never amounted too much, or he scared them off — until one day in 1883." She paused once again, and Colonel Fountain rose from his chair and offered her a goblet of wine from the tray. She took a full swallow and then set the goblet on the mantel.

"Less than a year after the two *patrons* had passed, two brothers from Boston, Whitney was their last name, harassed Manuel over their supposed claim on a large part of our *ranchero*. An Anglo judge had ruled against us. Manuel appealed and prevented the Whitneys from taking possession. On an August day, much like today, we received word that the Whitneys had tried to evict our Estancia *ranchero* managers at Antelope Springs.

Antonio rushed to prevent it. The land they tried to claim was critical to our sheep operation. It had lush grass and a large lake, fed by natural springs. It was our best land, and the large trees and flowering shrubs were beautiful.

"The Whitneys sent an armed posse to run-off our *vaqueros*. Our manager, Pablo Baca, and his sick wife and their three children lived at the Estancia ranch house. James Whitney accompanied the posse and told the Bacas to leave. When the Bacas refused, Whitney, his brother-in-law, and another man took over the front room where they drank whiskey and played poker all night.

"The next morning, my husband and two of our *vaqueros* arrived. It was August seventeen. I remember it like it was yesterday." Eloisa pulled her handkerchief from her beautiful dress and dabbed at her dark eyes. Colonel Fountain rose to comfort her, but she and Alfred signaled that she would be alright.

Eloisa glanced at her feet as she stowed her handkerchief. "Manuel knocked at the door and Whitney answered with his rifle over his arm. Manuel was only twenty-three years old. But he was mature beyond his years, and he was calm and polite despite the situation. He extended his hand and Whitney shook it as the two men went inside. The discussion became intense when Manuel asked for a court order as proof of the wealthy Bostonian's claim. Without warning, James Whitney pulled his pistol and shot Manuel, who was only a few feet away. In the ensuing shoot-out, Whitney's brother-in-law killed Manuel and Whitney appeared mortally wounded. Dr. Henriquez came with the *vaqueros* that accompanied Manuel to confront the Whitneys. The doctor did his best to cease the flow of blood from Manuel, but one shot severed his carotid artery. He held on until a justice of the peace arrived and with the last of his strength, he signed his statement."

Eloisa stood glassy eyed, reached for her goblet of wine, put it to her lips, but could not drink. She replaced the glass on the mantel and shuddered. "A rider warned us that the Whitneys had killed Manuel, but the sight of him in the wagon was the hardest thing for me in this life." Eloisa broke down into deep sobs and Mariana, Maggie and Marianita all rushed to her.

Mr. Bergère rose and said, "They did not try the man until 1884. It shocked the family when the court acquitted Whitney on the grounds that he shot Manuel in self-defense. We believe they bribed the judge. The dispute with the Whitneys has not been settled. So, you see, the immigrant opportunists have caused Eloisa and her family great suffering."

We all gathered round Eloisa to comfort and help her to a chair next to her husband. Colonel Fountain spoke about how honored he and his family were to know the truth of the matter in her words. When everyone had settled down, he asked, "So, what brings you to Las Cruces?"

Mr. Bergère walked to the hearth and turned to face us. "One day, I would like to move Eloisa and our family away from the turmoil that goes with her family's lands. We expect Santa Fe will be our destination, but when I worked for the Spielberg Brothers Emporium in Albuquerque, I met Martin Lohman. He had come to Albuquerque to buy goods for his Las Cruces store. He impressed me with his predictions for Las Cruces, and I thought we should visit to see it for ourselves before we made any final decisions."

Colonel Fountain stood and joined Mr. Bergère at the story-hearth. The two men clinked their goblets as the Colonel said, "Well, we are pleased and honored to have you all stay with us." He glanced at Eloisa. "I am sorry that our little town has not catered to your needs. However, I am confident that by the time you are ready to decamp from Las Lunas, Las Cruces will be a thriving metropolis. I, as the Immigration Commissioner, along with my family," he swept his hand in a motion toward them, "promote the Mesilla valley all across the world."

"Well, I can see you do not lack enthusiasm in your endeavor," replied Mr. Bergère.

The Colonel smiled with pride. "We have had some success. The town has thrived since we arrived from Mesilla a few years ago."

A bleary-eyed Eloisa said, "Colonel, I can tell you that many of our extended family acknowledge and appreciate your efforts on our behalf." She dabbed at the corners of her eyes and straightened her dress. "Now, enough about my woes. I am excited to hear the tale you promised earlier."

Just then, Jack came up the hall and said, "I heard we have visitors from Las Lunas."

Colonel Fountain introduced Jack to the visitors, and he sat next to his father.

Mr. Bergère said, "We had just heard from your father about the wonderful job he and the family have done to promote the Mesilla Valley."

"And I," began Colonel Fountain, "was about to tell the story of my escape from a Nicaraguan firing squad when I was a *Sacramento Union* reporter in the 1850s. But your appearance, son, reminded me I had not told your favorite story for several years about one of my clashes with the Navajos."

Eloisa spoke up. "The Nicaragua story sounds interesting, but my family has a long history of battles against the Navajos, and I for one would like to hear yours."

The Colonel shifted between his feet. He turned to place his wine glass on the mantel and said, "Well, it wasn't so much a battle as perhaps a skirmish, but … well, you be the judge."

# 17: Malpais Malaise

Colonel Fountain paced back and forth on the hearth for a moment to compose his thoughts. Then, quick as a cat, he turned, and the words flowed with his familiar theatrical gestures. "In 1863, with the Civil War in New Mexico all but decided, General Carleton, my commanding officer, sent an edict that warned the Navajos in the four corners region of their homeland." He stopped for a moment and posed, finger in the air. "The decree read, 'if you do not report to Forts Wingate or Defiance ready to relocate to the new reservation at Bosque Redondo on the Pecos, where you will be well provided for, we will march on your homes and destroy everything and kill those that remain.' "

"Colonel 'Kit' Carson assembled four hundred men for the raid. Their raids resulted in a Bosque Redondo crammed with Apaches and Navajos. Two more warring nations might never have existed. In addition, the promised goods and services were scarce, and soon diseases swept through the camp and the Navajos died like flies of smallpox. Soldiers and Indians died so often that the remaining officers ordered the Indians to dispose of all the bodies in the Pecos River. It was a horrible place. A place we should never have forced upon them."

Colonel Fountain paused dramatically in thought, finger to his chin. "But I was a soldier — a captain in command of the Army's Parje outpost. Our primary charge was the capture of escapees from the reservations. Mariana and my infant son, Albert Jr., were there with me.

"In June of 1865, I received word that several chiefs decided they had had enough and about five hundred Navajos decamped from the reservation and fled west. The Army had spotted them heading to the southwest, and the Army surmised they would attempt to cross the Rio Grande and disappear in the Black Range before dispersing into smaller groups to find their way back to their native lands.

"General Carleton suggested to Fort Craig's Colonel Rigg that I was the man to round up the Indians. Carleton told Rigg that we must recapture or kill the renegades before they cross the Rio Grande and Rigg relayed the message and ordered me to proceed forthwith. Carleton provided incentive by authorizing us to keep all the Indian horses as spoils. I decided I must make an initial reconnoiter of the passes through the San Andreas Mountains, as it was probable the Navajos would take that path to ford the Rio Grande and disperse into the Black Range before heading north toward their homelands."

Colonel Fountain paused for a drink of wine and Eloisa commented she was but a *bebé* when this happened, but her father and brothers talked of it often when she was older.

"It was a time when I began to feel pathos for the Navajo and Apache tribes, but my duty was my duty, and I could not question my orders. I hoped the Indians would submit and return to the reserve."

Colonel Fountain took another sip of wine, then spun back to face us. "But my duty nearly cost me my life."

Mr. and Mrs. Bergère gasped, while the Fountains restrained grins.

"I decided the Indians would detect a platoon, and so I determined it would be best to first survey the passes with the help of one of my able scouts. I chose a man, — Sanchez was his name, — who had an unequivocal reputation for the region we would examine. What I didn't realize was that he was a heavy smoker and not all that prudent about where he lit matches.

"We rode south along the foothills of the San Andreas and penetrated the known passes just deep enough to peer into the Tularosa. We reached Hembrillo Springs and camped in a small basin just below a rise that looked down upon the springs. At dawn, we lay at the crest of the hill and looked upon the area. There were at least a dozen Navajos camped there.

"I surmised they were a scouting party looking for the best route west through the Jornada and across the Rio Grande. We slipped away to the plain, then turned north, hoping to find the band's trail. In a short time, we found their tracks, and their sign showed twenty to thirty horses headed in a southwesterly direction toward Aleman. At that point, I realized their destination was the watering holes a few miles north of the Point of Rocks. We followed them through the night and caught up as the sun brightened the eastern sky. We waited for them to get ahead so they would not see us.

"When we restarted, I recognized the area and realized we were near the watering holes. We stopped in a small valley, and I sent Sanchez to reconnoiter the situation. Before I could check our gear, he returned on the run. As he approached, he threw up his arms and said the Indians had left."

"Oh my, you lost them," said Mr. Bergère.

Colonel Fountain let a hint of a smile slip before he made a 'just wait' motion. "After we waited and watched long enough that we were assured they had gone, we ventured to the water holes ourselves. Our mules raised a ruckus. It was all we could do to get them to drink. My scout and I realized the mules were reacting to the Indians' scents. They could not have left long before."

Colonel Fountain took the last sip from his wine glass and held it up in request of a refill, which Maggie provided.

"We watered our animals and re-filled our canteens before following their obvious trail. After about a half mile, we stopped, both of us dead tired from our overnight pursuit. We camped in a nearby grassy hollow to the side of a small arroyo, where our animals could enjoy ample browse. At daylight the next morning, we heard activity beyond the ridge. We approached the ridgeline from our downwind position where we saw the Indians' horses grazing. As we panned the area, we saw the Indians themselves. Some were lying down while others moved about. Sanchez was an excellent tracker and had superior knowledge of all things scouting, but his smoking put me off more than once. Several times, the scent of his cigarettes awakened me in the night, and I chastised him for it.

"While I peered through my field glasses over the ridge, he withdrew for a moment. I assumed he needed to relieve himself — pardon me ladies — but soon the Indians looked our way and made their alarming cries as they scurried about. It was then I noticed the wind had shifted. I turned to tell Sanchez, and there he was in the dried tinder of the hillside, cigarette in his mouth, trying to stomp out a growing fire as the smoke angled toward the Indian camp. They had already seen the smoke or picked up the fire's scent and they scrambled to their horses to investigate. I grabbed Sanchez by the arm and pulled him toward our camp. I quickly assessed our dire situation. As we reached the camp, I directed Sanchez to saddle our horses, which we had led all the previous day, while I threw our coats and blankets over two large soapweed. I hoped the Indians would think there were men guarding the camp. I knew it wouldn't hold them long, but reasoned any head start at all was better than none."

Sweat beaded on Colonel Fountain's forehead and he dabbed it from his brow. As Maggie topped off his glass of wine, she cupped her mouth, "Papa, this is more detailed than I remember. Usually, you just skip right to the ..." Colonel Fountain shook his head and put his finger to his wine-stained lips.

"You honor us with the telling of the full story," said Eloisa. "Already I am mesmerized by the tumult of your adventure. We know they did not kill you, as you are here, but the intrigue of your situation is enthralling."

The Colonel grinned and nodded his appreciation before continuing. "We gathered our weapons, canteens, and animals and galloped off down the arroyo. When we emerged onto the plain, we were just two miles from the Indian's camp. As we made our escape, I considered our options. My first thought was to return to Paraje and prepare to defend my family. But then my duty intervened, and I realized I would first need to get to Fort McRae where I could relay my information to soldiers that would then present it to Colonel Rigg at Fort Craig. If I could stay ahead of the Navajo scouting party, they would chase me all the way to Fort McRae, and I need not worry about my young family. So we turned to the northwest. We had scarcely gone twelve miles when we realized the Navajos had foretold our intent and had cut us off. Fort McRae was no longer a possibility. Paraje became our next best option, and we swung back to the north where we could gain the advantage of superior elevation. We rode hard and fast over the rolling hills at the base of the San Andreas. We could see faint signs of the Indians to our left — to the west — as we made haste toward Paraje.

"It seemed we had lost them, and I was about to congratulate Sanchez on our escape when he asked me for my field glasses, which had dangled from my neck all the while. We had paralleled the wagon road to Paraje some miles to the west, and Sanchez scanned the area for a few moments. With aplomb, he handed the field glasses back, pointed to the west, and said, 'There are the Indians. They are about five miles from us, on the road to Paraje. They have cut us off.'

"I raised the glasses and peered out but could see nothing that resembled Indians and yet, I had implicit faith in Sanchez. The Navajos had ferreted our intent and once again, we had become desperate. As you may know, there is but a narrow passage between the *malpais* of the Jornado del Muerto Volcano and the Frau Cristobal Mountains where the road to Paraje lies. Sanchez did not hesitate and said, 'We must cross through the *malpais*. That is our sole hope.'"

On its face, the story was gripping. However, Colonel Fountain's theatrical skills made it doubly so. The Bergères knew about the *malpais* and they gasped at the prospect of crossing the dangerous area. Many people had become lost there. A person could become disoriented, fall through brittle layers of dried lava into deep crevasses, or lose their balance on the uneven landscape and break a bone.

"We switched to our mules and crept north toward the craggy landscape. Our passage rose some five hundred feet above the plain. The path through the expanse of the *malpais* was a very narrow twisting rut through the hardened volcanic flows. When we reached the dreaded landscape, the lava walls rose menacingly twenty feet or more above the plain. It was the only safe trail through the bad land for many miles.

"We scrutinized the area in search of Indians that might attack us once we had entered the *malpais*, then returned to the pass trail head. I knew that the Indians occupied the pass somewhere despite our extensive reconnoiter. Sanchez and I changed our saddles to our horses. If we could navigate through the pass, our horses would provide the speed to make the last dash a few miles to Paraje. I then ordered Sanchez to retreat two hundred yards and take a position where he could cover my ascent and passage. When I reached the acme, I would signal him with my mirror and cover his ascent to join me. I said to Sanchez, 'If they should attack me, do not wait for the result. Make your escape, if possible, and carry our news to the nearest military post.'"

Mr. Bergère squirmed in his chair. "You must have been in fear for your lives."

Colonel Fountain, between sips of his wine said, "To be honest, sir, I don't recall fear — only an utter focus on the tasks at hand, but fear was about to find me.

"I entered the pass, carelessly astride my horse, I suppose. I held my Henry rifle in my right hand with the barrel across the saddle pommel. In my left hand, I grasped my rein and lariat. I remember that my stomach clenched, which reminded me I couldn't recall when we had last eaten. The perpendicular lava walls on either side rose to my horse's head and the width of the passage was so narrow there was barely enough room for me to keep my feet in the stirrups. About halfway to the summit, my horse reared, which pulled my arm back, thus causing my horse to pull up his head. The muzzle of a rifle was pointed at me from less than ten feet above. I glimpsed an Indian's head behind the rifle before it discharged, and my horse collapsed and died at once from the wound. I went down with him; my right leg pinned under his dead weight.

"A volley of shots followed, and an arrow passed through my left shoulder. A bullet entered my left thigh, and an arrow severed the artery in my right forearm. I wasn't certain whether I had fired a shot yet and blood gushed from my forearm. Before I could attend to it, the Indians rushed me. Fortunately, the narrow pass allowed only one attacker to approach me at a time. There was no time to sight the rifle. Pinned down by my horse as I was, I just fired from my repeating rifle as quickly as I could.

"It must have been the first time they had seen a repeating rifle in action, for in that short period I must have fired ten shots. I do not know how many I killed, for as they fell, they disappeared from my view."

Colonel Fountain paused and looked over his audience's heads. "I can still see the last villainous rascal as he charged with lance in hand to commit the coup de grâce. He was only six feet away when, with my left arm extended and rifle held steady as I could, I fired as if it were a pistol.

"In under a minute, it was over, and the war painted face of the Navajo lay just a few yards before me clad in nothing but his red breech clout. He did not disappear into the abyss as the others had and his contorted death convulsions played out in front of me while his tribal companions must have decided the threat of my repeater left them without a prayer of success. The brave took his last breath with the setting sun and at last I felt some relief as the cloak of the night sheltered me from further attack."

The Bergère's were on the edge of their seats as Colonel Fountain continued. "After a time, I realized I needed to attend to my wounds as my blood spurted from my forearm onto my chest. I could reach my knife with my left hand and cut the sleeve from my right arm, which I then bound around the severed artery. I used a section of steel whipping rod from the butt of my rifle to twist the sleeve-bandage tight, which stopped the flow of blood. Two canteens dangled from the pommel of my saddle. I drank from one until it was empty. I lay back, but my head contacted the dried lava wall and left me in an awkward pose, but I could do nothing about it as my horse's weight entrapped me. "

Colonel Fountain looked up. "The stars." he cried. And then at a lowered voice, "The stars." He stopped and looked skyward. "They were the brightest and twinkled as I had never seen them. I truly believed it was the last thing I would see, for if I lasted through the night, the Indians would be upon me with the rising sun. I did not know what became of Corporal Sanchez. The air grew icy, and my wounds stung. I hoped that death would spare me of a tortured living. Soon, out of exhaustion and my wounds, I fell into a fitful repose. If I had nightmares of my recent encounters, thank the good Lord, they did not awaken me, and I do not remember them.

"Meanwhile, Corporal Sanchez made his escape and spurred his horse away from the Navajos south twenty-five miles to Fort McRae. He arrived at midnight, rousted the commander, and informed him of the events that had transpired. Colonel Willis dispatched a detachment to my rescue. At dawn, I heard shod hooves on stone a long distance away, but it was distinct and familiar. I waited and waited … heard it again, much nearer … and then came the sound of a cavalry column as they crossed a rocky slope close at hand … and then the confusion and rattling stones coming down the slope from above me, letting me know the Indians had also heard the cavalry's approach.

"I shouted and discharged my rifle. A moment later, my good friend, Lieutenant Healey, was there beside me and I was saved."

The Bergères sighed in relief and then joined the Fountains in hearty applause.

Colonel Fountain held up his hands to quiet the audience. "An epilogue, if you please."

He took another sip of wine, then hands on hips, he began. "The rescue party took me on to Paraje, but my wounds were severe, and an army ambulance wagon transported me to Fort Bliss near El Paso where they surgically removed the arrow from my shoulder. After I recovered several months later, the Army discharged me. Several years later, that first face I saw that morning of my rescue — that of Lieutenant Healey — he ..." Colonel Fountain's voice cracked, and he hesitated to regain his composure. "In 1872, and at my heartfelt recommendation, Texas Governor Davis appointed Healey as a captain in a new law force called the Texas Rangers. It was a position he was eminently qualified for. Alas, enroute to his new assignment, he and a few local citizens learned of a predatory band of Comanche raids in the San Saba River valley. They lit out in pursuit, but never returned. How Healey died we never found out, but his memory is with me and will be, for all of my days."

# 18: Sacramento Home

Oliver was a good listener. His quiet manner often led people to say more than they should, and he recognized the value of keeping *his* plans to himself. So, when folks found out about the sale of all his cattle in the fall of 1889, they thought it was an astute move because soon after the markets declined.

Later, when the Tularosa fell into a disastrous drought, they thought of him as some kind of soothsayer. In reality, Oliver pursued the plan that he, Eph, and I worked out the previous month. Neither Eph nor I expected him to act that fast, but when Oliver recognized an opportunity, he didn't flinch. By then they knew the longhorn — Hereford crossbreed would not work. The sale of most of his four thousand head gave him the stake to establish a smaller herd of Hereford that was better suited to the type of graze in the area. After the fact, some Tularosans thought Oliver could forecast droughts, but the reduction in the size of his herd wasn't about a drought that he had no way of predicting. Instead, it was about a more efficient operation we had planned for over a year earlier.

Oliver kept all his deeded lands and irrigated hayfields and that meant his claimed range lands would go further. Meanwhile, his Hereford herd would do better during droughts and their gross weight and quality was better than longhorns.

## August 5

The Altmans, including Ed, made the trip down to Lee Well for another Sunday meal. We set up a temporary table under the porch with enough chairs for everyone, including the few hands that hadn't gone to town that Saturday night. Family gatherings always meant that George's death and the subject of his murder lurked just below the surface. Despite being on everyone's mind, no one uttered a word about it. Yet whenever Nettie's eye met that of a visitor, her grief and their sympathy passed without words. So, she kept her focus on her plate and they talked about the weather, the price of beef, Oliver's latest project, and often about the memories of their ranch back on Little Elm Creek in Taylor County, Texas.

Perry liked to talk about the old days. He loved his little brother Oliver, but he also liked to needle him with stories of their childhood. Even Nettie had to laugh when Perry told how a young Oliver nearly fell through the outhouse hole. Perry chuckled as he explained Oliver escaped his fetid fate by hanging on with his forearms and calves. Perry had heard Oliver yell, "Help, help! I'm stuck in the outhouse."

Even Oliver chuckled and smiled, but he was rarely without a response. "It wasn't so long ago, brother, that I remember when we saw the Tularosa you told me, 'This country is so damn sorry I think we can stay here a long time and never be bothered by anybody else.' Appears your idea of 'a long time' is mighty short. I might be the youngest in the clan, but I think I speak for y'all. We won't be run out of the Tularosa like we was Taylor County. Charlie and sister Emma's exodus ain't gonna be the start of another move for the family."

That put a damper on any further conversation. I helped collect the dirty dishes while the other men took their gun belts from the pegs next to the front door and went behind the adobe to practice shooting. When Mary saw the men had gone, she shooed me away and I joined Oliver, Perry, Ed, Eph, and Sixto. As I approached, Perry saw me and cupped his hand to shield his mouth as he said something to Oliver, who gave him a simple nod.

I knew better than to ask what they had said, but I couldn't help but remember George's murder still had not been settled — at least not to the Altmans' and Lees' satisfaction. At the time, my uneasiness faded when the men began their target practice, but it would return with a vengeance.

---

## August 12

It was a Sunday and as a rule, Oliver and his family were lenient with the work to be done on the ranch. Still, every Saturday there were some daily chores, and the foreman assigned a rotating schedule so that we had to work maybe one Sunday out of every month. Most of the other hands left the ranch on Saturday nights and stayed in town after some late-night fun. I read a book, wrote in my journal, or explored some of the local canyons that I hadn't seen.

On that Sunday, Oliver asked me to come with him to check out a hidden valley on the Sacramento River. We were to meet Cooper, Tucker, and Carr at a prearranged spot. Travel through the Sacramentos was rugged, and we brought a second mount, which we changed to halfway to our destination.

I had ridden with Oliver before when he scouted for new range. He would stop at a prospective grassy area and look for branded steers, which would suggest another rancher had claimed the area. If there weren't any, he would determine if there was a way to channel water from a nearby dependable source. By my estimation, on our way to meet the others, we had passed several prospects, but Oliver didn't even slow.

When we met them, Cooper had a pack mule that carried more supplies than necessary for a day or two and each of them trailed a second horse. While I gathered firewood and started the fire, the three of them stood down by the creek. A few times, their speech became heated. The only name I heard was Perry. It was obvious they didn't want me to hear, and that was fine with me.

After our meal, Oliver took me aside. He put his hands on my shoulders. "Hey-you, I realize I didn't ask if you wanted to be involved in this, but the fewer people that know about it the better. The rest of the hands go into town Saturday nights and once they get liquored-up, you never know what they might say." I nodded. "If some busybody asks for any of us, just tell them we are looking for new water and graze in the Sacramentos and you don't know when we'll return."

I glanced around. "Alright. Who's in charge at the ranch? Eph?"

"Yep, now look here, I want you to set yerself in that chair on the porch like you're on guard, 'cept I don't want it to look that-a-way, so keep busy fixin' tack and such. It's important that you let me know if somebody asks for us. Make sure you get their names and why they want us. As soon as you are certain they have gone, come up here and tell me what you know."

Oliver told me to let Eph know I was leaving and how to make certain no one followed me. "I told Ma and Nettie we have a lot of work to get done in several places up here, so they won't be askin' questions."

"OK."

"OK? What in tarnation does that mean?"

I squinted and put a hand on my hip and shifted my weight in that direction. "I guess it means alright, I agree, but I don't know where I've heard it before."

For me to get back before dark, I needed to leave right after the meal. As I saddled my horse and arranged my gear, I was deep in thought.

*I was certain something was up, but what? It would have something to do with justice for George's murder, but they wouldn't ... would they?*

Oliver must have seen that it disturbed me, for he came to the other side of the horse and acted as though he was retieing my bedroll as I double looped my canteen over the saddlehorn. "Don't worry Hey-you, everything will be alright. Just keep our location between you and Eph."

I nodded, mounted, and forced a smile. "I will."

On the way back to Lee Well, I jostled 'OK' around in my mind, as I tried to understand where I had heard the term before. I knew it was a clue, because Oliver had never heard it, and so it must be something that a certain area or person used. As hard as I tried to stop thinking about who I was and where I belonged, the vague, unusable clues kept popping into my head.

When I returned to Lee Well, neither Mary nor Nettie had heard of the term 'OK' and neither asked why I had returned without Oliver.

That night, I tossed and turned on my cot in the bunkhouse to the cries of tired cowboys: "Gol darn it, lay still will ya." and other less polite remarks. I felt torn. A part of me felt I should go to the law to prevent what could end up with more people killed, but on the other hand, there was no doubt the law had failed Nettie and the Lee clan. It didn't help that the primary deputy sheriff for the area — E. C. Rucker — was an employee of John Good. Oliver and the rest of the Lee clan liked to blame the Santa Fe Ring for the actions of the Goods, but it seemed to me deputy Rucker was where the workings of the sheriff's office got bunged up.

## August 13

The next morning, I forgot my assignment and rode with Eph and Virgil out to our delegated range, as we did every working morning. On the way, Virgil told about his Saturday night. He always had some humorous anecdotes about our cowboys that would be good ammunition in the never-ending playful verbal jousts between us.

"I sure am glad I didn't stop in at the Good's Ranch when I came in from up north," he said. "One of them boys was tellin' us about Walter gittin' all in a twist over his missin' paint horse."

I didn't hear the rest because my thoughts drifted to Oliver and the others up on the Sacramento River, and I realized I should have stayed back at headquarters in case someone would come for Oliver. When Virgil had to roust a calf from the muck at the edge of the stream, I told Eph that I needed to go back to ranch headquarters and I would send out someone else to take my place.

E.C. Rucker was there when I arrived, and Mary stood on the porch with her shotgun draped over her forearm — she had not invited him to dismount.

Rucker was saying, "... Walter's paint is missin' and I figure Oliver knows somethin' about it."

"Now, why would my son know anything about Walter's horse? Are you accusin' my Oliver of bein' a horse thief?"

Rucker seemed to know it would come to that, and he bowed his head and stared at his saddlehorn as he tried to decide how to respond. It was impossible to miss the polished deputy sheriff badge pinned to his vest. I decided Mary had things well in hand. I dismounted and looped my reins over the hitching rail, then walked to the porch and stood by her.

"You know what I'm gettin' at ... Mrs. Lee." Rucker said.

Mary adjusted the shotgun in a way that suggested she was prepared to do more than just hold it. "We don't know nothin' about no paint horse. And we 'specially don't know nothin' about Walter Good. Now, if you've said your piece, you're welcome to water your horse and refill your canteen from the well, but then I 'spect you'll be on your way."

Rucker got down off his horse and led him to the watering trough.

"Oh, and one more thing," yelped Mary. "Don't come back here with that badge on unless you're figurin' on arrestin' somebody."

I waited until Rucker had disappeared down the road to La Luz and then rode over to the bunkhouse. One of the cowboys picked out a second mount for me. I retrieved some jerky and dried fruit from the bunkhouse and left for the Sacramento River. On the way, I stopped by the range and told Eph what had happened, and he headed back for headquarters where he could send someone to take his place.

When I reached the camp, Oliver and the others were tolerating a staple meal of beans and rice. I told Oliver about Rucker. He nodded and smiled, but said nothing. I ate some of my food, had a drink from the cool, clean Sacramento River and then started back toward Lee Well. I wanted to retrace my steps to see if my news had caused some action, but I resisted because I knew Oliver wanted to protect me.

As I rode over the divide between Sacramento and Scott Able Canyon, I glimpsed four riders through the pine trees heading north up the Sacramento Canyon toward La Luz.

## August 14

That fateful Tuesday morning, Emma Altman appeared at the Lee's ranch yard in her carriage with an agitated baby. She said she had tried everything she could think of, but nothing seemed to comfort little Rena. It was pleasant in the porch's shade and so Mary pulled her rocking chair out there and the women took turns rocking the baby in their arms while I sat on my backless chair and whittled on a gnarly piece of cottonwood. After the women had taken a few turns in the rocker, little Rena released a fart you would have thought came from her father and that quelled the squalls. The women's eyes widened, and their lips puckered in surprise as they looked at one another. Then we all broke into a hearty laugh.

"She's a chip off her own father's block," quipped Emma, and we erupted into hearty guffaws.

When we had calmed down, Emma said, "I came over because I can't seem to find Stickney and Poor's Paregoric at Meyer's store in La Luz. I doubt you have any, but I was at the end of my rope. Her howls bothered Perry so much last evening that he rode over to the Good's Ranch just to get away. While there, he told them to tell Walter that his horse appeared at our watering trough the other day and to come and get him because we were tired of looking after him."

Mary and Nettie's eyebrows shot up as Perry was seldom that forward.

"That seems odd, don't the Goods corral their remuda?" asked Mary.

Emma shrugged. "Perry said that maybe one of our herd was in heat and the paint stallion caught a whiff of her. He said that if they gave him any grief, he would ask for damages for breeding our thoroughbreds, but I know he won't." She grinned and little Rena smiled at her as Mary and Nettie emitted adoring "ahhs."

While the ladies fawned over the contented Rena, I couldn't help but wonder if Walter's paint wandered into the Altman's ranch yard. It seemed August was a little late for a mare to come into heat. The Altman's place was several miles southwest of the Good's remuda pasture. While the prevailing south-westerlies could carry a scent a considerable distance, the Altman's place was in exactly the opposite direction.

My eyes drifted back to the ladies and little Rena, and there was something about the baby — something from my masked past. I gazed to the south at the face of the Sacramentos. When I looked back to my whittling, a baby appeared in my lap. I blinked, and it was gone.

# 19: The White Sands

**August 15, 1888**

After supper the previous evening, Oliver sent Eph to check on the Altmans. Since it was late, he took his bedroll and said he would return in the morning.

Mid-morning, Eph arrived back at Lee Well at a full gallop. Mary and Nettie heard the commotion and came from their morning chores.

Eph's horse was so lathered-up, I was hard pressed to tell its color; and Eph, eyes bulging, huffed and puffed with exhaustion and alarm. "Walter's horse," deep breath, dismount, "Altman's corral," deep breath, hands on knees, "Hugh Taylor ..."

Mary rushed onto the porch, held up her hands and said, "Calm down, Eph. Ain't nothin' gonna happen between the time you catch your breath and you tellin' us what's happenin'."

I got a ladle of water from the well and Nettie led him to one of the porch Windsor chairs.

Mary stood in front of Eph. "Now, take your time and tell us what has happened. We know Walter's horse has been at the Altmans. Emma came by yesterday and said Perry went to tell him to come git it. So, are you sayin' he came, and somethin' happened?"

As Mary spoke, Eph regained his composure and moved to the edge of his seat with his urgent information, but Mary was oblivious. When at last she finished, he said, "No ma'am, that's just it, Walter ain't never got there."

Eph relapsed into huffing and before he could recover, Nettie said, "You mean he didn't come?"

Eph swallowed hard to calm himself, "No ma'am, Walter's wife's brother — Mr. Taylor — say Walter lef' yesterd'y mornin' and he ain't never come back."

From behind me, I heard Nettie say, "Oh my," and I lost track of the conversation as my mind raced. My first thought was she was vengeful over George's murder, but then I wondered if she worried about the consequences of a feud. With all that had been going on with Oliver and his hired guns, him teaching me about guns, and all, it could have been a revenge attack. The thoughts and questions poured out of my head.

*Was I the sole person who didn't know what was happening? Should I be thankful for that?*

Something brought me back to the present and mid-conversation, I heard Eph say, "No ma'am, Perry say he ain't got no information and then Mr. Taylor, he took Walter's paint with him."

My mind wandered again to Las Cruces when Oliver suggested we would have to take care of Walter ourselves and then to Mary reciting Leviticus.

Once again, the ongoing conversation interrupted my thoughts. Eph said, "Mr. Perry say he gonna go lookin' for Walter. I begged him not to, but you know how he is. After a bit, I got him to wait 'til one of us can go along."

After considerable back and forth between us, Eph and I decided we should protect the women first. Since Eph was the better gunman, he stayed at the headquarters. I would stop in

Escondido Canyon to tell the foreman we needed good gun handlers back at headquarters. After, I would continue to the Altmans to search for Walter.

Why would Perry want to do such a thing? It seemed crazy because if he knew the family was behind Walter's disappearance, he would steer clear of its known location anyway, and if we found him, there would be accusations we knew where he was all along. It seemed a fool's errand, but Eph and I agreed Oliver wouldn't want him to go out there alone.

When I arrived at the Altmans, Perry told me he thought he should look for Walter to lend credence to their statements that they were not involved in his disappearance. I wasn't so certain of that, but agreed. We talked about where we should look while I let my horse water in the trough, and I filled my canteen. Emma called for me to get some trail food, and I left my canteen on the lip of the well. When I returned, Perry had mounted and was ready to go. I handed him his bag of jerky and dried fruit as he started toward the White Sands. I threw my leg over my saddle and followed.

We checked on the empty Graham Ranch before venturing into the fringes of the blinding white dunes. The White Sands could have been the ultimate resting place for more bodies than any New Mexico cemetery. It offered easy digging and people avoided it because it was easy to become disoriented. Between it and the malpais sinkholes and crevices, it was easy to hide bodies in southern New Mexico. In those blinding dunes, the 'planted' and the lost bodies appeared and vanished at the mercy of the shifting sands. With time, the sun-bleached skeletons went unnoticed as they disappeared against the alabaster grains.

Without a cloud in the sky, the relentless sun beat down on us. Our horses plodded through the loose sand. as we skirted the edges of the vast sea of dunes. "There ain't no chance of findin' Walter out here, Hey-you. We're gonna have to go in further."

Little by little we went deeper and deeper into the ominous landscape, then retraced our hoofprints out. We stopped and dismounted in one location, but the bones we saw were from an animal. Despite the cloudless sky and the heat of the afternoon, the sand was cool to the touch. How I knew why was a mystery, but I supposed someone had told me that the vivid white color of the sand reflected the sun's rays, which left the sand cool to the touch.

An hour or so later, we came across a bawling stray steer a quarter mile into the dunes. We would glimpse him and then he would disappear into the vast mounds of sand. Some of the dunes were higher than a house. I felt bad for the little calf — a spring calf, no doubt. He might have been from Charlie's herd. I thought that if I rescued him, it would show my appreciation to Oliver for saving me. Last time we saw him, we were near Graham Ranch.

"Perry, I'll go rope that steer and lead him back to the Grahams where he can get a drink. I'll meet you back there."

As I rode toward the calf and lost sight of Perry, the calf became energized and trotted further into the dunes. I knew I could just follow my tracks back out of the maze of landforms and so I chased him deeper and deeper into a landscape of cadaverous white wind whipped mounds topped by cerulean blue. I reminded myself a few times that there was no need to worry because I could retrace my horse's deep hoof prints.

When at last I got close enough to lasso him, he circled back and then feinted left. My horse wasn't a good roping horse, but he must have had some herding experience because he dodged back and forth and spun once as I grabbed for my saddlehorn. The calf continued to try to get past me. At last, he succeeded and trotted off toward the depth of the duneland. As he got away from me, I released my grip on the saddlehorn and threw the lasso. As it floated toward the calf, I became dizzy and disoriented. I recognized my symptoms as dehydration and reached for my canteen, but it wasn't there. The horizon spun, and I awakened to the view of the bright blue New Mexico sky. I remember the relief of the cool sand as its loose granules engulfed my body. Any pent-up worries about finding my way out evaporated, and I relaxed.

Whether I slept, was in a trance or unconscious, I don't know, but the dreams were stark and incontrovertible.

I dreamt of a large family in a town and the father was important. I saw a boy with a pompadour haircut next to him in his office. The man called the boy Jesús, and the boy called the man Zio. The man turned as though he looked at me and said, "Jesús, when will you return to us? We will wait for you here."

Perhaps they weren't dreams but … visions … for what else could you call them? And there were others. In one, on a frosty morning I sat in front of a store front where the sign read Las Cruces Telegraph office. A man leaned against the doorjamb, his legs crossed at the ankles … in another there was a tall man on a large white horse … buzzards circled … in still another several distinguished-looking men watched as one of them gave me an award … me sitting on a bench overlooking fields of cotton and chiles with an older man that looked like a farmer … a foreign soldier who sat with me and other soldiers around a campfire as he told of a harrowing trip across the seas … and others. Often, they were just brief glimpses, but they were vivid and when Perry shook me awake, I had a foreign and yet precious self-awareness.

"Hey-you, Hey-you." Perry coaxed. "Wake up. Wake up."

When he saw my eyes open and a smile creep across my face, he smiled. "Golly, I was afraid we had lost you there for a minute." He offered me his canteen.

I choked as my swallows were too large, and Perry took the canteen. Between gasps to catch my breath and clear my misty lungs, I said, "I don't know what … happened to my canteen … I remember filling … it at your …."

"Calm now, it's alright. You're fine now, don't drink too fast … and you lassoed the calf."

Beside me in the sand was the calf with a lasso around its neck.

"What happened?" asked Perry. "Well, I guess I know what happened, but why did you go so far?"

"I felt I owed you … and Oliver. I thought if I brought the calf back, it was the least I could do."

Perry smiled. "You do your part. No need to git yourself kilt over a calf." He grinned, stood and pulled on my hand. "Can you git up?"

If I hadn't been young and limber, I might not have, but as I rose my thoughts went back to the realization that my name — leastwise my first name — was Jesús. "Perry, I have something to tell you."

"Sure, sonny, what is it?"

"My name."

Before I could finish, Perry interrupted, "Yeah, Hey-you, I know. What happened? Did you forget that too?"

I paused. *What if the people I saw in my vision — my people — and the Lee clan were on opposite sides?*

Perry chuckled. "It's alright, you ain't the first and won't be the last."

He helped me onto my horse. As I tried my best to understand what I had just experienced, Perry took my lasso off the calf. He wound it into a coil and tied it off on my saddle, then cinched his lasso on the stray and looped the other end around his saddlehorn.

We arrived back at his adobe late that evening without finding Walter, but having found me.

# 20: Fooled 'em

**August 17, 1888**

*Jesús* .... I relished my name. My visions only gave me a first name, but it was a start, and I could see why 'Hey-you' struck me as similar. The next best thing was that I now realized Las Cruces was probably my home. The places I saw, St. Genevieve Church and the Las Cruces Telegraph Office, meant someone must know me there. It occurred to me that the people that had stared at me, but then turned away, thought they knew me. My beard and long hair threw them off. I needed a reason to go to Las Cruces.

---

Meanwhile, the cowboy grapevine produced the rumor that Cooper, Tucker, and Lee were at the Altman's house the night before Walter disappeared. I didn't know whether that was true, but my memory of them heading north as I went over the divide toward Moore Ridge made me consider the possibility.

John Good wasted no time. He went to the La Luz justice of the peace, Humphrey Hill, and without an investigation got a warrant against Cooper, Tucker, and Oliver for carrying weapons. John went with the posse to Altmans Ranch to make the arrest. As usual, Perry wasn't carrying a weapon, and he told them that Tucker, Cooper, and Oliver were camped in the Sacramentos. "Ain't seen 'em for quite some time."

John threw a tantrum. He stomped up and down in front of the Altmans' home and challenged Perry. Rena started crying and

Emma charged onto the porch. "John Good, you have awakened my baby with your carryin's on!" Little Rena squalled.

John turned to face Emma and chittered. "Well, ain't that just too damn bad? I've had it with you folks. I got a warrant, and I'm takin' your husband to La Luz for further questioning." Hill tried to interrupt John to tell him the warrant didn't include Perry, but John talked over him. As little Rena wailed, Hill refused to handcuff Perry. John snatched the cuffs from Hill and put them on Perry himself while he screamed at Emma, "Perhaps your yowling brat will sleep better without his father."

Perry said nothing, but Emma clenched her fists as her face turned bright red. "She's a girl, not a boy, and if that means she'll never have to deal with the likes of you, I'm thankful." She reentered the adobe and slammed the door, which fell half off its hinges.

Hill told one of the posse to fix their door as John stared arrows into the back of his head.

John and his son interrogated Perry for the rest of the day and overnight in a La Luz town office back room. He would begin with a question which turned into a rant of sorts. When he got nowhere with that, he bellowed threats and when anger and intimidation got no results, he resorted to a whiny, gentle cajole. Charlie was a chip off John's hotheaded block, but the youngest, Ivan, favored their pusillanimous mother. When John and Charlie wore themselves out or became overwrought with their lack of progress, they would leave the room and son-in-law Hugh Taylor and Ivan would let Perry doze. As the sun lit the sky toward morning, John gave up. "He ain't gonna talk. It'll be dawn soon. It's a good time to just string him up and get it over with."

John's histrionics didn't threaten his son-in-law, Hugh Taylor. "No, that will do no good," said Hugh. "It would only inflame the Lees." After considerable persuasion, John agreed to release him. But that wasn't the end of it.

**August 18**

John offered a reward of three hundred dollars for his son's
return dead or alive, plus one thousand for the arrest and
conviction of the killers. He had posters made in Tularosa to that
effect. In the meantime, area citizens petitioned the County Sheriff
— Guadalupe Ascarate — to come from Las Cruces and disarm
the factions.

Once again, the cowboy grapevine hummed, and when
Ascarate arrived, no one carried a firearm. He stood at the center
of town and declared, "The citizens of La Luz and the surrounding
area sent a petition with sixty signatures with a request that I come
and disarm the feuding factions. I departed Las Cruces the day
after I received your petition. I have walked your streets and
visited your businesses. I can find no one to disarm. I will now
return to Las Cruces, but my deputies here can continue to enforce
the law that prohibits weapons in town."

---

By the time I heard Ascarate was coming to La Luz, he had
already returned to Las Cruces. It was my best opportunity to find
out more about myself. If I waited for another chance, there was
no telling how long it would take. I decided to take some initiative.

Oliver and his men remained at their camp in the Sacramento
Canyon, or so I presumed. All of Good's attention focused on
Perry, which worried Mary and Nettie. As Oliver had instructed, I
whiled-away my days as I sat on the porch and waited for visitors
that asked for him or his small band. Tack repairs had run out, and
I sat in my old broken-down Windsor chair, wrote in my loose-
leaf journal, and read two-week-old El Paso newspapers and
month's old stockman's magazines. The Lees didn't have a novel,
unless you included the Bible. Mary offered it time after time.
"The stories in here are every bit as interestin' as anything you
might find in a New York library."

I thought I had read from the Bible, but I didn't know where
or how much. Each day, Mary marked stories for me to read. The

stories ranged from David and Goliath to the tale of Sodom and Gomorrah's destruction. But as I scanned her Bible, I noted many underlined verses in Proverbs. Most had to do with the righteous getting their just reward, while God punished those that could not or would not flourish. I could see how that fit with the Lees belief in a kind of natural superiority where only the toughest, strongest, and most determined thrived.

**August 20**

At last, John and Rucker wised-up and sent the Tularosa deputy sheriff to Lee Well to request Oliver and the others surrender. This new lawman was on the short side, but like most young men of the Tularosa, he was wiry and strong, and he rode tall and proud in the saddle. While he introduced himself as the Tularosa deputy sheriff, he wasn't armed and didn't wear a badge. He showed it when Mary questioned him, and then he returned it to his pocket. The young man apologized for taking them from their morning chores and Mary invited him to dismount.

He hopped off his roan and tipped his hat. "I can see Oliver and Perry ain't here about ma'am and I know it wouldn't be his way to go hidin' somewheres until I rode off. Deputy Rucker asked me to come and ask that Oliver, Perry, Tucker, Kellam, and Cooper turn themselves in. They can arrange the where and when as long as it ain't at none of your places."

Mary had come to the door with her shotgun. When she saw the deputy didn't pose a threat, she leaned it against the adobe. However, no one could fool Mary with shallow pleasantries. "So, it seems John's reward offer ain't turned anyone against my son and his friends."

The deputy smirked. "I wouldn't know about that ma'am, but your son seems to be playin' this thing right smart. Now, I don't know if they were involved or not. I'm jus' doin' my job. I hope you understand."

Mary shook her head, "Well sonny, it seems to me a salary puts a mighty cheap value on a man's honor, but I understand. Do as you must."

The deputy gritted his teeth, untied a rolled-up broadsheet from his saddle and offered it to us. I took the several steps to retrieve it from his outstretched hand and brought it back to Mary. She unrolled it, saw that it was the reward poster John had printed, and said, "This'll be right handy when I start the cookstove tomorrow mornin'." She turned and motioned for Nettie to follow her into the house.

The deputy let a brief frown cross his lips and tipped his hat to me. "Mr. Good didn't say y'all couldn't get the reward." He frowned as he realized how insensitive his words were, and I recognized how innocent he was. I wondered how Rucker had roped him into his task. He turned and galloped toward La Luz. I have sometimes wondered if that young man's experience that day led him away from the law or further into it.

I went inside where Mary had rolled the broadsheet out on the table. The word *REWARD* was printed in bold capital letters across the top of the page. The rumors we had heard about its content were spot on. At the bottom, in small print, read:

> *John Good will pay rewards at his identification of the body and/or a signed court finding of guilt of the accused.*

After I had read it, Nettie rolled it up and placed it on the cooking table next to the cookstove.

Mary had returned to chopping an onion. Without taking her eyes off her chore, she said, "I imagine you know where to find Oliver. Please tell him who brought word, and that he wasn't nasty about it." Nettie gave a half smile. "But make certain you ain't followed. As pleasant as that young man was, he made it clear where his loyalties lie."

When I saw the speck that was the deputy disappear over a slight rise in the flats, I mounted Ol' Nasty and doubled the lead on my second horse, brought him up beside me, and galloped off toward Escondido Canyon. I stopped several times at different intervals and listened for trailers, as Oliver had taught me. He had said that if Good's men stopped me, I could tell them I was going to one of his line camps in the area.

A few hundred yards short of Dripping Spring I stopped and whoever was behind me couldn't stop as soon. I heard their horses' hooves pound against the caliche trail above the wash. I dismounted. My play was to stay until the trailers decided I had made them and left, or they revealed themselves. I could also approach them, but I preferred they left.

After several minutes, the sound of their hooves resumed, and as the sounds got louder, I could tell there were several horses. I looked around. I needed an excuse for stopping at that spot. There were Indian paintings off the trail a short distance. I got down from Ol' Nasty and tied off my second horse to a bush. As I approached the Indian drawing of a horse and a lizard, I noticed several shards of rock before the etched images.

As I reached down to pick up a perfect arrowhead, the sound of the hooves stopped and a someone said, "You're mighty tricky there sonny — stoppin' and startin' oddly all the time — and you finally tricked us out."

I turned and looked back. It was John Good and E.C. Rucker. A third man behind them led a pack mule loaded with supplies.

"I don't know what you're talking about sir. My second mount gave me trouble and I had to stop now and then to sort out the problem. This little enclave is interesting, don't you think?" I held up the arrowhead I had found.

Rucker pulled his six-gun from his holster. "We don't care for your excuses, son. Just continue on to your meetin' with Oliver and Perry. We won't hurt 'em."

I was prepared for this and wanted to laugh but contained myself. With as much innocence as I could muster, I said, "Huh?"

Rucker opened the loading gate on his six-gun and spun the cylinder. "We know you're trailin' up to tell Oliver what the Tularosa deputy told you at Lee Well this mornin'."

"I never spoke with the Tularosa deputy." I hadn't, although I was present for his discussion with Mary.

"C'mon now, son," said John. "You're just startin' to piss me off runnin' us around the barn with your lies."

"I'm on my way to the line camp up the way …," I pointed up to my right toward the secluded pasture atop Moore Ridge where Oliver had dug a ditch to a tank the year before.

"Sure you are," snapped Rucker. "Just lead us on to their camp."

I shrugged, held up the arrowhead again, and slipped it into my vest pocket. It was a short trot to a small spring where I refilled my canteen, and the horses drank. There wasn't enough of a pool for Good and his friends and their horses, so they waited.

When I pulled my horses to the side, I thought they might stop for water also, but as I switched the saddle and gear to my second horse, they just waited. I suppose they thought I might make a run for it if they let their horses drink when I acted as though I was waiting for them. This seemed ridiculous and shortsighted to me, and later, I was proven right. I knew the next little canyon trail went up to the Moore's Ridge line camp. The last section of the rough trail onto the ridge was steep, and I figured my fresh horse would give me an edge there. I knew I could release Ol' Nasty and he would follow me through that last rocky, steep section of the trail. Even the main canyon trail narrowed as we rose into the Sacramentos. They didn't put someone ahead and behind me, and I realized I had the edge I needed.

When we reached the end of the trail, I let loose of Ol' Nasty and leaned into my mount's neck, dug my unspurred heels into his ribs, and urged him to scramble up the rocky slope. Between my two horses clambering hooves, loose stones flew down behind us and Good and his group had to rein their horses to the side to avoid the small landslide I had created.

This unforeseen calamity just added to my advantage. John swore a blue streak, and I turned to see the line camp shack thirty yards distant. A horse was tied to the hitching rail, and the cowboy, whom I didn't know well, came from beside the cabin to investigate the ruckus. I heeled my horse again, and we met at the hitching rail. As I swung down, I looked back to spot Good. He hadn't emerged from the slope.

I told the cowboy, "I'm being followed, and I need you to play along with what I say."

The cowboy nodded just as Rucker, John, and his hand crested the ridge and came toward us. Ol' Nasty cut in front of them as he headed for a drink at the tank a hundred yards to the south. Their horses veered in that direction as well, but Good and his men wrestled them back next to us. John swung off his horse so hard that I thought he might turn a somersault as his right leg flew hard behind him and his left foot became wedged in the stirrup. He did a quick hop and skip to regain his balance. The Lee's cowboy, whose name I didn't know, laughed as did Good's hand that had been leading their mule. I turned away and covered my mouth.

Ol' John turned redder than a dusty sunset. "I don't know what you think you're up to, but I have half a notion to have Rucker here arrest you for ... for ..."

Rucker turned to Good. "Now John, there was no malice in what happened. It's just a steep slope and well ..." Rucker threw up his arms as though to say, 'what did you expect?' "Now, it seems to me that the boy here was tellin' us the truth."

While Rucker and Good argued about it, I hustled the cowboy into the shack and filled him in at a half-whisper. I told him to get back to the ranch to let Eph and the foreman know I was being held by Good and Rucker and to send back six fully armed men the next morning.

When we left the shack, I said, "Alright Bob, I'll see you in a few days then." There wasn't time for me to ask the cowboy's name and I hoped neither Rucker nor John knew him. Fortunately, they didn't, and Bob, or whatever his name was, retrieved his hobbled second and secured his bedroll and gear. Bob started back toward Lee Well with a soft adios salute as I watched John's reaction. For all John knew, Bob could have relayed the message to Oliver, and I was just a decoy. But he was so flustered over his acrobatic dismount he didn't think to question us.

The message I needed to deliver to Oliver and the others wasn't urgent by any means, so long as they stayed hidden deep in the Sacramentos. Still, he'd want this information. I thought it sounded like a set up and I expected Oliver would think so, too.

Ol' Nasty had returned to chum with the other horses, while John's thirsty ponies edged toward the tank. John ordered his cowboy to take their horses there while he unpacked the mule and set up camp in front of the shack. I hobbled Ol' Nasty, got on my other horse, and rode out to inspect the small herd that occupied the high *mesita*. They were all longhorns. The majority were in good condition considering the time of year and lack of rain. The tank was a mud hole, and the steers hung around its edges where the grass regenerated almost as fast as they could eat it. I kept an eye out for any that suffered from injury or illness as I tried to think how I could leave and return without Good's knowledge. As I reined my horse around to head back to the shack, I looked for Good and Rucker. The shack was on a direct line between us. If I could find a way out of the back of the shack in the night and keep it between me and their camp, I could slip away and return and 'ol John wouldn't have a clue.

As I rode back, I made my plan.

# 21: Trust Earned

The moon was about a week past full. I had preferred a new moon to conceal my movements, but as it turned out, the light made my trek across the Sacramentos easier.

I needed to work fast while John and his crew set up their camp. As I tied my horse to the hitching post, I announced I would help them except that I needed to make some repairs to the shack before dark. Despite the elevation, it was still hot inside, and I removed my vest and shirt and took the hammer and whacked it against the wall a couple of times just to put in their minds that I was working with wood. I picked up the banjo shovel we kept there and dug from my knees into the compacted dirt floor near the back wall. The steel blade hitting the hard soil sounded like a pickaxe on granite. I pounded with the hammer a few more times and muffled the digging sounds with blankets and pillow against the door. I tried again, but harder this time. Thin chunks popped up, but it was clear this wouldn't do. I couldn't risk digging from the outside with Good just thirty feet away.

I wet the area with one of my two canteens. As the water splashed onto the hardened caliche, I realized the nearest drinkable water was back at Dripping Spring, and I would need what I had to get to Oliver and return. I set the canteen down on the floor and tried to figure out what I should do. Panic threatened to overtake me. I rubbed my face to quell my alarm and went outside, where the cool air made it easier to think. A few minutes of staring out at the tank calmed and reminded me that I needed to unsaddle my horse and hobble him closer to the tank.

When I turned back, I noticed that Rucker and his horse were nowhere to be seen and I surmised Good must have sent him to follow Bob. I glanced at the shack and saw boards stacked against the back wall. I remembered Virgil had said Oliver planned to re-roof several of the line camps that summer. They must have brought some supplies for this one. I examined the boards from about twenty yards, as I tried to figure out a way to use them to solve my problem. After a few seconds, I realized John was staring at me. I thought he might think I was staring at him, so I gave a half-hearted wave and he turned to resume whatever he had been doing.

An idea popped into my head, but I wasn't sure I had what I needed for the job. I went back into the shack and lit the kerosene lamp. Virgil would need other tools to fix the roof besides the hammer. A quick survey of the shack revealed a saw near the hammer, some nails on the table, and a sheet of leather hung from a nail.

The sounds of sawing and hammering wouldn't be as suspicious as digging noises. Before long, I had fashioned a board hinged with a piece of leather such that it would open out, but not in. The hole the board covered was just big enough for me to crawl through.

Removing the current pieces of board and batten was harder than I had expected. I must not have done any carpentry before because I ended up with several bent nails and a smashed thumb. I could hear Good and Rucker chuckle over my struggles, which assured me they did not know what I was up to.

When I had finished the escape hatch, I disguised it with loose boards on the outside and by placing the table over it on the inside.

I sat on a log across from John at the campfire and opened a can of beans. As I ate my supper of jerky and canned beans, I went over my plan. John's cowboy had returned from hobbling their horses and the mule the tank.

As the sun sank to the west, I tried to remember when the moon rose the previous night. I decided I might not recall because it had risen late, after I had gone to bed.

I was right. It was as dark as it could be as I whittled and waited for John and his cowhand to settle in for the night. When I realized they wouldn't rest until I had retired, I went inside and spread my bedroll on the cot. I lay there for a spell. When I got up and peeked through a slit in the wall. John hadn't moved. I lay down again and tossed and turned as though I was settling in. After a few moments, I made occasional snoring sounds. I needed to convince them I was sound asleep.

The next time I peeked, John's head bobbed up and down like a duck in a pond as he fought to stay awake. I slipped out the back and circled to find the Escondido Canyon trail. Before leaving the ridge, I glanced at John, still visible in the dying campfire. He stood and looked around, but the moon had not risen, and he couldn't see me. When I turned back, I couldn't see the faint path, but it was just as well because the rocks were loose from our previous use and I might have caused a noisy rock slide. Once I was far enough that they couldn't hear, I alternated walking and trotting along with my two canteen straps crossed at my chest.

The scents of the Sacramento high mountain forests are so different from the Tularosa flats. When I walked, I inhaled them, which kept me alert. I made the five or so miles in a couple of hours and found their fading campsite fire.

Just as I glimpsed the fire's glowing embers, a half-whisper broke the silence, "Who goes there?" I thought I recognized Jim Cooper's voice.

I slipped behind a small pine tree and half whispered back, "It's me Jim, uh …" for a moment I wanted to use my real name but realized that wouldn't mean anything to him and so I half-whispered, "It's me, Hey-you."

"Oh." The others rose from their pallets, and the man turned to them. "It's just Hey-you. C'mon in Hey-you. Is there somethin' wrong?"

Perry and Tucker stirred on their pallets but didn't rise.

"Well, I suppose so, but first, I need to pass on a message delivered by the Tularosa deputy."

We walked down to the camp as Oliver stood and put his hat on. "Tularosa deputy?" he asked.

That got everyone's attention and Perry and Tucker got up and pulled their Indian blankets over their shoulders.

"Yes, sir." I told him what the deputy had said and added that Mary said to tell him that the deputy wasn't nasty. "I thought he had an easier way than the deputy over in 'Cruces." After I said it, I wished I hadn't because Oliver still held a grudge about not getting his day in court. I looked around but didn't see the fifth man the Tularosa deputy said they wanted to surrender. Someone was missing. "Where's Kellam?"

Oliver smirked, "Unless he's standin' next to ya, ain't nobody ever knows where Cherokee Bill is. He could be anywhere from Lubbock to Tucson."

*Had Oliver baited Good away while Kellam ... no, no. I couldn't think that way. But, if that was what happened, Oliver and the others would be accessories to the crime. I wondered if he realized that.*

Tucker thankfully interrupted my thoughts. "Was there somethin' else?" asked Tucker.

"Yes, sir. John Good, Rucker and one of John's hands followed me up the Escondido, but I stopped now and then, as Oliver taught me, and they had to reveal themselves."

I told them how I had gone up to Moore's Ridge line camp and then escaped in the night to bring the message.

Oliver grinned and patted me on the back and said, "Right smart of you Hey-you." Tucker and Cooper came up and slapped me on the back also and chuckled to themselves about how, in their minds, a boy had outsmarted John Good.

"Oh yeah, I almost forgot. I told the cowboy you had stationed on the ridge to go back to the ranch and bring half a dozen armed men back in the morning to scare John and his bunch off."

Oliver was all smiles and the other three guffawed and slapped their thighs. "Well, sonny," said Oliver, "you may not be a ranny cowboy, but you sure make up for it."

Oliver said there was no way they would turn themselves in, which I expected, given our previous dealings.

We sat around what would have been their campfire and Perry gave me some dried fruit while Cooper dumped the stale water from my canteens and refilled them with clear, cold, fresh water from the Sacramento River.

While I munched on the dried fruit, Oliver said, "We've decided that it's time to head back home. We've heard about what they did to Perry and it's time we stood up to John Good. He ain't gonna bully us out of this valley."

Cooper spoke up. "Maybe we should come by there in the mornin' when your men show up?"

Oliver nodded. "I was just thinkin' the same thing, Coop."

## August 19

I slipped back into the shack undetected and managed an hour or two of sleep before John Good and his men banged around their campfire as they made breakfast.

I did the morning rounds, stopped by the back of the shack and stacked the wood planks that hid my escape hatch and then sat in front of the shack while I finished the can of beans I had started the night before. Scents of bacon and eggs frying over Good's campfire wafted past my nose. The aroma wasn't hard to withstand though because I knew what was coming.

I had left my six-gun and rifle just inside the door of the shack. When I heard the rumble of horses' hooves on the trail from the Escondido, I stepped inside and held the six-gun behind my back until Eph and the others revealed themselves.

When they did, Oliver's group must have circled and waited at the edge of the pine grove on my left. Just as John and his boys raised their weapons, Oliver, Perry, Tucker, and Cooper charged from the trees, putting the Good bunch in a crossfire.

John glanced at them and then back at me. His face was beet red. "What the hell is this?" He turned to Oliver and yelled, "I got a genuine deputy here to carry out a warrant for your arrest."

"Like hell you are, John." Oliver seldom swore, and when he did, the swears were on the milder side. "Your foreman is the deputy. He can't represent the county on this thing. Besides, the warrant is only good in the Town of La Luz, plus, we got the drop on ya, anyhow. Now throw down your weapons."

Oliver motioned to Eph, who told one of our cowboys to fetch their hardware.

John threw his handgun into the brush and another of our hands dismounted to retrieve it. "I know you did it, Oliver Milton Lee. I know'd it."

Oliver shook his head. "For goodness' sake, John, you don't even have a body do you? For all you know, Walter might have left his wife and run off with that pretty little senorita I seen him dancin' with on Saturday nights in La Luz."

John scowled and opened his mouth, but Rucker interrupted, "We're purdy certain he's dead. He's been gone now for near on two weeks."

That reminded me of my situation and that I had disappeared nearly four months ago. On second thought, I realized Rucker was probably right because anyone that had known me must have presumed I was dead. Meanwhile, the conversation continued as John's cheeks remained a brilliant red. "Give us our guns back and we'll be on our way."

Oliver chuckled. "No John, I'll send one of my men with them into the deputy's office in La Luz in the next day or two."

John looked as though locomotive-like steam would burst from his ears.

"Calm yourself John. Now, I suspect you think everyone is just as vengeful as you are but, I swear, I ain't seen Walter for at least three weeks. Sure, I'm still mournin' George. He was as much a part of our family as Walter is yours but until you get a body and can prove who did it — if indeed he is dead ... and you know John, them White Sands are mighty deadly ... folks get lost in there all the time and we never see 'em again."

John glared at Oliver. He spit to the side and signaled for Rucker and his cowboy to pack up. John mounted his horse with a little hop to get his foot in the stirrup. "This ain't over, Lee." He turned his horse, and they disappeared into the trees with the Lee cowboys on their tail.

I showed Oliver my escape hatch, and we took a brief ride around the small herd before we stopped in front of the shack. "I ain't sayin' I'll never turn myself in, but it will be a cold day in hell before I let John Good dictate to me."

―――――――――――――――――――――

When I returned to Lee Well, Bob came to me in the bunkhouse. "You surprised me when you remembered my name.

Purdy hard to forget Hey-you, though." He chuckled. "By the way, Good's hand followed me clear down to the mouth of the Escondido and then watched as I crossed the flats to headquarters. Those folks are mighty suspicious."

# 22: Do You Remember Me?

**August 22, 1888**

It seemed the Graham place would never sell. The previous evening, Eph decided to stay the night when he found signs that something had taken up residency in the adobe. Early in the morning, he heard someone yell "Hallo." outside. He didn't answer and instead took a pot shot through a window in the general direction. He listened but heard nothing, so he went back to bed, albeit with one eye open.

**August 23**

Then next morning, he found some small footprints on the roof above the door. Eph returned to Lee Well and reported to Oliver that he figured whoever was on the roof tried to draw him out for a clear shot.

That, on top of Good's attempt to follow me to arrest Oliver and several other strange goings-on led Oliver to ride over to the Altman's to see if they had further problems. Oliver and Perry shared information while they leaned against the corral and admired Perry's first-class ponies. They discarded the dangerous crazies out-of-hand and spent much of the conversation trying to distinguish between the honest-to-God truth and rumors. It was an impossible task and, in the end, they decided it was best for Emma and Rena to stay at Lee Well.

**August 24**

On the morning of the twenty-fourth, against Emma's protestations, Perry brought her and the baby to Lee Well. They used Oliver's room while he slept on the adobe roof.

After polite conversation with Oliver, Nettie, and his mother, Perry untied his saddle horse from behind their carriage and announced he needed to return to his ranch.

His mother objected. "Now Perry, there's no need to run-off. You've got a good foreman who can handle things for a day or two."

At last Perry relented, and he and Oliver spent the day assessing whether the Dog Canyon alfalfa field was ready for another cutting. They also stopped at Frenchy's place with the gift of a ham from the Lee's pig sty and smokehouse. Between stops, they talked about what John Good's next move might be. When they returned, they stopped by the herd where Virgil and I commiserated over what the rear-end of a steer resembled.

"Looks like the rear end of a steer. What in the devil else could it look like?" said Virgil as Oliver and Perry rode up.

Both men glanced at the steers in front of Virgil and me before Oliver said, "Seems like you have too much time on your hands."

Virgil tipped his hat, "Yes sir, boss." before riding off to feign a search for strays.

I removed my hat and wiped my brow. "Well, I am assigned to drag, and the herd hasn't moved, so what else should I do?"

Oliver and Perry chuckled, and I smiled. "We were on our way back home from Dog Canyon …." said Oliver.

Mid-sentence, my attention clamped on Dog Canyon as it always hit me like I knew it, but I assumed it was because it was such an odd name for a canyon.

Then I picked up another word, ... Frenchy ... something else that struck me as familiar. Maybe I should go see him.

"... we are headin' into El Paso tomorrow to stock up on ammunition and supplies."

I wasn't sure why he told me that. "Uh, alright. And you want me to do what?"

"I just told you," smirked Oliver.

"Sorry, I was distracted."

"Frenchy wants some of that wine we made last fall. I told him I'd have two small kegs brought over tomorrow. You can use Perry's two-seater."

As Perry and Oliver rode away, my mind returned to my predicament.

The rediscovery of my life sometimes excited me and other times left me fearful. Not all the dreams, unconnected faint memories, and visions promised a life well lived. Still, my curiosity wouldn't allow me to dispense with the former me. I needed to get to Las Cruces, but I knew in my heart that it wouldn't happen soon.

Whether the code the Lee's and others in the Tularosa lived by was a part of my life before or not, I now understood that loyalty was required in the largely lawless reaches of expansive Dona Ana County. As Darwin had written, it was survival of the fittest. That meant eat or be eaten. Allegiances prevented small fish from being devoured by big fish, and loyalty was how you confirmed your allegiances. A man had a duty to those loyal to him and his honor was strapped to that duty. That was at the top of the Code of the West. Oliver could have left me where he found me. Instead, he, Mary, and Nettie saved my life, and now I owed them. Word got around about what happened when men didn't pay what they owed. It was beginning to feel as though I would have to stay in the Tularosa, even if I didn't belong there.

Oliver and Perry decided they had not prepared for an attack from John Good once they found Walter. Besides, John might decide his vengeance didn't require a body. They took their freight wagons to El Paso the next morning so they could return with all the ammunition and supplies they could muster.

**August 25**

A soft light from the waning moon found its way through the bunkhouse window onto the foot of my cot as I tried to decide how I should approach Frenchy the next morning. *Had Oliver told him about me? Why should he?* Before I could decide anything, I fell asleep.

Most of the Lee Ranch cowboys had gone into town for their Saturday night carousal. Those that stayed behind opted to sleep on the adobe roof.

Some activity outside awakened me and I rose to see Oliver and Perry hitching their teams to the two freight wagons. The night before, they had discussed whether to wait until Sunday to leave and stock up on Monday or try to beat the Sabbath business shutdown by leaving before daybreak Saturday morning. I lay back down, but before I fell asleep, I heard the clip-clop of hooves against the omnipresent dust covered caliche. I wondered if they would stay over Saturday night in El Paso. An obscured moon on a cloudy night would make travel dangerous. What I didn't realize, and they had missed, was the vulnerability of the Altmans' place.

After I finished my bunkhouse breakfast, I backed the two-seater up to the root cellar door where we kept the wine. I wasn't sure why Oliver made wine since he didn't drink, and I had never seen Mary or Nettie tip a glass, either. I supposed he used it to barter with or as a special gift for friends. Anyway, I brought up the two kegs, one at a time, for although they were the smallest kegs made, they were full.

When I reached Frenchy's, seven or eight miles south of Lee Well, I was flummoxed over how to let him know I couldn't remember who I was.

As was the custom, I stopped a hundred or so yards below his ridge-perched stone home. I yelled, "Hallo-the-house," as loud as I could.

Frenchy stepped out from beside his home, shotgun held in both hands at his waist, and waved me in. Gosh, I was nervous, and forgot about the casks of wine. When I got out of the carriage, I just stared at him.

Frenchy pointed to the casks. "You bring wine from Oliver?"

"Oh, oh, yes sir." I walked behind the carriage to unload the casks. Frenchy, gray haired and a bit hunch-backed, collected the other one under his arm as though he carried an armful of hay. I didn't realize he had followed me and when I stopped short of his door and turned to ask where he might want me to put it, he almost ran into me. He slipped past and deposited his cask on the small table. I followed his lead.

"You want try?"

I was unsure. I didn't see any harm, and so I nodded.

"Oliver make good wine, but mine better." He winked, and I inferred that his comment should stay between us.

As the old man tapped the first cask, I regained my composure. "I think we might have met before. Do you remember me?"

As he screwed the tap into the oaken cask, he turned for a quick look inside the dimly lit cabin. "No." He took a second squinty look. "Think no."

It disappointed but didn't surprise me. He must have noticed my grimace. He poured us each a glass of the wine, then turned to me. "Go outside. My eyes not so good anymore."

We stepped outside, and he handed me the wine while he raised his to offer an informal toast. As they clinked together, he sized me up again. "No, don't know. Who are you?"

I grimaced. I thought it might come to that. At least I knew my first name. "Jesús." It was the first time I had said my name to someone.

"Jesús who?"

I looked out across the wide, flat Tularosa Basin for a way to explain.

"That's just it, I don't know. I had an accident ..."

"Oh, oh." His body straightened and his hand went into the air. "Oliver tell me you fall and lose your, your ... "

"Memory. Yes."

"But he say you smart."

Frenchy took another drink of the wine, and I welcomed the opportunity to avoid acknowledging his compliment.

"I'm remembering some things. A few days ago, I passed out in the White Sands and had some visions, which led me to believe that I am from Las Cruces."

Frenchy sipped his wine again and turned to look out over the vast desert toward Las Cruces.

"Ah, *oui*, White Sands ... haunted — is right word?" He didn't wait for my agreement. "Las Cruces ... Las Cruces ... I no go there much. When you think I see you?"

I shrugged. "I don't know that we have met for sure. Your name seemed familiar; that's all."

"Numa Reymond. You know his name? He owns store I go to sometime."

The name seemed familiar, but I wasn't certain. It seemed that sometimes I wanted things to be familiar so much that I made them so.

"I don't know." I frowned.

"You want so much … Frenchy understands." He paused in thought. "How old …?" He saw even greater frustration from me. "Oh, sorry. You don't know."

I finished my wine and Frenchy took my glass inside to refill them. When he returned, as he handed my glass to me, he said, "You look little like boy that come with Colonel Fountain. Bring maybe almost two year ago."

Had I heard that name before? I thought I had, but it had become difficult to separate what came from myself from the things that came from others.

"Oh, yes and me see the boy with Apache woman at Numa Reymond store maybe year ago. Later that year, he come with Colonel and the Apache woman to meet my Apache friend."

I had grown wary of connections. Each time something seemed to make sense, it tormented my mind as I paged through all the clues. Alas, I couldn't resist trying to solve the puzzle of my life. *'A boy with an Apache woman.'* Hadn't someone *mentioned something about a boy with an Apache woman and a military looking man?*

"Oui, but the boy, he much, much smaller than you. He look like maybe twelve years." Frenchy shrugged and drank his wine. "Can you help me move stone? Too big for me."

I helped him move the large rock into position as a corner stone for a stone fence he was building.

When I returned to Lee Well, Emma stopped me as I drove toward the barn. She held a satchel in each hand. When I stopped, she swung them into the back and ordered me off the carriage. Nettie held little Rena while Mary stood behind Emma and pleaded with her not to go.

Mary said, "You just can't tell about John Good and his family. The man is so crazed with vengeance he might do anything in one of those fits of rage that you hear about."

Nettie shifted the baby to her other arm, "Please sister, we got to stick together. Stay here where we know you and little Rena will be safe."

Emma put her hands on her hips. "Perry made me promise I wouldn't be ascared of nothin' out here. He told me it was wild and if we stayed together, we'd be fine. Our ranch hands are ever bit as sharp with weapons as yourn is."

I didn't want to get involved in family affairs but knew Oliver and Perry would say Emma should not leave until they returned. "Can't you wait until they get back tomorrow evening?" I asked.

The look Emma gave me confirmed my initial thoughts: I should have minded my own business.

Mary looked defeated, but she gave it one last try. "Like Hey-you says: Emma, please stay. You've only been here a couple of days. Oliver and Perry will be back soon."

But Emma refused, climbed into the carriage, and drove away. Mary asked me to follow her. By the time I saddled my horse and got on the trail to the north, I could only follow her dust cloud. Before the junction with the La Luz to Mesilla Road, she had turned toward Alamo Canyon. This confused me, but when I caught up with her at the Reynolds Ranch, I saw her buggy by one of their peach trees. She must have already gathered all the low-hanging peaches, for she stood in the crotch of a tree and leaned out to pick the golden fruit before she tossed them into a cloth basket held by Mrs. Reynolds, who placed them in an oaken bucket.

I dismounted and walked toward them. Emma turned round to pick some enticing ones from the western side of the tree. She gazed past the fruit to the northwest toward her house. Smoke spiraled up from that direction. She stretched to make out where the smoke was coming from, and I remounted my horse to get a better look. I confirmed my suspicions: there was a blazing fire at the Altmans' home. Emma scrambled down from the tree. She rushed toward her buggy with Mrs. Reynolds fast on her tail. Little Rena sensed her mother's alarm and screamed from her basket while Emma picked up the tether and climbed into the buggy. Mrs. Reynolds tugged her arm and begged her to stay with them. "You don't know what you'll run into over there and you can't do no good. Perry wouldn't want you to put yourself in danger. Wait here until tomorrow morning."

Mrs. Reynolds continued to try to convince Emma to stay until she could send her husband to see what was at hand. I sat on my horse, frozen by indecision. I seconded Mrs. Reynolds' pleadings, but I don't think Emma heard either of us.

A half hour later, she nearly drove her horse straight into the remnants of the conflagration. The place was awash with strange men, but it was the ravaged headquarters that consumed us.

Ashy vestiges of a pile of brush sat in front of the half-burned doorway where just a few days before, she had shrieked at John Good when he awakened her baby. The smoldering door lay halfway into the charred adobe section of the house. Emma leaped out of the carriage as the baby cried in her basket. Before she could reach the house, I had dismounted and rushed to hold her back from the scorched remains. She was strong. Accepted conduct between men and women of the time meant I struggled to restrain her. After several seconds, I held her at arm's length, but then she saw their puppy just off the porch. They had stomped the Altmans' collie dog into the dust. Emma's sudden urgency surprised me, and she escaped my grip and ran to the pup. She kneeled to comfort him. When she recognized his crumpled state, she fell to the side of the mangled corpse. She braced herself with one hand and covered her eyes with the other as she tried to unsee the carnage.

I went to her and tried to help her up, but she resisted and dusty tears dribbled down her cheeks. Between sobs, she said, "We didn't even have time to name him. Perry wanted Rena and the pup to grow up together." I stood there with her for a few moments while she collected herself. When the baby stirred, I reminded Emma of Rena. She returned to the carriage to tend to the baby. Emma wailed and her tears washed the dust from her face as they flowed faster than a Tularosa flash flood. She cradled little Rena who mimicked her tears and for a few moments they comforted each other in their misery — later she would say they were tears of anger and not fear and not a one of us doubted her.

# 23: Dust to Dust

The Altmans' place crawled with Rucker's posse. He would later say their purpose was an investigation, but several of his men ransacked areas of the Altman's headquarters without cause. Some walked in straight lines over every inch of the corral, while others dug under what remained of the floor in the wood-frame two-room addition. Perry had completed it just before Emma returned from Texas.

When Emma, baby cradled in her arms, got control of herself, she demanded that Rucker leave. He dismissed her remarks with a wave of his hand and walked away. Before he had taken a half-dozen steps, he turned and said, "A woman came into my office and said she saw you scrub blood from the floor on your hands and knees."

Emma, fraught with anger but despondent, shook her head. "It's nothing but gossip." Later, Perry told us he and Oliver had dismissed the rumors that led to Rucker's raid as crazy. One such crazy rumor purported that Perry had wrapped Walter's body in a blanket and hid it under their bed until he could move it to a better place. Another swore that they had hidden his body under the plank floor in the bedroom. There were also those that swore Perry, Oliver, Cooper, and Tucker tied Walter to a post in the corral and shot him up. They said the bullet holes might have pieces of his clothing and hair embedded in the posts. As a result, the posse removed some corral posts as evidence. I sometimes think that humans have a dark compulsion to imagine the worst when they don't know the facts.

John felt his son's blood was in the corral and he took soil samples to Fort Stanton for testing. Perry met with the surgeon who told him he couldn't determine if the blood samples were human. "They might have come from a horse or other animal."

It was clear we should leave, but despite the hopelessness, Emma insisted she stay. She was, and still is, a strong-willed woman, but after I had coaxed her for several minutes, anger overtook her despair, and she agreed to leave. As I turned the carriage around, Emma demanded Rucker tell her where Ed and the rest of their hands were.

"They didn't put up a fight, if that's what you're askin'. Must have run away with their tails between their legs." He glared at her for a moment and then cackled scornfully. Rucker walked a few steps, then pointed to tracks in the dirt. "Them tracks, what with their small foot and heel, are awful suspicious."

Emma glared at Walter's youngest brother, Charlie, who stood a few yards from Rucker. "They were suspicious on the Graham's adobe roof, too." Charley just stared back. Emma climbed in to the carriage and I snapped the reins on the Altmans' horse. Over the noise of wooden wheels on the gravelly desert dirt, she said, "Besides, it's my own dooryard, you damn fool."

Later, the accusations flew — each side accused the other. The Lees felt it was a vandal's attempt to force the Altmans out, while the Goods accused the Lees of setting the fire to wipe out the supposed criminal evidence of a body hidden there.

John justified his accusation because he claimed that the sewing machine and plow that was in the kitchen in the adobe part of the house had not burned. He told anyone that would listen 'They weren't even charred because they removed them and then set fire to the place.' There were many variations to John's accusations.

Somehow, word had reached Mary and Nettie before we arrived, and they came to meet us from the porch. As we crested the rise, Mary, Bible in hand, and Nettie, with some quickly picked posies, rose from their Windsor chairs. When we stopped next to the watering trough, the two women rushed to Emma. She turned to hand little Rena to Mary as Nettie held out her posies, then gasped at the puffy-eyed Emma whose still rage-triggered red cheeks bore dirty tear tracks. Nettie dropped the posies and clutched her hands to her face then reached out to help Emma from the carriage. They held each other for the longest time while Rena fussed in Mary's arms. Emma walked to the adobe, with Mary and Nettie on either side. As the baby continued to fuss, Emma reached for her, but her knees buckled with her anguish. While they made their way to the adobe, I stood next to the carriage helpless and angry. How could anyone be so cruel? What would Perry and Oliver do?

Jean-Baptiste Alphonse Karr wrote, 'the more things change, the more they stay the same.' The ranch hands continued to go into town on Saturday nights to spend their wages. I sat at the table in the oppressive bunkhouse to write in my journal and realized that my supply of paper was low. I wished I had asked Oliver to get some for me in El Paso. As wistful as I felt over the day's events, something drove me to write and continue to leaf through my papers for clues. The names of Colonel Fountain and the town of Las Cruces intersected. I resisted optimism because I had been disappointed before.

The Lee clan's hands, supported by Cooper's cowboys, found themselves in scrapes more often with the cowboys from the Good Ranch and others known as the big ranchers. People today call it a range war, but I'm not sure that would be accurate. First, there wasn't much decent range to war over. The occasional scuffles over the tiniest plot of alkali grass were the norm, and fisticuffs happened when cowboys challenged the pride of another ranch's outfit. Sometimes, disagreements led to brawls and even shootings over water holes, grass, and mavericks, but in reality, those were standard ranching events. If ranching was a factor in the conflict at all, it was because Oliver's superior cattle business skills threatened the big ranchers.

No, the so-called range war was just an old-fashioned feud … at that time.

---

The sounds of horses and wagons awakened me in the night. It was Oliver and Perry, returned from El Paso. The moonbeams shone through the window at the same angle it had when they had left the previous night. A twenty-four-hour trip, I thought, and then the reality of the previous day's events resurfaced. I rose and peered through the window across the ranch yard. A kerosene lamp's dim glow lit the adobe's front room. I returned to my cot and rehashed what I had seen. My thoughts shifted to my identity. When I concluded my recent discoveries made no sense, I turned onto my side and slept.

I couldn't tell if it was a few minutes or hours later, but several mounted cowboys thundered into the ranch yard. They yelled for Oliver, and I scrambled from my cot to see the few hands that hadn't gone to town raise their rifles above the parapet. Before the horsemen could rein in their mounts, I was outside and Oliver was on the porch in his nightshirt, six-gun at the ready. Perry stumbled out in his long johns with the women close behind, robes over their night clothes. At first we couldn't understand the liquored-up men and weren't sure who they were in the dim light. After a moment, we realized they were our Lee Ranch hands. They all talked at once — some in Spanish and others in English; all with drunken slurs. At last, we concluded that about the time Oliver and Perry had returned from El Paso, all hell broke loose as factions from the Good and Lee clans tangled in La Luz. Despite Sheriff Ascarate's edict, everyone carried their iron again. It was a wonder no one was killed. Rucker jailed several Lee clan hands for carrying a weapon in town, but not a single Good cowboy suffered even a questioning glance.

---

**August 26**

The next morning, Oliver sent Eph and me into town to pay the fines and get all their hands released. I didn't think I had carried so much money before. At the Justice of the Peace's discretion, the fine could be as much as one hundred dollars per violation, but Oliver said he rarely required that much. He gave us two hundred dollars for the four cowboys — two from the Lees and two from the Altman's. We stopped at the Justice's home, but it was Sunday, and he was at church and so we went to the jail. Thank goodness Rucker wasn't there, and the junior deputy allowed us to talk to the men they held. Before we could get back to the Justice's house, he, his wife, and their pretty little girl came into the deputy's office. His wife and daughter stood near the door and the judge stepped forward and put his hands on his hips. "Expect you're here to settle up on the fines for these fine young men."

Eph had told me he shouldn't say anything, so I said. "Yes, sir."

"First, I must bring my court into session." He picked up one of the six shooters the deputy had laid out on his desk, spun the cylinder to check it was empty and then, as he held the gun by its barrel, he pounded the butt end on the desk. "This here court of the Justice of the Peace of La Luz in the county of Dona Ana in the Territory of New Mexico is now in session. Now, how do your men plead?"

I hadn't realized that I would have to represent the men. "I guess guilty, your honor."

"You guess? Why are you guessing, son? Don't you know?"

I grimaced. "Yes, your honor, I know. They all plead guilty as charged, sir."

"I will now sentence the hoodlums. One hundred dollars each and time served."

I looked at Eph, but he was focused on his boots, so I turned to the judge. "Well, sir, we don't have that much."

"How much you got sonny?"

"Two hundred dollars … fifty each."

"Thank you for your figurin' sonny. Did you think I can't figure it for myself?"

"Oh, no sir … it was just …"

The Justice laughed, then picked up the gun and pounded the butt end on the desk. "Fifty dollars each and time served. Go fetch them deputy so I can get mama home to cook our Sunday dinner."

---

Lee Well was a beehive of activity. As I scanned the ranch yard, the way the hands stored the ammunition caught my attention. They took cartridges out of the original wooden boxes and concealed them in five-gallon cans with a layer of cornmeal on top. It never occurred to me that lawmen might confiscate ammunition.

Emma begged Perry to return to their home, such as it was, but he and Oliver had agreed they couldn't rebuild until they settled this thing once and for all.

When Emma heard Oliver had decided that she and Perry shouldn't go home, she threw a tantrum. She wanted her husband to decide for her and their family. "After all, ain't you the oldest? The Bible tells us Oliver should respect you. Instead, he has you kowtow to him like he was some sort of royalty."

Perry promised to look at the damage himself. He gathered a few of his hands and rode north. There, he took stock of what they could salvage while his men buried the puppy and tidied up the place.

When he returned, he and Emma took a walk while Nettie tended the baby. I couldn't see them, but I could hear Emma's sharp retorts to Perry's murmured comments. Then Perry made one last loud proclamation, and they returned with Emma a few steps behind her husband. She was a good wife to Perry. It's easy to imagine that living under Oliver's watch would bother her.

When Eph and I told Oliver about the fine, he shook his head. "Next time we'll just send twenty-five dollars each, unless Rucker is there, in which case we'll just have to break 'em out."

That evening, the Lees invited Eph and me to join them and the Altmans for supper. I wanted to tell them I had some new information about my identity, but the time wasn't right. And were they discoveries at all? Everything I heard and learned still felt masked in some sort of heavy haze that refused to lift. The harder I tried to ferret out my memories, the more it seemed they were pushed further back into my mind.

As all this rolled around in my head, Perry mentioned another name that caught my attention: 'Fall.' And then another: 'Fountain.' I had heard the name Fountain, but the name 'Fall' also seemed familiar. I considered where, but Perry said, "Cooper's foreman stopped by a couple of weeks ago. He said, 'That rotten Republican Fountain is running for the territorial legislature and he's certain to get in unless the Democrats can find a sure-fire opponent. They're talkin' up a fella from Kentucky by the name of Albert Fall.'"

Oliver shook his head. "We got no chance in the election. Fountain is married to a Mexican, and he has them lassoed and hog-tied."

Oliver's words about Fountain weren't as damning as his expression and tone. *Perhaps my previous life wasn't in concert with the Tularosa Texan's code. Las Cruces was a Republican town. What was I to do?*

## August 27

Oliver sent a few cowboys to tend the herds. The rest prepared for an all-out war. Everyone they could spare moved the Altmans' fine horse herd into the alfalfa field at the foot of Dog Canyon. Oliver reasoned putting Lee Well between Good and Perry's prized horses would protect them. It would also mean he would have to reseed the alfalfa next spring but, when the family was involved, no cost was too high.

## August 28

The next morning, Jim Cooper came down from his place and arrived after Perry had made a careful count of his horses. He decided his herd was fifty or so short.

Oliver made certain they secured the ranch during the morning. At the noon meal, he suggested we recount and by midafternoon they confirmed the herd was short fifty horses. As a result, we went with Oliver, Perry, Cooper, and a couple of neighbors to find them. We left armed, which had become the norm.

Unbeknownst to us, one of Good's search parties found Walter's remains that afternoon in the White Sands. He had been dead for two weeks. The coyotes and insects left only his bones, remnants of his clothes, a unique piece of jewelry and the new boots he had purchased at Numa Reymond's store in Las Cruces a few weeks before. Those items, identified by his father, along with his unusual height, made identification a certainty.

John and fifteen of his men came across Walter's emaciated corpse at the hottest time of the day. The sight of the body, half the flesh gone, must have sent John into a wailing fit that turned into a vengeful rage. When he had regained his usual despicable character, he left two men to guard the evidence of the body and he and his other sons and a couple of hands — five riders in all — started back to La Luz to fetch the coroner and deputy sheriff.

On the way back to the Altmans, we rode past the Malone Ranch. As we crested a little hill, a group of men on horseback appeared. As they approached, Oliver put up his hand, cavalry style, for us to stop.

"That man in the lead's John Good," said Perry.

"And that's Rucker and John's sons and a couple of his hands with him," said Oliver.

Cooper stood in his stirrups. "And I'll bet he and Rucker are heading to your place, Oliver, with arrest warrants."

Oliver looked around. "We best give them the chance to just pass us by. Let's head over into that little arroyo there and see what happens."

We dismounted and turned our horses loose. The six of us scrambled up the eroded arroyo bank. After dismounting and checking our guns, we peered over the slope to see what John would do.

Later, rumors circulated that we ambushed the Good party. Perhaps he thought that. We had no warning that he was on his way to La Luz to report the grizzled discovery of his son's body. Anyone that knew John, knew rage would soon replace his tears and he would have been loaded for bear. It did not surprise us when John's group prepared for battle. They disappeared into a cornfield some hundred and fifty yards away as the six of us braced ourselves. Perry lay down on the eroded bank behind a gobernadora bush with his new revolver. Someone from the Good group fired first. They hit one of our horses in the head. She fell with the start of a panicked whinny. The other horses reacted with shrilled whinnies as they pranced all about, but as they had been trained, they stayed in the arroyo near their riders. All but Perry's prized black, Old Black Joe that is, who, despite exceptional training, skedaddled along with Perry's new Winchester in the saddle scabbard.

Perry, overcome with the expected losses at his homestead and his best horse and rifle, fired back, and then every gun from the cornfield must have returned fire.

We ducked as Oliver said, "Hold your fire. The last thing we need is another killin'. If they come at us, shoot over their heads."

Sure enough, John Good led a charge until everyone from our side fired high and they fell back into the cornfield. This little game of charge and retreat repeated itself several times before Good and his men retrieved their horses and rode off in a rush toward La Luz.

Later, some folks said the two factions fired over two hundred shots, but I doubt they could find a hundred shell casings in the arroyo. After the Good gang had gone, we retrieved our horses, minus Perry's Old Black Joe. We later learned that he had circled round the Malone Ranch where one of the Goods caught him. Good and Rucker sent him to Las Cruces as evidence, where the sheriff stabled him at Shields and Bennett's Livery.

Bill Carr was on his way to meet us at Perry's place but stopped in La Luz. While there, he found out that when Good and crew arrived shaken, the justice of the peace sent Deputy Armijo and the coroner to fetch Walter's body and another horseman to Las Cruces to alert Sheriff Ascarate. Ascarate arrived the next day with a twenty-five-man posse and added twenty-five local men, with deputy E. C. Rucker in charge from the La Luz area.

When we arrived at the Altman's, it was pretty much as Emma and I had described. Perry's men had cleaned things up a bit and replaced some of the removed posts, but the corral was still dug up.

We could repair the physical damage; it would only take time and money. The real question was whether this escalation would gather steam and how many people would die.

# 24: Cross the Rubicon

**September 7, 1888**

It had become clear that E. C. Rucker was a foreman in name only at the Good Ranch. He used his title to strong-arm John Good's enemies and spent little time on anything to do with ranching. Oliver and his followers believed the Santa Fe Ring had influence in Dona Ana County and they had appointed Rucker a deputy sheriff to protect the vast cattle operations managed by Good on their behalf.

As the date of Walter's burial approached, the Lee clan and allies met to decide their next move. They could not tolerate the constant threat of attack any longer. They gathered in the Lee's front room. When the room had quieted, Oliver stood. "We don't need to do much. Ol' John will hang himself, but we have to give him enough rope. We just need to bide our time and keep everyone safe."

---

Walter's father buried him on September seventh under a cottonwood tree next to his family's expansive adobe, where just a few weeks before Walter half-joked, 'That's where I want them to plant me when the time comes.' None of the Lee clan attended the funeral and so we didn't learn until later that day that the coroner's jury declared that Jim Cooper, Oliver Lee, Tom Tucker and Perry Altman had murdered Walter Good.

A neighbor that had remained neutral stopped by to tell us the news. The neighbor said Sheriff Ascarate had attended the funeral and promised to lead the posses to make arrests. "Ascarate said he would stay in the area until he caught the murderers."

We hadn't expected that. As the man disappeared down the trail, Oliver scowled. "Ain't no doubt now. They've turned up their hand. It's a showdown."

The Lees didn't fear a fair trial. But given the influence of the Santa Fe Ring and John Good, they couldn't accept that a fair trial or even a lawful arrest would occur. During those times, the only thing that separated an outlaw from a lawman was a badge, and putting up your hands didn't always assure you wouldn't get gunned down.

The ten days between the discovery of Walter's body, the dust-up with Good and his family near the Malone Ranch, and Walter's burial were a pure hell for those that stood accused of Walter's death. The men avoided the posses by scattering into the desert and Sacramentos, but the women suffered constant questions and pickets at Lee Well. Nonetheless, Mary, Nettie, Emma, and little Rena stuck together while Eph, Ed and I took turns on the porch.

Good and Rucker learned the accused men had fled Lee Well. The accused spent their nights at line shacks in the mountains or camped in the desert, where we would smuggle them food and supplies.

I sometimes wondered how the Good women had fared. Were they comfortable in their confidence that their husbands and sons would protect them, or did they toss and turn in their beds with the suspicion that the Lee's had lain in wait outside their house for the darkness of the night? I didn't know Mrs. Good. Supposedly, Bertha was a timid woman. What other kind of woman could stomach a life with a man like John? I imagined that she and his mild-mannered middle son felt John had brought this on himself. It wouldn't have surprised me if the two of them would have embraced a way out of John's mess.

The feud affected all the eastern side of the Tularosa. The *Rio Grande Republican* reported that businesses in La Luz and Tularosa were all but shut down. Anyone that had a gun carried one — everywhere — despite the penalties, and those that didn't when the feud started bought one.

---

### September 8

The coroner's jury edict didn't amount to a legitimate arrest warrant, but if Rucker didn't need one before the coroner's jury, now he needed one even less. If Rucker could get rid of Ascarate, we expected the harassment would increase, and suspected Rucker would lie to Ascarate to accomplish that. If Ascarate's reputation was accurate, he would go back to 'Cruces for the slightest excuse. That would leave Rucker and his now 'legitimate' vigilantes to act on the 'facts his eyes and ears' gave him.

As time passed, the Lee band's perseverance ebbed. Perry didn't want his wife and child bothered any further, while Jim Cooper seemed to dwell on how he had disappointed his folks and whether he could lose his ranch. They and neighbor Bill Earhart teetered on the edge of surrender. Earhart was a curious case. The coroner's jury hadn't charged him, but he was involved in the dust up near the Malone Ranch. I figured he just enjoyed being a part of the group.

Oliver couldn't decide what to do for Cooper. In private, he said, "When a man starts feelin' like he's embarrassed his parents … well, he best cross the Rubicon and make the best of things, but *I'm* not ready to give up."

Late that evening, Oliver, Perry, Cooper, and Earhart came to Lee Well to meet with several of their supporters. Even Cherokee Bill Kellam appeared, albeit late, and he didn't stay long. He stopped at the door. "Wish you boys luck. I got nothin' to tie me down. I'll just disappear into the Sacramentos."

It was a crowded room. The accused and I sat around the table while several other men stood in close quarters behind us. We discussed our options well into the night. You would not have known the accused were the only threatened people in the room. Every person spoke as though their names were on the indictment. Some wanted to turn themselves in, but Oliver felt the surrender of less than all would put those that didn't surrender at risk. "I don't doubt your loyalty, but if the men surrender to the wrong people, they might shoot you down outright or, if they survive Good might torture them for information." There were nods around the room.

Just after midnight, Perry and Cooper announced they would turn themselves in if they could do it risk free. Earhart's position changed with the wind, but between the lines I was pretty certain he wanted to surrender as well.

When Oliver tried to discourage Cooper, he shot back, "I ain't got near the spread and loyal hands you've got, Oliver. With this dry spell, I'm near to havin' to sell off my herd, anyway."

"All the more reason not to give in, Jim. They ain't got any real proof, so I don't think they can hold us for long."

"You 'don't think,' but you know no more than I do and what we know is they haven't 'xacly played by the rules so far. They's just as likely to string us up and lose us in the White Sands or throw our bodies in ol' mama Gomez's kiln as take us to jail."

I had talked with Oliver about our situation several times over the last week and I could see by the look on his face that he couldn't argue Jim's point, but he also didn't like their prospects if they turned themselves in. The discussion got heated, and the voices rose with each exchange. So much so that Mary appeared at her bedroom doorway. She pulled her night coat across her breasts, "Alright, I've been listenin' — what choice did I have with how loud y'all are? Ya'll ain't gonna agree tonight. Best let things settle for a few hours. 'Sides, y'all need some sleep. Sounds like a long day tomorrow."

The men at the table studied each other. First Oliver, then Perry, then another and another mumbled or nodded and left the house for their camp behind the barn.

Perry, Oliver, and I slept in the bunkhouse. Oliver folded his clothes and placed them at the foot of his bed. He stood before us in his long johns. "I want to trust that none of these men would give in to torture, but I just can't."

Perry tossed his clothes onto the foot of the bed. "Oliver, each of those men trust you to the hilt. They would die before they would betray you, and if you asked them to take an oath, they would."

Oliver shook his head. "That's just it. I wouldn't want them to do that on my account."

***

## September 9

Everyone appeared at the makeshift porch breakfast table, groggy but eager to resolve their problem. Between sips of rich black coffee, they continued their discussion without the previous night's rankle, over fried eggs, ham and sour dough biscuits topped with sweet butter and honey.

As the last of us finished our meal, Oliver stood at the end of the table. "I never asked to lead this … group." He cleared his throat. "I hope you are all here of your own choice." He ran his fingers through his hair. "If you aren't, you should leave."

The men looked around the table. No one moved.

"Fine then. I trust you all and I hope you trust me. Some of us have more to lose or a family to concern themselves with. I'll understand if you end this now."

Perry, Cooper, and Earhart glanced at each other with faint grins.

"So, we'll make certain that we can leave the women-folk secure, then saddle up and ride into Tularosa where we can get a message to Ascarate that we wish to surrender. It's up to y'all, but if you want to surrender, I think you best present yourselves to Ascarate and only Ascarate. If you surrender yourself in La Luz or to anyone other than Ascarate, it could mean the end of you." Oliver shifted from one foot to the other. "One last thing. Bring all the iron and ammunition you can carry. If they don't fear us, they'll just gun us down and be done with it."

I realized later there are few men that could hold sway in a moment like that. Oliver Lee is one of them. There was a calm confidence about him. If he recognized his leadership qualities, perhaps it began then.

Oliver, Perry, Bill, Cooper, Tucker, Earhart, one of Oliver's best cowboys with a gun, Sixto García, and I departed about two hours later. We steered clear of the major roads and trails and tried to space ourselves out, so we didn't present a conspicuous group.

We stopped to rest a few miles west of La Luz on the La Luz Creek arroyo under the shade of a small grove of desert willows. A roadrunner, with a small snake in its beak, flushed while a Cooper's hawk soared above us. The men's anxiety left them oblivious to the roadrunner, but the hawk grabbed their attention and Earhart remarked it was an ominous sign.

Those that wanted to surrender were excited to get it over with, while Oliver and the others worried about an ambush.

As we passed a canvas water bucket around for the horses, Oliver half-whispered to me, "I'm not so sure about this plan now, Hey-you. I can't trust Ascarate much further than I can throw a road apple."

"Sounds like we need a go between. Is there someone in Tularosa that both sides will trust?"

Oliver removed his hat and ran his fingers through his sweat darkened hair. He kicked at the loose arroyo sand, then stopped, one foot in the air, "Yes, I have just the man."

I helped Oliver compose a note to Tularosan Charles Moore. In it, Oliver asked him to intercede on our behalf. He asked that Moore find Ascarate, let him know the accused were ready to surrender to him and only him, and that we would meet in Tularosa that evening.

When I arrived at Mr. Moore's home and presented the note with the explanation that it was from Oliver Lee, he invited me in. Several mature cottonwood trees made the dark interior quite comfortable despite the still torrid temperatures outside.

Moore invited me to his office and offered me a lemonade. I sat and relished the tart thirst quencher as he read our note. When he finished, he sat back in his chair. "Can't fault Oliver for not trusting Good and Rucker. Not one bit, and I think he's right to deal only with Ascarate, as useless as he is. What's your name, son? Don't think I've met you before."

The name 'Hey-you' had become uncomfortable for me. "Jesús. I've been with the Lee's since May."

"I see. Can I get you something to eat or refill your canteen?"

I accepted an empanada stuffed with ham and queso. While I gobbled down the delicious victuals, Mr. Moore's house girl refilled my canteen, and he wrote a response to Oliver.

He put down his pen, blotted the paper, and then asked if I knew the contents of Oliver's note. I replied I had helped compose it. He seemed impressed, and we talked about the feud for a few minutes.

"I hope this gives us some peace. Folks around here are as nervous as I've ever seen them. Even Patrick Coghlan never set souls afire like John Good has since he arrived." Mr. Moore read his response to me. He agreed to Oliver's request and said he would fetch Ascarate and make certain Good and Rucker would not find out. He agreed to meet us at the described place, but only after he was certain the meeting could take place without risk.

I rode back to the arroyo and handed Mr. Moore's note to Oliver, which he read and nodded. "You know what it says?"

I nodded, and we settled in to wait through the heat of the afternoon. The men took watch shifts as the others dozed in the dappled desert willow grove shade.

When Mr. Moore arrived, he said he could not locate Ascarate, and no one seemed to know where to find him. He left word with reliable people for Ascarate to meet him at Coghlan's in Tularosa. "I said nothing about you, Oliver, or any in your group, and I have handled the whole affair on the sly. Instead, I summoned several friends of you and Cooper. They will gather in front of Coghlan's store to meet us and there will be safety in our numbers."

# 25: Surrender?

We arrived in Tularosa in the late afternoon, and Mr. Moore led us to the hitching rails in front of Coghlan's store. Eight armed men riding into town sent people into a tizzy. The arrival of Charles Moore and the marshal allayed their fears. As Moore had promised, there were at least a dozen local friends gathered around us, which garnered an air of relief, especially from Jim Cooper, whose ranch was closest to Tularosa. Several of them greeted him with slaps on the back and shook his hand while he introduced the rest of us. Soon, someone brought a fiddle out and Jim, an accomplished player, played everyone's favorite tunes. One of Jim's friends lived close by and had his wife prepare a meal for the famished men.

Well-fed and watered, we waited into the night. The atmosphere was festive, but Oliver and his bunch remained alert and on edge. Near midnight, a rider came into town and asked for Moore, who came forward. Moore spoke with the other man, then he approached Oliver. "I can't find Ascarate, and no one seems to know where he is. Sorry Oliver, we did everything we could short of tellin' why we were lookin' for him."

That put a damper on our mood and, as the crowd dispersed, we huddled with Moore to determine our next move.

Moore scanned our group. "I'm sorry that our plan didn't work out fellas. Rest assured that I'll follow through to get this done."

Oliver nodded, "Thank you Charles. We appreciate that you've done your best and gone out of your way to help. I don't know about you fellas, but I need to go home to make sure … well, it's so sorry that it's come to this, but to be certain Tucker and Good haven't harmed our families or torched our spread."

The men tightened their saddles cinches for the trip, but Bill Earhart stood motionless, head down. It got everyone's attention and then he shifted his weight right to left a few times. "Uh, uh, I, uh, probably," he paused and scratched the back of his head. "I guess I shoulda said somethin' earlier, but, uh, my cousin works for Good and … well uh …" Earhart scuffed the hard baked street with his boot and wiped his hand across his mouth, "… well …. he's deliverin' a letter to him tellin' John and Rucker not to pressure us 'cause we're headin' to 'Cruces to turn ourselves in." Oliver frowned.

Mr. Moore shook his head. "After all the trouble I went to, to keep this all secret."

Earhart couldn't look us in the eye. "I uh, I was scared Good and Rucker would ambush us and I wanted to warn them off."

"Ain't nothin' to be done about it now," said Oliver as he checked the cinch on his saddle.

As Jim and the rest of our group saddled up, Mr. Moore put his hand on my shoulder, looked at me, and said to Oliver, "Where'd you ever find a smart young fella like Jesús? He's too clever to just punch cows, isn't he?"

I didn't think Oliver had heard my name before, and it felt like I swallowed a yucca pod. Oliver eyed me. I wanted to explain, but this wasn't the time or place.

We walked our horses all night to Lee Well. I must have slept in the saddle. When I smelled bacon frying, I awakened with a start. The sun peeked over the Sacramentos. I breathed in the delicious aroma of breakfast frying. Somehow, Mary and Nettie knew we were on our way back.

**September 10**

Nettie bounced around the table as she set plates and utensils. Eph and two hands took care of the horses while we dug into fried eggs, bacon, and buttermilk biscuits.

During the meal, Moore reiterated he would see this thing through. Oliver said he would stay home and as I expected, Perry, Cooper, and Earhart planned to ride into 'Cruces to, as they said, 'get it over with'. Oliver asked me to go with them, then over emphasized my name as he announced to the group, "Jesús won't let them use some legal talk to take their rights away."

Once again, it wasn't the time and place to talk about my identity. I wasn't sure what I could tell him, anyway. I gave him a tight-lipped smile and went to help Ed get fresh horses ready.

A trip across the Tularosa always left plenty of time for wandering mind. I considered my situation frontwards, backwards, up, down, kitty-wampus and every which way I could think of. The realization that Lee and Fountain families would never have Sunday dinners together made a difficult situation worse. For the first half of the trip, I tried to sort it out, but I knew too little.

We avoided the main trails again. The Forresters had sent word we were welcome anytime, and we sent a rider ahead to let them know we would arrive that evening. We hoped to stay the night at the Forrester's ranch near the White Sands. When we came upon the main La Luz - Mesilla Road, we saw a group of riders some distance to the east. As the five of us approached, Rucker, John Good, and eight other men rode up behind us. They stayed on the road as we crossed into the Forrester's place.

The Forresters had graciously prepared a feast. While we ate and chatted with our hosts, I knew no one had forgotten that Rucker and Good awaited us on the road.

A messenger came to the door and handed Moore a note. It read, 'keep moving'. After discussing our next move, Mr. Moore decided he would talk with Good to let him know we intended to turn ourselves in to the sheriff in Las Cruces. He warned him not to crowd us.

When Mr. Moore returned, he said that Rucker and Good weren't cooperative and said they had sent a man by the name of Buchanan ahead. They gave Moore no reason for this. It seemed we would be driven like a herd to the slaughter. We couldn't help but believe they had set a trap and so we called the whole thing off. After our meal, Cooper asked Moore to go ahead to 'Cruces to get the proper papers and negotiate a way for them to surrender without the risk of vigilante attack.

We were only a few days past the new moon. Perry, Cooper and Earhart waited until they were sure that Rucker Good and their bunch had set up camp and then walked in the dim moonlight to the Forrester's remuda with their tack. They saddled up without a peep and rode into the San Andreas Mountains to the west. Moore and I accepted a gracious offer of cots for the night by Mrs. Forester. The next morning, Rucker and Good had gone. Charles Moore headed west for Las Cruces to take care of the paperwork for their surrender, and I, with a bead on Dog Canyon, headed east cross-country.

## September 11

When I got back to Lee Well, I was saddle tired and cactus sore. I dropped onto my bunk and fell fast asleep. The next morning, I slept through breakfast in the bunkhouse and the usual morning banter between the cowboys. They must have felt sorry for me because I had seen over-sleepers get half-drown with a bucket of trough water.

Yelling awakened me as several men came into the bunkhouse to get their rifles.

"What's happening? I asked.

Felipe said, "Hombres a caballo."

By the time I got outside, Eph had put a ladder up to the adobe section of the house so six of our hands could hide behind the roof parapet. I looked to the north. In the distance, a wispy cloud of dust floated behind several mounted horses. The rumbling sound of their pounding hooves was faint, but alarming. "Are we under attack?"

Eph said, "Got word yesterd'y that Rucker was comin' to get the ladies to take 'em to La Luz for questionin'." As the last cowboy rushed up the ladder, Eph put one foot on the first rung, "Mama Lee ain't havin' none of dat."

"Well, where's Oliver?"

When Eph reached the top, he pushed the ladder away, and it fell to the side, "Ain't quite sure. Said he needed to tend to some bidnez down south and he left not long after you did yesterd'y."

As I considered what I should do, the thunder of hooves left me with no choice. I went inside the house and took a rifle from the gun rack. I ran rushed to the door, but Mary stopped me. "You stay in here and keep a bead on that good for nothin' John Good. They're here for me and Nettie and Emma." She paused, then and with a little extra oomph, "I'll handle this." I closed the curtains so there was a slit for me to aim at whomever came forward to do the talking.

The group violated the custom of 'hallowing the house' from a distance and rode right up to the porch. Before the morning easterly breeze could blow the dust cloud over them, one of them unnecessarily yelled, "Hallo the house!" It was Rucker and his so-called posse. The porch roof overhang prevented me from seeing his head and so I swung my rifle on this heart.

Before the man could finish his summons, Mary opened the door. She held her shotgun stock under her armpit while her right finger flicked at the trigger guard. She stood in the doorway and said just as loud, "State your business."

Rucker pulled out a piece of paper and read it in Spanish as the dust settled. Why he would come with a document in Spanish puzzled me. Perhaps they thought it would confuse us long enough for them to gather the women. Mary interrupted him with a couple of demonstrative stomps on the porch floorboards. "We ain't Mexicans. If you want to read any papers to us, you go back and get 'em done in English. Then we'll see."

A horse pawed at the ground over by the new windmill. I looked through the adobe's side window where a stranger was on horseback with his pistol drawn. I moved my head to the left. Nettie stood next to the man's horse with her hands in the air, while Emma held little Rena and tried to keep one hand up. I thought Mary must have thought Rucker would try to torch the house and so she sent them to hide.

Mary must have heard the horse, too. She closed the front door and ran along the porch to the side of the house where she could see the windmill. "Stay back," she said to the stranger. "What do you want?"

She caught the spooked cowboy off guard. He glanced at Rucker, tried to swallow, and said, "A drink. I been eatin' dust all the way …"

At first, I thought the man didn't belong to the posse, but Rucker's reaction proved otherwise, and Mary said, "Then drink out of the horse trough. It's good enough for you."

That's when Eph and the others emerged above the parapet with their rifles aimed at Rucker's posse. They left without another word.

---

## September 12

Emma wasn't happy that Perry hadn't come back with me to Lee Well, but we all did our best to comfort her. Nettie couldn't nurse the baby, but she took over the rest of Rena's care while Mary handled all the cooking.

Eph and I were back to spending our days close by the headquarters. He tended to repairs and training horses. Me? I wrote a little, read whatever two-week-old or older newspaper that found its way to the bunkhouse and whittled on desert willow sticks. I got so good at the whittling that I considered whittling replacement spindles for my broken Windsor chair. But whittling can be a mindless undertaking and most of the time I tried to think of an excuse for going to 'Cruces. I wanted to be ready when Oliver made one of his infrequent surprise appearances.

If I went alone, there wasn't anybody that could stop me, but I knew it was wrong for me to leave then. It had been almost five months since I awakened in Oliver's bed. Perhaps people that knew me had moved on with their lives. Maybe I shouldn't go.

Between the worries over my past and the constant threat that Rucker or Good might attack, not to mention what had happened to Perry and the others, I couldn't sleep and wasn't hungry.

It had been a little over two weeks since I had brought Frenchy Oliver's wine to him. Our discussion about my identity and my probable connection to Albert Fountain continued to bother me.

That night, I stared at the *latillas*.

*How important can identity be, anyway? I don't need to reclaim my life. Maybe I should just leave and start anew.*

And yet, my curiosity lingered. No, it was more than that. I couldn't think of a word to describe it in my journal, but it gnawed at my soul, and I remember the feeling to this day.

Frenchy was the one person I had met that had met me before my accident. I needed to return to Frenchy's place.

# 26: Tai Chi, Frenchy Style

**September 13, 1888**

I called, "Hallo," but there was no answer. I rode up the hill into the morning sun. When I got within about thirty yards of his stone cabin, I glimpsed Frenchy. He was sitting cross-legged in front of a smoldering lump on a rock. As I came closer, he appeared to inhale the smoke. I approached. He noticed me and scrambled to his feet.

"Ah, Jesús. It good to see you again. You join for breakfast?"

I smiled, "No thank you. I'm not hungry."

Frenchy eyed me. "Why you not hungry? You eat at Lee Well?"

"No, I'm just not hungry."

Frenchy nodded, then arranged things on his outdoor cook stove. As he cracked a couple of eggs into a bowl, he chopped a slice of ham, a pepper, and half an onion and put a glob of butter into his cast-iron skillet.

"You sad about ... who you are?"

I looked at the ground and shuffled my boots in the loose gravel in front of Frenchy's cabin. That was, of course, the reason I came, but to hear someone come right out and say it like that made me feel like an oddity, like someone that should perform out of the back of a huckster's snake oil wagon or in a circus side-show.

Frenchy did not seem to notice my embarrassment as he went on about cooking his breakfast. When the butter bubbled, he tossed the onions and peppers with some seasonings into the pan. As he did so, he glanced back and forth between his task and me.

"You no want to talk about it?"

"I do, but …" I couldn't find the words. I stood in the doorway and thought about heading back home.

Frenchy removed the now soft vegetables and ham from his pan and whipped the eggs in the bowl with a fork into one yellow semifluid mix. "I know why you no eat."

He poured the eggs into the skillet and turned it while he lifted the thin egg layer so that all the egg mixture cooked.

As he placed ham, onions, and peppers on one side of the egg layer and then sprinkled some crumbly white cheese into the mixture, he turned to me. "You worried that Fountain and Lee not friends."

He then folded the other side of the thin egg layer over, added cheese crumbles to the top, removed it from the burner and covered it with the pan lid. It was a like another dish I had seen made with corn masa instead of egg, but I couldn't place it.

I had sat at his little table and after a few moments, he removed the lid from the pan and slid the stuffed egg dish onto a plate. When he turned to me, he said, "Now you eat while I make my breakfast. It no help if you no eat. Your belly hurt because you no eat."

He turned back to his stove and cracked three eggs into the hot skillet, along with a thick slice of ham. As the eggs popped and crackled, he turned back to me. "I know. You want to know …" he lifted the cooked egg edges, then pointed his spatula at me …

"but you not want to know." He returned to his task and used his spatula to make certain the eggs wouldn't stick to the pan, then turned to me and held the spatula high in thought.

"You no remember, but when you here first time, Colonel Fountain say some things about me and the stairs at Chapel of Our Lady of Light in Santa Fe." He flipped his eggs and the slice of ham.

"I build the stairway but not like he say. I study ... how you say it, arch-i-tect-ure with *Compagnons du Devoir et du Tour de France* and devote myself to the work. Quintus Monier and I were friends ... in France. He come to Santa Fe to build the Chapel of Our Lady of Light but he not like the stairway another architect design to reach choir loft. He think of me."

Frenchy slid his ham and eggs into his own plate and sat next to me, knife and fork held upright with either hand to the side of the plate of food. Between bites, he told me his story. I nibbled at his egg creation. It was delicious, and I dug in, pausing between bites to listen to his story.

"I build many staircase — but not same — in Europe. Archbishop Lamy hire me build staircase and pay half to begin. I build in workshop in France, then take apart and ship to Santa Fe. Go with, but somehow got separated and when arrive in Santa Fe ... no staircase.

"Wait one week ... two week ... ready go see Mother Magdalen Hayden and the Archbishop. Feel *malade* ... sick in my belly. I think, what if staircase not come? No money to pay back."

I looked at my plate and it was empty.

Frenchy saw me, smiled, and continued with his story. "One day as thought must beg archbishop for forgiveness, I meet China-man in Santa Fe who help build railroad. Him decide railroad building not for him and he stay in Santa Fe. He see I ... worry. Tell me he help. Take me behind buildings where it private and showed me this ritual. This called Yang Tai Chi, and the man, wish could remember name, he say from town in China where invented." When Frenchy had finished his meal, he looked at me, then said, "This help you. Come with me."

I followed him to Dog Canyon Creek and a small island of pure, fine sand. A young cottonwood cast its luxurious August shade across the length of the sandy spit. There were footprints everywhere — all barefoot. The scene was typical for a southern New Mexico mountain stream, but there was something more to it. There was a scent that was foreign to me. I looked around and there were shrubby plants that had pale purple blooms. They weren't native. I had never seen plants like them. There were also rocks balanced on top of each other in a sort of impromptu sculpture. When you added in the soft gurgle of the rushing water, all my senses felt relaxed. This place was special.

Frenchy noticed as I breathed in the scent while looking at the plants. "That lavender. Smell nice … eh?"

I nodded.

"Take off boots." We sat on a rock at the edge of the island. I removed my boots and stockings. The cool sand yielded a hint of a massage to the soles of my feet. "You stay on rock and watch careful."

He began with his feet shoulder width apart and his hands by his sides. "This called Prepare Form." Then he slowly raised both arms until they were shoulder height and parallel to the ground. He paused there with his eyes closed before he dropped his arms in a wavelike motion back to his side. All his movements were slow and deliberate.

"That called Opening". Next, he turned to his right, lifted his right hand a few inches, then crossed it over his left. He spread his arms. Left hand higher than right, he shifted his weight right and then back left, still facing right.

Every movement was deliberate, slow, and smooth as silk. He took a step forward with his right foot and leaned forward over it, then turned further to his right with his right palm open, then returned to the previous position with his right palm facing me. Next, he leaned forward while he placed his left hand on his right forearm. After a momentary pause, he pushed outward with both hands, then recoiled and repeated. He turned to me, "That called Grasping Bird's Tail".

He returned to "Prepare Form" where he stood still with his eyes closed for a moment. I felt mesmerized by the deliberate and yet continuous movements that required his complete focus. Tai Chi was as beautiful as any dance I had seen and just watching it brought a calmness. And what was the word ... spirituality?

"Now you try." We exchanged places.

He watched and gave me cues with his hands and body. Not long after I had started, he stopped me by waving his hands and standing. "You no breathe." I had been so mesmerized by the movements that I hadn't noticed his breathing. I realized I had held my breath. "You must breathe slow and deep with movements."

I began again and with his cues, got the hang of a slower inhale and exhale. In fact, it seemed to make the slow movements easier.

"Jesús, this help you feel better. Do each morning before you eat. Make a place with sand."

We walked into the pure running stream and rinsed the sand from our feet, then returned to the rock. As we waited for our feet to dry, I thought about his staircase story.

"So, what happened? With the stairway, I mean."

"It came the next week, but no handrail and other pieces. The conductor say other pieces stolen. Not have right wood to turn for handrail. Feel bad and then come here."

"What was that smell when I first saw you?"

"Oh, that. That lavender and I have oil, too. I not have enough plants to make oil. It come from Roualt's store in Mesilla. He get special for me. It help sleep. I give you some now. When you go meet Colonel Fountain, you buy more and bring to me, and you can have half."

We put on our boots and went back to his stone house. Once again, he asked me to move a stone with him, which I did.

That night, I put the oil on my pillow, and I slept like a baby.

---

**September 14**

The next morning, Virgil, who slept in the bunk next to me, said, "You smell like a sportin' house." He turned to the other cowboys and humored them. "I didn't know there was a sportin' house close enough for you to ride there and back in one night. You must be mighty quick on the draw." The bunkhouse roared and I must have turned beet red, but whenever they teased me, it felt oddly satisfying.

Throughout breakfast the men made light-hearted comments like, "Hey-you, do you favor calico or chintz for the curtains in the bunkhouse?" and "Is lavender your daily scent or do you tend toward ambergris except for special times?"

I laughed with them. "Laugh all you want, but I slept better than I have for months."

That got some attention and later, Virgil and a few of the men asked to try it. The bunkhouse smelled like a cathouse and it was quite the subject of discussion with the Lees.

---

Emma was fit to be tied when Perry didn't return home, and her angst resulted in an increase in little Rena's crying fits. Between the tension over the males' situation and little Rena's agitation, the women at the Lee adobe were in a constant state of emotional dread.

Rucker and Good's attention had shifted away from Lee Well and toward hunting Perry, Cooper, and Earhart, but that didn't calm the women. Their worries shifted to their absent men's whereabouts, and the respite from harassment was short-lived.

Oliver wanted me at headquarters and spent considerable time on the porch in my broken Windsor chair. With all the hullabaloo over my lavender scent in the bunkhouse that first morning, I forgot to try out my Tai Chi. It was near noon when I realized I had forgotten to do it that morning. I sat on the porch with my eyes closed and tried to recall the moves, but I couldn't remember the one after "Opening." After several minutes, I opened my eyes and looked around. There was no one in sight. I could hear the women in the house as they chatted over some chore. The possibility of splinters meant I couldn't remove my boots. With my eyes closed, I stood and took a step away from my chair. As the moves came, I felt relaxed and focused, and accomplished the full three positions and movements. It felt good, although not quite what I had experienced at Frenchy's. Still, I smiled and opened my eyes.

Nettie faced me from just in front of the porch. "What on earth are you doin'? You look like … like … well shoot, I ain't never seen nothin' like that."

I shrugged. "It's something Frenchy taught me."

"Frenchy? Why, in God's name, would you go to that old hermit?" I knew why, but was reluctant to share the reason, so I stared off over the desert. Nettie tapped her foot on the plank porch floor. "Does it have anything to do with your name being Jesús?"

My eyes met hers, but I looked away. "Yes, yes it does. I think Frenchy knows who I am."

"When were you going to tell me … your name?"

"I don't know. The time never seemed right."

I walked onto the porch and sat in my broken chair. Nettie picked up the next chair, placed it opposite me, then sat and crossed her arms and legs. "How's now? Is now a good time?"

I slumped forward, my upper body resting on my thighs and my hands over my eyes. Nettie would not leave until she got an explanation. I told her what happened the day Perry and I searched for Walter Good's body in the White Sands — about the visions I had and the realization that my first name was Jesús. She frowned, and I added, But I'm not sure of anything else.

"Oliver told me you had discovered your name was Jesús. I can see why Hey-you struck a chord with you." She smiled for a moment, but then her brow wrinkled. "That — your name being Jesús — that's not the reason you wouldn't talk to me though, is it?"

I swallowed and scratched the corner of my eye. "No, I'm somehow connected with Colonel Fountain."

"Oh." She rose from the chair, turned away and looked toward the Sacramentos, hands on hips. "So, your last name is … Fountain."

I had hoped not. "Suppose so." I stood and drew my hands to my hips, then back to my sides. What could I say to her? Without thinking, my gaze swung toward Frenchy's place.

"Does Oliver know?"

"No. I don't think so."

She turned round to face me. "You should leave. Now." She turned back to the mountains.

"I know … but I can't."

Before I could finish, she started toward the barn. Without looking back, she yelled, "For the sake of George, you owe me that."

I returned to my broken Windsor chair as Mary came out of the house wiping her hands on her apron. "What's all the yellin' about?"

"Nettie will tell you."

She shrugged, returned to the house, and muttered, "Time to eat."

"Not hungry."

---

I didn't see Nettie the rest of the day. She was my responsibility, but we didn't want to be near each other. I stewed over what to do for the rest of the afternoon.

That evening I forced down a few bites of the bunkhouse cook's usual fare — beans and rice bulked up with a chunk or two of beef. I wasn't hungry, and I went to find a place for my Tai Chi. I wanted to do it then, but the sun, low in the sky, was still relentless against the windowless west side of the bunkhouse. There was no other place private enough for me to relax. When I tried to use my boots to scrape away the rocks on an eight-by-eight space, it just brought new rocks to the surface. I would need pure sand to get the full effect of the calm focus I experienced at Frenchy's. I wished for the pure white grains of The White Sands.

---

## September 16

The weekend was calm — the quietest it had been for weeks. That is, until the Lee Well ranch hands returned from their Saturday night carousing. More than usual came home before dawn Sunday morning, which caused a ruckus. By the time we got the strait of it, or thought we had, word was that Rucker planned another raid — this time to secure physical evidence of Walter Good's murder. One cowboy said he heard they still wanted to bring the women to the La Luz jail where they could question them as they pleased.

We had moved Perry's stock and his hands back to the Altmans. Perry and Oliver were there. I asked Mary if I should fetch him. "Oliver's doin' important things for Perry. Whatever Rucker and Good want ain't as important. 'Sides, I've been handlin' them just fine … haven't I?"

I laughed. "Yes ma'am, I think you have."

However, Mary feared that evidence collection might spill over into robbery, and so she gathered all the cash and valuables from the house and ranch hands. She paced off twenty steps from the corner of the corral, dug a hole, turned a Dutch oven over the valuables and cash, and covered it with manure.

Mary must have thought they could kill us all and no one to tell the tale, and so she told Nettie to sleep in the chicken house, where no one would think to look. Nettie refused. She mumbled she didn't care what happened to her now that George was gone. Emma's refusal left no doubt. "Chicken house? Why, I wouldn't allow my child to sleep in a barn, let alone a chicken house."

Mary threw up her arms, then collected everything with a sharp edge and brought them inside. At first, I thought she had carried things a little too far, but then I realized Good and Rucker would do anything to make Oliver's life miserable. Cutting tools and guns were the most valuable items a ranch required.

Her anxiety amused some because the nighttime raids had become routine. It seemed clear that if Rucker would do anything, he would have done it by then. Nonetheless, she ordered us, "Don't do anything unless they try to break in. Then do anything you can to them."

Mary had Eph and I sleep on pallets in the front room and several other men bedded down on the flat roof. There were strange noises in the night, mostly whistles and animal sounds, but that was all.

Before sunrise the next morning, I started to the outhouse, but I saw Oliver asleep, sprawled out in one of the Windsor chairs, with his hat over his face. He must have heard me at about the same time because he jumped up and his hand went to his pistol.

I raised my hands. "Sorry to wake you. I was headed to the outhouse." He relaxed with the sound of my voice. "We had prowlers again last night." I also mentioned the signal calls we heard and that the women were upset about a claim that Rucker wanted to question them at the jail in La Luz. "I doubt the women slept a wink. They'll probably sleep in this morning."

Oliver chuckled, "You know Ma better than that. I don't care if she wrestled a bear all night. She'll have Nettie and Emma jumpin' and breakfast right on time."

It was too dark to see much, but Oliver looked around anyway. When I finished in the outhouse, he joined me back on the porch. After a few moments, he said, "Looks like they tied their horses up behind the chicken coop."

"They did? My goodness, your Ma wanted Nettie, Emma, and the baby to sleep there last night for fear Rucker's posse might murder everyone, but they refused."

Oliver put his hands on his hips. "Nettie often seems to have a feel for things … except George, I guess."

A thin orange slice of the sun peeked over the Sacramento ridgeline as I considered the state of my situation. Without looking at Oliver, I said, "Nettie knows my name is Jesús and … well, I might be a Fountain."

Oliver didn't blink or make any move. He stared at the crest of the Sacramentos as though he expected to see his response revealed. "And?"

"She wanted me to leave when I told her … two days ago."

"Why didn't you?"

"I promised you I would stay here and watch over her and your Ma and Emma."

"You did?"

"Well, not in so many words, but I felt like I had."

Oliver took off his hat and ran his fingers through his tawny hair. "If nothin' else, I guess you learned from us how to live a right life."

"I've learned a lot from you ... you and everyone here. I don't want to leave, but ..."

"You must. You'll have to go sometime and the longer we wait ... It ain't fair to you ... nor to us and 'specially not to Nettie. But that's just how it is."

The sun grew larger, and I heard the rattle-bang of pots and pans and faint sizzle in the kitchen as the 'down-home' aroma of smoked bacon wafted through the open windows. I looked toward the kitchen and muttered, "So much for sleeping in." Oliver grinned.

"Do you wish you had left me to die that day last April on San Augustin?"

Oliver turned in his chair to look me in the eye. "Not for a minute have I wished that, and no matter what Nettie or Ma might have said in the heat of the moment, they ain't neither."

I sat with my thoughts. Moments like this had become all too frequent. I wanted time to stop and yet I knew it wouldn't. Oliver read my mind.

"My pappy used to say that his pappy told him, 'Time nor tide stops for no man.'

"Should I leave now?"

"No, not this minute, but today, and I've got news that will mean you must go. Neither one of us knows what the future holds for you or us. The only thing I ask is, that you promise me you'll see that Perry and the boys get treated right in 'Cruces."

# 27: Revelations

## September 16, 1888

Oliver wanted several of us to join him for breakfast and so we had to put together the temporary table on the porch. As we set it up, I couldn't help but consider where things stood with my identity. I expected Mary knew I had discovered my name, and Eph and Ed may have as well.

*Later that day, I would be on my way to Las Cruces. Was it relief I felt? Maybe, but it was also mixed with just about every emotion you can name. I would go home soon ... it sounded so odd. Lee Well had been my home for all the time I could remember. There would be new people ... at least it would seem they were new. Had they assumed I was dead or had left for parts unknown? I wondered what it was like to have someone you thought was dead appear before you.*

There was a nudge to my upper arm. Eph held out the platter of ham. I took two slices and passed it on to Nettie. I hadn't noticed that she had sat next to me. She half-whispered, "I'm sorry about what I said ..."

I smiled, "I understand ... at least I want to."

Another nudge from Eph. It was the fried eggs. I tilted the platter and slid three into my dish.

*Seems my appetite is back. Maybe I shouldn't have acknowledged to Nettie that I might be a Fountain. After all, they might be some other relationship to me. And after what had happened in the saloon in Las Cruces, I didn't think I had anything to do with the law there.*

As I handed her the platter of eggs, I said, "You know I'm sorry about George and ... and I don't know what I can do, but I will do what I can to see that the courts hold John Good responsible."

Mary brought two platters of fresh buttermilk biscuits, which went into the center of the makeshift table next to two pots of coffee.

When everyone had eaten their fill, Oliver stood. "Perry, Cooper, and Earhart want to ride into 'Cruces tomorrow to surrender." There were nods and mumbles of approval. "However, they still don't have the paperwork to make it legal like."

"There still ain't no warrant?" asked Ed.

"We don't know why exactly, only that there is some mixup in the district court office. Without the paperwork all signed and all, we need to have as many men as I can spare ride in with them so nobody can jump 'em."

Sixto held a fork of ham above his plate. "How we know theese, señor Lee?"

"I ain't gonna tell you how I got the message, but Charlie Moore has still been workin' to get this done."

There was a murmur around the table about how Charlie was a dependable sort.

"Some of you know what I'm about to tell you. Hey-you has discovered that his real first name is Jesús and that he is from 'Cruces. He is going with our men to make sure — he has promised me so — the law treats the boys right. When he has done that, he will live with his real kin."

"Jesús!" said Sixto. "*absolutamente!*"

I was thankful Oliver didn't say I was a Fountain.

Oliver pulled the napkin from where he had tucked it under the top of his shirt. "I realize it's the Sabbath men, but I believe even the good Lord would say that the work of protecting your family and neighbors on his day is not just alright, but downright necessary. We leave in two hours." As the women cleared the table, Ed, Eph and the other hands congratulated me and Oliver raised his voice over the din, "Get what you need and meet here next to the well."

As I started toward the bunkhouse, Oliver pulled me aside. "Pack everything you've got. You'll stay in 'Cruces."

"All I have is what I wore that day you found me."

"No, you've earned at least what we've bought for you." He handed me an envelope. I peeked inside and saw there were several dollar bills. The first one I saw was a ten.

"Thank you, Oliver. I ... I don't know what to say."

"No need, now. I also want you to pick out a horse and tack to keep. Oh, and don't forget your gun belt and the pistol and rifle. And make sure you load up with ammo."

That didn't make my departure easier. I blinked and wiped my mouth on my sleeve. "Thank you, Oliver. I won't forget it."

I picked out Ol' Nasty from the remuda and saddled him. It didn't take long to gather my things from the bunkhouse. The last thing was the jacket I wore when Oliver found me. When I picked it up to fold it into my saddlebags, the letter fell out. I perused it. I didn't think I could have written that letter, but now I knew I did. But why hadn't I sent it? Nettie and I had talked about it not long after I awakened. Why had I forgotten about it until now? I unfolded it and reread it to myself:

*Dearest, I'll call you whatever you like,*

*I miss you and expect to come to you soon. I have
surprises for you. I hope the trial will be over next
Thursday, but it could end as late as the following
Saturday. If I can get Zio's permission, I'll come
earlier, but I know I can't count on it.*

A couple of hands interrupted and wished me well. The rest of
the letter was just some closing comments. As I refolded it, I
stopped when one closing line hit me and I read it aloud. "You are
as sweet as *tres leches* cake."

There was a name that came with that sentence, but it was
buried deep in my mind. As I stood next to the bunkhouse table, I
tried on names aloud: "Alejandra, Aletta, Alucia ... no, no, it's
Lucia." I heard sniggers from the other end of the bunkhouse and
looked up to see two or the hands gawking at me.

The taller of the two said, "And you best not stumble around
like that next time you see her."

The two of them laughed, and so did I, with the simple joy of
a memory returned.

"Luna. Lucia Luna was ... is her name." My grin must have
been as wide as the Rio Grande.

The smaller of the two said, "That sweet young thing that is
Juan's daughter at Luna Well? If she is sweet on you, you best
make haste. Every cowboy in the basin wants a chance to woo
her."

The two cowboys left, and I glanced back at the letter. I
wondered how I had overlooked the second sentence when Nettie
and I had read it months ago. *It said something about a trial
holding me up from visiting Lucia. What was my place in that
statement — accused, defense attorney, witness, or prosecutor?*

There was another name — I had spelled this one out, and I
read it aloud, "Zee-oh." It rolled around in my head a bit and then
another name came to me, "Mee-uh Tee-uh." I wrote the names in

my journal and without thinking, my mind guided my hand, and I wrote: 'Zio' and 'Mia Tia'. I recognized 'Tia' as aunt in Spanish, but 'Mia' was not Spanish. '*Mi*' would be Spanish for 'my' and 'Zio' was close to '*Tio*' for uncle in Spanish. So, 'Zio' was probably my uncle, and Mia Tia my aunt, but the mystery of the language still puzzled me, and it didn't confirm I was a Fountain.

Oliver and many Tularosa Basin folks watered at Pellman's Well. I went to Oliver and asked if we could stop at Luna Well instead.

"I don't think we should. The stagecoaches go there, and the place is like a quiltin' bee the way gossip flies out of there."

My expression must have puzzled him. "Is there something there from your past?"

"There's a girl there I know, well knew ... when you found me, the letter in my breast pocket was to her."

"Ah, well then, that's a good reason to pay a visit. I'll tell you what, when we stop at Pellman's you go on to Luna Well and we'll meet you at Sunol."

When we reached the spur to Pellman's, I could barely contain myself with anticipation. Before the rest of the group could make the turn off the main road, I had encouraged Ol' Nasty into a fast lope toward Luna Well.

When I arrived, a man was walking toward the *porche* of the station house. His name came to me with no effort — Juan. He saw me and stopped just before he opened the front door.

When I had brought Ol' Nasty to a halt and pushed my hat back on my head so he could recognize me, Juan said, "hey there stranger, can I interest you in a ..." He stopped mid-sentence. "I

... I think ... no, it cannot be. He opened the door and yelled, "Come, mama!"

A woman in a black dress and scarf came to the doorway. She held a pitcher of something. When she saw me, her face turned to stone. "Where is my Lucia?" She and Juan glanced here and there. I recognized the woman ...she was Elena, Lucia's mother, and the man was Juan, her father. I dismounted but didn't know what to say, and just stood there with the hope Lucia would appear. They looked at me and something dawned on them. Elena went into the house and there was a scream and the sound of pottery crashing onto the wooden floor. I looked around and recognized the places I had seen in my visions.

Juan went to her, and I followed him, but stopped just inside the door. Memories crowded the scene of Elena on her knees with the dark stain of a liquid surrounding the scattered pitcher shards.

As Juan helped her up, I walked over to pick up the shards from the clay pitcher. Elena turned to see me and wailed, "No! No! get away from me, you, you .... If she's not with you ... I knew it." She peered up at Juan, who pulled at her shoulders as he tried to comfort her. "I knew it." She took a deep breath. "I knew I needed to wear black."

After a few moments, Juan helped her to a chair and scooped her a dipper of water from the well bucket. He looked at me and pointed out the open door. That shocked me. "What happened? What? Was it my fault?"

When Juan got me outside, he was near tears himself and almost as angry as Elena. "Where is my daughter? Where have you been? I trusted you. I let you woo my daughter. Why are you here now? Colonel Fountain said you were missing, and we thought ... we hoped ... and ... and .... What happened?"

I apologized over and over and tried to explain, but he couldn't hear me. I felt panicked. "Where is Lucia?" I asked. "Where is she?"

At last, Juan realized I knew even less than he did. "Gone." He fell to his knees with his hands over his face in the dusty station yard. I hadn't noticed the wind when I had been on horseback. Now, it whistled through the gobernadora bushes and bent Juan's slouch hat brim up. He pulled his hands away as I kneeled next to him.

"Gone where?" I whispered. He looked at me through a contorted face and I understood ... *Lucia was dead.* He covered his face again and bent over until an exposed shock of his coal black hair swept across the fine Tularosa dust.

"What happened?" I said louder, but Juan couldn't speak. "What happened? What happened?"

I stood in front of him, without a clue about what to do. After a moment, Juan pulled his hands away and looked up at me. "She loved you and you left her. She was lonesome before ... you ... and when you were gone, she was ...." He spread his hands as though he didn't have the words or didn't want to say them.

I offered my hands, and he took them. I pulled him up and gave him a hug. He shuddered again and when he stopped, I explained, as best I could, what had happened to me.

I cocked my head and murmured, "It was only yesterday that I remembered Lucia and you all. What happened? Was she sick?"

Juan had composed himself and his tone became combative. "Yes, she was sick in love with you. For weeks she sat on the *porche* waiting for you. We didn't know what to do. One morning a few weeks ago, she said she wanted to ride over to see the salt lake west of White Sands and then to the Lucero's Ranch. We were relieved that it seemed she showed some interest in something other than you.

"She never came home and the next day we had a dust storm. We tracked her into the White Sands, but the winds covered her tracks, and we had a hard time finding our own tracks when we came out." He stopped to gather himself. "We thought ... hoped ... the two of you had ... run-off and, and ..."

I felt horrible. All this time, all I could think about was how difficult this had been for me.

*I didn't know about Lucia. But I should have, and now she's gone.*

"We searched there for days but found nothing."

The memory of the story of a ghost that floated through the White Sands as she searched for her conquistador husband struck me. I looked out across the dunes and mumbled, "She felt like the Spanish girl in the legend."

"Yes," Juan responded. "I think that legend always stuck with her."

I wondered how I could have missed hearing that kind of news. Surely, it was passed around. I must have heard it, but it meant nothing to me. I was so preoccupied with my own thoughts that I must have disregarded it. *It wasn't all about me.*

When Juan and I had overcome the grief of our stories, he told me they planned to leave the Tularosa Basin. At first, I wanted to ask why, but I thought before I spoke and instead, I said, "I understand. Have you sold the place then?"

"The stage company bought it from us, and they have someone that will take over."

"Where will you go?"

"We are returning to live near family in Veracruz. You have family there as well, I believe." We walked to my horse. Juan held Ol' Nasty's bridle while I put a foot in the stirrup. "But your father and mother, hmm, they aren't in Veracruz, no. Was it El Porvenir?"

It sounded familiar, and for the first time, I felt like I could trust it. I stepped out of the stirrup. "I'm sure you are right. Things still come to me in bits and pieces." I turned to stare off toward Dog Canyon. "Perhaps I should apologize to Elena."

"No, it is not necessary. She still will not understand. Someday, I hope she will, but now she, well, I hope you never have to experience the loss of a child."

On the one hand, I thought I should stay and help them, but it was clear that Elena did not want that. I had felt nothing quite like the shame that draped over me in those moments. I told myself over and over it wasn't my fault, but the shame lingered. After a few quiet moments with Juan, I looked at the low angle of the sun and realized I had several miles to go to meet Oliver at Sunol.

As I swung up into the saddle, Juan said, "Who did you say you lived with for the last several months?"

"I didn't say, but it was Oliver Lee."

Juan gulped. "*Madre di Dio*. No wonder Colonel Fountain never found you. You know ..."

I nodded. "Yes, I wonder what is ahead for me. I'm so sorry Juan. I hope for the best for you and Elena. Please let her know how sorry I am."

"*Si*, Jesús. You will need all the good wishes you can find. Please tell Zio and the family about our plans to leave and thank them for their devoted friendship. *Addio amico mio*."

I looked to the east and raised my hand to flick Ol' Nasty's reins, but I stopped when I realized Juan hadn't used Spanish to say 'goodbye, my friend.' And '*madre di Dio*' wasn't Spanish, and there was that name 'Zio'. The words were close, but not exactly it, and ... I just couldn't .... I put my reins hand on the saddlehorn and said, "Juan, that wasn't Spanish that you used when you said 'goodbye' and 'mother of god', was it?"

"Why no, but you understood me, didn't you?" I must have appeared perplexed because he said, "We share our Italian heritage. Your father is Italian, and we are Italian. You grew up with his language sometimes."

"Ah, and Zio is uncle in Italian, and that is the variation in my aunt's name — Mia Tia."

Juan smiled, winked, and said, "*Addio mio amigo.*"

# 28: Homecoming?

By the time I arrived at Sunol where I was to meet Oliver, Tucker, and Sixto, at least thirty other riders were there with Perry, Earhart, and Cooper. Everyone was armed, but Oliver clarified we should fire no weapons unless someone tried to waylay Perry, Earhart and Cooper. If that happened, we were to fire high and skedaddle back to the Sunol camp.

When he had made it clear how the surrender was to play out, he said, "Tucker and I are not ready to turn ourselves in and we will return home. One of my best hands, Sixto Garcia, will lead. Perry, Earhart, and Cooper will ride in the center of the group as you ride through town. Jesús," he pointed to me, "is coming along to make certain the law treats our men right since they haven't finished the legal paperwork. Jesús will also stay to take care of his personal business. We leave in the morning. Tucker and I will not turn ourselves in, so we will wait here for you to return and let us know how it went. Then we'll head back into the mountains until Moore can produce the proper paperwork."

When Oliver had finished, he took me aside and pushed a paper into my hand. I looked at it and there were five names:

**Albert Fall**

**Waddil and Young**

**Newcomb and McFie**

Oliver said, "I spent a night at W.W. Cox's place last week. Albert Fall was there for the night after stumping in Roswell for the election. Cox introduced him to me and recommended him as an excellent lawyer for us Texans. I talked with Fall, and we hit it off right away, but he hadn't registered with the Bar in New Mexico yet and was busy with politics. He recommended the other two firms. Fall told me either would do well by us, but I think we should hire both."

He handed me a wad of cash. "This should be enough to get them started. Tell them to get in touch with me when the funds are low, and I'll replenish their purse. Oh, and please tell Mr. Fall that I will be in touch and thank him for the attorney's recommendations."

I was reluctant to take on this additional task. Despite my attempt to keep my concern to myself, Oliver, ever keen on reading people, noticed. "That's all you need to do. Tell them that any other discussions should not involve you. I'll not ask anything else from you. I do hope we see you now and again after you've gotten yourself settled, but we'll understand if you decide to cut the lead for good."

━━━━━━━━━━━━━━━━━━━━━━━━━━━━━━━━━━━━━━━

As we topped the San Augustin Pass and started back down into the valley, the view struck me as familiar. I couldn't decide if it was because I had made this trip a couple of months before or because I remembered from other times … *when I was Jesús*.

We arrived just north of town and stopped to get organized. Our intent was to wrap ourselves around Perry, Cooper, and Earhart and, if possible, to dominate Las Cruces' wide Main Street while we rushed through to the sheriff's office. With over thirty riders, we spanned the dusty street, but as we approached the bustling town at a near full gallop, Sixto saw people filled the street. He held up his hand cavalry-style and slowed us to a walk. Even though our entrance into town wasn't as dramatic as we would have liked, people noticed and there were excited discussions as they pointed our way. Well-dressed couples were walking up and down the boardwalks arm in arm. It seemed there were far more people there than this little town could support. As

I looked around for anyone that might look as though they planned an attack, I noticed a handbill with '2$^{nd}$ Annual Southern New Mexico Fair' in large letters across the top.

*It's fair time! And ... yes ... my family lived in El Porvenir, Mexico, as Juan had said, and then I remembered, I had visited there, and we had planned for them to come to the fair ... this fair. All my people were here ... somewhere.*

People looked at us and ... and applauded. They must have thought we were part of the fair.

*So, my name's not Fountain ... it's Meh, Mess ... yes, Messi.*

As we reached the end of the street and approached the courthouse and sheriff's office, the men that wanted to turn themselves in made their way forward through the other riders. I followed them and we tied our horses to the hitching rail.

While the rest of the men stood guard outside, Perry, Earhart, Cooper and I entered the sheriff's office. The same deputy that had been there a few months before was again leaning back on his chair with his feet on the desk. This time, he must have been asleep for the sound of the door latch caused him to start, and the chair, balanced as it was on its rear legs, flew out from under him into the desk and he landed on his backside. He jumped to his feet and positioned the chair against the desk.

"Uh," the deputy blinked several times as he tried to focus. "Uh, what can I do for you fellers?"

Perry spoke up before I could respond. "We're turnin' ourselves in."

The deputy rubbed his eyes and yawned. "What for?"

"I'm Perry Altman, and this here," he waved his hand to his right, "is Bill Earhart, and this," he waved his left hand to his left, "is Jim Cooper."

"That s'posed to mean somethin' to me?"

I didn't know why, but my instinct told me I should take control. "We understand the court hasn't finished the paperwork, but there will be a warrant for their arrest for the murder of Walter Good."

"Which we didn't do," Cooper added.

Earhart must have decided that was the time for him to plead his case. "And all I did was get into a little scuffle ... with guns ... near the Malone Ranch with John and Deputy Rucker."

The deputy shook his head and shuffled through some papers on his desk. "I ain't never had nobody turn themselves in afore the warrant was served."

It was clear I needed to take control of the situation.

"Deputy, John Good and Deputy Rucker have harassed these men and their families for weeks and they have decided they do not want anything to happen to their properties and families, so they wish to turn themselves in."

"Hmm." The deputy scrunched up his face. "C'ain't do nothin' without a warrant."

Perry's brow wrinkled as he tried to restrain himself, and Cooper had his hands on his hips.

"Deputy," I said, "These men are in fear for their lives. Even though you don't have the warrants, you can jail them for their own protection, can you not?"

"I ain't quite sure ..."

"I would like to speak with the sheriff."

"He's over at the fairgrounds helpin' with settin' up."

I didn't need to look at them to know that Perry and Cooper were about to explode. "Deputy, please believe me, you can do this. Now, I need it settled because I have about thirty-five men outside that are unhappy about how unfairly the Dona Ana County Sheriff's office have treated them and ..."

"Alright. But wait, you look familiar, but ... who might you be? You don't look old enough to be a loyer."

"I'm ... Jesús ... Messi." It seemed odd to say it, but comfortable as well.

The deputy pushed his hat back on his head. "Not Colonel Fountain's junior assistant? Why, I thought you's dead. The whole town think you's dead. Where ya been?"

"It's a long story, deputy. Can you please jail these three men? I will hire lawyers for them as soon as you can do that. How much will their board be?"

After settling-up on meals for the three men for a couple of days, the deputy walked them back to their cells, and I went outside and told the men that had come with us they could return home.

I led Perry and the other men's horses over to Shields and Bennett's Livery, where I paid for several days in advance. When I gave Perry's name as the owner of the strawberry roan, the attendant said, "We've already got Mr. Altman's horse here. Been here for three weeks now. You'll have to pay up on his black before I can take any other horse of his."

I paid him what he owed; plus the amount I had given him for the other horses, and turned back toward the telegraph office. There was something about that storefront that was pulled me there.

I removed my hat as I approached the door, but before I could open it, the door swung open and a middle-aged blonde-haired, blue-eyed woman appeared that looked familiar. When she saw me, she seemed stunned and stared as she rushed past me onto the boardwalk. I ignored her but thought I might have to get accustomed to people's odd reactions when they saw me for the first time. I entered the office. Memories came flooding back.

*It's Miles, and he's a good friend.*

Miles had his back to me as he tapped out a message, but there was no doubt it was him. I walked in and stood at the counter. When Miles had sent the message, he pulled the pencil from his ear, licked the lead, and made a note on the slip of paper in front of him. As he turned to me, he said, "What can I do for you sir ..."

I forced a smile and Miles cried, "My God, son. Where in the devil have you been?"

"It's a long story, Miles. Suffice to say that only at this very moment, I have recognized who you are."

At first, my riddled response confused him, but then his face contorted, and he swiped a tear from his cheek. He opened the pass through on the counter and hugged me with such verve that for a moment I thought I would have to push him away. I could hear subdued sobs and gasps and so I waited until he had composed himself. When he stepped back, he pulled out his handkerchief, wiped his eyes, and blew his nose.

"I'm sorry Miles, I don't have time to talk much right now. Can you tell me where the Fountains live?" He gave me a blank stare. "Honest, I barely remember who you are." My hand went to the spot on my head where there had been a sizeable gash. "I fell off my horse and hit my head when I was on my way to Luna Well and I ...." Someone else entered and I didn't want to go through the complete story.

Miles' eyes widened. "Of course, Jesús. I think I understand."

"Oh, and Miles, who was that lady that left just before I entered?"

"That was Mrs. Ascarate. I think at one time you had eyes for her daughter, Bella."

He told me where to find the Fountains. I remembered that the Ascarates lived down the street from the Fountains. Memories surfaced of me sitting on the Ascarates *porche* with Bella and her mother, shelling beans. *That's where I learned how to shell peas.* I mounted Ol' Nasty, and we trotted back down the street to the south before I turned east. As we approached the cross street where I was to turn left, I noticed some people gathered in the far corner of a cemetery that had just a few headstones.

I turned the corner. *A windy winter day appeared before me. I carried a valise. Tumbleweeds flew about, a dog scampered past in pursuit of a cat, and I could hear a baby ... Little Henry it was ....*

I stopped in front of the house and got down from Ol' Nasty. There was no hitching rail and so I led him to the *porche*. I took in my surroundings. The *porche*. I remembered seeing it for the first time.

How inviting it was then ... and was still ... the floral printed fabric covered chairs with footstools for each. There were barrels and boxes between the chairs for placing your drinks. The multicolored flagstone floor was swept clean.

I tied Ol' Nasty to one of the *porche*'s posts and walked up the trimmed path to the adobe. Just as I reached for the door, I realized perhaps I shouldn't just walk in like nothing had happened. I paused and heard a small voice inside. "a-a-a-a-a." I grinned. As I reached to knock, the door opened. A young woman ... *Rosa* .... She turned before she saw me because the baby ... *Little Henry* ... had crawled away from her. When she turned back to me, her eyes got as big as yucca pods and her hands went to her open mouth. Her knees buckled and her eyes closed. I reached for her waist and stopped her fall, which brought me against her midsection. I reached back and closed the door with my foot, gathered her into my arms and took her down the hall. Little Henry crawled after us as fast as he could go babbling, "do-a-ma-ma-a-by."

I stopped midway down the long hallway and looked at the open doors.

*Right for the boys and left for the girls.*

I turned into the girl's room, and it hit me. 'You're never to go into the girl's room for any reason.' "Well, I doubt Mia Tia or Zio thought of this circumstance," I mumbled.

By now, Little Henry had reached the doorway and after I laid Rosa down, I picked him up and we went to the kitchen, where I found a glass and some lemonade. I returned to Rosa with Little Henry in one arm and the glass of lemonade in the other.

She came around as I placed Little Henry next to her. I kneeled at the side of the bed. When she could focus on me, she said, "Where have you been?"

# 29: The First Supper

**September 17, 1888**

As I explained what had happened to me, Rosa interrupted to ask if I had seen Lucia. I told her what the Lunas had said and added, "I guess they hoped that she and I had eloped."

Lucia's fate shocked, then saddened Rosa. After a moment, she tilted her head and said, "She was smitten with you. We chatted a few times. She had no close friends or brothers or sisters. I can understand how disheartened she must have been. I imagine she didn't want to return to that loneliness."

Her words reminded me of the unsent letter I had carried, and I reached for it in my pocket. That was when I found Oliver's wad of money.

"Oh my gosh, Rosa, I have to go. I need to do something for Oliver."

"Oliver? Do you mean Oliver Lee?"

"Yes, that's who rescued me, and his mother and niece nursed me back to health. I promised him I would do something, and I have to go."

Rosa sat up and Little Henry reached for her. She put her arm around his waist and he hugged her shoulder. "You do know that he and the Colonel are on opposite sides of the law, right? The Colonel is the prosecutor for the Walter Good murder case."

Tight-lipped and eyebrows raised, I shrugged. I wasn't sure if I knew that. "I'll work it out somehow. Where are they, by the way?"

"Oh. Oh my. *Madre de dios*. They are with your parents and brother and sister at the cemetery for a memorial service for you."

*That was who I saw on my way.* "I … I must go. Please tell them I am back and that I'll return as soon as I can."

～✦～✦✦✦✦✦～✦✦✦✦✦✦✦✦～✦✦～✦✦✦✦✦✦✦✦✦～✦✦✦✦✦～✦✦✦✦✦✦✦～✦✦✦✦✦～

The lawyers recognized me, which led to confusion about why I would help the Lees. I gave them a brief explanation, and they confirmed that Colonel Fountain was assisting the prosecution on behalf of the Territory.

After I paid the jailhouse board for the men and for stabling their horses, the remaining amount wasn't enough to cover the two firms' fees. The district court session would start in a couple of weeks, and both firms said their preparation would require their full staffs. I would need to go back to Lee Well, to tell Oliver. Both offices gave me a written fee estimate, which I needed to get to Oliver.

On the way back to the Fountains, I wondered why the lawyers recognized me now, but not a few months before. It seemed likely that at least one of them would have been in the Alhambra Saloon as I spouted legal terms. After I thought about it, I realized my hair had been much longer and I still had a scruffy beard. Still, it seemed someone would have said something. Perhaps it was also that I didn't look like someone that belonged there. I wore Texas cowboy garb and not what the local ranchers wore, which was like the Mexican *vaqueros*.

I passed the cemetery where, unbeknownst to me, I had seen my family. They were no longer there. At first, I didn't want to see if there was some kind of gravestone, but I couldn't resist.

In the late afternoon light, I saw the small stone slab etched with the inscription:

**In Memory of**

**Jesús Perez Contreras Verazzi Messi**

**who disappeared April 21, 1888**

A fresh mound of soil made it easy to find the small stone. The mound wasn't big enough for a casket, but it stood out.

---

Over the years, the humbling experience I felt that day is never far from my thoughts.

*A few words on a headstone does a life no justice — is it the final reckoning of just how inconsequential we all are? I hoped that people who knew me would remember, but would later generations take note of Jesús Messi's life? Did it matter if they didn't? Did Jesús Messi make the world a better place? If I had died on San Augustin Peak, would I have been forgotten in a year ... five ... ten?*

It was a disturbing sensation. I felt what I imagine it feels like to be disemboweled. Yet many years later, it had the reverse effect on me. I realized it isn't who remembers you, but why, and it made my life precious. I still had my moments, but the image of my "headstone" reminded me to let the troubles of everyday life go. That, and loving thy neighbor as thyself, helped me make the most of my time on this earth.

---

By the time I got back to the Fountains, Rosa had informed them of my return. Everyone was at a makeshift table in the backyard. Mateo saw me first, and he came out from the stable with his arms raised and said, "¡Aleluya¡ Gracias, Señor. My goodness, you have grown." Indeed, after Mateo gave me a hug, he took Ol' Nasty into the stable. As he led Ol' Nasty away, I realized I was taller than him and that seemed odd.

As I approached the table, everyone stood. I stopped and scanned all the faces. As I focused on each one, my memory cleared, and I knew them. No one sat at the head of the table. On either side was my mother, Madre; and Mia Tia with Katie sitting tall on the Sears catalogs. Their husbands, Zio and my father, were next to them. On one side of the table were my sister Angelina, my brother Miguel and Tommy Fountain. On the other side sat Albert Jr., Marianita, Maggie, and Jackie.

When I smiled, my mother and Mia Tia rushed to my side as the others followed. Family members didn't think to introduce themselves and for that, I was thankful. It would have been awkward. There were tears, handshakes, pats on the back, hugs, and a hundred questions. I didn't know whom to address first. Rosa stood in the kitchen doorway and waved when our eyes met. In the end, Zio took charge. "You have remembered us, and we are thankful, and as you can see, we have not forgotten you."

Having just visited what amounted to my gravesite, I felt his words were hollow. He continued, "We must hear your story, but let's enjoy this wonderful meal Rosa has prepared for us and we'll hear it all tonight from the story-hearth."

As we gathered around the table, I still felt like a stranger. Their faces were familiar, but something had changed. When Rosa, along with Marianita, Maggie, and Angelina, went to gather the platters of food, I noticed how much taller Angelina was and I realized just how much I had grown. In Spanish, my father said, "Chuy, you have turned into quite a young man. I never thought you would grow so much or become so strong."

His use of my nickname flooded memories to me faster than I could make sense of them other than to realize that most were tinged with sadness.

As they passed the platters, I realized they had planned this meal before they knew I was alive. It was my funeral meal.

Several of the Fountains and my family couldn't wait for the evening story-hearth, and they asked me questions as we ate. Fortunately, short answers were all that was required because my discomfort with their gathering's original purpose distracted me.

My uneasiness left me without an appetite and I answered the few questions they ventured with simple answers. As I pushed the food around my plate, I noticed their reticent glances. By the end of the meal, everyone eyed me with measured smiles, which didn't quell my uneasiness.

Madre and Mia Tia notice my anxiety and held my hands, while Papa reminisced about how Zio and I had discouraged the Mexican government from their plan to route their railroad through his land. Zio said the attorneys for Terrence Mullens had never appealed the conviction we got on the day before I left. The floodgates opened and questions came fast and furious until Zio stood and said that their questions should wait until we've heard my full tale at the story-hearth.

A time or two, I thought Zio stared at me. I expected Rosa had told them about Oliver. Perhaps Zio doubted he could trust me. As I considered my situation, I wondered if Oliver still felt I was loyal. Oliver and Zio might have reacted the same.

*Perhaps neither man would trust me ever again.*

Tommy's voice broke into my thoughts, "Thank goodness you are back cousin, now I can go back to my militia position."

Zio laughed and said, "Jesús, do you want to return to work with me?"

I didn't want to answer that, and before I could respond, Mia Tia said, "Leave him alone. He has only just returned. He needs some time." My mother and Mia Tia smiled at each other and squeezed my hands.

Maggie said, "Did you remember that your family planned to come to the fair?"

It was all happening so fast. I wasn't sure what or when I remembered. "Uh, yes. I … I … saw the posters in town. It starts tomorrow?"

Mia Tia said, "Yes, and Maggie made those posters for Papa to print."

For a moment, I wondered why I could remember the fair and my family's attendance but couldn't recall Maggie's artistic ability. As my time back with the Fountains progressed, those kinds of inconsistencies with my memory weren't as frequent, but for a time they persisted, and I sometimes lied rather than explain.

The evening story-hearth went well enough. Marianita's husband Carl, Albert Junior's wife Teresita, and their son, little Albert III, Rosa, and Gene Van Patten joined the two families. I kept it brief and tried to portray myself as neutral. When I told them about my visions in the White Sands and Frenchy's part in learning my connection to the Fountains, Maggie stood and said, "Wait, are you saying that you knew you belonged here long ago, but didn't come?"

I looked around the room. They all awaited my response. My reason wouldn't satisfy them. "You might not understand this, but I couldn't leave the Lees then. It was just a few weeks ago. I owed them so much and they were under constant scrutiny by John Good and Rucker. I … I wanted to come, but I couldn't."

Maggie demonstrably crossed her arms on her chest and said, "It sounds like you wanted to stay."

There were murmurs, but nothing more was said. I wasn't sure I wanted to continue. I stepped off the hearth. Zio stopped me by holding up his hand and said, "This is a difficult situation for us all. Please continue Jesús. We need to hear all of it."

I stayed off the hearth, but continued with how Good and Rucker harassed the Lees and Altmans. When I told them the Lucia story, I didn't want to include how the Lunas had blamed me and I feared they wouldn't understand that my feelings for Lucia hadn't returned. I didn't want to appear indifferent. I paused, put my hand to my mouth, and turned away. When I turned back, I wiped my eyes and said she disappeared in the

White Sands. Everyone stared at me for a moment. I thought they didn't believe me, but then the tearful women gathered, and the men patted me on the shoulder.

After, Zio pulled me back onto the hearth and said, "Well, this has been, uh … well, I just want Jesús to know he has thrilled us with his return. When I was in the California Column, a private got kicked in the head by a pack mule. As a result, he also lost his memory and sense of who he was. I don't remember how long it took before he regained his senses, but it was perhaps just a week or two." He turned to face me. "Yours must have been quite serious. I find it miraculous that they nursed you back to health without a doctor." He paused and looked me over. "When you finally came around, they must have worked you hard to be as strong as you are. I wonder how much quicker you would have recovered had we found …." He stopped mid-sentence because I think he realized it made me uncomfortable when he insinuated the Tularosa folks were backward.

After, Gene Van Patten approached me. "A.J. and I looked for you for several days. We scoured the Tularosa, but we didn't go to Lee Well. A.J. was afraid our presence might cause a ruckus and we reasoned that if they had brought you all that way, someone would have seen your body over a horse and remembered. No one did." He put his large hands on my shoulders. "I can't imagine what you have been through and what's coming ain't gonna be no picnic neither." He asked if I remembered where he lived. I said I did, and he told me I could come talk with him anytime.

Madre and Mia Tia stayed with me while the family approached with their thoughts. Mostly, they told me they were happy I was back where I belonged. I wasn't sure I agreed.

I lay in my bed that night and wished I could hear Virgil snore or Sixto speaking Spanish in his sleep. At the Lees, I wanted to know who I was and where I belonged.

*What happened?*

# 30: Banking on Me

**September 18, 1888**

At Lee Well, I had gotten accustomed to rising with the eastern sky's first light. The Fountain adobe became active a little later, so I dressed, started the stove, and made coffee. As I looked through the previous Saturday's newspaper, the problem of letting Oliver know the lawyers asked for additional money interrupted my reading.

It was wrong to leave my family after they had come so far. But they didn't expect to see me. *Perhaps I should leave right away.*

I folded the paper, placed it on the table, then rested my elbows on it with my chin in my hands. *Perhaps the lawyers will know how to get the money they need.*

The coffee was ready as Rosa arrived to make breakfast. Zio had a quick cup of coffee and went to help with the final preparations at the fair.

The fair wouldn't open until noon and there was plenty of time to sleep in. However, the smell of breakfast cooking must have awakened everyone. I was still a novelty at the table, and I noticed a few of the family shook their heads as though they couldn't believe they were seeing me. I finished my meal and walked downtown to see Judge McFie of the firm, Newcomb and McFie.

He had been the first of the lawyers to recognize me, and he also reminded me he had put the Colonel onto the San Marcial Ring.

When I asked if there was another way to get word to Oliver fast, McFie rose from his desk and stood next to me while he massaged his chin in thought. "Well, as you know, the telegraph hasn't reached La Luz yet, although, I hear they are stringing a line now. But to your question, perhaps we could send a telegram to the telegraph office in El Paso for delivery at Lee Well, but there's no tellin' when it might get to him. One other possibility would require a trusted go-between. If you know someone that Oliver trusts, we could send it to them, and they would see that it gets to Oliver right away."

My visit to El Paso with Perry and Nettie immediately came to mind. "I might know his banker. His name is Joshua Jefferson. He's President of the First National Bank in El Paso."

"Perfect." said McFie. "We'll send the telegram to him, and if Oliver and he have a good relationship, he might even feel comfortable wiring us the money without Oliver's approval. Let's see here …. I'll tell you what. you said you hired Waddil and Young also, correct?"

I nodded.

"Well then, I'll go right over there and put this thing together for you. If you come back in, say, an hour, you can send it with Miles. You know Miles, right?"

"That sounds just fine, sir."

"You can call me John, son. As I recall, your name is Jesús?"

"Yes, sir."

I walked outside their office onto the east side Main Street boardwalk. It occurred to me that Zio had cautioned me to avoid the east side businesses: 'They're all Democrats. If they know you're a Republican, you might as well spit in the wind as get help from them.'

I walked across the still peaceful street and started back to the south toward the Fountains. On a whim, I entered the only bank in Las Cruces. There was no line or teller at the teller's window. I looked over the counter and saw him thumbing through some papers.

I tapped on the counter. "Excuse me sir, can I get a balance on my account?"

"Why sure sonny. Now let's see." He squinted. "Are you the Fountain's Jesús that disappeared and came back yesterd'y?"

The teller was an older, white-haired man, maybe five feet tall. All I could see above the bottom of the teller window was his head. Round spectacles were perched on his nose.

"I am. I don't have my account book. Can you look it up for me? My last name is Messi."

"Oh certainly." He took out a long wooden box with alphabetized dividers that separated the index cards. "Now let's see here, hmm ... M - M - M-e - M-e, M-e-s, M-e-s-s, ah yes here it is, Jesús Messi." He wrote something down on a slip of paper and handed it to me.

$548.38.

"And that includes your interest from August."

A twinge of guilt hit me. "When was the last deposit?"

"September first, just like every other deposit — first of the month."

I thought about depositing what Oliver had given me. The envelope was still in my pocket. *No, I'll put it on Mr. McFie's legal bill.*

"I want to withdraw twenty dollars. Can you do that for me?"

"Why certainly Mr. Messi, would you like that in paper or hard cash?"

"A double eagle if you've got it."

As I walked back to the north toward Freudenthal's store, I thought about how my family and I had planned for them to atttend the fair and they followed through.

*Did they come for those reasons, or did they need to know my fate for themselves?* My intuition told me it was the latter.

I had forgotten Freudenthal's store had burned down a short time before my accident and so I looked around before I found Numa Reymond's mercantile, which now had the name of Lohman's.

As I entered, the familiar smell of the sawdust-covered floors with hints of spices and gunpowder greeted me, along with Mrs. Lohman. I didn't think I had met her before, but she turned from other people that had entered in front of me and took my hand. She half-whispered, "It's so nice to see you've come home." Her friendly smile dissolved my discomfort as I tried to remember her name.

The clothes I had brought from the Lees were for rough work and riding, and I knew that whatever clothes Mia Tia had kept wouldn't fit me.

"I'm so sorry, ma'am. I guess I don't remember your name."

She grinned, put her hands on her hips and cocked her head, "Well, from what I've heard about your accident, that's perfectly understandable." She introduced herself in a way that allowed me to escape embarrassment. Perhaps it was her smile … she *always* had a smile.

I told her I needed two new sets of clothes and shoes. After she showed me around. I changed into them in the storeroom and paid with the gold coin I had gotten from the bank.

Mr. Lohman looked surprised, flipped the coin a foot or two in the air, caught it and then bit it before he checked it for his tooth marks. "Ayup. It's real." He pointed to the indentations he made with his teeth in the gold coin. "We don't see many of these here in the store. How did you come across this one?"

"The bank. Our bank, here in Las Cruces. You suspected it was counterfeit?"

"Can't be too careful where them Texans are concerned."

I frowned, took my change, and had my old clothes and boots bundled and wrapped in butcher paper.

When I stood before Judge McFie in my new duds, he did a double take and smiled. "Feeling a little out of place in your old clothes, were you?"

"Well, that outfit wasn't exactly suited for the fair, sir."

Judge McFie chuckled. "My first thought was that you have switched sides. But then I realized just how difficult your position is. How do you plan to manage it?"

Speechless, I gazed out the storefront window. He recognized my discomfort. "It won't be easy, but I'm sure you'll manage." He handed me a folded page. "Go ahead, you can look at it." I unfolded it, thought better of reading it, and refolded it.

*The less I knew, the better for me.*

Judge McFie's eyebrows rose, and he smiled. "I think you've got the hang of it." He tried to hand me two dollars and some change, but I wouldn't take it.

"I won't need it, sir. Oliver gave me some money when I left."
I reached for the envelope of cash in my pocket. In fact, please put
this toward Oliver's legal bill. I'll keep enough to cover the
telegram."

Judge McFie studied me and shook his head. "I can see what
Colonel Fountain thinks the world of you, Jesús." He took my cash
and put it into a till on his desk. "Oh, and you may not remember,
but Mr. Newcomb handles all cases for Democrats."

I tipped my Stetson — the only thing I still wore from that
morning and walked across the street and headed a block south to
the Telegraph Office.

The bell tingled my entrance, causing Miles to turn from some
task at his desk. "Aw, so glad you're back … I mean that doubly."
I remembered that Miles always had a different way from others.
I had the feeling that he and I had had several chats about serious
matters. "Oh, and I heard about your girl — Lucia, was it? So
tragic." He sighed and wiped his hand across his mouth. "S'pose
life goes on." He pointed to the slip in my hand. "Somethin' for
me to tap out?"

He reached across the narrow counter and took the paper from
my outstretched hand.

"I have to get this to Oliver Lee through El Paso."

"I see. So, you're workin' for him now?" He knew that wasn't
the case. Perhaps he felt it was better to clear the air and not let
something like that fester.

"No, although he *did* save my life — he and his mother and
niece. I figure I owe him this much."

Miles nodded, as though he already knew what I had told him.
He counted the words on the note and calculated the telegram's
cost. "That'll be one dollar, even."

I handed him the folded dollar bills Oliver had given me and that I had left from what I gave Judge McFie. "Does Judge McFie have an account with you?"

"Why, yes, he and Mr. Newcomb keep one for their law office." Miles scratched his temple.

"Can you credit the rest to their account, then?"

Miles counted it. "Sixteen dollars. Those lawyers don't need your money, Jesús."

I scratched my temple. "It's not my money. Besides, I want to keep a clean slate."

Miles smiled. "That's right smart of you Jesús."

I shrugged, "I'm not sure how this will all turn out, but I respect Zio and Oliver, and I don't want either to think otherwise."

"Perhaps you can keep it that way, but there may come a time …"

"I hope not."

# 31: Fair Recrudescence

Zio had hired a special wagon so all of us could ride to the fair together. When I returned to the Fountains, the livery had left it parked on the street in front of their adobe. I took my belongings inside and looked for my razor and shaving mug. Tommy saw me rummaging around. I asked him if he knew where my things were. "Sorry, but maybe Rosa knows. Here," he handed me a box of his personal care things. "Use mine for now."

As I finished shaving, I heard Mia Tia call everyone to the wagon for the ride to the fair. They all complimented my new clothes. I told Mia Tia I had used some of the money in my bank account and how thankful I was that had continued to pay into it while I was missing.

As we bumped along toward the fairgrounds, the family couldn't help glancing at me with broad smiles. I would see them and they would look away, but their smiles would persist. Their reactions to my sudden reappearance were understandable. I tried to show the joy our reunion should engender, but I struggled to match their giddiness. I hoped it wasn't obvious. Since my visions in the White Sands a month earlier, I knew I would eventually return to my previous life. All the people I had known would still be there. They had no expectation of my return, and they may well have thought I was dead. I couldn't shake the feeling that my death was so easily accepted.

*Coming home after such a long absence should have been exciting, shouldn't it? I didn't realize it would be so difficult. Now and then, I yearned for the easy friendships at Lee Well.*

Maggie's voice interrupted my thought, "You seem to have matured beyond the months you've been gone — emotionally, I mean."

"Have I?"

"Yes, you seem less adolescent — less like Tommy."

Jack laughed and Tommy snapped, "I don't know how you could get more mature than a soldier. Besides, if you want to suggest someone is adolescent, why wouldn't you suggest that of the person who pretends to be a cowboy?"

At first, I thought Tommy meant me, but then I saw Jack in his vaquero garb. We had sat in the back of the wagon on our haunches. Jack half rose and said, "You think so? I do a hundred times the work you do behind that desk."

"Maybe so, but I can still lick you." Tommy also rose.

Mia Tia turned from her seat next to Madre and said, "Now, boys, settle down. Shall I tell your father about your argument?"

As they sat back on their haunches, Maggie mouthed to me, "See what I mean?"

Maggie and I snickered out of the boys' view.

Zio had met us at Wil Rynerson's farm exhibit. My friend, Fabián Garcia, was Wil's farm manager and Fabián came to me as I helped Maggie and Marianita off the wagon.

"Jesús, I did not know you were missing. I've been so busy here at the farm. I never go into town and Mr. Rynerson brings us whatever provisions we might need. It's so good to see you again, my friend."

His words were refreshing after the 'I thought you were dead' look on people's faces. I introduced Fabián to my family and the Fountains and we walked out across his chile fields, which looked even better than I had remembered.

While we talked with Fabián about the farm, the women helped Fabián's grandmother, who had prepared Mexican cookies and her special wine and lemonade elixir. They munched on her snacks and sipped on their drinks as they sat under their massive Cottonwood tree while we inched closer for the treats.

Papa and Miguel seemed happy with Fabián's description of his irrigation system and seed selection methods. Miguel even took some notes.

When we left, Fabián wished me luck and asked that I come visit whenever I was in the area. I made a mental note and helped the women back into the wagon. Our next stop was the exhibition hall, which was busy, although not as busy as I thought I had recalled from the previous year. I asked Zio if there were fewer visitors. "The Exposition in Albuquerque moved their fair to just a couple of days after ours and so we must have lost some visitors to that event. It's a shame because I think our produce exhibits are even better this year."

As we wandered through the exhibits of fruits, vegetables and various ores, people stopped us many times to shake my hand and express their thoughts about my reappearance. Some were compassionate, while others stated they thought I was dead. A few said nothing, but their faces expressed pity. One boy who held his father's hand said, "Papa, is he a ghost?"

We all laughed at the boy's innocence, but people's insensitive reactions wore on me, and I wanted to leave, but I felt obligated to remain with my family and the Fountains.

We came upon an exhibit of peaches. "Hey-you," the exhibitor said, "fancy seeing you here. Where are Emma, Mary and Nettie?" It was Mrs. Reynolds from the homestead where Emma had first seen the smoke from her burning home.

The Fountains and my family looked uncomfortable, and Zio pointed to a booth across the way. "Oh, look at those nuts. I don't think I've seen them here before." Everyone moved toward the display of pistachios.

"The name is Jesús." I wiped my hand across my face. "Hey-you is from when I couldn't remember my name ... or where I belonged ... and, well, those people are my family, and this is where I am from ... Las Cruces."

Mrs. Reynolds put her hands on her hips but let them fall to her side. "Oh. I see, well then ... um, what can I do for you? The peaches are especially good this year because of all the moisture last winter and early this spring."

"Where is Mr. Reynolds?"

"Oh, heavens knows. That man can't sit still for one minute. I imagine he's gone to find some new machine or other contrivance."

*Perhaps the Reynolds could get a message to Oliver about the lawyers' fees.*

I wanted to trust Judge McFie's plan to get the money they needed from Oliver, but the probability of some problem lingered. I decided a message to him from me should reassure him about the telegram to his banker. "Do you have a paper and pencil?"

She reached under her makeshift counter for her writing instruments. "Of course, but I can just pass a message along if you like."

"I'd rather you had it in writing and also you'll have the paper as a reminder." I smiled to quell thoughts I didn't trust her.

"Whatever you say, uh, Jesús."

I scribbled my message, folded it and wrote on the outside, "Oliver Lee".

"Should I not read it?"

I had rather she didn't, but I didn't want her to think I didn't trust her. "No, it's alright, you can read it."

She read through the note while I tried to move my foot around in one of my new, unbroken-in shoes.

"Oh my. So, Perry, Cooper, and Earhart turned themselves in?"

"Yes ma'am. Yesterday. That reminds me, I need to stop at the jail to make sure everything is alright there."

"Where can Mr. Reynolds find you if there is a problem? He'll want to take care of this himself."

"I live with the Fountains, ma'am. I'm sure Oliver will appreciate your husband's help."

"The Fountains. Not Colonel Fountain?"

"Yes ma'am, I was his law apprentice before my accident."

"Oh, my, oh my, oh my. My goodness, son, whatever will you do?"

I grinned briefly. "It certainly is a dilemma, ma'am. However, you can rest assured I won't do any harm to Oliver or the folks in the Tularosa. I owe Oliver and you folks that much.

"If your husband wants to advance the money himself, he should go to Judge McFie at the law offices of Newcomb and McFie on Main Street, across the street from the bank. Here, I'll write it on the note." As I jotted down the lawyer's names and location, I realized the whole thing might get confused and I said, "Oh, and be certain to have him remind the lawyers to send a telegram to Oliver's banker in El Paso."

As I turned to leave, Mr. Reynolds arrived. After his wife explained, and I supplemented where necessary, he said he would handle it that afternoon.

After I shook his hand and thanked them for their good wishes, I turned to see everyone had gone except my mother. She met me in the middle of the aisle and in Spanish said, "My son, I see how people look at you and I'm afraid you are in a bad spot. Maybe you should come home to El Porvenir? You could start a law office there. We could use a wonderful lawyer in the village. The railroads seem to have given up, but your father still worries."

There were wrinkles on my mother's face that I couldn't remember. Her eyes exuded a compassion for me that was equally unfamiliar. I took a deep breath. Leaving the Zio and Oliver dilemma behind was attractive, but there was something uncomfortable about my family and El Porvenir. It was just a feeling, but I knew it wasn't right for me. Her wistful expression made me realize I needed a delicate response.

"I'll think about it Madre, I'll think about it."

In the rush to catch the rest of our party, a blister developed on my left foot, and I stopped to try to adjust my shoe. I waved my mother on and sat on a bench. When I looked up from my shoe, I was looking at the booth location where Lucia and I had sold her and her mother's crocheted goods. I blinked and she was there smiling at me. I looked away and when I looked back she was gone.

After I caught up with my family, we had a few more encounters with people that were inconsiderate of my situation. I was tired and sore, and I said to Zio, "These new shoes aren't broken in. I'm getting blisters. May I take your horse back ... to the adobe?" I couldn't say 'home' ... not yet.

"Of course, Jesús, I'll drive the wagon back home."

# 32: A Little One

**September 18, 1888**

I stopped at the sheriff's office. He wasn't in again. A different deputy was on duty. Jose Lucero said he was helping during the fair, but he looked too young for the responsibility. He must have been told that before because as we walked to the cells, without a prompt, he said, "I'm older than I look."

The men were in good physical condition, but confinement frazzled them. I told them what I had done for their defense. Perry said Mr. Newcombe came by that morning to talk with them.

"Did he say anything about the warrant?"

Perry got up from his cot, "Yes, he said he 'spected the sheriff's office to git it by the end of the week."

"Today is Tuesday, so just a few more days." I hoped that would smooth their frayed nerves.

"That's four days!" said Cooper.

Earhart threw his hat onto his bunk. "I cain't take it much longer!"

Perry walked to the bars. "Does that mean they will release us, then?"

"What did Mr. Newcombe say?"

Perry wiped his hand across his mouth. "I was so happy to hear a date for the warrant that I forgot to ask him about our release."

I shook my head. They wouldn't like what I had to say, but they needed to prepare themselves. "Well, it's a murder charge — well, not for you, Mr. Earhart. They should release you soon." Perry and Cooper groaned at the realization they would be in longer. "You'll have to wait until the court convenes on October first so they can determine whether you are bail eligible, and then set the bail amount."

Perry and Cooper's expressions left no doubt to their fear, anger, and despair. They were still being held 'for their own protection', and after a brief discussion, Perry and Cooper told me, they would just leave. Perry called for the deputy to come let them out. I reminded them that when the sheriff swore the warrant, the law would come for them. "I thought you were tired of Rucker and John Good harassing your families." That calmed them.

Perry sighed, "I s'pose that's why I came in the first place."

Cooper said, "Yup." And Earhart nodded and sat hard onto the thin mattress.

After a few moments, I sent the deputy back to his desk, and they settled down.

"How is it going with your family?" asked Cooper.

I tried to smile. "Oh, just fine."

Earhart broke in, "I'll bet it's hard. Did they think you was dead?"

"Bill!" said Perry. "I'm sorry, Jesús. Bill wasn't thinkin'." He directed a scowl Earhart's way. "I know Oliver is hopin' for the best for you. Once we get outta here, I hope you'll stop in at the ranch and say howdy now and then." Perry sat on his cot. "Will they serve the warrants right away to us here?"

"I expect so. The fair might interfere, but it shouldn't."

I left Deputy Jose to twiddle his thumbs and rode at a walk back up the hill toward the Fountains' home. When I arrived at the stable, Mateo was nowhere to be found. I unsaddled Bella and gave her a quick brush before I released her to drink from the watering trough in the small corral.

As I left the stable, Mateo emerged from the back door of the adobe. He picked up a shovel that was against the wall. When he turned and saw me, he jumped in surprise. "Oh, señor Jesús, you *alarma* me."

I smiled, "Sorry Mateo, what is the shovel for?"

"What?" His eyes batted back and forth. "Oh, oh, this shovel?" He pushed it toward me. "Oh, this, this shovel … uh … this one … uh oh yes, um … the Colonel, he use it to dig for worms last night for fishing."

Before I could ask another question, he rushed off to the stable. Rosa had come to the door. She smiled sweetly. "Why are you back so soon?"

I explained that my new shoes had caused some blisters, and she said she would prepare a pan of hot water and Epsom salts for me to soak.

I went to the bedroom to find more comfortable shoes. When I opened the bedroom door, there was a crate next to my bed. The boards were nailed tight. I looked around to see if I could find something to pry open a slat. Tommy had left his Bowie knife beside his bed. I forced it under one edge of a slat and pried up and down several times until one end popped up. I moved it nearer to the window and opened the curtains. There was some clothing inside. I put my foot on the box and pulled off two adjacent boards. They were my clothes from six months ago. I pulled off the rest of the top boards and removed the shirts and pants. Bits of something flew off them. Underneath were my razor, shaving mug, and other things I had owned. I removed them and at the bottom of the crate were my pen and ink wells, junior bar association certificate, and my two journals. When I looked over my things more carefully, my shaving mug had dirt in it.

---

I still needed to find Albert Fall and give him Oliver's message. I didn't want to forget what he said and so I took the pen and ink well from the crate, drew a piece of paper from my bedroom desk and wrote what he had said. My feet, my left one in particular, hurt from the new shoes, and I decided to wait until the next day to find Mr. Fall.

After I wrote the note, I went back to the crate and removed everything. The clothes were of no use to me, and I tucked them under my arm and went to find Rosa to ask her where I should put them. She was on the *porche*, and Little Henry stood with his two little hands on Rosa's knee as he braced himself. I startled her when I appeared at the doorway, and the baby's face scrunched up with a hiccupy gasp prelude to a wail. Rosa smiled at me while she reached to pick up Little Henry. He calmed soon after she touched him and then he laughed as Rosa bounced him on her knee. She noticed me. "Oh, there you are. Your foot bath is ready. Can you watch the *bebé* while I get it?"

She moved Little Henry's hands to the half-barrel side table and motioned for me to sit where she had. Little Henry looked up at me. At first, I thought he would cry again, but his expression changed, and he broke into a toothy smile. He looked funny, and I laughed, which started him laughing and I had the feeling we both were remembering the times before my accident when I held him on my lap and made foolish faces.

She returned with the small tub and took Little Henry from me. "He seems to remember you."

"Yes, I think we had an awakening."

We chuckled and Rosa sat on the chair next to me with the baby on her lap. I soon realized that talking to each other side by side was awkward. I left my old clothes on the chair and moved the small tub in front of the chair across from her. When I had removed my shoes and stockings, I tested the water with my toe. It was too hot and so I settled back into my chair.

"Are those clothes from the crate?" she asked.

"Yes, they won't fit me. What should I do with them?"

"Yes, you've grown and changed. Your face is a little different as well." Rosa stared at my face as she spoke, which made me feel a little self-conscious. "It's no wonder no one recognized you while you were missing." She paused before putting Little Henry down so he could stand by supporting himself on the side table again. "I doubt they will fit Tommy or Jack, either. You can put them back in the crate and remove whatever else you want. Señora Fountain will take them and other things to the church. Father Lassaigne gives clothes we donate to the poor."

I nodded and tested the water again but withdrew my foot as I drew in my breath. My things in the crate came to mind. I wanted to ask why they buried them, even though I knew why. The need to lash out boiled to the surface, but I resisted. "Do you know why they buried my things next to the memorial stone?"

Rosa wetted her fingers and tried to flatten Little Henry's cowlick. "I think you should talk to the Colonel or your mother about that." The cowlick persisted, and she tried again as she said, "You don't talk about your family very much."

"They sent me away … and they didn't want me in the family. That much I *do* remember."

"It sounds complicated."

"No, it's not complicated at all, but from what I read in my journals today, I guess I had forgiven them."

"Are you not happy … were you not happy with the Fountains? It seemed to me you were."

"I think I was … but I was also happy with the Lees."

"Do you want to return to them?"

"No … Yes. I don't know. Everything is different. Is it me, them or …?" I threw my arms in the air in exasperation. "I can't figure it out."

"I think you will. You're the smartest person I know for your age, but don't you think it will take time?"

I looked into her dark eyes and saw a genuine concern for me. I grinned and nodded.

When it had cooled enough, I eased my aching feet into the soothing salt water. Little Henry's attempts at words were all that broke the silence, and I closed my eyes with the soothing douche. I could hear Rosa shushing Little Henry as he squirmed to get down. I opened my eyes as she stood him by the side table again. After a moment or two, he broke away to walk on his own, but Rosa stopped him and raised him onto her lap.

"I guess you have to watch him all the time," I observed.

"*Si*, it started a month or two ago. He's a fast crawler and now he wants to walk. It's time for his nap and I have some chores in the kitchen. You can leave the tub on the worktable when you finish."

After the water cooled, I rose and, barefooted, emptied the tub in the yard and brought it into the kitchen with my old clothes and new shoes under my arm. As I passed Zio and Mia Tia's room, I heard the rhythmic creak of the old rocking chair and Rosa's sweet voice as she coaxed Little Henry to sleep with a Mexican lullaby.

I resumed reading my journal and made some notes for a future entry, but soon grew drowsy and fell asleep. I don't know how long, but I dozed until I heard someone clear their throat.

Rosa was at the doorway with a tray of food. She used her ever present red bandana to tie back her raven hair at her nape. The filtered light from the window made her skin glisten from the effort of her evening chores.

"Thank you, Rosa. I hadn't heard anything for a while, so I assumed you had gone home."

"Oh, no. I still have the *bebé*. He should wake up from his nap soon. I was late putting him down."

"I ... I was wondering. How old are you?"

She grinned and tilted her head. There was something about the way she moved. I hadn't felt like that for a long while. "I am eighteen years old. Why do you ask?" The allure of her head turn and smile happened again as she brought the tray to my desk. My loins stirred.

It embarrassed me and I looked across the room toward Tommy's desk to avoid her eyes. "Oh, I don't know. I just thought you were older. When is your birthday?"

"It is funny, you ask. It is tomorrow, but I have never told the Fountains ... and yes, they have asked, but they have so many birthdays to celebrate. I didn't want them to make a fuss. Besides, I would have to make another *tres leche* cake!"

We laughed, and I bit into the sandwich she had made.

"Yum, you are a wonderful cook, Rosa."

"Well, not for much longer. I must leave to help my grandmother in Paso del Norte next month. She is losing her mind ..." she stopped, sensitive to my situation. "Oh, oh, I am sorry. She is old and ...." Her light olive cheeks turned rosy.

"No, no, it is alright. I'm sorry to hear that."

Rosa turned her head toward Mia Tia and Zio's bedroom before I heard anything. "I think he is awake. I better get him now because he tries to climb out of his crib."

While Rosa was gone, I returned to my journal. I was so glad that I had written so much because it helped me remember, but my insecurities puzzled me. It seemed my law work was all I was confident about.

I heard baby noises and turned to see Rosa in the doorway with Little Henry in her arms and I said, "Oh, hello. Uh, I can watch him if you want to go home."

She seemed uncertain. I picked up a lariat that was behind my desk. "I can tie a rope around me and him so he can't get away too far ..." Her eyes got as big as yucca pods, and she raised her hand to cover her open mouth. Before she could reply, I said, "I was joking. I would never do that, but seriously, I can watch him."

Rosa relaxed and grinned. "You *are* different, you know."

"Well, the bunkhouse cowboys joked like that a lot. I guess I picked it up from them."

"Is that all you learned?"

"I learned how to play poker."

She laughed again and put Little Henry down so he could stand. She held his hands above his head and 'walked' him over to me. "It is nice of you to offer to watch him, Jesús. I left some food in the larder for a snack for the Fountains and your folks when they return." She looked at me as I took Little Henry's hands from her, and he dropped into a sitting position on the tile floor. As I reached to pick him up, Rosa leaned over and kissed me on the forehead.

# 33: Airing Out

When Rosa had left, I said to myself, "I wonder what that meant," and then thought, *two years' difference in our ages? That's not so much.*

Little Henry and I played for a bit before I coaxed him to walk on his own, but he tottered after just a step or two and I had to catch him. I thought he deserved a treat for his efforts, so I brought him into the kitchen and tied him into his highchair with the tea towel. The larder held a Marlboro pie — one of Zio's favorites from his childhood — and I cut a small piece for each of us. Little Henry wouldn't open his mouth when I held a small spoonful in front of him, so I shifted my attention to my slice. When I glanced back after a couple of bites, the little man was shoving the custardy apple concoction into his mouth, but he missed with gusto and hearty laughs between swallows and licks of his lips.

When he finished, I returned our plates to the sink and washed the dishes. By the time I returned, he was fast asleep, and I carried him off to his crib.

Everyone returned home long after dark, full of excitement over the day's experiences. Tommy, Miguel, and Jack chatted about the baseball game. I overheard Tommy brag to Miguel that Larlo was an expert player. When I noticed them again, the three had gone outside to play catch in the moonlight.

The women were excited about canning techniques the Sisters of Loretto displayed and the impressive artwork that Maggie had submitted. Meanwhile, my father and Zio sat at the business end of the parlor, smoked cigars, and talked about the difference between U.S. and Mexican politics. They seemed to conclude that politics is politics, no matter the country.

Mia Tia asked where Rosa was, and I told her I sent her home. She said, "Well, she put Little Henry to bed with his face and shirt covered in Marlboro pie."

"Oh, no Mia Tia, that was me. A couple of hours ago, I told Rosa I would keep an eye on him. He fell asleep in his highchair after we each had a slice of pie. I guess I forgot to put his bib on. I didn't want to wake him, so I didn't wash his face before I put him down. Sorry."

My mother was there beside Mia Tia and they both laughed. Madre said, "Oh *mijo*, you will make a wonderful father." Before she had finished, I thought, *and Rosa will make a wonderful mother*.

Since my family did not speak English, the adobe was full of Spanish. Mia Tia remarked at how nice it was to hear the adobe filled with her native language, and it seemed to spark old memories for me. My journals helped as well, but whatever the reason, for the first time, I felt confident I would remember everything at some point.

Later, as everyone prepared for bed, I heard low voices in the kitchen. When I peeked around the doorway, I saw my mother sitting across from Mia Tia, each with a glass of milk. It was a familiar scene.

I went to the kitchen, poured myself a glass of the fresh milk and sat next to my mother. They welcomed me with a pat on my hands and then returned to their memories of their childhoods.

I listened with interest, but the image of the dirt in my shaving mug lingered. The thought that they had given up on me wouldn't disappear. After a bit, their conversation paused, and I said, "I saw the memorial stone. Why did you bury my things? Did you think

I was dead?" I turned to my mother. "And why did you come here?"

Their shocked expressions shouldn't have surprised me, but they did. My mother's brow wrinkled, and her eyes widened. "We came here for the fair and to see my sister and her family, yes, but also because we wanted to know ... to see for ourselves what happened ...." She looked away for an instant. "But of course, there was nothing to see. It has been a horrible six months. Angelina has gone to the post twice a day with our hope for word of your return. She has worn out two pairs of shoes."

Her words didn't comfort me. The pressure of trying to live between the Lees and Fountains was getting to me. At the time, it seemed my accident wasn't mine; that somehow what happened to me only happened to them.

She paused and looked at Mia Tia, who extended her arms. "You were ... just gone. When we realized you did not arrive at Luna Well, Albert and Mr. Van Patten looked for you for days. We offered a reward and Maggie created a handbill. Zio had hundreds of them printed and we put them up everywhere, but no one had seen you. Well, yes, there were false reports. An Indian reported a body in the White Sands, and Albert followed him there to determine if it was you." She paused and she and my mother 'crossed' themselves. "We questioned ourselves — whether you might have left because of something we did." Her hands went to her face.

My mother wiped a tear from her eye. "Now, we know why no one recognized you. You have grown and your face is ... is a little different ..."

Mia Tia interjected, "And the sketch we showed people of you that Marianita had drawn was before you had a beard." As an afterthought, she added, "And, as Marianita had said, the likeness was not what she had wanted."

My mother pointed at me. "You have changed a lot in appearance, my son, but you have also changed in your demeanor. You are stronger in your character."

Their words spelled out how my questions hurt them, but it was their facial expressions that conveyed the debilitating worry they carried. I felt ashamed I had doubted them. I didn't reply and sipped my milk as I thought about what they had said.

I knew I shouldn't have said anything when I sat with them, but I couldn't escape the feeling I had been ... abandoned? They hadn't said they thought I was dead, but they had erected the memorial stone. That thought relit my anger because, to me, it meant that they had given up on my return. The three of us sat quietly for a time. I finished my milk and took the glass to the washtub. As I turned to walk up the hallway, they resumed talking about their Mesilla home and brothers and sisters. It bothered me they could just move on so quickly from our discussion. I recognized it had been twenty years since they had seen each other. Still, their words and emotions stuck with me and their expressions said more than their words: They didn't want to admit it. They *had* believed I was dead.

It had been a busy day. I realized I was tired and walked up the hall toward my bedroom. I paused at the door to the boys' bedroom when I heard a muffled, "Damn them to hell." It sounded like it came from the office. I hadn't gone there since my return and, as I knocked on the door, I wondered if my desk was still there.

"Come in Jesús."

That startled and distracted me from dwelling on what had just transpired. I opened the door but stood just inside the impressive office. "How did you know it was me?"

"It's quite simple. None of my sons knock and when the girls knock, it's ever so faint. Rosa's knock has a certain rhythm to it and Mateo stands at the door and shouts '*señor* Fountain.'" He chuckled at the sight in his mind. "Mariana never comes here and visitors come to the parlor door. I don't recall you knocking before and so, when I didn't recognize your knock, I knew it must be you."

He motioned for me to sit in one of the two chairs that faced him, but then rose from his plush leather desk chair and came toward me with his arms spread. We embraced. "I'm so relieved to know you are OK."

There was that word 'OK' again. I had forgotten about it. I couldn't remember whether anyone else had used it, but the story came to me about how he picked it up in his youth from the Dutch immigrants in New York City.

We stepped back from each other, and I said, "There was a time when I wanted to give up hope."

"I can only imagine how frustrating it was. I trust the Lees treated you well?"

"Oh yes, Perhaps I *should* have died … and would have had Oliver not found me."

"Yes, I'm sure. On the story-hearth you said you were about to shoot a mountain sheep on the San Augustin. Perhaps you can tell me what on earth possessed you to do such a thing?"

"I can't remember all of it, but it had something to do with jealousy. Juan Luna had hired a young hand, and in Lucia's last letter, which I saw tucked in my journal, she seemed to favor him."

"Yes, that explains it … to a degree. Perhaps you thought a mountain sheep for the Lunas would restore Lucia's interest? Some of the lawyers talk about hunting them a lot. Maybe you overheard them and thought it would be an easy way to boost your credibility with Lucia."

"I should have known you would figure it out. Yes, your theory helped me remember. That was exactly it. And I had a good place to conceal myself with a nice ram in my sights when …"

"The mountain lion jumped you."

"Yes, and I fell and ... well, the rest, you know."

The Colonel flicked the ashes on his cigar into the ashtray. "I found the spot — the place where it happened."

"Oliver said that it looked as though Sinsin must have trampled the mountain lion." I hadn't thought about that before. "She probably saved my life ... also." The thought flashed that Sinsin's killing of the mountain lion reduced the importance of what the Lees did for me. "I thought she would have returned home, but she isn't in the stable."

"No, she didn't come home." He took a puff on his cigar. "I imagine she was so spooked that she ran off through the cactus and brush and ripped her hide to where she either bled to death or a predator got her. We found her over on the Lucero's Ranch. Wasn't much left of her, and the saddle was gone."

She was such a great horse, and I felt responsible. "It never occurred to me that she wouldn't make it back home." My voice cracked a little. "I'm sorry. I'll pay to replace her."

Zio discounted my offer with the wave of his hand and I sat with a memory of Sinsin.

Speaking of payments reminded me of my bank account. "Why continue to deposit my earnings into my account at the bank? I went there today, and the teller said the deposits were on the first of the month right along, just as you had ... before. I know you all thought I was dead, so why?"

Zio crushed the cigar stub and leaned back in his chair. "I was responsible for you. I promised your parents I would see to your safety and I ... uh ... well, it appeared that I had failed. The money in your name — your wages — was to be given to your folks when they went back home. I knew it wouldn't make up for .... Well, anyway, it's yours now. I see you used some of it to get some new clothes."

"Why does Oliver hate you so much?"

"He does?"

"Yes, he and Perry, Oliver's half-brother, say you're a part of the Santa Fe Ring. Are you?"

"What do you think?" Eyebrows raised, he waited for a moment, but I was afraid to say anything. "Do you remember when I told you about the Republican Territorial Convention two years ago when I battled it out with Catron and his men over the nomination of Wil Rynerson for our U.S. House seat?"

"Vaguely."

"People equate the Santa Fe Ring with all Republican politicians, but the Ring's shenanigans aren't tolerated down here. How about the San Marcial Ring? Do you remember that one? We had the final hearing with that rat Mullen. Now, *he* was connected to the Santa Fe Ring."

"Can't you see how it looks, though? George McDonald gets killed and there's no action, but when Walter Good was killed, there are indictments and arrests. The difference I see is that Good's foreman is a deputy and Good works for Mr. Catron."

Zio shifted in his chair and picked up another cigar from his drawer. "Has your accident affected your law sense? Surely you realize that there were no eyewitnesses to McDonald's death, but there has been to the accused murder of Walter Good."

"Wait, what?"

"Ed King has come forward and testified before the grand jury that he was at the Altman's homestead and witnessed the murder of Walter Good."

"Ed? Not negro Ed?" Regardless of what Zio said, I knew Ed would not have come forward. I was convinced John Good and Deputy Rucker had captured and coerced him.

"The very same."

As I lay in my bed later that night, there was a lot to consider. I accepted my families had thought that I had left them or died. How could they have thought otherwise? What hope could there have been?

It was Ed's apparent testimony that dumbfounded me. He would never do that, even if he witnessed what they said. I racked my brain to remember if Ed was at the Altmans' that day.

# 34: Fall for What?

I continued to doubt Zio's news about Ed King. I didn't know him as well as Eph because Oliver had sent him to work for the Altman's and to keep an eye on the Graham's place. Ed might have been at the Altman's, but if Good's accusations were true and Ed saw what Good and Rucker claimed, then I just couldn't believe that Ed would sell the Lee clan 'down the river'.

As I considered why Ed might do such a thing, I recalled Zio's profane declaration as I stood in the hallway. It reminded me of the reactions Zio had over the lack of payment by the New Mexico Attorney General for his services as a special assistant district attorney. I wondered if they still weren't paying him.

---

**September 19**

The next morning, I begged off attending the fair again with the excuse that my feet still hurt. That disappointed my parents, but I promised to join them for the midday meal at Wil Rynerson's Mesilla Park project.

My first stop was the sheriff's office to check on Perry and the others. They were fine, although growing ever more impatient. From there, I stopped at the offices of Newcombe and McFie. Judge McFie confirmed that Mr. Reynolds had come by, but Oliver's banker had already confirmed by telegram that he would wire the required money and notify Oliver.

I needed to go to the telegraph office, but I remembered that day was Rosa's birthday and stopped at Lohman's to buy her a gift. Mrs. Lohman welcomed me back to their store and asked me to call her Aminda. She showed me a few things, then asked, "Is this for someone special?"

At first, I didn't get her meaning, and she clarified, "Are you courting this woman?"

"Oh, no, no, ... she is special to me in that she works for the Fountains, and she looks after my domestic needs."

Aminda leaned close to me and said, "You mean Rosa? You could do a lot worse; you know. How much did you want to spend?"

I showed her the change I had gotten when I bought my clothes the previous day. "That's all I have right now."

"Well, you work for the Colonel, am I right? We could set up an account for you."

The offer surprised me. I hadn't decided whether I would continue to work for Zio. After a few seconds of indecision, I agreed, but only if the cost of the gift exceeded what I had in my pocket.

Aminda looked around the store in thought, and then said, "Rosa comes to us often on behalf of the Fountains. She is a delightful girl." Aminda's eyebrows shot up as she thought of a suitable gift. She strode off toward a case in the back of the store as I struggled to keep up. She flipped open the counter pass-through and said, "I have just the thing. We got these French scarfs in last week; I think Numa must have ordered them before we bought him out. I doubt the ladies here will buy them to be worn as they do in Paris." She reached into a case and pulled out a small crate. "I haven't had a chance to put any on display yet. They are made with the finest French silk." She took one from the box and unfolded it on the counter. It was beautiful.

"Why don't you think the ladies here will wear them?"

"Well, they aren't in style here. Rosa wears a common cotton red bandana in her hair." She mimicked how the women wore their bandanas. "Now one of these can be worn in many other ways," she pointed to the one she unboxed, "although not this one because its colors wouldn't befit her."

The one she spread out had a black background with red roses intertwined throughout. Aminda rummaged through the crate and found a yellow one, which she lay folded on the counter. Something about the color reminded me of Lucia, and emotion threatened to overtake me. I turned away and dabbed at the corners of my eyes with my handkerchief.

"Oh, I'm sorry. Did I say something that saddened you?" she asked.

"No." I turned back, took a deep breath and said, "It's just that something reminded me of ... of a dear friend."

"Was it Lucia Luna?" Aminda's face expressed her regret that she had mentioned her name. "I'm sorry. We hear everything here and ... well, all I can say is I'm very sorry ... uh ... about all of it."

"It's alright. Her loss hadn't hit me fully yet ... and it caught me by surprise, just then. New things come to me all the time now, but the emotions don't always accompany the memories. It's difficult to describe."

Aminda put her hand over mine on the counter. "It's understandable. I once knew someone that had a head injury. He was never the same ... but you seem to come out of it fine."

"Thank you, Aminda. By the way, I don't mean to tarnish my relationship with Lucia with the purchase of Rosa's gift. As painful as it would be, I wish I could feel the emotions I felt for Lucia from before my accident."

"Perhaps I overstated my empathy. I can't say that I understand," said Aminda, "but I will say that perhaps the accident has spared you considerable grief and you shouldn't feel as though you have shamed Lucia's soul by doing that. There is plenty of grief in our lives out here, so don't let your purchase bother you." She unfolded the yellow scarf. It had an exquisitely faint floral display at each of the corners. "I think Rosa would be beautiful in this — not that that matters to you." She winked at me. "And because it is larger than her red bandana, she could wear it in far more ways."

The price was more than I had, so she opened an account and then wrapped the gift in butcher paper, tied it with twine. I glanced at the wall clock. The time had passed quicker than I expected. *How might I find Mr. Fall's office?* I considered asking Aminda, but realized my question wouldn't remain with her. The last thing I needed was suspicions about my loyalty to the Republicans. It was enough to have seemingly hordes of people tell me they thought I was dead.

I left with my purchase and walked down the street to the north before crossing to the Democrats' side of Main Street. I came to a barbershop with a sign that read:

### Albert Ellis

### Fashionable Barber

### Hot and cold baths

The name seemed familiar, but I couldn't quite place it. Regardless, I thought, a Democrat barber will know where Mr. Fall's office is.

As I entered the shop, a negro boy asked for my hat, which he took outside and vigorously brushed. When he finished, he returned and handed it to me. I accepted it and turned toward the barber, but he moved with me. I didn't know why and so I sidestepped him and went to introduce myself to the barber. The boy walked alongside and then stood next to me. He stared me at me as I tried to focus on the barber, also a negro, who was lathering a customer's face. When the barber saw me, his expression changed. He stopped me as I began to introduce myself and placed a towel over the customer's face. The barber said, "Mista Messi, here for your bath this mornin'?" He nodded to me as he spoke, and I got his cue.

"Yes, uh yes, that's why I'm here."

"Good then" He looked at the boy and said, "Now Freedom, get on over here and shave this gentleman while I show Mista Messi where his bath is. You'll get your penny tip for dustin' his hat when he pays for the bath." Albert Ellis walked past Freedom and motioned for me to follow him into the back room.

"What you doin' here, boy?" he whisper-shouted at me. "Don't you know you cain't be on this side of this here street?"

"Do I know you Mr. Ellis?"

"What you want? I ain't got no time … don't you know that if'n you seen here, I'm gonna have big trouble?" He winced and threw down his hands in alarm.

"I'm sorry. I guess you remember me, but I don't remember you. Can you direct me to Albert Fall's office?"

I thought Mr. Ellis would have a conniption. "He's upstairs from that new stationery store at the end o' the block. Now, for both our sakes, go out the back door and don't never come back, hear?"

I pulled a penny from my pocket and handed it to him. "For Freedom."

I walked down the alley, which, given what Mr. Ellis had said, seemed the prudent choice. Soon, I came to the cross street and then walked out to Main Street and entered the corner stationery store. I paused just inside the front door to take in my surroundings. There was a staircase that paralleled the outside wall

I had just walked past. A sign hung on the wall opposite the first step that read:

### Albert Fall
### Attorney-at-Law

Underneath the sign was an arrow that pointed up the stairs. I climbed the stairs two at a time. At the top was an empty desk. There was a door. Just before I knocked, I heard voices on the other side. A man's voice said, "We think you're the man to beat Fountain. If you won't run now, we'll have to put you at the bottom of the list for the future. Now is the time."

Then the other voice, also a man's, said, "I don't have time now. I've got to get my family here and can't do that until my businesses are stable. Then I need to get my Bar membership in order."

"I'm telling you, it's now or never. You're a newcomer and Fountain has nothing on you but give him another two years and he'll make you look like you arrived in Las Cruces ahead of the law."

I knocked.

"Yes, enter if you must," said the voice in a twangy accent.

I opened the door, and a man smoking a cigar sat behind a huge ornate desk. He said, "Who are you? I thought you were my secretary. Where the devil is that woman?"

"I, uh, don't know, sir. No one was at the desk there." I pointed behind me.

"Oh darnation. That's the second one this week. Isn't there anyone in this town that wants to work for a livin'?"

"I don't know, sir."

"What's that in your hand, boy?" He rose from his chair and started toward me.

"Oh, this sir?" I held up the package for Rosa. "Oh, no sir, this isn't for you."

"Then what the devil do you want? Can't you see I'm busy?"

"Uh, yes sir. Uh, you are Albert Fall, correct?"

"Who wants to know?"

"Well sir, I have a message for Mr. Fall from Oliver Lee."

"Who?" His head bobbed and then he glanced around the room. That seemed his way of remembering something. "Oh, yes, that Texas rancher over in the Tularosa. Met him at W.W. Cox's Ranch. A right smart young man. Well, spit it out boy, I haven't got all day you know. Yes, I'm Fall."

"Well sir," I unfolded the slip of paper with what Oliver wanted me to say and read it. "Oliver says that he wants to thank you for your referrals to the lawyers and that he would be in touch with you soon."

"That's all?" he snarled.

"Well, yes sir, he told me it was important to tell you that and I promised I would."

Fall shook his head and flicked cigar ashes on the floor. "Alright then. If that's all, go on about your business and close the door ... oh wait." He reached down beside his desk and picked up a signboard and pushed it toward me. "Hang this on the wall downstairs on your way out, if you would."

I took the sign and hung it where the dust ghosts suggested it had hung before. The sign read:

**Wanted:**
**Secretary**
**Inquire Within**

I walked out the door and crossed to the west side of the street. The afternoon sun usually brought a more vivid view of the Organ Mountains. Every pinnacle, needle, canyon, gorge, escarpment, outcrop, and ledge seemed visible in that light. On this afternoon, clouds masked the midsection of the ragged peaks as the spires jutted through the puffy layer. I admired them for a few minutes until a well-dressed man said as he passed, "What's a matter sonny, ain't you never seen mountains afore?"

# 35: Rosa

I took the shuttle train from the depot to meet the Fountains and Messis for lunch at Mesilla Park. As I approached, I could hear them conversing in Spanish. Maggie saw the butcher paper wrapped package that protruded from my pocket and asked what it was.

Rosa didn't want the attention. I wasn't sure what to do. I must have paused too long because my father sensed the situation. In Spanish he said, "Perhaps it is a thank you gift for the people that saved his life — it was the Lees — am I correct?"

I nodded, hoping I had squelched any talk about the Lees, but I was more relieved that I didn't have to reveal what Rosa's birthday gift was. Besides, I sensed that a birthday celebration just between the two of us could be romantic. I wondered if she felt the same.

As in the previous year, the food at the Mesilla Park Fair exhibit was excellent and the ice cream was even better. I remembered how Lucia and I furtively brushed our hands together and risked an occasional covert eye lock. Even so, the love I must have had for her didn't return, and a sense of guilt flooded over me.

My expression must have shown some discomfort because my mother asked, "Do your feet still bother you?"

"Well, yes, but I'm wearing my cowboy boots today. They fit me like a glove. I still have a couple of blisters from the new shoes, but I think I can join you all for a while."

We returned by the shuttle train to the depot and walked the short distance to the fairgrounds to the west. As we toured the exhibition hall again, we came to the Democrats booth. The man I had seen in Mr. Fall's office was there. Zio bantered with the men that sat behind a table piled high with their handbills and copies of the *Mesilla Valley Democrat*. Zio could engage his adversaries in raillery that left both sides with smiles or even hearty laugh, but later, on further reflection, his political opponents would realize just how cutting his remarks were.

I tried my best to stand back away from the booth so that the man I had seen in Fall's office wouldn't recognize me. I wasn't sure I had succeeded. It seemed prudent to let Zio know.

As Zio led us down the aisle toward the minerals displays, I caught up with him and whispered that I needed to chat with him alone. When the rest of the family had passed to gather round the judges, I said, "That man that sat at the center of the Democrat's table … I saw him this morning in Albert Fall's office."

"Albert Fall's office. Why were you there?"

"I promised Oliver Lee I would deliver a message to him."

"I see." He looked back toward the Democrat's booth. "The man at the Democrat's booth is Thomas Bull. He's taken to calling himself T.J. Bull. He runs things for the Democrats now." Then, he turned to look at Mr. Bull, and said, as though thinking aloud, "So, he is talking to Fall." He touched his finger to his lips, then said, "Did you hear what they said?"

I had a fleeting sense of disloyalty to Oliver. "Yes, Bull asked him … no, he pled with Fall to run against you. He told him that now was his best chance because if you got to know him in the next two years, you would use all you knew about Fall to defeat him."

Zio snickered. "Well, if that isn't the pot calling the kettle black …." He looked back toward the Democrats' booth and said, "I'm glad you let me know, but Fall's a neophyte and he won't have a chance against me if he runs.

Zio turned to join the family, but I stopped him. "One other thing, when I was in Mr. McFie's office, he told me that Newcombe would handle the Walter Good murder case because he handled all the cases for Democrats." Zio nodded.

Then, as an afterthought, "Why don't you have a partner that is a Democrat? He seemed to say that all the lawyers had paired-up that way."

He took off his hat and ran his hand through his hair. "With politics and how we run our governments, I am a Republican. There can be no doubt. However, for prosecutions, as an assistant district attorney, I feel that politics are extraneous to guilt or innocence and therefore, it should be so in my private practice as well. Often people that come to me for help don't come because of my party affiliation but because they have seen or heard of my courtroom successes."

I nodded slowly as I parsed what he said. When he could see I understood, he continued. "I'm not sure you would have asked me that question six months ago." He pursed his lips and looked away. When he turned back, he said, "Jesús, I need you to come back to work again. Tommy's heart isn't in the work. With the election coming up, I've reduced my cases, but we still have lots of contracts and wills and you can screen new clients, so I don't take up my time with that. I need you, Jesús."

How could I deny him? But my loyalties were jumbled. "I know I owe you for my law experience, but I owe Oliver my life. If I work for you again, it seems like that would be disloyal to him." At once I regretted what I had said, and I looked away from his stare. He just walked away toward the family, who by now had entered the needlework room.

I stood in the middle of the aisle alone. I wondered if I could coexist between these two men.

For the rest of the afternoon, I trod along with the others, quiet with my thorny thoughts. The Messis and Fountains had gotten to know each other better. As they made up for lost time, they were oblivious to my moods.

They all stayed for one of the tournament baseball games, and I thought it best if I left them to have their fun. As they looked for a bit to eat, I begged off with my painful feet complaint again. Besides, I wanted to have as much time alone with Rosa as I could.

When I reached the Fountain home, I entered without a knock and found Rosa asleep with Little Henry on a bed in the girls' room. Despite my desire to lie down next her, I realized we shouldn't be alone in the house. So, I pushed myself to go to the kitchen for a drink and left Rosa's gift on the kitchen worktable. I wrote a note across the butcher paper wrapping that read, "Happy Birthday, Rosa." After making a fresh pitcher of lemonade, I brought my journals out onto the *porche* to read. When the front door opened, it startled me. Rosa stood in the doorway with Little Henry on her hip and the scarf in her hand.

"Jesús, you didn't need to …"

I interrupted her. "I know. It's just that you've done so much for me, and I've done hardly anything for you. Come and sit. I need to refresh my drink, and I'll get one for you as well."

She tried to take my glass from the table next to my chair, but I snatched it before she could reach it. I gave her a stern look. "It's your birthday, and this is my treat. You just sit and entertain Little Henry."

I found some wine and poured us each a mixture of the wine and lemonade. It reminded me of the pleasant visits I had had with Fabián Garcia and his grandmother.

When I returned to the *porche*, Little Henry was in my chair. I put the two drinks on the side table between Rosa and me, picked up Little Henry, and put him on my lap as I sat. He looked at me and laughed.

Rosa straightened his clothes. "He is a happy baby."

"I remember him as not so happy." I grinned.

"Oh, yes, those were tough days, but when you visited your family in Mexico, we got his colic under control, and he has been all smiles since."

I nodded, and we sipped our drinks as I played with him. She rose and excused herself while promising to come right back.

When she returned from the adobe, she had replaced the red bandana with the scarf I purchased. Mrs. Lohman was right; she was beautiful in it. The scarf was long enough that its ends draped over her lean, but strong shoulders. The color complemented the plain blue dress she wore. She pranced around and twirled to show it off and I said, "You are beautiful, Rosa."

She held out the ends of the scarf that draped over her shoulders. "I know. I just love the color and the length."

"No, I mean *you. You* are beautiful. The scarf only magnifies your best features."

Rosa smiled and blushed a little, then turned her attention to Little Henry, who acted as though he might want to walk. I put him down, but he just stood next to me, one hand on my knee for support.

"Yesterday, you said your family sent you away. I don't understand why they would do such a thing."

"It's still a bit hazy, but I remember I couldn't do any of the work on our farm, but I'm not sure why they sent me away. I spent all my time with books."

"You were much smaller, then. Perhaps you were too small to do the work. I mean, when you first came here — gosh, it seems so long ago, but it was just what, two years ago?"

"Yes, two years the first week of this month. Your comment reminds me; yes, that was the reason. I didn't feel a part of my family." I paused as I tried to pull the memories from my head. "Yes, a lot has happened since." I tickled Little Henry, and he giggled and put out his arms for me to hold him. I returned him to my lap. "The simple answer is they didn't want me. At least, that was how I felt. I didn't even say goodbye to them."

"Why doesn't your brother, Miguel, is it?" I nodded. "Why doesn't he talk to you?"

"Oh, he told me he was glad I was back. As I recall, he always teased me about how small and weak I was — he and my oldest brother."

"Well, you surely aren't *that* anymore."

That was good to hear. I knew I had grown and gotten much stronger from the ranch work, but hearing it from someone else … well, it reinforced the good experience I had at Lee Well.

The late afternoon September sun waned from the fiery days of June, July, and August. The shift in the weather seemed to lift the spirits of plant and animal, alike; perhaps not unlike their emergence from the cold winters of the north. The blustery winds of spring were behind us as well and the glorious, albeit not as colorful as some locales, harvest time had arrived. It was still monsoon season, but as often happened, the clouds would pile up and drop all their moisture on the northwestern side of the Robledo Mountains, skip Las Cruces, then do the same on the west side of the Organs. It was dry and not even an occasional cloudburst could pry loose the drought's talons that clenched both valleys for years.

I gazed over the bluish, then orangish tinged Organs and thought about Rosa. She knew me so well. I felt some guilt because I couldn't remember thinking of her as anything but the hired help. Meanwhile, she played simple hand games with Little Henry. Our eyes met. "It's such a wonderful time of year to be here on the *porche* with you Rosa." We smiled at each other, and Little Henry made 'goo-goo, gah-gah' sounds and laughed at himself, which caused the two of us to chuckle, also.

I rarely felt that any of the people in my life could understand what I was going through … and how could they? I was so confused. The slightest misspeak left me feeling alone and angry. At least, Rosa tried.

I looked back to the Organs and said, "Things seem so different from before — from the little I can remember."

"Not much has changed since your accident. Perhaps you are thinking about what things were like when you first arrived here." Little Henry pulled at the top of her dress, and she feigned pulling his shirt down while she removed his hand from her breast. "Were the Lees good to you?"

"Oliver saved my life."

"Yes, I know, but did they treat you like family, the way the Fountains do here?"

"I don't know. Oliver and I were the only males … that is, if I was a part of the family, so …" I wagged my head back and forth a few times in indecision. "I guess that everyone that worked for the Lee's felt like they were a part of the family, to a degree, just as I imagine you feel that way toward the Fountains."

She smiled. "Yes, yes I do, to a degree, as you say."

Little Henry wanted down and so I stood him up and put his hand back on my knee. He let go a time or two as I thought further about Rosa's question.

"I had to earn my keep, and they expected me to take on a man's responsibilities. I learned what it was to have people depend on you."

"Hmm."

"I guess that doesn't sound like I was family to you, but things are different there. It's a wild country and a man's commitments are as serious as life and death."

"Oh look, look, he's walking."

Little Henry wobbled across the flagstone. He stopped once midway before reaching for Rosa's skirt and falling, exhausted, to his knees. He looked back at me and laughed. Rosa hoisted him to her lap and brought her wine and lemonade drink to his lips for a sip. "He's such a different baby than he was those first several weeks." She shifted him in her lap. "Will the family be coming back for supper tonight? If so, I need to start it."

"I think they will stay for the ballgame and get something at the fair. The Las Cruces team is playing."

Rosa crossed her legs. "I'm surprised Larlo didn't come back for it." Little Henry reached for her glass, and she gave him another sip. "This will knock him out for his nap." We chuckled.

Little Henry pestered Rosa for more to drink while we sat in silence. She resisted his attempts without harsh words or pushing him away.

"We missed you very much, you know," she murmured.

"I suppose I do."

"That's an odd comment." Her tone alarmed Little Henry and his babyish face screwed up to prepare for a wail. She picked him up and patted him as she cooed in his ear. While Rosa's expression let me know I had hurt her feelings, Little Henry looked at me and smiled as a tear dribbled down his cheek and across his lips. I wanted to smile at him. I knew Rosa needed an explanation, but I couldn't seem to come up with the right words.

With Little Henry recomposed, Rosa said, "You don't know what it was like." She told me how the family remained hopeful despite Zio's own withdrawn behavior and Sinsin's failure to return. The constant questions from family and friends about whether there had been any word or sign wore on them all. Rosa said people peppered her with questions when she went to the grocer and butcher. "In July, we got a letter from your mother that said they wanted to come for the fair, although it seemed you wouldn't be here. She also wrote that they wanted to understand for themselves; that it didn't seem real without seeing where your accident had happened. The day before you appeared, Zio rented a carriage, and we all rode up to the spot where you ..." her voice cracked and faltered.

I looked to the east, where orangish hues tinged the Organ Mountains. "I'm sorry. It's my selfish nature, I guess."

Rosa took her handkerchief from her sleeve and dabbed at the corners of her eyes. "I don't think I could ever think of you as selfish. I've never known you to make anything about yourself. Even now, you feel remorse because you couldn't feel what we felt. But who could?" Little Henry fussed, and she touched the glass to his lips without a sip, which quieted him. "When you find out how others feel about things that involved you, you don't accuse them for their words or actions. No, Jesús, I think the problem is you think too little of yourself."

She paused for a sip of her drink. My thoughts went to the previous night and my outburst with my mother and Mia Tia.

*If she had seen that, she might not be so complimentary. Perhaps she doesn't know me as well as she thinks.*

"We all think well of you, and I imagine the Lees did as well. I have heard your mother tell Mia Tia that the work on their farm is all-consuming and that they couldn't give you the attention you should have had. But they realize that is in the past and your future is here with the Fountains."

That puzzled me. "That's odd, because just yesterday she suggested I come home with them and avoid all this." I sat up in my chair and swept my arms wide apart. "Sometimes I think I've decided and then something happens and I'm back to questioning myself."

"But Jesús, I think you make it about who wants you. We all want you. If you go back to the Lees, you will be a cowboy and maybe someday a rancher. If you go home with your folks, you'll be a farmhand and someday, maybe, you will own a farm. Would you rather have either of those lives over the life that the Colonel has offered you? You are a smart man and yes, you could buy a lot of books and read all the papers and maybe become active in politics, but it won't be like the life you would have in a community like Las Cruces."

"I have thought about all that, but what about the debts I owe to people that have helped me?"

"Your biggest debt is to yourself. For me, I could do much better than this job for the Fountains. Other work has been offered to me. Despite how I feel about the dangers the Colonel is exposed to, I stay with them because this family is ... oh, what is the word ... *estimulante*. I enjoy them and they appreciate me. I've learned so much and my world is much bigger than if I was a chambermaid at the Commercial Hotel or a clerk at Lohman's. But the possibilities for me don't compare to what you can achieve."

She surprised me with how well she understood her situation. The mention of Zio and the threats against him reminded me of the time he crashed in the blizzard and Rosa was beside herself with fear for his fate.

I paused as Little Henry attempted to attach himself to her breast. Rosa got up and deftly pulled his hand away. "He's tired."

I walked with her to Zio and Mia Tia's bedroom and waited at the door while she placed the baby in his crib. When she turned, Little Henry had pulled her dress down so her bodice and the hint of a well-rounded breast were revealed. She covered herself with the flick of her hand at the back of the garment. Her movements proved her embarrassment, and she turned to me and whispered, "He still doesn't understand that I have no milk for him."

When she emerged from the bedroom, we returned to the kitchen to refill our glasses, but there was not enough in the pitcher for the two of us.

I put my glass in the washbasin. "You go ahead, you should have it; it's your birthday."

Rosa cocked her head in the way I found so attractive. "No, I want to share it. I'll share my glass with you."

It was a small gesture, but an intimate one nonetheless, and I smiled as I realized she had feelings for me, too.

We returned to the *porche* and as we sat, I asked if Zio had gotten any more death threats.

"If he has, they have not been through me, *gracias a Dios*."

I nodded. "He seems ... I'm not sure of the word ... detached, maybe?"

"It's the campaign, I think. Politics this year are dirtier than ever, and the other side has made nastier accusations than usual. That and without his usual load of cases, finances might be tight, but I do not know that for certain. All I know is what I hear from the women. You realize that none of what I have told you leaves this house, right?"

I nodded. "Do you know when my family intends to leave?"

"I think the day after tomorrow, but you should ask them."

"Yes, I suppose I should. So, I doubt they will want to go back to the fair tomorrow. They have probably seen everything by now."

"They might want to go to the rodeo tomorrow evening. I think Miguel said something about that. Maybe all you men could go fishing tomorrow morning?"

"That sounds like a wonderful idea, and it would give me a chance to spend some time with my brother and papa."

# 36: Dripping Springs

**September 20, 1888**

The next morning, all the men except me jumped into the wagon and Zio drove us to the Rio Grande. I rode Ol' Nasty because I needed to stop at the jail on the way back. It had been a dry year, and the river was low. We set up on a sandbar that projected into the channel. In some of the shallowest places, the water's surface roiled and dorsal fins flashed as they fought to get to deeper water.

We cast our lines, but soon, Tommy — oh, he of little patience — was chasing the fish trapped in the shallows. Miguel and Jack had joined him when they saw how much fun Tommy had. My father, Zio and I peered over the glistening water as we sat on the sandy bank.

"I don't suppose we'll catch any fish with that ruckus," said Zio in Spanish.

Father and I nodded as we watched Tommy and the others make fools of themselves as they tried to corral and pick up the fish.

My father turned to me. "I know we have talked about this before, my son, but you might not remember." He sat next to me with Zio on the other side of him. Zio feigned disinterest as he seemed to focus on his bobber amongst the rippled flashes of reflected light. "I don't mind telling you this again and I will do it yet again if I must, although I hope this will be the last time." He paused and pushed some sand with the sole of his shoe toward the river. He gazed across the water. "We never meant to hurt you when we sent you to live with your Mia Tia and Zio." He looked at me. "I love that name — Zio — by the way." He chuckled for a moment, remembering the influence his Italian heritage had on the Spang-lian mixture of Spanish and Italian in our house.

He put his hand on my leg. "You are my son." I remembered I had questioned that. "You should have no doubt about that. Your mother told me she said you could come back to live with us, but the reasons we sent you here haven't changed. We are thankful that your Zio has scared away the railroad and our government. However, there still is not enough land to bequeath to you and your brothers." He pulled his hand from my leg and bowed his head, but then looked at me. "But I should not despair because, this," and he motioned to Zio, "has been better for you than we could have imagined. To us, your disappearance isn't what it was for the Fountain family — not that we didn't ... mourn you — we did, but you had been gone for almost two years." He frowned and put his hand over his mouth. He moved his hand enough to say, "I'm not saying it right. I don't want it to sound like we didn't care."

Zio patted him on the shoulder. "I think Jesús understands ..." Zio looked at me. "Don't you?"

I nodded, but deep down, there were sour feelings that wouldn't go away. My father held something against me. I knew it and he could say what he liked, but words pale to actions.

My father pulled his hands away. "We just work so hard. I always worry we will not have enough. We didn't have time ... I know it sounds insensitive ...." His voice trailed off, and he gazed out over the sparkling water.

Zio bobbed his head up and down as he tried to avoid the glare that obscured his bobber. We sat for a moment, each with his own thoughts.

*I forgive you, papa.* I thought it but didn't say it because I sensed I couldn't remember all that happened to me back in Mexico.

The commotion from the shallows subsided, and I looked to see why. Miguel was running toward us with a good-sized fish in his hands. His eyes were on me and the essence of the memories of his and Jacinto's mocks and taunts flooded over me in a split second. With those times in mind, I expected he was about to embarrass me somehow. Strange as it may seem, I hoped he would. The negative thoughts of his orneriness cleared and memories of my brothers lovingly teasing each other filled my mind. I was jealous then. I smiled because I sensed I was about to be privileged with the brotherly love I had craved for so long.

Miguel laughed, and I closed my eyes, but he knocked my hat off and swept past me. Instead, he knocked off Papa's hat with a swipe and rubbed the slimy catfish into his hair. I recognized there was no expression of scorn or ridicule on Miguel's face, and my father laughed. Instead, it was one of joyful mischief, but it hurt. Miguel dropped the fish next to me, then ran back to the shallows. Everyone laughed except me.

*Was it jealousy or something else?*

On the way back to the Fountains, I stopped at the jail to check on Perry, Cooper, and Earhart. As I entered the sheriff's office, a racket erupted from their cells and the deputy on duty rolled his eyes when I asked how they were doing. Perry and Cooper voiced their anger that the court had appointed someone they did not know to look after their ranches. I had no explanation. As I rode to the Fountains, I racked my brain for something more I could do for them.

When I got back to the Fountains, I asked Zio why the court appointed ranch managers unknown to the accused, but he shrugged and said he had no say in those matters. I tried to put that and my brother's snub aside so I could spend the rest of the day enjoying my family.

The women had put together a picnic. Mia Tia, my mother, sister Angelina, Maggie, Katie, and Little Henry were poised to make the ten-mile jaunt to Dripping Springs, a favorite picnic spot in the foothills of the Organ Mountains.

The men had horses, while the women and Little Henry got into Zio's rented four-seater. Maggie drove and Mia Tia and my mother sat in the back seat. Rosa had brought Little Henry out along with his accouterment of extra nappies, toys, and other items, which she put in the small storage area behind the back seat, along with the picnic baskets and blankets.

I sat on Ol' Nasty behind the carriage. After Rosa loaded the last of the things we would need, she turned to me with a forlorn look.

I had a thought. "Can't Rosa come to? I can put Angelina in front of me and Rosa could hold Little Henry."

Rosa's eyes brightened. "No, no. That's alright, I have plenty to do here while you are gone."

Mia Tia said, "No, I think Jesús is right. Angelina can't hold Little Henry, and my sister and I will have to put Katie between us in the back seat. Besides, Little Henry always behaves better when Rosa is with him."

The men arrived before the ladies and we 'staked out' a spot near the giant rock overhang where a man locals referred to as *El Ermitano* lived twenty years before. Although it had a been a dry year, it was still monsoon season and thunderstorms near the mountain were always a threat. The rock shelter, which many people referred to as a cave, thus *La Cueva*, had provided shelter for many years, as evidenced by pottery shards, arrowheads and rock chippings, and other material people often left behind.

When the women arrived and we had spread our blankets and placed the picnic baskets, Zio suggested the men accompany him on a walk up to the Dripping Springs. It was an easy, although uphill, walk for a couple of miles. We tramped single file on the narrow trail as it serpentined through several kinds of high desert vegetation. I wondered if every trail turned gently back and forth like that until someone cleared a direct path. I remembered other paths that layout in elongated esses. Zio was behind me. I turned and asked if he had noticed it as well.

"Yes, I have. I came across an old trapper once back in California that told me that if you don't have a landmark to aim at, you'll walk in circles. I think a trail like this confirms what he told me. People walk and look around, then look up to their destination and must correct their direction."

That made sense to me. As we continued through waist high side-oats grama grasses and flowering coreopsis with an occasional live oak and desert willow, I wanted to test the theory out for myself. I considered closing my eyes and walking for a distance, but I was afraid someone would stop in front of me, or I would wander off the path and the others would question me.

The mountains got more rain than we did in the valley and yet, all kinds of cacti dotted the area amongst the other plants. As we rose higher and higher, juniper and pinion trees, along with various shrubs, teemed with wildlife. Deer grazed in a meadow to our right as the path bordered a brushy area along the nascent arroyo. As we neared the gorge where the spring emerged, sage, desert willow, and scrub and live oak formed thickets. Along the way, we had to duck under branches.

Zio said, "We should have brought a hand axe with us to maintain the trail."

As we approached the rocky box canyon terminus, it reminded me of the place where Oliver and I had buried George McDonald. A modest waterfall fell from above us onto the rocks, where it sheeted into a humble pool surrounded by dense vegetation. The trickling sound seduced us to the pristine pool where we sat on our haunches and enjoyed the cool, peaceful alcove.

I couldn't get George's murder out of my mind. I wished Zio would explain why he couldn't see that Rucker and Ascarate had mishandled the investigation. Tommy, Miguel, and Jack gulped handfuls of the cool fresh water and splashed it over their faces. Zio scanned the rocks above us, as was his habit, to avoid Indians or animals that might lurk. The memories of George's murder persisted, and I wanted to broach the subject, but the context of the conversations didn't offer an opening.

My father noticed me staring at Zio. In Spanish, he asked, "Are you bothered by something, *mijo*?"

Zio spun to me, "*Hay algo mal?*"

I looked to the rocky crags and the small pool and said in English, "This place reminds me of the spot where Oliver and I buried George McDonald." And then said to my father, "*De nada, Papa.*"

Zio stood, hands on his hips. "Oh, not that again. I thought I straightened that out for you."

My father understood enough English to know that there was indeed something wrong. "Well," said my papa to me in Spanish, "it appears not. What bothers you, my son?"

I didn't want my father involved and so I continued in English, "I am certain there was foul play involved."

"How can you be so sure?" asked Zio in Spanish. "The deputy there investigated, and the sheriff looked over the location and talked to the people that Lee accused. What else could we do?"

I continued in English. "I suppose I don't know. But there's a lot you and the sheriff don't know that rules out suicide."

My father looked concerned, but I knew he wouldn't support me. I took a deep breath and shook my head with the realization that my arguments wouldn't convince Zio and no one would stand up for me. It was no wonder Tularosans felt the way they did about Dona Ana County law.

I hoped my next words would be the last on the matter. "I knew George, and I was … am close to the people that knew him well, including his betrothed. And I know George wouldn't do that. I don't think you realize how much bad blood there is between Good and the other ranchers."

Papa put his hand on my shoulder, but I didn't acknowledge his attempt to calm me. Zio squatted, leaned back on the haunch of one leg while he flexed the other in front of him.

I lowered my voice, "Perry and I told Oliver he needed to let the law handle it and we came to you … well, not you, but to the sheriff and no one would listen."

Zio pointed at me, and said in Spanish, "Your witnesses filed their statements, didn't they?"

I replied in Spanish, "Yes, they did, but to what end? The sheriff and his Deputy — Rucker — are nothing more than John Good controlled puppets." I wanted to leave.

Zio continued in Spanish. "I wouldn't go that far. Granted, Sheriff Ascarate shies away from conflict, but I read his report and between the two of them, I think they did a thorough investigation, which is why the grand jury refused to indict."

In Spanish my papa said, "Jesús, listen to your Zio. He knows what he is talking about."

I replied in Spanish, "Papa, please stay out of this. Zio doesn't have all the facts, and I don't think he wants to know them. I now understand why Oliver and the others wish to handle their affairs on their own."

Zio shifted against the other leg and said in Spanish, "You should listen to your father. Besides, ranchers are always in some kind of conflict. It comes with the open range. Most of the time, they work it out amongst themselves."

I continued in Spanish, "Well, why is it when the Good's work it out by killing George it's alright, but when Oliver and Perry get accused of murdering Walter Good it isn't? And why hasn't the sheriff sworn out a warrant so Perry and the others can be bailed out? They turned themselves in without a warrant nearly a week ago. And …" I stood up, "and why did the court appoint someone unknown to Perry and Cooper to manage their ranches? And … and … and …?" I had said too much, and I wanted to leave, but I still hoped Zio would take my outburst as an expression of my exasperation and finally listen to me.

Zio stood as he brushed off the dust and pebbles that had stuck to his hands. In retrospect, it was an innocent gesture, but at the time, it felt like a brush-off. He sometimes used that gesture to put an end to uncomfortable conversations. I recognized, not for the first time, that we were nearly the same height. That emboldened me as I listened to him say in Spanish, "You forget, perhaps because of your injury … or perhaps because you have lived amongst those rebels too long, that in the early seventies I introduced the bill, and ushered it, against great odds, through the Texas Senate, permanently establishing the Texas Rangers as the Texas State Police force."

As I waited for him to finish, I decided on an equally piercing retort, but the anger on his face shocked me and I realized that the conversation had gotten out of hand. He had resorted to boasting about his law enforcement background in Texas. He wouldn't listen to me. I turned back down the trail as Zio called after me in Spanish, "I understand quite well what these Confederates parading as Democrats want."

As I walked away, I could hear him tell my father. "He should ask himself why Oliver Lee had to hide in the Sacramentos."

Whether it was because the trail to *La Cueva* was a quick downhill walk or because I was so aggravated, I arrived at the picnic site before I had calmed down. I walked past the women and stood at the mouth of the rock shelter. After a few moments, I walked further into its dark recesses. I couldn't think, and I hoped the darkness would clear my mind. I looked to my right and Rosa was standing next to me. She put her hand between my arm and my side. "Something happened. What is it?"

I hooked her arm with mine. I was still angry, and my whisper came out louder than I wanted. "Why can't Zio understand that … that …" I looked at the women to see if they heard me. They were involved in their own discussion. "I don't know. It just feels like all this is going in a dangerous direction, but I can't explain it so he will listen." She turned in front of me as I released her arm, and she reached out with her right hand. "Here, I have a burrito for you. It's your favorite."

"Thank you, Rosa." I accepted it in my left hand. I wasn't hungry, but I took a bite. It was indeed my favorite. She had stuffed the flour tortilla with *carne asada* and *queso fresca*. I forced down a bite. "It is delicious, but I am not hungry. I can't eat when I'm upset like this."

She laid her fingertips and the base of her palm on my chest. She half-whispered, "You must give it time. Your Zio has a lot on his mind. The election is only a month and a half away and the land grant agricultural college has taken up a lot of his time."

I covered the hand she had placed on my chest with my own. "But this is important. If the Tularosa Texans believe the law is one-sided, they will handle things themselves and people will die. They were pushed out of Texas over these same kinds of problems. Granted, they might be a bit touchy, but I've heard them say no one will push them out of the Tularosa."

"I don't know about all that, but I do know that the Colonel feels their witness is all they need to convict."

*How did she know that?*

I pulled my hand away and shifted my weight in surprise. "I know Ed. Not well, but I know he would never testify against the Lees unless someone threatened him."

"Threatened?"

"Yes. John Good runs things over there, and his foreman is the deputy. They already tried to force Perry Altman to confess. They even threatened to hang him. Imagine how a negro boy would react to hanging threats after he had seen or even just heard about lynchings? I would wager Good and his foreman threatened Ed until he swore to the events the way they wanted it told. I'd bet they have him locked up somewhere until the trial."

Rosa sighed. "Oh, my. I did not know about all that. I wonder why the Colonel hasn't seen through it?"

"The Tularosans think he and Wil Rynerson are part of the Santa Fe Ring along with John Good, but I know that isn't true, and I tried to tell them, but they won't listen to me … either. If I could just talk to Ed."

Rosa moved her hand from my chest to her lips, then removed them and said, "I suppose I shouldn't tell you this, but the Sheriff came by yesterday while you all were at the fair. He wanted the Colonel. When I told him he was at the fair, Ascarate grumbled something about not spending all afternoon looking for him and then said to me. 'Just tell him the negro boy is safe at the Colony.'"

"The Colony?"

"Yes, the Shalom Colony." Just then, Little Henry started crying and Rosa turned to go to him, but I threw out my arm to block her. She shrugged and said, "That's all I know."

I remembered The Shalam Colony was where we had placed some women and children after the Bronco Sue trial.

After our lunch, my two families engaged in activities that brought them closer together. Zio and my father talked about whether Mexico would reelect President Diaz for a second term. Mia Tia and my mother reminisced about their parents and when they were young, and Angelina played some game with Maggie, Katie, and Rosa.

I felt like an outcast for a few moments, and the memories of my loneliness back in Mexico resurfaced. Alas, I blamed myself.

# 37: A Fly on the Wall

We couldn't stay long after our picnic meal if my family was to watch the baseball tournament finale at the fairgrounds. When the girls finished their game, we packed up and headed back to town. I trailed everyone, deep in thought, and asked Ol' Nasty lots of questions.

"Should I tell Oliver where Ed is?"

"Should I see if I can talk to Ed first?"

"Should I try to talk to Zio again?"

I nixed that last one almost as soon as I said it. Zio was wonderful to discuss topics where he didn't have a stake, but when he did or he felt he was right, his manner and language could leave people feeling beat upon. "No, I don't want to go through that again," I said to my horse. Ol' Nasty didn't utter so much as a snort, and yet I continued to ask him questions.

"Should I go to the Sheriff and explain why I think they coerced Ed?"

"Should I steal away to some faraway place with Rosa where no one knows us?" I smiled at the thought, but I knew it was just a fanciful dream. "Buuttt," and I cocked my head with eyebrows raised, "Rosa and I feel sparks."

Miguel, on the horse ahead of me, turned around. *"¿Qué Pasa?"*

I replied, "*De nada*," but resolved to keep my thoughts to myself.

*Who should I believe? If Ed saw Oliver and the others murder Walter Good, then he should stay in a secure location unknown to anyone but the law. On the other hand, if they coerced Ed, the sheriff shouldn't hold him, and they should arrest John Good and his 'so called' deputy for witness tampering.*

When we returned to the Fountains, I helped Mateo unpack the carriage and stable the horses. I was in another world and didn't hear Miguel when he asked if I would go with the family to the baseball game. When he repeated the question, I realized I didn't want to spend the evening near Zio at the Fountains' adobe, so I went.

It was a good match that ended in a tie. Several others were between my father and me, and my afternoon harangue didn't come up. I never would have expected a game would interest my family, but they cheered and booed along with the rest of us. When they didn't understand what happened, they asked me. It was our last evening together. I only gave Ed a passing thought, and I had the best time I could remember with my family.

---

When at last I fell asleep, Zio startled me when he gently shook me and said, "Your folks are leaving. Don't you want to say goodbye?" I sat up and squinted at Zio. He placed his hand on my shoulder and said, "I thought you might want to drive them to the depot. When they have gone, you can return the carriage to the livery and pick up the telegrams and mail."

My grogginess still hadn't left me, and I didn't remember what had transpired the previous day. I just nodded and swung my feet over onto the chilly tile floor, which brought me quite awake. By the time I had rubbed the crusty goo from my eyes, Zio had already gone. When I had finally fallen asleep the night before, I still hadn't decided what I should do about Ed.

It was a tearful farewell between my mother and Mia Tia. My father had a concerned expression, and he promised they would return soon. Miguel surprised me when he said he had told Tommy he would come back for the fair the next year, regardless of whether his parents came.

For once, the train was on time and my mother, with Angelina stuck to her side, cried again as we hugged on the platform. She uttered something about me coming back to her, but her sobs left me without the specific words. Miguel shook my hand and whispered aside, "I can see why you want to stay here, brother." I couldn't help thinking that he had no empathy for my situation. My father shook my hand, then grabbed me by the shoulders. "We are so glad you … you didn't … you are with us again." I looked for signs of a tear, or even a sniffle, but no emotions matched his words. He released my shoulders, and my mother came back to me. Her tears still flowed, and she jumbled her words, but I could tell she wanted me to return home. But, none of them simply said, "We want you to come home."

*It would be easy to leave all this behind, but they didn't say it. Would I? Would I go if they had a ticket for me?*

Before I could resolve the question in my mind, the conductor called "All Aboard — last call for passengers to El Paso and points between — ALLLLL-ABOARD."

Miguel and Angelina had already boarded. They hung out of the windows and waved as the iron horse chugged its way south. I watched the smoke pour out of the smokestack and disappear into the sky … *wish I could do that.*

I stopped in front of Shields and Bennett's Livery, where Mr. Shields and his boy met me as I climbed down from the carriage. "You're early, sonny. The Colonel paid through supper time."

I shrugged and moved away as his boy snapped the reins and drove the two-horse team into the stable. "Guess he didn't need them any longer," I said.

"Some folk would have just kept them hitched up and tied to a tether all day, just cause they could. Not the Colonel, though, no siree. Shucks, I'll bet he hoped I could rent them out to someone else today. That uncle of yours is a peach, Jesús. Say, it's right nice to see you back here and we — my boy Archibald and me — we hope to see you more oftener. Any idear when those fellers from Tularosa will get out of jail so they can settle up on the boardin' of their horses?"

He reminded me of Gabby, the livery owner in Silver City. *What was it about livery folks? Seemed like they all wanted to talk your leg off.*

I smiled and shrugged but made a mental note to talk to the lawyers. I picked up the mail and then entered the Telegraph Office. Miles was standing on the counter. I expected the unexpected whenever Miles was involved. I didn't ask, but he explained, "There's a darned old fly buzzin' round here for more'n two days now and ... well, I just had enough."

"Did you get him?"

"Nope." He got down from the counter and retrieved our telegrams. When he handed them to me, I must have looked like something bothered me because he asked what was wrong.

I replied nothing. I must not have convinced him because he came through the counter pass-through and gave me the evil eye. "Yes, something is bothering me, but do I have to tell you every time I have a problem?"

Miles scratched his head. "Well, not if ya don't want to, I s'pose. But ya do want to ... don't ya?"

I didn't know whether to laugh or cry. "Miles, what would you do if you had a friend that you thought told a tale because somebody threatened him?

Miles rubbed his chin in thought and then I added, "And it could mean life or death."

"For the person tellin' the tale?"

"No, for the people he's telling the tale about."

"Oh, now that's a little different, I s'pose." The fly he had hunted buzzed around his head. It lit on the wall, then flew at Miles before it hovered a couple of feet in front of him. His eyes widened and crossed as the flittering menace buzzed closer and landed on the tip of his nose. With his eyes still crossed, he said, "Whack it for me, Jesús."

"No, I'm afraid I'll break your nose," I whispered.

Miles raised both hands slowly. He paused for a second, then slapped them together, catching the tip of his nose and missing the fly that had flittered away an instant earlier. His anguished expressions added to the tears that dribbled down his cheeks.

I reached for my handkerchief, but he said, "No, no. I'm alright. Whew. Did I get 'em?"

"Nope." I pointed to Miles' desk. "And now he's on your sandwich."

"Aw dagnab it." He grabbed a *Rio Grande Republican*, rolled it into a column and swatted at the fly. He missed it, but sent the sandwich on his desk flying across the room. Miles swore and swung at the sound frantically as the fly buzzed around his head.

I picked up a small piece of the bread from the sandwich and held it in front of me. The fly came to it, and I walked him out the door. When I returned, Miles said, "Why ask *me* for advice?"

# 38: Friend or Foe?

**September 21, 1888**

After waving goodbye to Miles, I went to the lawyer's office. Judge McFie and his partner were away, but one of their understudies asked if he could help me. After I asked him to alert Newcombe about Mr. Shield's livery bills, the young man said he had heard about my accident, and he wished me well. That turned into a discussion about Oliver Lee and his case.

I didn't have to prod him much to learn the sheriff would free Earhart soon after the third district court fall session opened on the first of October. They would also file Perry and Cooper's bond paperwork then. They had assembled the required cash to cover the projected twenty-to- thirty-thousand-dollar bonds. He said that W.W. Brazel and L.S. Reynolds had put up ten thousand dollars each and some of their less prosperous friends had made up the rest.

He also told me that Judge Newcombe, who was the lead on the case, had requested a change of venue. They felt the *Rio Grande Republican's* one-sided reporting before and after Walter's murder tainted the jury pool.

We got deeper into the case, and I expected they did not know where Ed King was. I wondered if I could tip them off without it getting back to Zio.

"The testimony of Ed King will be critical, don't you think?"

The young man rose from his seat. "Well, it's our only eyewitness, so yeah, I expect so."

"I know Ed King a bit. He's been with the Lees a long time. I never thought he would testify against them."

"Who knows why people suddenly turn on their friends? I'm sure you've seen it in your work with the Colonel."

"Oh yes, yes, I have. Say, do you suppose they will move Ed from the Colony to Socorro because of the venue change?" I covered my mouth, as though revealing Ed's location was a slip. "Oops, I can't believe I said that. Can you forget you heard me?"

"Sure," he winked. "From one apprentice to another, even now I can't recall what you said."

I walked back to the Fountains with guilt and elation in each step. If what I did got back to the New Mexico Bar Association, they would never admit me.

⟡⟡⟡⟡⟡⟡⟡⟡⟡⟡⟡⟡⟡⟡⟡⟡⟡⟡⟡⟡⟡⟡⟡⟡⟡⟡⟡⟡⟡⟡⟡⟡⟡⟡

A letter from my family arrived a few weeks after their departure. They wrote the trip was uneventful except that Paso del Norte had become Ciudad Juarez. That shocked many people. More than once I heard, 'How could they change the name of a place that was known otherwise for so long?' Zio reminded us that the citizens there revered Benito Juarez for his resistance against the French occupation of Mexico in the mid-1860s.

⟡⟡⟡⟡⟡⟡⟡⟡⟡⟡⟡⟡⟡⟡⟡⟡⟡⟡⟡⟡⟡⟡⟡⟡⟡⟡⟡⟡⟡⟡⟡⟡⟡⟡

The next two weeks passed in a blink for me, although I imagined it dragged for the men in jail. Rosa and the women canned vegetables and dried herbs, chiles, and fruit. Their loud discussions and laughter accompanied the sounds of their chores throughout the adobe.

I had decided to work for Zio again, which allowed Tommy to return to his regiment. Jack still cowboy'd at Wil Rynerson's ranch and Zio was off on one of his then frequent political stumping trips.

You can do only so many basic wills before boredom sets in. Mr. Anderson's was about as lifeless as they come. The sounds from the kitchen didn't just distract me, they seduced me, and I made several trips there for drinks and snacks. Rosa's presence might have been part of the seduction. I hoped Rosa's eyes would meet mine … but they never did … well, not in the way I had hoped.

*Perhaps I had made more of our chats than I should have.* After several attempts, I ran out of excuses for going to the kitchen.

All of Judge McFie assistant's suggestions were spot on. The judge signed the warrants and bail was set and arranged for 25,000 dollars. By the end of the first week in October, the sheriff cleared the jailhouse, and Perry, Cooper, and Earhart left for home. However, Oliver and Tom Tucker were now officially fugitives from the law.

Zio came home with the news. He entered the office with eyebrows raised. With a deep sigh of relief, he said, "I believe you have now fulfilled your promises to Oliver Lee. Let's hope we can return to the way things were before your accident. I sincerely want that, Jesús. I have written to the Bar Association, and they wrote they would simply add five months onto your apprenticeship to make up for the lost time. If I'm elected, I'll be in Santa Fe for two months and I'll need you to captain the ship here."

At that moment, I believed I had breached the ethics rules when I revealed a key witness location to the defense attorney's staff. My devotion to 'reading law' hadn't returned, but I didn't want to stir things up with Zio again. So, I smiled, "Thank you. I'll do my best."

Zio left for one of his political appearances. As I sat at my desk, I wondered if things could ever be the same. I had my doubts. Despite my feelings about how Zio and the Dona Ana County Sheriff had handled Oliver's case, the Democrats nasty political tactics made me feel compassion for him.

The last month before the elections was quieter in the office than I expected. Throughout the month of October, Zio traveled to the far reaches of the district, while I stayed and handled wills, contracts, and the mundaneness of a legal practice. He would often come home and complain about Democrats' dishonorable efforts to derail his election.

At the time, the territory restricted how towns could fund their governments. The vast did so with a liquor tax. Republicans knew that inhibited efforts by towns to deal with problems associated with saloons. Some communities even wanted to outlaw whiskey all together. Therefore, the Republican platform included a plank that would allow towns to fund their governments in other ways.

The Democrats labeled it a bane against the temperance folks because it would make whiskey cheaper. They called it the "Free Whiskey" proposal and suggested the GOP intended to buy votes with their nonsense. At every stop, Zio would have to explain that the GOP proposal would have the reverse effect because it would allow towns to collect taxes in other ways. He would tell his audience that their proposed law would reduce the town's dependence on the whiskey tax and could allow them to outlaw whiskey sales, if they desired.

As I have written here before, the Santa Fe Ring was among the most aggressive in acquiring Spanish and Mexican granted lands with suspicious methods. They, and others, had somehow avoided conviction in northern New Mexico, but Zio had several successes in the south and his courtroom prowess threatened them.

It alarmed the Santa Fe Ring when the Federal Democratic Administration appointed Zio as a Special Assistant U.S. Attorney in March of 1886. They specifically wanted him to prosecute land grabbers that violated the Homestead Act and other land laws. Soon after his appointment, the Santa Fe Ring hired a man by the name of R.P. Walker to besmirch Zio. Walker's report concocted several accusations against him, which the Santa Fe Ring used to try to remove him from his duly appointed post. While some thought it incredible the northern Republicans would so aggressively go after one of their own, southern Republicans knew it was because Zio would threaten their methods of stealing lands from unprepared Spanish and Mexican land grant holders.

Walker's report claimed that while Zio was in the Texas Senate, he was a known carpetbagger and that his actions there required him to flee to New Mexico. It also said that in the past year, Zio had received a one-thousand-dollar bribe to suppress indictments in three cases against ranchers and land jumpers. The report stated the offenders were as good as convicted if Zio had presented the evidence.

The Santa Fe Ring sent the spy's fraudulent charges to the Democratic Federal Commissioner of the General Land Office, A.J. Sparks. Sparks then forwarded them to Attorney General Garland, who referred them to Colonel Thomas Smith, New Mexico's U.S. Attorney, for investigation. Colonel Smith's investigation discovered the truth, and he responded to his superiors that the report was false. He suggested that citizens that feared Colonel Fountain paid for the report. Its aim was to remove him from his special appointment.

When the attorney general cleared Zio's name, Colonel Smith sent Zio a copy of the correspondence and Walker's report on October 29, 1887. In his letter, Colonel Smith not only dispelled all the 'Ring's' accusations, he praised Zio again and again.

The following year, local Democrats found out about Walker's report. They used it to sully Colonel Fountain's reputation, in that the Republicans themselves originally commissioned it. For a time, all Zio could do was deny the accusations. As the election approached, the result appeared in doubt. Then, on November 3, 1888, three days before the election, The *Rio Grande Republican* printed all the correspondence. Editor Metcalfe concluded the accusations did not damage Colonel Fountain. Instead, he suggested they added to his "brilliant reputation as the ablest and most successful advocate in New Mexico." Their smear campaign could have widened the already significant schism between the southern territorial Republicans and the northern districts, led by the Santa Fe Ring. However, Zio must have had an ally in the editor of the Santa Fe *New Mexican* because he soon touted Zio as perhaps the ablest legislator and best candidate for Speaker of the House.

Election day on the sixth of November was clear and pleasant. On the tenth, the *Rio Grande Republican* reported that Democrats had treated forty or fifty Mexicans to whiskey all night, then herded them to vote at the nine o'clock opening of the polls. How editor Metcalfe knew they all cast straight Democratic tickets is anyone's guess, but that is what he reported. I had volunteered to monitor the polls for the Republicans. While many Democrats milled around throughout the day, there were no fights or arguments. Republicans erected a bulletin board to display the vote tally in front of Lohman's store. Results poured in by telegraph, and Miles' young son hustled back and forth while Judge McFie posted the results. Because New Mexico was a territory, we could not vote in the presidential race, but that didn't quell interest. It looked tight.

The final tallies on all the national and local elections weren't available to the *Rio Grande Republican* until the seventeenth. Locally, the Republican party made a significant comeback from the '86 election and regained nearly all their lost seats.

There was a hiccup, however, when Santa Teresa's commissioners refused to report their results because their poll clerk had filled out only one poll book. The *Republican* reported that someone appealed to Judge Henderson to have the votes counted, but he denied the *mandamus* because the time limit had expired. The *Republican* suggested it didn't matter because all the votes were for Republican candidates. That seemed unlikely.

In the end, Zio won, but reports of the vote margin seemed influenced by each newspaper publisher's party affiliation. The *Republican* publisher Metcalfe reported that a Democratic weekly wrote Zio won by just two votes, while the Santa Fe *New Mexican* reported a sixty-one-vote victory. Metcalfe reported in the *Republican* that the margin was forty-two.

Contentious elections were a staple of New Mexican politics, but dirty electioneering spread throughout the nation. For the third time in history, and a second time in twelve years, the electoral vote overturned the will of the people in the presidential election. In 1876, Samuel Tilden beat Rutherford B. Hayes by 200,000 votes, but fell a single vote short in the electoral college. Many voters remembered the querulous congress that ensued until Hayes was at last confirmed in March of 1877.

In 1888, Republican Benjamin Harrison won the electoral vote and defeated Democrat Grover Cleveland despite Cleveland's 90,000 popular vote margin.

That alone riled the country. Accusations of voter fraud against Republicans brought the entire country to the brink of a hard boil. While Harrison continued with his campaign slogan of 'a pure, free ballot … the jewel above price', Democrats accused Harrison of ballot buying and stuffing ballot boxes, among other things. The election laws were so varied and full of holes that election officials expected and tolerated chicanery. Case in point, in Kentucky, all a person had to do was show up at the polls and voice their vote to the poll tender.

Alas, there was a limit, but the GOP seemed oblivious as they took advantage of every opportunity. Pennsylvanian Matt Quay, the Republican National Committee's president, raised extravagant amounts from businessmen and spent heavily to buy Democratic leaders in the big cities. He also sent Pinkerton detectives to the southern states to protect negroes that wanted to vote Republican in Democratic districts.

In one instance, Republicans transported voters from Pennsylvania to Indiana. Harrison had a solid majority in the Commonwealth and the shift likely gave him Indiana, which was critical in the Electoral College count. In another, Quay must have had a limit because he stopped a scheme by his party's campaign treasurer that advised ways to vote multiple times. Not to be denied, as the election neared, the GOP's firebrand treasurer sent an indiscreet directive to the Indiana party boss. He instructed him to "divide the floaters into blocks of five and put a trusted man with necessary funds in charge," and to "make him responsible that none get away and all vote our ticket."

In the end, Harrison was sworn into office, but the *coup de grâce* came when he claimed that providence determined his election. In response, Quay said, "Providence hadn't had a damn thing to do with it." Quay felt his help entitled his cronies to key appointments, but Harrison ignored him. The feud became public, which further stoked the corruption boiler.

The apparent crooked actions led to election reform and by the 1892 election, thirty-eight states voted by secret ballot based on Australia's New South Wales model. Still, suspicions of voter fraud and other election shenanigans persisted for many years.

As December arrived, Zio came to me with a letter. He laid it on my desk. I was certain the New Mexico Bar had found out about my interference. I looked at him, but his poker face was unreadable. I thought the worst and almost blurted out that I was sorry. By good fortune, I scanned the sheet of paper first. It was an official court document from September notifying Oliver Lee's lawyers that the court had granted their change of venue request. I hoped my relief wasn't obvious, and when I looked up, Zio had already turned back to his desk.

Zio's prosecutorial duties kept him from Santa Fe until the day before the legislative session started. Throughout December, rumors made Zio the unopposed next Speaker of the House.

There was also a letter from Oliver's mother, Mary, that arrived the week after Christmas. She wrote there had been an incident between Jim Cooper and John Good and his hands. The Goods had been out rounding up some of their horse herd. Jim was on his way home from La Luz. He cleared a small rise and found John and his cowboys coming directly toward him. Several people were along the road in front of Fletcher Thomas' house and neither Jim nor John would embarrass themselves by yielding to the other.

One of Good's men pulled his Winchester from his saddle scabbard as Jim came alongside him. Jim said, "Don't do it." The man didn't, but another man aimed his six-shooter at Jim. When he cocked the hammer, John's son pushed the man's arm down. The gun went off, and the round went into the ground. As John and his bunch rode off, Jim heard John Good holler, "Stop it!".

Mary hoped this signaled the end of hostilities. There was further hope when Jim Cooper's brother Ira corresponded with John about ending the feud. By then, much of John's anger had dissipated. He invited Ira Cooper to come and stay with him while they commiserated over the state of things. By the end of the year, it seemed Ira was successful because John leased his ranch to C.P. White of Tularosa and moved his family to Las Cruces, where they lived in some rented rooms. It seemed like the beginning of the end for the Good family in Dona Ana County. Nonetheless, John was the tinder for the growing feud between the two valleys.

Rucker lost his job with the election of Sheriff Barela, and John Good left the area. That didn't relax Rucker's dander. Although he was no longer a deputy, he demanded people call him that. He refused to bury the hatchet. In Nettie's next letter she wrote that Rucker and his friends continued the surveillance and harassment at Lee Well, and that Oliver and Tucker continued to hide out in the Sacramentos.

---

My journals have been invaluable to me as I wrote this chapter. As I reflected on the 1888 election, I have concluded that having survived it, we as a nation will persevere, for I see no possibility that we will ever face such corruption and discord.

As I reflect on the trials and tribulations I have written about so far, I must wonder if I would have been better able to deal with circumstances, had my accident happened earlier in my time in New Mexico, when I had the benefit of naivete.

---

# 39: Mr. Speaker

Zio had insisted that if he won the election, the family would come with him for the start of New Mexico Territory's twenty-eighth legislative session. Mia Tia had to be cajoled by Maggie and Zio before she finally relented. Albert Jr. got an offer to serve as the Copy Clerk for the Legislative Council, but their young daughter, Ermindita, who was born the previous April, was sickly and he was reluctant to leave his family for the two-month session.

One day, not long after the election, Albert Jr., Teresita, and their children visited us, and the subject of his appointment came up. I could see that the family had mixed emotions. It was an important step for Albert Jr.'s political aspirations, but no one would dare suggest that he leave behind little Ermindita in her moribund state. When at last a decision was necessary, Teresita said, "She is in God's hands now, my husband. The doctors can do nothing more."

Mia Tia crossed herself. "I think you should come with us for a few days, Teresita. You need a break and Rosa can watch young Albert and Ermindita."

Teresita mimicked her holy expression. "Rosa shouldn't have to watch them all day and all night."

Mia Tia gathered Teresita's hands in her own. "I've already arranged for Marianita and Carl to watch Little Henry, and I'm sure they won't mind adding Albert and Ermindita, but I'll ask them later today when they come by. We only want to stay for a few days, anyway."

Teresita seemed relieved — the mental and physical exhaustion of tending to their sick baby had worn on them both, but Teresita had been with the child every minute since she was born.

Marianita and Carl agreed to stay at the Fountains and tend their niece and nephew when Rosa wasn't there. As soon as the election results were official, the women, Teresita included, replenished their wardrobes. The suit of clothes Zio had bought the previous January for my attendance at the New Mexico Bar Association meeting were too small. When Zio ordered a new suit, he had his old suit altered for me. At the last minute, Tommy decided he would go, and he wore his militia uniform.

---

## December 31, 1888

The first day of the legislative session was a Monday. During the opening ceremonies, the color guard brought in the flags and Tommy, a last-minute fill-in, paraded the territorial flag. There was the swearing ins and a motion by Socorro's Michael Cooney to appoint Zio as Speaker of the House. As his nomination was about to come to a vote, John S. Sniffen nominated Felix Martinez of San Miguel. The roll was called and Zio got fifteen votes, Mr. Martinez's vote included, while Martinez got just eight votes, including that of Zio. The two men had voted for each other. I thought that must be a tactic to show mutual respect to promote cooperation.

It was moved and seconded that two members escort Colonel Fountain to his dais desk. He stood before the other twenty-three legislators and gave an impassioned, patriotic speech without notes. Zio thanked his fellow members for the honor of their selection. He also expressed his intention that the legislative session would promote well-conceived and composed laws that held the best interests of the people of the Territory. Colonel Fountain praised his fellow legislators at every turn and diminished his own role, despite his position. He closed with a "request that his fellow legislators pay particular attention to the education of the youth of both sexes of the territory."

Eyebrows raised at this statement because, to date, New Mexico had relied on the Catholic faith for education. The idea that girls would have equal access was rare nationwide. It spoke volumes about Zio's sagacious mind that he left this powerful statement of his own objectives for his closing. The room was in his hands. And while their approval may have been alcohol induced, no one knew how much.

The House adopted rules, made position appointments, and carried out their initial business formalities without incident. However, Mr. Sniffen, of Socorro County, looked as though he would be a 'stick in the mud' as he continued to offer unsuccessful amendments and challenges for roll votes.

That evening everyone attended a gala ball. It was something! The finest fashions of the day adorned the ladies, and the men looked smart in their evening wear. Patriotic trappings decorated the hall and waiters wandered amongst the crowd with trays of champagne and whiskey, while the orchestra played pleasant background music. Many of the territory's lawyers attended. Several told me they had heard of my accident and that they were happy I had returned to the Colonel.

Attorney Field, the past president of the New Mexico Bar, spotted me. I remembered how his calm voice and words got me through my first occasion in front of a gathering. He made the usual comments about my accident; they seemed heartfelt and reiterated what his letter had said about how I could gain full member status.

I wondered if my relief showed. "Thank you, sir. I look forward to that day."

Field smiled and put his hand on my shoulder. "Of course, you realize we will review your record and any complaints made on your ...."

I couldn't hear another thing he said because all I could think about was my violation of ethics when I revealed the location of the prosecution's star witness.

Field must have recognized my guilt because he asked, "You haven't done something wrong already, have you?"

"Oh. Oh, no sir, I was just thinking how dishonorable denial would be."

"That's right, son. You just keep that in mind and there won't be a problem." He spotted someone across the room he wanted to talk to and left me with an abbreviated wave.

Zio stood with a magnificent smile as people crowded around to congratulate him. As he had predicted to me, legislators dropped subtle hints about the bills they would later lobby him more directly about. Each one would eventually ask for preferential treatment so that Zio would present their bills and usher them through to the governor's desk. Zio loved it.

Off to one side, I heard one of his admirers say, "Tell us the story about the time the Kinney Gang outlaw tried to escape from you."

Zio demurred, "Ah, that was a long time ago when outlaws ran rampant. We need to focus on the problems that our civil and industrious society will face during statehood."

Another man said, "Oh come now, Colonel, can't we relive the past for a short time? It will help us relish what we have and where our future will take us."

Zio grinned and took a sip of his champagne. "Well, OK, I suppose you are right." He tipped his champagne flute again, cleared his voice, and started. "Many of you will recall, what has it been — five? No, nearly six years ago now ..." He gazed above the crowd as he reflected on those times. "I was a Major, back then ...." Zio shook his head as he reckoned how much time had passed. Then, with a flourish of his arms and elevated voice, he began. "John Kinney and his gang had terrorized southern New Mexico. Governor Sheldon ordered me and our militia to investigate the gang, their criminal methods, and find the locations where they hid.

"After a couple of months, we understood their *modus operandi*, and had located their hideouts. The governor gave us the authority to do as required; 'to act in every way upon my own best judgement.'" Zio paused and raised his finger. "And those were the governor's precise words, gentlemen.

"Little by little, we gathered up the miscreants. We knew that one of their secret lairs was in La Mesa, fifteen miles south of Las Cruces. I had sent Company B under the command of Captain Francisco Salazar to surveil the area and with instructions to take whatever gang members he could when the opportunity presented itself.

"As reported to me, Salazar and his men surrounded a cantina where they knew five of Kinney's men had imbibed all evening. The confusion of our raid allowed Doroteo Sains and his brother to escape through a window, but we captured two of the other men and shot down a third as he tried to escape."

Zio motioned for a waiter who brought the Colonel a flute of champagne, but he demurred, and a second waiter brought his tray of whiskey and tequila shots. The Colonel downed the whiskey in one gulp and the crowd erupted, but he held his hand in the air to restrain his supporters. Zio held the empty whiskey glass with the last two fingers on his right hand as he selected a second shot glass of tequila with his index finger and thumb. In a demonstration of unity he promoted between the latino and white legislators, he gulped down the tequila and replaced the two shot glasses on the tray with a smile for the waiter.

The now tipsy gallery went wild. Not everyone had gathered around him as he told his story, but there were plenty of Democrats that stood within earshot. While one or two of them mocked his theatrical manner occasionally, they believed the tale because the rumored version was well known throughout the territory.

"While the Sains boys got away, our citizens could see that law and order had prevailed. They knew it was only a matter of time before John Kinney and his band of bad men would get their due. Captain Van Patten brought in seven additional prisoners the next day and deposited them in the Las Cruces jail, where I reinforced the sheriff's staff with a militia detail.

"Other than that, I kept all my companies in the field searching for the rest of the gang. Soon a telegram arrived from Texas Rangers Captain John Baylor. John wrote he had captured Doroteo Sains and two others of the Kinney gang and he asked if we could pick them up in El Paso. At the time, Van Patten was near Rincon and Company A was in Lake Valley.

"John Kinney was still a fugitive from justice. I knew he would be in either of the two places I had positioned my companies and I couldn't pull any of my key personnel from there to escort Sains et al. back to Las Cruces. So, my son Albert ..." Zio motioned across the room to Albert, "and I went.

"I met Baylor at the depot. Despite his rather brutal confederate war tactics and against Indians, John and I have become friends, and we had a pleasant discussion while we waited for the train north. Just before I boarded with the prisoners, John rebuked me for not cording my pistol to my gun belt. He told me all the Rangers had done so to prevent the loss of one's gun in a scuffle. I thought that sounded like a good idea and Baylor detached his own cord and looped one end around my belt and the other to my pistol.

"After we got under way for a time, I saw someone back in the car that I needed to speak with. I left young Albert to guard the prisoners. We handcuffed the three prisoners and sat them opposite him in the front seat. Albert sat on the coal box.

"Everything was fine until the train slowed for the Canutillo station. I heard a commotion up front and turned. Albert and Sains had vanished. When I reached the platform at the front of the car, I could see Sains had kept his feet while Albert had not. Sains had run toward the mesquite thickets along the river. I jumped from the still moving train and rolled twice before I reestablished myself."

Zio became frantic in his gesturing and his voice hastened with the emotion of the moment. "The fear of the loss of my prisoner gripped me and I grabbed for my pistol, but it wasn't in the scabbard. I assumed I had lost it when I jumped from the train. I gathered myself to run after Sains. When I took the first step, something hit my shin. My gun dangled there from Baylor's pistol cord. I dropped to one knee, sky-lined Sains at the crest of a little hill, and fired four quick shots into the prisoner. Sains dropped to the ground and was dead before I could reach him."

The gathering was in a frenzy. Fists flew into the air with salutary shouts, but Zio hadn't finished, and he held his hands high to stifle the crowd. When the assembly had quieted, he continued in a calm volume and manner.

"But that is not all, my fine men. Kinney's men wouldn't talk, but within a week we had located, captured, and arrested John Kinney and the rest of his lieutenants at Ash Springs on the Gila in the Arizona Territory."

The crowd erupted as Zio repeated his unifying gesture of downing shots of whiskey and tequila. Maggie, who sat next to me, said, "That's the reason Governor Sheldon created the First Cavalry Regiment, New Mexico Volunteers. He also promoted papa to colonel and put him in command of the new First Regiment."

The legislative session was only two months and abbreviated ones at that. It ended with the short month of February. During that time, the speaker's job was Zio's total focus. The House didn't hold sessions on Sundays, and I suppose he must have caught up on sleep then, but at the end of the session he returned home thinner and exhausted. Zio had taken a room in a nearby Santa Fe hotel where many of the elected officials stayed.

I've never known a man more devoted to his family and yet I don't think he came home once while the legislature was in session. He did write. We got letters several times a week. Often it was just a few lines about what occupied the House chamber, but he always concluded with a version of: "I miss you all so very much and think about you every day."

I had assumed the House would not meet on January first, but I was wrong. They adopted the rules from the previous session *ad infinitum*, but then spent much of the morning debating motions to review and revise them. Zio expertly guided them away from their rules debates to the resolutions and appointments that were required for the House to begin its work.

During the initial roll call, Mr. Sniffen did not respond even though he was present. Perhaps his failings on the first day discouraged him. I wondered how someone with so little perseverance could get elected. It would seem the campaign alone would disqualify him.

By lunch, the assembly had 'set up house' and Zio dismissed them for the day. He joined us for lunch in one of Santa Fe's finest restaurants where we rushed through a meal so that Mia Tia, Teresita, Maggie, Tommy, and I could catch our early afternoon train south.

# 40: Electoral Shenanigans

**January 1, 1889**

When we arrived back in Las Cruces, to the pleasant surprise of all, Ermindita had rallied under Rosa's care. As a result, Albert Jr. stayed in Santa Fe and completed his obligations. The baby smiled and even giggled when Little Henry and Katie ran in circles around her. It seemed that her illness had resolved.

Often rumors of the legislature's activities came to us before Zio's letters. When his missives arrived, he sometimes included clippings from the Santa Fe *New Mexican,* which detailed the activities of the House and Council daily sessions. One such event was the controversy over the Taos District election where Democrat Henry J. Young appeared to beat the incumbent Republican Bonifacio Martinez. There had been disagreement over the vote tally, in part because many people had voted for variations of Mr. Young's name. Henry J. Young occupied the district's seat while the responsible committee reexamined the election and presented its report. It found that the final corrected vote tally was:

> **Votes for Henry J. Young - 860**
>
> **Votes for J.H. Young - 48**
>
> **Votes for H.H. Young - 80**
>
> **Total votes for all variations of Young's name - 988**
>
> **Votes for Bonafacio Martinez - 989**

Therefore, regardless of whether voters intended to vote for J.H or H.H. Young, Bonafacio Martinez still won the seat by one vote. The clerk read the report before the assembly. It included a resolution to seat Mr. Martinez and remove Mr. Young.

Two majority and one minority members comprised the committee that prepared separate reports. The minority member's report contended Mr. Young had won since it was clear the votes for J.H. and H.H were for Henry J. Young. He stated there was no serious intimidation of Republican voters by the U.S. Marshals or others and that sixteen Pueblo Indians had voted for Martinez (ballots were not secret). Furthermore, he suggested that officials should have removed those sixteen votes from the tally. Somehow, the minority committee member, Mr. Mascarenas, concluded that Mr. Young had won by a margin of twenty-seven. How he arrived at that number is anyone's guess.

After the House completed its business of the morning, the legislature returned from lunch and Mr. Mascarenas moved for adoption of his report. After a brief discussion, the assembly voted to table the matter until the next day.

The next morning, after the House had convened, and counter to Mascarenas' motion, Mr. Foster moved adoption of the majority report of the committee, which meant they would install Martinez in the seat occupied by Young. Zio removed himself from the Speaker's chair and, along with two other Republicans, became embroiled in a heated discussion with three Democrats over the merits of the two opposing reports. Sadly, it took just over a week for the camaraderie and goodwill Zio had crafted to end.

In conclusion, a closer examination of the minority report revealed that there weren't sixteen Pueblo Indians that had voted — perhaps only one — and the other irregularities were based on hearsay and speculation. In contrast, the majority report noted there was a second Young in the district. Jack H. Young (J.H.) had run against Henry J. Young in the primary and lost. In addition, Jack Young lived in the only precinct that recorded votes for J.H. Young.

The Republicans stated they had gone into the committee room and reviewed the facts. They concluded Martinez was the clear victor. The assembly raised the previous motion to accept the majority report and remove Henry J. Young from the district's seat and then install Bonifacio Martinez as the rightful winner. Mr. Sniffen requested a roll call vote, and the ayes had it 15-5.

Later, Young would say it was an attempt at humor, but hardly anyone cracked a smile when he told the assembly some of his friends had hinted there might be a funeral that day. If so, he thought the House should now appoint pall bearers.

---

**February 10**

It was a Sunday morning and Mia Tia, and Maggie had taken Katie to church. Rosa had the day off. I volunteered to stay with Little Henry and while he played with some blocks on the floor; I worked on Mr. Anderson's will. Little Henry would stack alphabet etched blocks between my desk and Zio's, opposite the open door to the hallway. I sipped my coffee, smiled at Little Henry's attempts to stack the blocks, and then looked back at Mr. Anderson's confusing form. Little Henry made an unfamiliar sound, and I looked up. A cowboy stood in the doorway with his back to me. It wasn't Mr. Anderson. For a moment, I panicked and stood to fetch Little Henry.

The man turned my way. It was Oliver Lee in all his Texas rancher glory, although he looked a bit dingy. "I never considered you might have a little 'un Hey-you. Sorry, I mean Jesús."

I opened my mouth to speak, but Oliver's presence in the hall stunned me. He sensed my surprise and said, "I knocked at the back door."

I remembered hearing a knock, but others always answered it and so I must have ignored it.

"Should I leave?" asked Oliver. "I knew Fountain was in Santa Fe and I figured his wife and kids would be at church … I thought …"

"I don't think you should have come, Oliver."

My tone of voice scared Little Henry, and he got up and 'ran' into my arms. I hoisted him up and sat him on the desk in front of me.

"I know, but well, the last time I saw Nettie, she asked after you. We all hope you are …"

"I'm fine and my memory has returned … well, most of it. But Oliver, there's a warrant out for you and Tucker … is he here?"

"Yeah, he's mindin' the horses out behind the stable."

I had forgotten Mateo had the day off. "Well, why are you here?"

"Got word of the trial date in Socorro. My loyer told me where they were holdin' Ed, and I need to plan out rescuin' him."

I knew it would come to that, but with Oliver's words, I realized how awful what I had done was. "I don't want to know this, Oliver. Wait, did your lawyer tell you how they found out?"

"Yep, he said you told 'em. And I'm mighty obliged you did."

My face must have shown my disgust for myself. "Yes, well…Oliver, please turn yourself in. Evading the law makes you look guilty."

Oliver looked toward the backdoor. I thought he might leave, but he spun to face me. "It's been over six months since Walter Good died. Perry, Cooper, and Earhart turned themselves in. Why have they sat in jail for over two weeks waitin' for bail papers?"

I grimaced. I couldn't explain why it took so long.

"My loyers say they filed some papers to get us released if we turn ourselves in, but the court is waitin' for Fountain to give his reasons for holding us until trial."

"Well, Oliver, you can see that Zio isn't here. He has shared nothing about your case with me. I don't know about any of that." I lied because I didn't want to give him any reason to doubt my loyalty.

"Zio, who is Zio?"

"It's Colonel Fountain ... oh and by the way, I'm not a Fountain. My last name is Messi. The Colonel is my uncle and Zio means uncle in Italian."

"Italian?"

"Yes, well, it's a long story. I'm sure Colonel Fountain will do it as soon as he returns from Santa Fe next month." I wanted to move the conversation away from how much I knew about his case.

Oliver took off his hat and ran his fingers through his sweat darkened hair. He repositioned his hat just so and said, "I also came to talk to Albert Fall. He says the Bar should recognize him soon."

"Will he represent you? It seems to me McFie and Newcombe have done a good job."

Oliver's normally calm demeanor disappeared. "How can you say that? I've been livin' rough in the mountains for near-on six months now waitin' for the law to do right by me and mine. I have to manage my ranch on the sly and my family is under constant stress because deputies question them about my whereabouts day and night."

Little Henry whimpered as he reached for me, and I gathered him onto my hip. There was nothing I could say that would make either of them feel better.

"Mr. Fall says the Constitution says I'm entitled to a speedy trial by my peers. He says that if he was my counsel, this would never have gone on this long."

"He's not wrong — about the Constitution, I mean."

"Can't you write up the required paperwork in Fountain's absence?"

"No, Oliver, I can't. Judge Henderson would just send it back to us."

We stood there in silence for what seemed like forever. I sat back down and put Little Henry on my knee.

I guess Oliver took that as his cue to leave. He said "Well, you've got a nice lookin' boy there Jesús — raise him up right,"

Before I could correct him, he was gone. I was left with the little boy that wasn't my son but was nearer and dearer to me than my own brothers. Little Henry looked up at me and I said, "How did I get myself into this mess?"

Little Henry smiled and then broke out into one of his convulsive laughs.

# 41: A Not So Boring Will

To say that Zio worked hard for his constituents and all New Mexicans would be an understatement. Long before he ran for the territorial legislature, he established himself as someone that would work to improve his community and help his fellow man. His experience as president of the Texas Senate in the 1870s allowed him to avoid many pitfalls that befell other first-time speakers. But it was his reputation as a man of integrity, bravery, benevolence, oratorical skill, and perseverance that endeared him to Mesilla Valley residents and propelled him to the legislature.

In his leadership position as Speaker, he appointed all committees and chaired the rules committee. This enabled him to set agendas, which he used to establish his priorities of statehood, public education, and placement of the state funded colleges.

Once they had appointed standing committees, the Colonel called for a resolution to establish a joint House-Council committee that would urge the U.S. Congress to authorize a Territorial Constitution Convention to prepare for New Mexico statehood. His leadership included activism as well, as he wrote and introduced several bills. Of the first seven bills presented, Zio authored two. The first was also the first to be signed by the governor. It standardized Supreme Court practices. The second sought to resolve land grant claims, some of which robbed people of land their families had occupied for centuries.

He introduced and adopted several resolutions, rules, and procedures that made the proceedings of the House transparent. Among them was a special committee to "devise ways and means to improve the acoustics of the chamber". A resolution held that "every official of the House ... shall at all times extend every possible facility to the members of the press..." Many of these practices persist even through this writing. The Santa Fe *New Mexican* applauded his parliamentary procedures and overall management as he facilitated 'the business of the House'.

The previous session, two years before, had left the House bathrooms unusable. Zio allowed a resolution that instructed the janitor 'to clear out the bath rooms ... and see that said bath rooms are placed in condition for use.' One newspaper reporter wrote: "One can only guess how legislators might have made a go of it."

---

**February 20**

Besides his expansive duties as Speaker, Zio served as chair for the resolutions committee. When the first anniversary of Archbishop Jean Baptiste Lamy's death arrived, it fell to him to appoint someone to deliver a commemoration speech. Before long, his grandiloquence and theatric presentations made him the favorite inside and outside the House chambers. Zio hesitated because his persistence in getting public schools established and funded in New Mexico didn't always align with the Archbishop's advocacy for Catholic schools. In the end he agreed with the hope it would assuage those that doubted his words when he defended his public-school plans as not damaging to the Catholic schools. He gave a beautiful speech that didn't touch on the public-school controversy. Within House order, he also resolved: "That we trust in the almighty mercy that Archbishop Lamy has received the everlasting crown he deserved for the self-sacrifice he made of his life and person on behalf of suffering humanity, and that he is now enjoying the great reward promised by our Savior to those who have faithfully served him in the world of misery; and...

"*Resolved further*, That with feeling of profound respect, veneration and gratitude, the memory of our great and lamented benefactor shall always live in the hearts of the Catholics of New Mexico."

**February 22**

A couple of days later, I needed to meet with Mr. Anderson to wrap up some details of his will. Zio's desk beckoned my occupation while he was in Santa Fe. It would be easier than moving the two client chairs to face my desk, I thought. I even sat in his plush leather chair for a while before I decided I belonged at my own humble desk.

Mia Tia and the girls had helped Father Lassaigne make special preparations to mark the anniversary of the archbishop's death. They gathered so much material that they devoted the entire month to his memory. It was the last Saturday of the month. Mia Tia and the rest of the women had gone to work with Father Lassaigne on his final homage to the archbishop.

Mr. Anderson arrived at the mid-morning appointed time. Rosa showed him in, and he removed his hat and took the chair facing my small desk.

"Thank you for coming in, Mr. Anderson. I have a few questions so I can complete your will and record it at the courthouse."

He wore a long black coat, black Derby and pants, and a fresh white shirt garnished by a neat, black string tie. He had a neatly trimmed thick beard and when he removed his Derby hat; it exposed a gray, almost white, head of hair. Mr. Anderson was tall, as I had observed was common among Scandinavians. However, he was so thin his cheek bones protruded so that it made him appear almost skeletal. He must have noticed me 'sizing him up', for he cleared his throat, projected his chin, and said with a thick Scandinavian accent, "Yes, vhat do you need to know?" with a slight lilt as the sentence ended.

"Well, first sir, in the form I asked you to fill out, you did not specify who you would like to carry out your last will and testament. Perhaps you have had time to think about it."

He ran his finger around the brim of his Derby but remained silent. Zio hadn't told me that Mr. Anderson was shy.

I prompted him. "We can manage the executor duties for you, sir, for a nominal fee."

He nodded.

"It says here," I held up the form he had completed, "Your first name is Amund, but you have also written that your wife's name is Amund … and your son's name is Amund, also?"

Just then, Rosa tapped on the door, and I invited her in. She held a tray of lemonade and two glasses. Little Henry toddled past her as fast as his little legs would carry him, past Mr. Anderson, and into my arms.

"I am so sorry." exclaimed Rosa. "He was sitting on the floor in the kitchen with a cookie. I thought …"

Just then, Mr. Anderson let out a tortured howl, and he covered his face with his Derby.

Rosa put the tray on my desk, and I put Little Henry down and we both rushed to Mr. Anderson's side.

"I'm so sorry, sir," said Rosa. "Here." she poured a glass of lemonade and offered it to him.

He placed his hat on his lap, took a sip, and nodded to Rosa. "I'm sorry, it's just that the little boy reminded me of my son."

"We are sorry if Little Henry brought unpleasant memories. Did he pass recently?" I asked.

"Oh no, no." A tear escaped his eye, dribbled down his chiseled cheek and paused before it dropped onto his hat. His face scrunched up, then under his breath he said, "He won't come."

I looked at Rosa, and she shrugged. Little Henry tugged on my shirt as he tried to climb into my chair. I looked at Rosa and mouthed, "go." She retrieved Little Henry as Katie squalled in the kitchen. Within a few seconds, she was gone; the room was quiet, and I returned to my chair.

"I'm so sorry for the interruption, Mr. Anderson. Why don't we start again? Sir, what is the matter? I realize it may be none of my business, but if you want a will …"

"My vife died last veek, and my son vill not come for her funeral. I buried her this morning."

I was stunned.

"The little boy … he reminds me of Amund vhen he was …" Mr. Anderson broke down again; this time with deep sobs.

I walked around the desk and sat next to him. When I reached out, he grasped my hand.

"Ve, I mean my vife Asmund, and I came here for her tuberculosis four years ago. Ve bought a farm … an excellent farm with irrigation … but she got sicker … not better. She began coughing up blood and so I put her in Dr. Huber's sanitarium, but she died."

"I'm so sorry, Mr. Anderson."

"You can call me Amund. My vife and I had the same first name. It seemed right for our firstborn to be called Amund, as vell."

I nodded as I checked the form notes he had provided. "And when you notified your son, he said he could not come for her funeral?"

"He never vanted us to leave Visconsin. It was Door County vhere vee had a fine farm. My son took it over vhen vee left."

I released his hand and stood. "Do not fear, Mr. Anderson, I will help you. I'm not sure how, but I will."

He looked at the cerulean blue sky through the office's high window. "I vant to go back to Visconsin, to bury my vife there."

"But you said you buried her this morning?"

He looked at his hat in his lap and nodded as tears dripped onto his Derby. He tried to shake them off, which seemed to renew him, and he straightened his back, put on his hat, and looked at me.

"I must carry on. Amund, my love, vould not have me behave this vay." He stood. "There is no reason for a vill, now."

"No, wait, I can help you."

"I am too old to drive a vagon all the vay back to Visconsin."

"I know, I mean, you don't have to."

As he turned to go to the door, he stopped, but didn't look at me.

"I can get an order to exhume your wife's body and you can accompany her on the train to Vis … I mean Wisconsin."

Mr. Anderson's head jerked toward me in surprise, but then turned back and said, "Vhat about my farm … and all our … my things?"

"You can ship them with you on the train — whatever you can afford, and we can sell your farm for you and wire you the money when the sale is final."

"You can do that?"

"Yes, sir, we have done that before." I shuffled through the papers on my desk. "Your farm was part of the land owned by Wil Rynerson. Is that correct?" He nodded. "Well, he might buy it back, or if you aren't in a hurry, we could advertise it in the *Rio Grande Republican.* You might get a better price that way."

The old man's shoulders slumped, and he sobbed as he said, "You vould do that for me?"

"Of course, sir. There will be a fee, but I could draw up the papers to give us power of attorney and you could leave tomorrow if you like ... well, it will take a few days for me to get the order to exhume your wife's casket."

Amund broke into a wide smile. "I must go to the telegraph office and send a message to my son." He left in a rush.

Within the week, I had made all the arrangements, and Mr. and Mrs. Anderson were on their way back to Wisconsin.

# 42: Making Sausage

**February 23, 1889**

With the desire for statehood, came several requirements imposed by the Congress. Zio took it upon himself to see that he and his colleagues met all their conditions. Among them was the establishment of state institutions. Zio had long understood what a state institution would do for a city. He wanted that and the recognition it would bring for Las Cruces. When the U.S. Congress' Morrill Act offered funding incentives for agricultural colleges, the fruitful Mesilla Valley became its natural location. He, Hiram Hadley, Numa Reymond, George Bowman, Wil Rynerson, and Eugen Van Patten had laid the groundwork with their Las Cruces College organization. Under that precursor to the agricultural college, they assembled land, facility, and funds.

But Las Cruces wasn't the only location considered for the state college. One plan had all the higher learning institutions in Albuquerque and another proposed Socorro for the agricultural college and experiment station.

In the end, the Las Cruces' committee's preparations and lobbying helped Zio gain the needed votes. However, the Colonel had little control over the Senate, or Council as it was called then, and that presented problems. His power was limited, but he did all he could to assure the Council's proposed locations matched the House Bill's.

On the final Saturday of the legislative session, all hell broke loose. The Senate saw the bill to establish state institutions (the Agricultural College in Las Cruces included) fail on a six-to-six vote. Parliamentary antics and a failed filibuster failed to resurrect the measure, and the Council recessed until its evening session.

That evening, the Council leadership regained control. Their members voted to pass the state institutions bill and refer it to committee to resolve any differences with the House's version.

Meanwhile, in the lower chamber, panic set in over the removal of public education from the omnibus bill. Gallery guests and angered Council members fanned the flames of discord as they milled about the Legislature's chamber during their Council recess. The chamber became chaotic. Members attempted to make several motions as visitors bellowed over disagreements carried over from the Council side. In a chaotic scene, the Colonel attempted to listen to his members as another tried to get the sergeant-at-arms to clear everyone except members from the room.

The Colonel mumbled, "These members are acting like a parcel of children." He therefore gaveled the session to "adjournment until Monday morning at 10 o'clock."

All day Sunday, he stewed over the events of the previous evening. He wasn't one to stifle debate, but he expected it to be respectful and pertinent. The Colonel decided he would speak to the House about it the following Monday morning.

His speech was eloquent, as always. He led with an acknowledgment that some members disagreed with his decision to adjourn the previous evening. The Colonel also scolded them because they ignored his calls to order and refused to take their seats. He admonished them for 'unparliamentary language' and their failure to come to order upon several of his gaveled requests. To conclude his remarks, he told them: "When the speaker of this house was elected ... he took an oath to maintain order, ... to maintain dignity of the house ... and he asks members to credit him with the intention of doing what ... he regarded as necessary for the preservation of the dignity of the house ...."

Later that day, H.B. 186 designating Las Cruces as the site for the Agricultural College and Experiment Station received its final reading and, despite attempts to amend, it passed by a vote of 16-7. The two chambers agreed on minor revisions and Governor Ross signed it into law on Monday, February 25, 1889.

The telegraph lines hummed with the news of the designations for the state institutions, and Las Cruces erupted into an impromptu celebration. When the Colonel returned, there were more formalities and celebrations, often with him as the master of ceremonies. Despite this, he remained frustrated. The territory still did not have the genuine public schools required for statehood.

The Santa Fe *New Mexican* reported that the Colonel "acted in the best interests of the people and the Republican party." It always struck me as odd the *New Mexican* supported him when the Santa Fe Ring and Zio were often at odds. Perhaps their editor recognized the Ring's corrupt ways as they gobbled up land from powerless Spanish land grant holders.

Zio's biggest disappointment came with the Education Bill failure. Those that had read the new bill viewed it as a revision of the 1884 Public School law. That version didn't allow local authorities to support their school's infrastructure or operation through taxation. The creators of the new Education Bill patterned it after Iowa's, which was considered the best education legislation in the land. But they could not guarantee passage.

Most in the legislature believed Governor Ross favored the new law. In fact, rumors suggested he would pocket veto the omnibus bill unless the Education Bill passed.

Issues of taxation and the pervasive objections of the Catholic Church often resulted in heated debates over the Education Bill. However, after considerable wrangling, the House sent it on to the Council. All Zio, the rest of the House members, and governor could do was wait for the Council to act. At the eleventh hour, they approved the bill, albeit with twelve amendments, which meant it had to be returned to the House.

The House clerk read the amendments and several members jumped to their feet to object to them. Once again, the members of the House became unruly, but adjournment would mean defeat. In the end, they refused the Council's amendments by a vote of 15-9 and returned it to the Council. Whether the Council refused to reconsider the bill or simply ran out of time, midnight struck, and President Chaves of the Council ordered the adjournment of the body without action on the Public Education Bill.

As a footnote, despite Governor Ross's rumored veto, he signed the omnibus bill. Still, the lack of a bill that would establish true public schools for New Mexico deeply troubled the Colonel.

The Santa Fe *New Mexican* was one of the few newspapers that reported the complete events of each session of the House and Council. Their reporting didn't put the blame for the failed public school bill on anyone. Meanwhile, the local Democratic leaning newspaper, the *Las Cruces Daily News*, condemned Zio without the background that the Santa Fe *New Mexican* published. I've rarely seen him so riled. As soon as we received a copy of that 'rag', he fired off a lengthy letter to its editor.

During the nine plus years that I knew Zio, his two years as an elected representative and Speaker of the House were his best and happiest. The two months when the legislature was in session were the penultimate period of those two years. I believe it had little to do with the power of the position and everything to do with him being able to do his best for the citizens of the Territory, and in particular, for his constituents in southern New Mexico.

# 43: Back in the Middle

Zio stayed in Santa Fe for an extra few days after he adjourned the twenty-eighth session of the New Mexico House of Representatives to meet with allies and plan for a state constitutional convention.

Back in Las Cruces, Albert Fall partnered with a man named Lowry and they opened a real estate, stock, and mine brokerage business. Notwithstanding his narrow defeat in the 1888 election, Fall piled up achievements. He must have felt financially secure enough to bring his ailing wife and family west in late '87. In the spring of '89, he had gained influence as he formed the partnership with Lowry and the New Mexico Bar admitted him. He was elected to the office of Irrigation Commissioner and became active in the Dona Ana Democratic Party, which allowed him to attend various social and political functions.

At the end of March, Zio returned to the office after one of his meetings. I assumed it had to do with the Oliver Lee case because he didn't tell me where or who he met. He shuffled papers and mumbled. I turned back to the will I was working on, but then he interrupted my thoughts when he seemed to speak to no one, but ostensibly to me. "That Ed King sure is a strange one. Newcombe says nothing about his behavior, but every time I talk to him, he seems scared. I mean, I suppose it's natural …"

I didn't hear another word he said as my mind raced back to what I had presumed was my violation of pre-trial ethics.

*Newcombe had talked to Ed King? That was acceptable? Perhaps all my law knowledge hadn't returned.*

"Is something wrong, Jesús?"

My face must have revealed my confusion and disappointment in myself. "No, no. I think it must be difficult for Ed to be separated from his brother Eph and prevented from roaming free." I made a mental note to revisit the pre-trial rules.

*Perhaps I should revisit all the things I had learned before my accident.*

Regardless, it was a relief to know I hadn't violated lawyer ethics after all. I drew a deep breath as I realized that my memory hadn't been fully restored.

"Are you sure nothing is wrong?"

"It's only that I haven't recovered … at least not in full, but come to think of it, how can I even know that? Everybody seems familiar now and I remember the town and how to find places, but uh … it's hard to explain, I guess."

Zio stood and came to my desk. "It's OK. You might be a new you and that is alright, as well. I'm no expert, but I should think that it isn't good to pressure yourself."

"I read my journals and they seem familiar … but it doesn't seem like me."

"Like I said, try to relax. Besides, there might be things you may not want to recover. Perhaps I shouldn't say it, but your self-confidence is much better. Accept yourself for who you are and go from there."

I nodded and leaned over my desk with my hand to my chin. He had a point. While my journals helped me remember some things, they also reminded me of feelings and attitudes that I might have been better off not remembering. I shook my head to clear my mind. *Best to think about the here and now.*

Zio turned back toward his desk and I said, "Do you still think that Ed King told the truth about Walter Good's murder?"

He stopped and turned back to me. "King swore an oath that it was." Zio's quizzical expression made me think he wasn't certain. Then he surprised me when he asked, "How many times have you spoken with Oliver?"

I felt distrusted. "Are you sure you want to hear about this?" I paused. I wished I hadn't taken his bait. "You *do* realize that Walter made enemies with ease?" Zio stared at me. "Ed is just a pawn in this. He shouldn't be 'locked up'."

"Well, if King was free to return to the Lees, we believe they would re-school him on the truth. If he changes his story, our case is gone. It'll be a shame if Ed King goes to prison for perjury over this."

I had thought of that, but hearing it from Zio struck home.

Meanwhile, Lee and Tucker continued to live rough in the Sacramentos. Somehow, they got through the spring roundup. I supposed that was the worst of it. I knew they wouldn't turn themselves in without some assurances of their safety. But even if Zio suggested they would do so, and perhaps they had already, the word would never reach Oliver because John Good and his puppet deputy E. C. Rucker would never pass it along.

Zio could see something was on my mind. "If you know where he is …" he sighed. "I don't want to know, but if you go there, tell him he's not helping himself."

"I told him …" I stopped, but it was too late.

"You've talked to him?"

"Well, yes, but I didn't tell him anything."

"He was here in Las Cruces? Why?"

"Yes. He needed to talk to his lawyers and Albert Fall." I neglected to say Oliver stood not three feet from him when he told me that ... and more. I felt horrible, and I wanted to tell Zio everything ... rid myself of the burden ... but Oliver and his mother and Nettie were like the family that Zio, Mia Tia, Little Henry, Maggie, and the others *were* to me.

"Jesús, you have tread dangerously close to abetting an indicted criminal."

"He's not a criminal."

"Well, perhaps not formally, but a person who evades arrest is a criminal. We could probably charge him with that now."

---

A nationwide movement to form organizations to honor and assist veterans of the civil war had gained steam. Zio saw it as an opportunity to formalize the Memorial Day gatherings of his California Column veterans. On April fifteen, he applied to the territorial office of the Grand Army of the Republic to form a post in Las Cruces. A month later, just in time for Memorial Day, the territorial office notified Zio of their admission as the Phil Sheridan Post #14. They designated Zio the commander, and he wanted to make the Memorial Day celebration extra special that year. Every attendant from the California Column joined the Grand Army of the Republic. They honored him for his service with a handsome gavel as their commander and for his service as the Territorial Speaker of the House of Representatives.

We heard through the grapevine that Albert Fall refused to accept the Democrats nomination for sheriff in the '90 election. Zio remarked it seemed rather early to select candidates. I imagine Zio felt as though he had little chance to relish his elected term. Fall told the Dona Ana Democratic committee that he had enough of politics in the last election, but Zio reckoned he was still smarting from his defeat six months prior.

"I know a competitor when I see one. That man will be back."

About that time, Albert, and Teresita's little girl, Ermindita, lapsed back into her poor health and fell into a coma-like state. Within a few days she had passed, much to the heartache and distress of all the Fountains and many friends in Mesilla. Larlo, Tommy and all the Fountains went to Mesilla to comfort Albert Jr. and Teresita and to mourn their little cousin. I saw firsthand how the family reacted to the poor little girl's sickness and death. It gave me a first-hand look at how they might have reacted when they thought I would not return. We buried her a few days later in the little Basilica of San Albino cemetery at the end of Calle de Guadalupe in Mesilla.

## May 21

A couple of weeks after we laid Ermindita to rest, the new sheriff, Mariano Barela, came to speak with Zio, but Zio was in Rincon. Rosa showed the sheriff in. She wore her scarf in a way that I had not seen before, and it distracted me from Barela's question.

Barela frowned and said, "I said, when will A.J. return."

I stood and in one motion pushed my chair away with the backs of my legs. "He didn't say, sir. He went yesterday to speak with someone in Rincon about some land."

Barela frowned again. "Well, they have assigned Judge McFie to the Oliver Lee case, and he wants it off his docket. I tried to explain that Lee, Tucker and Kellam were not to be found, but he wouldn't accept that."

"I can let Zio know when he returns, but I don't think he is rounding up suspects anymore."

"Yes, I realize that. My intent was to ask him to send you to talk to Lee and arrange for a deputy from Las Cruces to escort him here so he can have his bail hearing."

Just then, Zio entered from the parlor. "Ask me what?"

Barela repeated the question and Zio replied, "I don't think Jesús should go alone. I don't want to see him become entangled in this. We've prevented that so far. In fact, I don't want him to go at all."

Barela frowned again. *Was that his habitual expression?* I reached onto my desk and fiddled with the keys on the typewriter in thought.

Barela shook his head and said, "I don't want this. It's Judge McFie. He wants this off his docket by the end of next month. This needs to get done today. Can you do it?"

"Zio," I said, "If you go, they won't talk to you and you're the last person they would tell where to find Oliver and the rest. If I go, they will send word to Oliver, and he will meet with me."

It was Zio's turn to frown. The two of them stood a few feet in front of me with the god-awful-est frowns you ever saw.

A knock at the door interrupted us. It was Miles Wilson from the Telegraph Office.

"Colonel, this urgent message just came through and I thought I ought to deliver it to you right away."

Zio took the message and read it. His fingers and thumb framed the area between his eyebrows, as he was deep in thought. "I must go. Larlo has been in a mining accident in Lake Valley. I must tell my wife and Maggie before I leave to see to his health."

Barela, frown still pinned to his face, said, "Oh, I am so sorry to hear that A.J. is there anything I can do?"

"I don't think so, Mariano, but thank you for asking. But how do we proceed from here?"

"The judge says it has to be done no later than tomorrow. He wants Lee and the others to surrender to Tom Williams on the twenty-sixth … that's uh, let's see …"

"That's Sunday," I said.

"Right," confirmed Zio. "The judge's never let the Sabbath stop him from giving assignments. Well, OK then, Jesús can do it, but I want it understood that Jesús will do so on behalf of the prosecution so that they cannot accuse him of abetting the suspects."

I hadn't thought of that. The sheriff shrugged with disinterest. I asked, "Should I wait on some paperwork?"

"No," said Zio. "I'll take Sheriff Barela's word for it."

"You have it A.J." The two men shook hands and Zio exited into the hall.

Barela turned to me. "How long will it take to get in touch with him?"

"I'll have to ride hard to get there tonight, but I think I can do it." It was fortunate that the days were long, with a good amount of daylight.

"He won't be there, though, will he?"

"No, sir. I'll have to send word to him. Unless he is further away from his ranch than I expect, I should see him tomorrow evening. That would be Wednesday. If he agrees, which I think he will, they should have time to put their affairs in order before they come in."

Barela frowned again and said, "And that would put you back here no later than Thursday evening, the twenty-third; am I right?"

"I believe so, sir, again, if everything goes as planned."

"I want Williams there the morning of the twenty-sixth, so he and his prisoners will not overnight on the road." For some reason, his frown deepened, and I nodded.

"That will give us a couple of days in case I have trouble finding Oliver. Do I know Tom Williams?" I asked.

"I believe you do. The two of you monitored the polls on election day. Every time I looked, you seemed involved in a discussion."

"Oh, yes, — Tom. He seems like a straight shooter. I have your word Oliver can trust him?"

"Yes, I would swear it on my mother's grave."

"Well then, it seems like a good plan."

Barela concluded with a grimace-tinged nod, "Right. This better work, or McFie'll have my bee-hind." He turned and left.

I threw together a bedroll with a few things, Rosa handed me some jerky and two canteens, and I went to the stable where Mateo waved as Zio galloped north toward Lake Valley. Between Mateo and me, we had Ol' Nasty saddled, and I was on my way in no time.

# 44: The New Me

I planned to stop at Luna Well and exchange Ol' Nasty for a fresh mount, but then realized the Lunas had probably left. Still, I would need a fresh horse. When I got there, a young man greeted me. He introduced himself as Mark Jamison. He said his wife, whom he had married a few weeks before, had supper ready. We had a friendly talk, and he made the temporary exchange for Ol' Nasty. I asked about the Lunas, but he only knew they had left the country. As I rode away, I spotted the rustic bench behind the adobe. One side had broken down. My vision blurred as I remembered Lucia and me sitting there. As I refocused, Lucia sat, gazing over the vast sea of cacti and brush. Her vivid black hair had an iridescent glow against the flowing cream-colored dress she wore for her birthday party. She scanned the basin. *What did she seek? She was looking for me.* "For me," I mumbled. I blinked, and she was gone.

I arrived at Lee Well shortly after sunset as the orange-tinged sky faded to the western horizon. Before I could get within 'Halloo' distance, someone jumped from behind a clump of gobernadora and demanded my name.

"I'm Jesús Messi. I'm here to see the Lee family."

"They ain't taken no ...." He must have recognized me in the dim light because he stopped mid-sentence and said, "Hey-you? Is that you?"

"Virgil?" I got off my horse to shake his hand, but he grabbed me by the shoulders and gave me a big hug.

He held me out at arm's length. "Well, ain't you a sight for sore eyes? Go right on in."

"Well, how have you been Virg? Did you forget how to shave?" He sported about a week's growth.

"Nah, just ain't had hardly a minute. Good and Rucker and that bunch come buzzin' round here near-on every day. It's gittin' real tense. The women folk ain't been into town since about the time you left. The boys go for supplies. It's downright nasty hereabouts." We started toward the adobe, but Virgil stopped and turned to me. "By the way, how *is* Ol' Nasty?"

"Oh, he's fine, I exchanged him for this nag at Luna Well. Aren't you coming in with me?"

"Cain't. The boss says I gotta stay out here 'til I get relieved." He peered to the west, where the night's visual serenade threatened the fading sunset symphony. "Cain't be no more than an hour or so. I'll come to the adobe when Billy shows."

"I'll look for ya, Virg."

When I turned the corner of the adobe, a dark figure was in 'my' old spindle-less Windsor chair. He held a Winchester across his lap and when he heard me step on some gravelly sand, he stood with a start and said, "Who goes there?"

I recognized the voice. "It's me Eph, Jesús. I've got news for Oliver."

Nettie and Mary must have heard the ruckus. They came to the door with shotguns. "Oh Jesús," said Nettie, "Is there somethin' wrong? Have you come back to us?"

She handed her shotgun to Eph and threw herself into my arms.

"Nettie," cried Mary. "You're a betrothed woman now. You cain't be throwin' yerself into other men's arms."

"Betrothed?" I yelped.

"Yep." Nettie and Mary broke into huge smiles. "I'm gittin' married." Nettie spun with such energy that we had to back away to avoid colliding with her.

"Do I know the lucky man?"

"Nope. His name is Bill McNew. We met last fall."

"How did you meet?"

Mary returned to the threshold, leaned her shotgun against the inside wall and said, "Come on inside, you two. I'll warm the leftover stew for Hey-you, I mean Jesús. You must be starvin'."

I followed Nettie and Mary inside and Eph returned to my old chair, Winchester at the ready. He saw me and said, "I done ate. 'Sides, I'm on guard." I nodded and went inside.

Nettie was excited to tell me how she met McNew. She said that one day the previous fall, Oliver found himself pinned down by gunfire in an arroyo by several of Good's men that wanted to collect on John's reward. Bill McNew heard gunshots as he rode past and investigated. Later, he told Oliver he didn't know who was right and who was wrong, but he didn't like the odds. Together, they chased off the attackers. Oliver brought him back to their camp and the next time he came home, Bill came, too.

"Oh, Jesús, it was love at first sight." said Nettie. It was good to see her in high spirits again. I didn't think that would ever happen after George was murdered. "And I think Oliver likes Bill better than he did …."

It seemed like a good time to interrupt her. "That's great Nettie." Mary brought my plate of stew and a fork. "I'm afraid I'm here to talk with Oliver."

Mary spoke up, "I ain't got no more biscuits tonight Jesús … we don't know where Oliver is. He says that keeps us safe."

"Well, someone must. You still send him messages, right?"

Nettie had gotten up to get me a napkin, which she placed next to my plate. "Eph took over that job after you left. Shall I get him?"

The jerky I ate while in the saddle had done little for me, and I was famished. I forked a chunk of beef and pointed to the door with a nod. Nettie went outside and then returned without Eph. "He has to fetch Sixto to take over — he says it was about time for his relief anyhow."

While Eph went for Sixto, Nettie sat down across from me. Mary had taken the slop bucket out to the pigsty.

I had focused on my plate, but when I looked up to pour a glass of water, Nettie was solemn. I couldn't help but ask, "Is there something wrong Nettie? You're gettin' married of your own free will, aren't you?"

Her smile broke out again, and she said, "Oh, no, I mean yes. Yes, I love Bill, but when I saw you … well, it just reminded me about George … you know, sometimes I wish he had just shaken danged ol' John Good's hand that day in front of the mercantile."

I grimaced. "Yes, I suppose that is natural, but you know what Oliver would say, don't you?"

As I finished my stew, Eph returned. I didn't realize that I had missed Mary's Texas style meals so much, but that stew was the best I ever had. Mary always said, 'the longer you keep stew around, the better it gits.'

Finally, Eph said he knew where Oliver was, but he couldn't tell me. "I done promised Mr. Oliver that I wouldn't tell nobody nothin'. 'Sides, you rode all 'dis way. You must be plum tuckered out. You stay here and git some sleep and I'll fetch Mr. Oliver for ya. We orta be back by daybreak."

Eph left, and I sat down to a hot cup of coffee with Mary and Nettie. "So, when will this happen, Mrs. McNew?"

Nettie giggled, and Mary frowned. "June twelfth. Bill made an appointment with the justice of the peace." Mary frowned again. Nettie didn't notice her aunt's expression. "We ain't got no Methodist ministers over here and Oliver wouldn't hear of us goin' to that new one in Las Cruces. I didn't even ask him cause I knew …."

Nettie went on and on about William McNew while we sipped our coffee. Mary seemed to have mixed feelings, which I expected. Six months of courting wouldn't have satisfied her. Still, she smiled more than not, and so I presumed she felt it was better to see Nettie happy again than to deal with her moods.

"You can have Oliver's bed if you want Jesús … gosh, it seems odd to not call you Hey-you," said Mary.

"Thank you, Mary, but I think I'll sleep in the bunkhouse tonight. I want to talk with the boys a bit. Besides, if Oliver gets in early, he might catch a few winks in his own bed."

Nettie and Mary nodded, Mary filled my mug with coffee, and I half-skipped with anticipation across the ranch yard to the bunkhouse. When I walked in, nobody said a thing. Playing cards and matchsticks lay on the table in front of Stumpy, Willie, Benito, and Eliseo (I noted it was toward the end of the month and wages were long gone). In the corner, Felipe strummed a somber Spanish ballad on his guitar. A couple of new recruits darned their socks, while Shorty, Chuck, and Lorenzo read dime novels in their bunks. There were plenty of open bunks, and I surmised those men were on guard somewhere. I just stood in the doorway with my mouth agape. When it seemed they didn't see or hear me come in, I said, "Hello boys."

Just when I was wondering if I had done something wrong, Virgil came through the door with two pies. All the boys jumped up with big smiles as they gathered round me. They asked how I had been and how was Ol' Nasty and was I still using lavender on my pillow, and did I still dance around early in the morning? Most of them called me 'Hey-you', but I didn't care. It was nice to feel comfortable with the people around me.

We had a wonderful time. No one asked why I was there. I think they must have known it had to do with the warrant for Oliver.

**May 22**

The next morning, the sound of the door opening and closing right away awakened me. In my groggy state, I had forgotten where I was. Virgil shook me fully awake and said, "Hey-you, Oliver is on the porch. He's been waitin' for you for over half an hour."

I jumped out of my cot with apologies flowing, but when I looked around, Virgil had gone. When I came around the corner of the adobe, Oliver had turned his chair, so he faced toward the bunkhouse. "Well," he said, "I guess it doesn't take long for a man to fall into bad habits. Seems you've already forgotten that daylight is for workin'."

"Sorry, Oliver. I guess I was tired from the hard ride over here yesterday. It's good to see you." If I had insulted him with what he might have thought was laziness, I hoped my greeting would restore a harmonious visit.

He smiled, took off his hat, and ran his fingers through his chestnut hair. "Well, what's so important that they couldn't come to tell me themselves?"

I wasn't sure what he meant by that. "They were afraid you wouldn't talk to them."

He laughed and replaced his hat. "Do tell. I wonder why they would think that." He remarked sarcastically.

It didn't need a reply, and I knew he was waiting for me to explain my presence.

"It's wonderful that Nettie is getting married. Her fiancé seems like someone that would fit right in here."

"What do you mean by that?" Oliver stood and walked toward the barn. I didn't know how to respond, and I just sat there. After a few steps, he turned to me. "I'm sorry ... Jesús. None of this is on you. It's just that I'm gittin' real tired of lumpy bedrolls and moldy biscuits, and Mary and Nettie shouldn't be locked up inside like they are." He took a deep breath. "Now, what did they send you to tell me?"

I explained the plan and told Oliver I didn't know Williams well, but we had chatted on election day. Oliver said "pfft," at the mention of election day but didn't interrupt me. I told him I felt Williams was a stand-up young man, and he would carry out his orders to the letter.

"Pfft," again. "And why should I believe their orders aren't to handcuff me to a cholla and shoot me?"

I shook my head and looked out toward the ominous wall of the Sacramentos. "He wouldn't do that. Besides Zio ... the Colonel hasn't ordered it."

"Well, who the ...who is it, then?"

"Judge McFie ordered Sheriff Barela to send me. He wants you, Tucker, and Kellam to turn yourselves in to Williams and allow him to escort you back to Las Cruces so you can have a *habeas corpus* hearing."

Oliver chuckled. "I don't need no *habeas corpus* hearing. We all know they want me jailed. What about bail?"

"Well, a finding of lawful detention will follow that, and they could release you the next day pending your trial."

"If I come, how soon would this hearing take place? I ain't gonna sit in jail for weeks and weeks like Perry and Cooper did. And I need to be back in time for Nettie and Bill's weddin'."

I wanted to tell him I trusted Zio's word. I thought about that all the way across the Tularosa. Too much had happened that made me skeptical, but I was there to see that Oliver and his bunch surrendered. I wouldn't have agreed to do it if I hadn't believed it was best for them.

"The sheriff said that if you surrender, they could schedule the hearing right away." Barela hadn't said so in so many words, but Oliver would not have agreed to anything less. It would be better for Oliver and Tucker to get it over with. He probably wouldn't agree with that now, but I knew he would eventually.

I wasn't sure the judge and sheriff would follow through, but I told him Judge McFie wanted it off his docket and I thought that was as close to a guarantee as he would get.

"McFie? I thought I hired his firm to represent me?"

My little fib about scheduling a hearing right away made me nervous. I stretched my legs out to relieve some of the tension. I hoped Oliver didn't notice and so I stretched my arms out above my head and faked a yawn.

"Well, yes sir, you did, but Judge McFie is a uh ... well, not just a judge by name."

Oliver had gotten a little red-faced. "Well, how can he be the judge in a case where I hired him?"

"He won't because he's the court administrator — he schedules hearings and that sort of thing. Judge McFie hears cases, but he won't hear yours because he would have to recuse himself *since* he represents you."

"I suppose it's too much to hope that he would do it so he could dismiss my case. Don't answer that."

He turned again and walked to the end of the porch, then turned back and paced back until he faced me. "Alright, I'll do it and I think I can talk Tucker into it too, but I do not know where Cherokee Bill went."

"You mean Kellam?"

"Right."

---

**May 23**

The next day, my stop at Luna Well for Ol' Nasty went without a hitch, but the image I had seen before of Lucia on the bench haunted me. I feared a glance in that direction might trigger another vision or worse yet, tears. As a dust devil appeared out of nowhere and moved across the stage parking area, the new attendant and I had a brief conversation about how dry it had been. He hoped the monsoon would mean plentiful rain. His wife interrupted us when she called from the adobe doorway.

"The pie is ready, Mark." It reminded me that his name was Mark Jamison. I had my back to the adobe and when I turned, there stood Lucia in the forest green dress she wore when she surprised me at the Fountains for the first fair. She beamed at the prospect of our future week together. My heart sank, and I blinked. Once again, her image was gone and in its place was Mark's sunny wife. She wore an apron, and a bandana held her blonde hair at bay. "Invite your friend for a slice," she called.

I had mounted Ol' Nasty and Mark looked up at me. My eyes had turned glassy, but he didn't notice. "Would you join us, please? It's mighty lonely out here."

I demurred with the best smile I could muster and said, "Sorry, but I must be back tonight." I reined Ol' Nasty, and we started up the trail toward San Augustin Pass. Mark called after me, "Another time then, maybe?" I waved with a thumbs up and broke Ol' Nasty into a slow lope while I bawled my eyes out.

The full impact of my relationship with Lucia and losing her unshakeable love hit me. All the way up the mountain, I forced myself to feel what she must have. My emotions grew, and as I crested the San Augustin Pass, the heartache that would not allow her to go on struck me hard. I dismounted. Tears streamed down my cheeks as I peered over the expansive White Sands. How could I not feel some blame and yet I could have done nothing to allay her grief and loneliness?

As we started down the pass, I felt a sense of relief — not that I could ever forgive myself, for in the final analysis, it was my jealousy that led me to that apocalyptic event on San Augustin Peak a little over a year before. My accident put my immaturity and lack of experience on display and nearly killed me. I hoped the resurfacing of my feelings for Lucia marked the end of my transition back to my true self. If not, perhaps it was as far as I needed to go. As Zio had said, I needed to accept myself for who I am *now*. Considering all I had experienced, he made sense. Now, if I could only accept this true me.

# 45: Oliver's Anguish

**May 24, 1890**

The day after I returned to Las Cruces, Zio arrived from Lake Valley in time for supper. He gathered everyone in the parlor and told us about Larlo's accident. Bad luck seemed to pursue the Fountains, and I wondered if it was a trend. Larlo was injured when he had just begun a temporary assignment in a mine at Lake Valley.

Zio stood before us without a hint of worry. "He was in a shaft, about seventy-five feet down, when someone dropped a pail of dirt from above. Fortunately, it was a glancing blow, for a direct hit would have killed him. He had no broken bones, and he wasn't gravely injured, but suffered abrasions and a deep gash. I wanted him to come home with me to convalesce, but he refused. Larlo says he will be fit to work in a few days, but I expect he will rethink that. He will be OK with some rest and seeing to his wounds."

The next day, Zio was off again. This time he went to Silver City to lobby for the upcoming statehood constitutional convention. He was to return home before going to Santa Fe for the Republican Central Committee's meeting, but he didn't appear in time to catch the northbound train. Normally, he would have telegraphed us if his plans had changed, and so Rosa worried that foul play was afoot.

After a day or two, I noticed her and Maggie whispering in the kitchen. That Saturday, the *Republican,* based upon a Silver City *Sentinel* article, reported that Colonel Fountain was indisposed with a sickness for ten days. The *Republican* editor, Charles Metcalfe, also came by to tell us the same issue of the *Sentinel* had an article about problems they had with severed and downed telegraph lines.

---

## June 7

While Zio was away, Sheriff Barela kept a campaign promise to water Main Street. He found a converted wagon contraption and used prisoner labor at no cost to the taxpayers to spread water across the areas that experienced the bulk of the traffic. As I did my daily rounds, I observed the contraption the prisoners used to try to spray water evenly across the wide street. Oliver and Tucker were among the prisoners. What we got was a mess, with puddles everywhere and caliche caked onto people's boots and shoes. It was quite a sight. Anyone that crossed the street had to stop and use the edge of the boardwalks to scrap the mud from their shoe bottoms. They left little piles up and down Main Street next to the boardwalks. However, it lessened the dust issue, and people seemed willing to tolerate a little mud in exchange. Each time the practice continued, their technique improved and before long, the *Rio Grande Republican* reported that Las Cruces had the best conditioned Main Street in the territory.

## June 11

Oliver's and Tucker's surrender went off without a hitch on May twenty-six. Although I had no responsibility to do so, I visited them at the jail every few days. They kept them in two separate cells, which was just as well, because Tucker always seemed like a dangerous man to me. Like Oliver, he was quiet, but a certain evilness about him made me uneasy.

On a Tuesday, I stopped by after my daily errands to exchange books I had loaned Oliver from the Fountain's library. He was fit to be tied.

"Jesús, I gotta git outta here. Nettie's gettin' married tomorrow, and I have to be there."

I pursed my lips. The news wasn't good, and I wondered why the sheriff hadn't told him. "There's some bad news, Oliver, and I wish I wasn't the one to tell you about it."

Oliver threw up his arms. "I'm stuck here — I knew it. Did you know it was going to take this long?"

"Won't they delay the wedding until you get out? By the way, why would they get married on a Wednesday?"

"No, it's bad luck to change your weddin' day. I don't know why the Justice of the Peace sets marriages for that day. Maybe cause it's Weds day?" He was serious, but then caught the terrible pun and we snickered.

"I'm sorry Oliver. I hoped they would schedule it sooner, but yesterday, Zio told me he wouldn't be back until June twenty-ninth and a judge by the name of Whiteman will come down from Santa Fe."

"June twenty-ninth? My goodness Jesús, that means I'll be in here longer than Perry and Cooper were. You knew I didn't want to be locked up this long."

I sympathized, but knew the heavy docket was the reason and that the court heard cases in the order filed. All I could do was shrug and say, "I'm afraid there's a lot of lawlessness in the county and you'll just have to wait your turn."

Oliver turned his back and took two long strides before he stopped facing his bunk. He turned ninety degrees and took another step before he stopped next to the thunder jug against the other wall. "I think you could have warned me about this."

"Yes, I could have told you it might take the greater part of the month to get your hearing, but I didn't know that for sure. If I had, would you have given yourself up?" I paused, and Oliver appeared in thought. "Because if you hadn't, you would still live rough in the Sacramentos and when you finally turned yourself in, your hearing wouldn't be until the fall session."

Oliver grimaced with the recognition that I was right. "Well, can you tell Ma and Nettie?"

"Sorry, I can't, but they say the telegraph line has been extended to La Luz. I can send a telegram to somebody there if you like, and they can deliver it to Nettie and ... Bill, isn't it?"

Oliver nodded. "I s'pose that's the best I can do. But, I'm still not happy about being kept here for nye on a month." He wiped his hand across his mouth. "Ya know Jesús, after the time you spent with us in the Tularosa, you should know that if the law would just let us settle things for ourselves, they wouldn't have your heavy dockets."

I got a paper and pencil, and we agreed on the message. He offered me a quarter for the telegram, but I refused. The fee was thirty cents, but I felt I owed him far more than that.

Oliver was a voracious reader. He had finished *Moby Dick*, so I exchanged it for *The Adventures of Tom Sawyer*. As I turned to leave, he said, "Does that uncle of yours have *War and Peace*? I heard the publisher translated it to English a couple of years ago. Fall doesn't have it, but I thought you might know someone that would."

*Fall? I knew he meant Albert Fall. I knew Oliver was impressed by Fall, but I hadn't expected that they would become close.* "No, Zio doesn't have *War and Peace*, but Mrs. Branigan has a wonderful collection of books. I'll check with her."

"Good! Thank you. Fall has been teaching me Greek, and I'm getting' mighty tired of wading through those Greek tales. The one about the wooden horse is my favorite, though."

As I left the jail to continue my errands, I reflected on the sympathy I felt for Oliver. But that wasn't quite it. The more I thought about it, the more I realized it was empathy. For I was in my own kind of prison. While there were no bars or jailer and my cell allowed me to roam, my 'cell' kept me in a kind of biblical limbo.

It turned out that Mrs. Branigan had a copy, and she offered it to me for Oliver. Several years later, she and several other Las Cruces women formed the Women's Improvement Association. They eventually owned a building for their club headquarters. Shortly after, they pooled their books to loan to the public and Las Cruces' first library was born.

---

**June 25**

That afternoon, as I toiled over a contract, Zio burst into the office and said, "Someone has taken Ed King."

He cast an accusing eye toward me, but then said, "Please tell me you know nothing about this."

While my false guilt lingered, I knew nothing about it. The defense knew where Ed King was before I did, and that rat-faced assistant to Newcombe made it sound like I had revealed privileged information. "I knew where he was, but so did his lawyers, long before me. They must have told Oliver." As Zio left the office, he mumbled he needed to speak with Judge Newcombe, Oliver's lawyer, about it.

By now, the twists and turns of my stories had made me doubt myself. After Zio left, I couldn't reconstruct the entire mess well enough to decide if I had indeed told Oliver.

When Zio returned, he said that Judge Newcombe told him that their assistant had let Oliver know where Ed King was by mistake. "The man apologized vehemently, but I think the Bar should know about this." He sat down and wrote a letter to the

Bar. I never knew if he sent it, but my relief was palpable, and fortunately, Zio didn't notice.

# 46: Only the Innocent

**June 28, 1889**

Judge Whiteman came from Santa Fe to hear the last case in the district court's spring session. The judge called the *habeas corpus* hearing to order amid an early summer heat wave. Despite the clerk's and bailiff's efforts to encourage a wisp of a summer breeze, the courtroom was sweltering.

The district court held the bail hearing, called a *habeas corpus* hearing at the time, in Las Cruces for the convenience of all except the judge. Per Oliver's lawyer's filing, the actual criminal trial would be in Socorro at a future date.

Everyone in town knew that Zio was handling the prosecutorial duties and that the sheriff had held Oliver and Tucker in the Las Cruces jail for some time. In those days, courtroom dramas were as close to theater as folks could get. Nearly every Tularosan had an interest in the case and lots of Las Crucens would want to attend as well.

I wanted to avoid the hearing but decided to go because I hoped I might see Nettie and Mary and perhaps one or two of the hands. I arrived a little late and had to stand behind the gallery next. The people next to me said they came every time Colonel Fountain prosecuted. They asked who I was. When I told them, they asked about my accident. Thankfully, Judge Whiteman gaveled the court to order and I didn't have to hear how some friend got kicked in the head or something and never survived.

The variety of stories people will tell you when they think it will comfort you amazed me.

The judge took up the application of the defendants, Oliver M. Lee and James Tucker, for bail. He read the charges. I knew there was other court business to be resolved, which included a complaint filed by John's wife Bertha.

Many friends of the Lees made the seventy-mile trip to see justice done and support their neighbor and friend. The Goods were the sole attendees that favored the prosecution, although there were many local people that attended to witness the drama play out. John, ever the egotist, had insisted he sit at the prosecution table alongside Zio.

A *habeas corpus* hearing can agitate the people attending that want to support their accused friends. If the judge accepts the accused's application and evidence, he might only call on the prosecution's witnesses. This can appear to the accused's supporters that the judge intends to rule against them.

Court procedures require the accused to file a writ requesting release on the grounds of improper imprisonment with supporting causes. The prosecution must then show the accused is too dangerous to release. In this case, the judge must have accepted Oliver's lawyers' pleadings as substantive reason to permit bail and so he questioned the prosecution's pleadings and witnesses all day Friday.

As I expected, Oliver's supporters read this as a bias by the judge since he didn't allow Oliver's lawyer to rebut Zio's version of the events. The Judge began by asking Zio to read his response to the request for release into the record. He did so with his usual theatrical gesticulations. It amounted to John Good's account of how he and deputy Rucker believed Walter met his end. The gallery grew increasingly restless. The judge had to gavel them down several times when Zio mentioned Oliver and Tucker's accused crimes.

Zio's account did not surprise anyone, as the *Rio Grande Republican* had published a lot of it when Ed King testified before the grand jury. Zio read from his filing that the Lees plotted to separate Walter Good from his family and friends, and when they had done so, they then questioned and killed him. They then hauled his body in a wagon into the White Sands, where they attempted to bury him. As the day wore on, Zio had few chances to sit, as the judge asked him question after question. He answered without hesitation, but with a subtle bias against the accused.

When John Good took the stand, the onlooker's uproar caused the judge to threaten to clear the gallery. But the judge could not restrain Oliver's Tularosan friends. When the judge questioned Deputy Rucker, derogatory murmurs filled the court. The judge demonstrably raised his gavel as he stared into the gallery, and the rabble calmed.

Late in the afternoon, Ed King was called to the stand. He wore a neat white shirt with a bolo tie and a tattered but clean slouch hat, which he removed before the bailiff swore him in.

"Do you solemnly swear to tell the truth, the whole truth, and nothing but the truth, so help you, God?" stated the bailiff.

"Yes. suh, I certainly do."

The judge leaned over from his perch. "Mr. King, you have heard what the assistant district attorney read into the record about the events of August fourteen and one Walter Good. Is that right?"

"Yes suh, judge."

"Now, Mr. King, I understand you testified to these facts at the grand jury hearing. Is that right?"

The stark whites of his eyes against Ed's ebony skin exposed his nervousness as they went from Oliver Lee, at the defense's table, to Perry in the gallery.

"Now listen to me, son," said Judge Whiteman. "Do you understand what I asked you?"

Ed looked down at his old slouch hat in his lap. The judge leaned further and as the judge repeated his question, Ed muttered, "Yes, suh."

"Uh-huh," acknowledged the judge as he peered out to stare down an interruption from the gallery. "Now, is all that you heard from Colonel Fountain accurate … I mean to say, did he say anything that didn't agree with your testimony or that he left out something?"

The court was on edge. Everyone thought they knew why Perry Altman and his men had taken Ed King from the Shalom Colony a few days before and they hung on every breath from the middle-aged black man.

The judge sensed the tension, and he pushed on. "Now uh, Mr. King, you do remember that you are under oath to tell the truth, do you not?"

Ed turned so he could make eye contact with the judge. "I do, suh."

Zio stood a few feet away from Ed, about halfway between the judge and the prosecution's table. He took a couple of steps toward Ed and glared at him as he put his hands on his hips. It was a subtle move, but I recognized it as a tactic he used to intimidate witnesses.

The judge knew it as well, and he said, "Now Colonel, I can manage this myself. You have paced around this courtroom all day. You must be exhausted. Please take a seat. I can handle this from here."

John Good had tried to get Zio's attention throughout the proceedings. As Zio sat at the prosecution table, Good tried to whisper something to him, but Zio hushed him by putting his hand out toward John. It incensed John, but a glance from the judge quieted him.

"Now then, Mr. King. Let's get back to the matter at hand, shall we? You understand you are under oath. Now, did Colonel Fountain leave anything out or did he say something that you feel was not right?" The judge simplified his questions for Ed. What he didn't realize is that Ed was well read. It wouldn't have surprised me if Ed had found a way to study up on how the proceedings would go.

Ed took a deep breath and let it out slowly. "Yes, suh"

The judge looked at Zio, who could see what was coming. Zio had put a hand over his mouth. It was a signal to the witness to stop talking, but Ed looked away.

"And would that be, you have more to offer the court, or you disagree with something the Colonel said?"

"All of it, suh."

The courtroom gasped and Zio stood and screamed, "Objection, your honor. The accused have tainted Mr. King's testimony …"

Before Zio could finish his objection, the judge said, "Denied. I cautioned you about this before this hearing, Colonel."

Zio put both hands behind his head and leaned over until his nose nearly touched the table.

Judge Whiteman turned back to Ed. "All of it? Mr. King, do you mean to say that none of it is true? You testified to these very facts at the grand jury hearing in uh … uh," the judge leafed through some papers, "November 1888, I believe."

"Yes, suh, judge." Ed kneaded his hat with his massive hands and his feet jiggled around like he needed to pee.

The gallery buzzed with delight as the judge shook his head and made veiled threats to the troublemaker's by swinging his gavel up and down. Their conduct was sufficient reason to clear the room, but I think Judge Whiteman ordered a ten-minute recess because he was so distressed over what Ed had said. As I turned to leave, Tom Williams, the deputy that had escorted Oliver and Tucker to Las Cruces, told me I could stay.

I sat in the back row next to two other attorneys. Ed got up after the judge left, but he didn't know where to go. He sat back in the witness' chair and continued to mangle his hat and tap his feet. I felt so bad for him. He had become a pawn in a life and death game. However you viewed it; those that could influence Ed had victimized him for their own benefit. *Now, we may never know what really happened.*

Ed looked up and caught my eye, and I smiled. I hoped it would comfort him, but he cowered and put his hat over his face.

When the judge returned, he called the court to order and reminded Ed of his oath, then repeated his question. "Mr. King, do you mean to say that nothing you told the grand jury is true?"

Ed dropped his hat into his lap, which revealed penitent trails of satiny tear tracks on his cheeks. I wanted to cry also and hate them all for what they did to this poor man.

Ed looked at the judge, gathered himself, and clear as day said, "Yes suh, ain't none of it the truth. I never saw any of what I said I did."

Zio raised his hands in exasperation and Oliver's attorney, Judge Newcombe, raised a fist in victory. Ed put his hat back over his face and his shoulders shuddered as he struggled to restrain the sobs that tried to break free.

The judge stood and glared at both lawyers. After a moment, he pounded his gavel and ordered the sheriff to remove the witness and charge him with perjury. He then gaveled the session in recess until the following morning. When I emerged from the courtroom, everyone had gone their separate ways.

There were fewer people in the court the next day. Most expected the result was decided. They were right, and the judge cut the hearing short. Although Judge Whiteman wasn't required to issue an explanation, he told the court he needed to be back in Santa Fe the next day and the last train would leave within the hour. I doubt he could bring himself to admit hia court had been made a sham. It was a victory for the Tularosans that had come to support their neighbor and kin, for in their opinion, justice had been served. Unfortunately, the pawn paid the price.

I spent many hours going over what happened in that courtroom that day. Every time I entered the courthouse, I thought about Ed. *There were no answers, only more questions.*

So, after a full day and half of judicial review, Judge Whiteman allowed bail in the amount of ten thousand dollars each. J. Bull, James Cooper and Charles Graham were Oliver's sureties, while James's father, J.C. Tucker, Bill Earhart, Oliver, Mary, Bill McNew, Perry Altman and a host of other Lee family friends and neighbors became sureties of Tucker. It surprised me to see that previous Democratic Dona Ana County Sheriff S.P. (aka James) Ascarate also pitched in on Tucker's bail.

---

Zio got a notice that they released him from prison a year later, but I never saw Ed again. Whether he simply stayed 'out of the way' or fled the mess that had been foisted upon him, I never found out. *Either way, who could blame him? Yes, it was a fine mess.*

(We learned later that Judge Whiteman had told mutual friends in Santa Fe that he 'would have dismissed the entire case, there and then, if he had the authority.' As a result, the case dragged on for months.)

John Good had lost in his vindictive bid against the Lees. He also lost his beloved ranch and moved to Las Cruces where he temporarily rented some rooms before moving west. The Good family were downtrodden and financially ruined. Meanwhile, Oliver changed his courtroom representation. He fired Newcombe and McFie and the other firm and then hired Albert Fall to represent him and his family. Fall filed for delay after delay, and after Bertha Good requested the dismissal of her suit, the remaining civil suits fell by the wayside.

In the end, with their only witness jailed for perjury and no one to push for action, the case against Oliver and the rest resolved out of neglect. I won't discount Albert Fall's expert handling of the case, but the departure of John Good and his family to parts unknown also made the matter less vital.

The courts may or may not have resolved the Good–Lee feud, but Oliver and his small rancher friends would be forever leery of the big outfits in the Tularosa. Their suspicions sometimes found their way out of the saloon backrooms.

It didn't take long for Oliver to accumulate more land, cattle, and horses and, with it, Tularosa power. People often speculated that he grew his ranch on the back of his gunplay. In reality Oliver knew how to find and develop a southwest rancher's gold: Water. Most importantly, he knew how to keep it.

# 47: **Blinded**

Zio's joint House and Council Committee had drafted a method to apportion constitutional convention seats to the counties. Democrats grumbled about the GOP's convention seat rules because they felt their counties were underrepresented. However, they couldn't do anything about it. Republicans felt statehood was their destiny. They weren't about to shortchange themselves at the Democrats' behest. Republicans were so confident they made tentative appointments to the federal positions that came with joining the union.

Even before the Republican Central Committee met in Santa Fe in early June to select constitution convention candidates, a confident Zio wrote considerable portions of the proposed constitution. One day, as I tapped away on the typewriter, Zio rose from his desk. He paced back and forth in thought before stopping in the middle of the room. He turned to me. "Perhaps it sounds rather vainglorious, but I have aspired for some time now to be the first Senator from New Mexico."

I didn't know what to say. It didn't surprise me, but I hadn't expected him to state it so matter-of-factly. He started back to his desk but must have thought I disapproved because he spun back and said, "Not that I want the recognition for the notoriety, mind you. I just think there will be much I can do for the people of New Mexico, and I want to help our citizens to better lives. Besides, New Mexico is misunderstood in Washington, and I want to set our government right on that point."

I nodded, resumed my typing and he went back to his desk. There were times I thought Zio was a bit 'full of himself', but as I write this, I believe that impression was because of his extensive vocabulary and theatrical nature.

Once he had won the party's nomination for the ballot, he focused on lobbying for a prominent position within the convention, which earned him chairman of the Education, Ways and Means, Rules, and Revision and Adjustment committees.

Since that first day in the House chamber, Zio was a man possessed. He even put his dramatic performances aside. He campaigned throughout the district for a seat at the constitutional convention and stuck to the GOP's talking points about the benefits of statehood. While his performances were on hold, he spoke about his goal for a proper theater while stumping in the Las Cruces area. No one could doubt Zio knew how to denigrate political opponents in a conventional campaign, but this was different. Rather than lash out at an opponent, he seemed to relish the opportunity to stump on the positives he could offer. Much to my surprise, that allowed him to use his oratorical and acting skills even more.

Zio won his seat to the constitutional convention handily and in early September, the convention convened without a single Democrat. Albert Fall's planned boycott was a bold move. They risked everything. The result might well have been that the union would admit a New Mexico that the Democrats would have abhorred. In Albert Fall's mind, a constitution without legitimate Democratic representation would amount to the same thing. He convinced his fellow Democrats that, in fact, they risked nothing.

The Republicans offhandedly brushed aside the Democrats. I suppose that when they had refused to send any delegates; the GOP figured the Democrats had surrendered. It was a big mistake by the Republicans. They never dreamed the Democrats might try to invalidate the whole thing. And yet, that is exactly what they did.

Democratic leaders ordered counties they controlled to boycott the constitutional convention delegate elections. Their territorial committee reinforced that position when they refused to nominate anyone. Unphased, the Republicans charged ahead with the convention, drafted their constitution, and journeyed to Washington to report to their Republican allies in control of their legislative branches. The convention selected Zio and twenty others to go to Washington to lobby for New Mexico's admittance. I hoped Zio would need me as an aide, but once again, he needed me to stay at the office. The delegation must have spent as much time on the trains as they did in Washington. When Zio returned, he was near exhaustion.

He rested the first day he was back, although I couldn't be certain because pile upon pile of notes and files hid him.

That evening, he took to the story-hearth to tell us about everything he did in the nation's capital. He hadn't been to the district in some time and was excited to tell us how it had changed.

"At last, they have filled that ugly Washington City canal. It was little more than an open sewer the last time I was there — a vile scar on the public grounds, which people now call the mall. Oh! And the architects have finally finished the Washington monument. It is a wonderful terminus for the mall. On the whole, the place looks like the national capital the country deserves."

It surprised me he seemed more excited about the theaters than the city and government interactions. He told us about some wonderful American playwrights' works he saw performed at beautiful theaters. "I walked past Ford's Theatre where Booth assassinated President Lincoln. Sadly, it is only used to store military records now."

When he resumed work, he revised the portions of the proposed constitution that he and the delegates had agreed required attention, but he also made time to get in touch with some of the amateur actors in town and propose a finer dramatic club.

He rallied them to form the organization and later, at the end of August, they proposed to find a permanent theater for performances.

"Jesús, I was so pleased to see so many young people in those theaters in Washington. I think a formal theater would give our idle young a far more formative and healthful alternative to saloons. I think we must see this through."

The Republican's trip to Washington bolstered Zio and his compadres' optimism. They felt certain the Congress would welcome New Mexico as a state when they completed the required tasks. It was beyond their imagination that the citizens of the territory would vote down full membership in the Union. After 'resting' at home with us for a few days, Zio returned to the convention to finish the revisions to their prized state constitution.

**August 24**

That Saturday morning, I had slept in after a late evening party with Zio and Mia Tia. It amounted to a Republican rally. The wine flowed and while it had been several months since my return, I still had to revisit the entire episode for the occasional person. Usually, it was someone that I had not met since. A couple of times, return inquisitors wanted to revisit the tale because they 'just couldn't fathom what it must have been like.' Often, they offered a glass of wine or a savory as an enticement.

I sat in my usual spot at the table and Rosa greeted me with a cup of coffee. "What would you like this morning, Jesús?"

I took a sip of my coffee and looked up at her cheery face and a carnal thought came to me. While I was hungry, I looked back at my coffee and said, "I'm fine, Rosa, thank you."

To distract myself, I picked up the *Rio Grande Republican*, folded where Zio had left it. The front page had Metcalfe's usual "What and Why" column. On that day, it focused on the popular subject of the agricultural experiment station. It would accompany the college that Zio pushed through the legislature. Page two featured an article about artesian wells and explored the prospects for deep water wells in the Mesilla Valley. Nearly a half-page of advertisements included one that announced the thirty-first session of St. Michaels College in Santa Fe. Classes would begin on September twenty-third, which was still a month away. I imagined that their hidden message was 'plenty of time to enroll.' I entertained enrolling to put some space between myself and Zio and Oliver. Alas, we were busy, and I soon dispelled the notion of a formal education.

Page three contained the perennial "Local News" column. It announced the comings and goings in the community: births, deaths, marriages, visitors, and that sort of thing. I scanned it for names I recognized and discovered that Judge Henderson had traveled east. It was also noted that Zio had returned from Silver City on Thursday and further down that he had been there to attend to his court obligations, along with several other Las Crucens. It was also noted that an advocate for artesian wells was in town. *Thus, the article on page two,* I reasoned.

An article in the next column requested a second meeting to organize a senatorial committee escort. The Senators were to review the community's plans for the agricultural college. My eye caught another piece down the page that reported on a plan to hire a railroad car for farmers of the valley to fill with fruit and vegetables for display around the country. Zio's Immigration Office had developed the plan to attract new people into the area. His plan included railway cars from other sections of the Rio Grande Valley, as well. An attendant would accompany the displays to remove unsightly perishables and replace them with fresh samples. He would also answer questions and inform visitors about the bounty of the Rio Grande Valley.

Below the fruit and vegetable car piece was an article about several Las Crucens that went north along the Rio Grande to a clear lake near Dona Ana. It must have been quite an organized affair because the *Republican* noted a Mr. Armstrong was the master of ceremonies. Men and women, all in beautiful bathing suits, bathed and seined all day. They caught about eight hundred pounds of fish. One weighed over twenty pounds. *Sounds like a fisherman's tale,* I mused.

I turned the page, and my eye caught a lengthy article about the Shalam Colony in the upper left-hand corner. The article originated in the *San Francisco Examiner* and gave the usual description of Dr. Newbrough's organization and religious teachings. I tried to stay abreast of the Colony's operation but had seen little for a while. So, it surprised me when they quoted Newbrough saying he had given up on adult converts. Instead, he now focused on babies in need of homes. That change in their focus resulted in six babies being transferred to them from New Orleans. This made me wonder what had happened to the women and children we had placed there two and a half years before. I made a mental note to investigate further.

That evening, Zio chaired the meeting about the senatorial committee visit that was called for in the *Republican*. When he returned that night, he sat with Maggie and me in the parlor and talked about the political situation.

"I had a lot of time to think on my way back from Silver City. While there with Judge McFie and Judge Newcombe, we talked quite a lot about how current politics had divided our territory. They told me about Albert Fall, and I came away impressed with his wit, perseverance, and tenacity."

Zio continued as I thought about my concerns about <u>Fall</u>. Whereas Zio appeared boastful to some at first, I believed it was because of his confident and outgoing nature. Fall, on the other hand, struck me as conceited, tactless, and heavy-handed. Granted, I might have been slightly biased since he had ignored me in our first meeting when he came to see our typewriter. As I considered these things, Zio said something that caught my ear.

"… at our meeting, I appointed him to form a committee to arrange escorts for our senatorial contingent."

I looked at Maggie and she had her hand over her mouth in shock. "But papa ..."

"I know, I know. He ran against me last year, but wait. McFie and Newcombe assured me he wasn't as close-minded as he would seem in a conversation with me. They said he would need to feel some sense of amity between us. So, I decided that this gesture could allow us to learn how to work together."

That shocked us. Don't get me wrong, partisanship had gone from bad to worse over the statehood question, but ... well I guess in the end it pleased me that Zio would live up to his espoused philosophy and put his pride aside for the sake of his cause.

Zio lifted his chin and pushed out his chest a bit. "Fall then moved that the committee should choose me to preside over the visit. And then ... then," Zio raised a finger in the air. "Then I appointed him to a committee of three to make recommendations for escorting our visiting senators."

"Sounds like a lot of committees, papa," said Maggie.

I restrained a laugh and said, "Perhaps you should have appointed a committee for your mutual admiration society as well. I find it hard to believe you think this will last."

"Wait, that's not all." In Zio's excitement, he didn't hear me.

Maggie and I looked at each other with widened eyes.

"You know about the fruit car exposition — right? Well, I appointed Albert to the committee to make those arrangements."

Democratic tactics and accusations angered him plenty of times over the years, but the prospects of a productive relationship with Fall and the Democrats excited him. While the Fountain vs. Fall rivalry persisted, he hoped there could be healthy cooperation. I think he also wanted his own collaboration theories confirmed.

A week later, we learned Zio had won the constitutional convention seat. On September third, he journeyed to Santa Fe for a convention session that ran the greater part of a month.

# 48: What'd I Do?

**September 24, 1889**

The convention finished its work on the twenty-first and ordered its beloved state constitution printed in English and Spanish. Along with the document was a request that all county officials inform their citizens by public dissemination in every way. While Republican delegates did just that, Democrats took a far different tack. They told their constituents a vote for the constitution would be a vote for the Santa Fe Ring's collusion and flimflammery. Incredibly, they suggested the proposed constitution was so worded that Republicans would have full control over the state for decades. If that wasn't enough, they said Republicans wanted to invoke clauses that would validate ten million acres of land claims by the Santa Fe Ring. But the *coup de grâce* that I believe swung the vote their way was the suggestion in no uncertain terms that religious rights would suffer under Republican rule.

Democrats passed a Spanish flyer between catholic Mexican families in Dona Ana County that read:

> "It is the declared intention of the enemies of our religion to send delegates to that convention who will ... force you to deny your children all kinds of education excepting that of the world. The plan is ... that you be obliged to pay taxes to sustain public schools, notwithstanding you can not(sic) on account of conscientious scruples

permit your children to be educated in said places. No faithful son of the church, nor any man of the Mexican caste ... will submit to this ... great is the danger that this execrable, wicked education will be forced upon us ... to take our houses and possessions from us."

Zio had already suffered from a nasty association with the Santa Fe Ring from Tularosa folks, but the label soon spread into the Mesilla Valley. At last, Zio and the Republican party realized they needed to defend themselves.

One day, the *Rio Grande Republican* editor Charles Metcalfe came to the office to interview Zio. I went into the kitchen to put my coffee cup into the washbasin. Rosa was restocking the shelves with supplies she had gotten that morning.

She thanked me for the cup. I realized I wanted to be with her — just the two of us. "I have to go to Wil Rynerson's office in town; is there anything more you need?"

Rosa turned to me as she placed a can on the shelf. "Well, yes, there is, but I'm not sure how to explain what I want. I think I will go with you."

A brief early morning shower had dampened the streets. Its damp scent lingered in the air. We walked side by side as Rosa carried a woven tote for her purchases. She wore her old red bandana in her hair, and I wondered why. Before I said anything, she noticed my glance. "Your scarf — the one you picked out for me — was dirty, and I didn't have time to wash it last night."

"Oh, no, no, it's not mine, it's yours. Perhaps you need another scarf?"

Rosa smiled. She had such a wonderful smile — broad and bright. "It was nice of you to buy the one already."

"It was your birthday. There's nothing special about a birthday gift for someone you like ... a lot."

"Still…." She cocked her head with a grin that sparked my desire for her.

She wore her daily work clothes and yet, to my mind, she couldn't have been more attractive in the finest gown.

I had to discuss a legal issue with Wil. It would be improper for her to come with me into his office. We stopped on the boardwalk in front of Wil's office. I stood and made small talk as I tried to think of an excuse to stop her from going inside. "Well, where are you going?"

"Lohman's."

"Why don't you go on? It will just take me a moment at Wil's office, and then I'll join you there."

She looked away for a moment. I feared she would conjure an excuse and refuse. "Besides, if you fill that tote with items, you may need someone to help you carry it back to the Fountains."

She laughed. "Yes, I suppose I might."

After my brief errand at Wil's office, I arrived at Lohman's. Mrs. Lohman, whom we now called Aminda, tallied Rosa's purchases in the Fountain account, and placed them in the tote. Rosa had her back to me as she looked at something on the shelf behind Aminda. I reached around Rosa while 'accidentally' touching the back of her shoulder and pulled the side of the tote back to reveal her purchases.

"Oh!" said a surprised Rosa, to Aminda's amusement. "Jesús! How did you get here so fast?"

"I told you I only needed to drop off a file. I would have been here sooner, but Wil's assistant wanted to chat."

The tote contained a bag of *masa harina* and some herbs and spices. I felt flirty. "What? Nothing for yourself?"

"Oh, Jesús, you know I would never buy something for myself on the Colonel's account. I can't believe you would even suggest such a thing."

Aminda put her hand to her mouth, but her eyes expressed her amusement at my coy flirtation.

"Let's go down this way." I picked up the tote and placed my other hand on the small of her back as I guided her along the counter toward the back of the store. Aminda had already guessed our destination, and she had rushed ahead to remove the boxes of French silk scarfs.

As we arrived in front of Aminda, she pulled out an unusually colored one. I had seen the shade somewhere but couldn't place it.

Aminda let the feather-light sheer material flutter as she shook it out to its full length. "I've wanted to show this scarf to Rosa for a long time, but I feared she could not afford it. The French call the color 'pru-nay'. Mr. Rouault was in the other day, and he told me 'pru-nay' translates to plum. Isn't it just …. Perfect?"

Plum. Yes, that was it. There was a pink three-lined border around the entire scarf and when Rosa folded it to place on her hair, it complemented her and her personality so well. Aminda fetched a mirror for her while Rosa turned to me. "Oh, Jesús, it is so, so beautiful. I love it, but I cannot accept it."

"But why? Wasn't your birthday last week? You said last year that you didn't want us to bother with your birthday, but I can't resist."

Rosa blushed through her olive tinted skin. "You remembered after all," she whispered. Aminda feigned disinterest as she refolded and packed the scarves she had ruffled when she pulled the plum one from the box. In truth, I hadn't remembered Rosa's birthday until I entered the store, but I had thought about buying her a gift. It was only then I realized her birthday was about then and that gave me the excuse to give her a gift. However, it hadn't seemed like a year had passed and I was still uncertain of the exact date. I chanced I was within a week.

She tied the beautiful headsquare in place and turned to me with a firm hug. It was only after that I realized her breasts had been firmly against my lower chest. I regretted I hadn't relished the moment. I wanted to kiss her, but even in my altered state of mind, I recognized that would harm her more than me. Nonetheless, the thought excited me. Aminda gave her a hand mirror and Rosa admired the scarf against her raven hair. She glanced at me through the mirror. "It is so beautiful, Jesús. I ... I ... I am speechless."

Aminda asked, "Would you like to wear it home?"

Rosa nodded. She pursed her lips as she placed the mirror on the counter and reached for my hand.

Aminda folded Rosa's old bandana and put it in the box the new scarf came in. I accepted the box and with my chest pushed out said, "Can you put that on my account, Aminda?" I glanced at Rosa with the hope I had impressed her. She smiled as I placed the box in the tote. Arm in arm, we walked out of the store.

On the way back, we heard a ruckus as we passed the Commercial Saloon. The fight spilled through the batwing doors, past us, and into the street as both combatants flipped over the hitching rail and fell amongst the tethered horses. Rosa clenched my arm so hard I thought she might cut off circulation.

One man was a rather heavy immigrant. He lost his hat, revealing a ghostly white bald scalp. The other was a much taller and wiry cowboy. They found each other in the middle of the street. Horses and wagons passed as if it was a normal occurrence, but I couldn't remember a fight spilling out of a saloon earlier than sundown. Somehow, we found ourselves at the front of a crowd where a cacophony of voices yelled for them to stop or for one to kill the other.

A couple of onlookers from the boardwalk shouted for the sheriff, and someone ran toward his office. It was fortunate neither of the combatants carried a weapon and I expected that when one or the other got the upper hand, it would end. Instead, they raised Main Street dust as the advantage shifted back and forth until the cowboy pinned the heavy-set bald man to the ground.

"Stop them Jesús." cried Rosa. "He's going to hurt that man."

I gawked at her as I wondered what in the world she expected I might do. The cowboy seemed to relax. He must have expected that the rotund, bald man had had enough. Before I could tell Rosa, the fat man had relented, he rolled all his weight to the side and, quick as a cat, pinned the cowboy's arms with his knees.

Again, Rosa said, "Stop them. Stop them somebody." But instead of searching for a powerful man in the crowd, her eyes never left me. I had already sized up the heavy man and realized I could not restrain him. As I looked for help, Rosa pointed to the two tangled men and screamed.

I looked back to see the cowboy's arms and legs flailing about and then saw why. The fat man had buried his thumbs to his knuckles in the cowboy's eye sockets. Fluids with bits of flesh had splashed into the caliche street while blood oozed down the sides of his face. Rosa turned and pressed her face against my chest in horror. I had heard street fights could get ugly. Zio had told me it wasn't uncommon for men to attack the soft places in the body, but I had never witnessed it. The man's screams were blood-curdling. A deputy arrived and pulled the heavier man off the aggrieved disfigured cowboy who jumped to his feet and hopped around like a wrung necked chicken.

Rosa couldn't look any longer, and she was close to me with her face against my shoulder. Had what we had just seen not disturbed me, I would have realized how pleasant our juxtapositions were. Alas, she sobbed and walked back to the boardwalk without me, as I was mesmerized by the people attempting to calm the maimed cowboy. When I noticed she was gone, I ran to catch up with her as she walked briskly south toward the Fountains. As inexperienced as I was, I didn't realize that something had changed between us. But when I offered her my arm, she refused and walked faster. After a block or so, I dared to look at her. There were tear tracks down her cheeks, unchallenged by a handkerchief. She said nothing, and I wasn't sure whether it was just the spectacle of the event or if she believed I could have stopped it.

Later, I discovered it was the latter.

# 49: Stormy Times

Autumn passed with little to record, and Rosa ignored me for the most part. It wasn't overt. I might have been hypersensitive to it, but things were different between us.

I brought up the issue with Zio one day in mid-October as we sat in the office. He told me I made too much of nothing. "Besides, I don't want to lose Rosa, and a failed romance would make that a certainty. I won't tell you to stay away from her, but if you want to court her, you better be certain that it won't end badly."

Meanwhile, Zio and Fall continued to get along well. The senatorial visit to examine the region's agriculture led to the culmination of Zio's planned display of the Valley's produce. Several flatbed cars toured the Midwest with an attendant that doubled as a *Rio Grande Republican* correspondent. He wrote a weekly column about the raves Mesilla Valley produce got from people from all over the country.

As usual, Zio had Third District Court duties for the fall session in October and into much of November. The circuit began in Las Cruces on the first Monday in October and took five weeks or more. The lawyers and judges often traveled together by carriage and horseback as they would cover several hundred miles.

Fall took his first court case in the fall session at Las Cruces when he served as associate counsel in C.T. Williams' civil complaint against Fitzgerald Moore. Zio heard Fall provided valuable input in his role.

At the end of October, the circuit court finished in Lincoln, and they were to proceed to Hillsboro, the county seat of Sierra County. That stop always soured Zio. Five years before, the Santa Fe Ring helped a rebellious lot unceremoniously lop off a chunk of Dona Ana to form Sierra County. Zio couldn't prove the Santa Fe Ring was behind it, but Zio knew they held a grudge against him because he and the Dona Ana Republicans wouldn't bow to the Ring's control. At the very least, the legislators they controlled provided enough votes that the new county was approved.

Not long after the Las Cruces District Court had adjourned, Zio left town and Fall began publishing the *Las Cruces Independent Democrat* newspaper. Oddly, he listed his father as the editor.

When Zio returned and I informed him, he shrugged. "I published a paper called the *Mesilla Independent* when I first came to the Valley. As that paper did for me, I imagine Fall's will prove a suitable vehicle for him to get his opinions known on important topics. Don't worry, Jesús, he's still behind me, and I doubt he will be much of a challenge again in the next election."

At last, all the circuit locations had access to telegraph and, without exception, Zio notified us of his arrivals and departures. On Friday, the first of November, he wired he was leaving Lincoln on that day, and they expected to reach Hillsboro in two days' time to open court the next Monday.

The storm hit just after sundown on Saturday night and continued through dawn on Sunday morning. All telegraph lines were down throughout New Mexico. There was no way to find out if Zio and the others had arrived in Hillsboro.

The storm dumped seven inches on Las Cruces and the surrounding area, and everything came to a standstill. We awakened to a rising sun and a brilliant white landscape. It was a sight to see. The glistening chill brought me back to the sled rides with the road clearing crew down the mountain a couple of years before. There was occasional snow on the Organs in the winter during most years, but to see it so completely covering the valley was a rarity. Rosa hadn't arrived for work yet and Mia Tia, Jack, and I gathered at the windows to look upon the wondrous alabaster blanket while Maggie made coffee. As we held Katie and Little Henry up to see, Rosa plodded down the alley in what looked to be her father's boots. When she came close enough to us, I noticed her wrinkled brow and recognized her concerned expression. Rosa stepped inside and removed her serape and red cotton bandana as flakes of the icy particles flew from her hair. She shivered as she asked if Miles had delivered a telegram to us the previous evening. Rosa was always the first to worry about Zio. It was a manifestation of her character; she allowed herself to feel close to most people she met. Still, it seemed odd, since Maggie and Mia Tia rarely showed any outward concerns for him when he was away. Perhaps they had become accustomed to it.

Mia Tia and Maggie gathered around Rosa and made her sit at the table as they brought coffee. After several minutes of gentle words and hugs, she calmed down. I sat across the table from them, but whenever I tried to catch Rosa's eye to convey a look of concern, she would look away. An hour later, Tommy appeared at the back door in his uniform. He said he had been called with his company to help clear the tracks in certain places and their commander had sent thirty of their company to clear twenty inches of the snow at Nutt Station. When I asked Tommy about the telegraph lines, he said despite the amount of snow they got, lines were still up to Nutt Station. However, when he stopped to check for a telegram from his father, there weren't any, and Miles figured the lines were down into Hillsboro.

This sent the women into a tizzy. I went to get Tommy a cup of coffee, but I stopped short when he said, "Let's have a snowball fight."

It seemed odd for Tommy to suggest a fight of any sort with the women in their state, but then, I realized: that was Tommy. I wanted to suggest it might not be the right time. Besides, I didn't know what a snowball fight was.

I squinted. "What is a snowball fight, Tommy?"

"I ain't quite sure." I hadn't heard him use that contraction before. Perhaps the other soldiers had influenced his language usage. "One man in our company is from Iowa and he told me about it this morning. Come outside with me and I'll show you."

Jack and I put on our jackets while Tommy went outside. When we opened the door, he greeted us with a hail of icy snowballs that didn't break up much when they hit us. We picked up the remnants and hurled them back; and the 'war' was on!

Between icy hands and feet, we only lasted a few minutes. We returned to the kitchen with shivers and boasts about how many times who hit who. I glanced at the table where the women sat glaring at us. After I removed my shoes and jacket, I realized that Mia Tia's and Maggie's focus was on Tommy and Jack, while Rosa fixed her eyes squarely on me.

Rosa stood, and the others looked at her as she said, "Jesús. How could you?" Whereupon everyone stared at me.

I glimpsed Tommy, who had the remains of a semi-thawed snowball in the middle of his forehead. The melt dripped off the end of his nose. I couldn't help but laugh and before you could say 'Jack Robinson', the tension in the room was released as everyone pointed at Tommy and laughed.

When we had gotten control of ourselves, Mia Tia, whom I didn't think was aware of the threats against Zio, said, "Oh, Rosa, why are you so worried? You've been here long enough to know Albert always comes home. He's like a cat with nine lives."

Later that morning, I went into the office with a cup of coffee. There, on my office chair, lay Rosa's two French scarves. I didn't know when she had left them there. It hurt, but I also remembered what Zio had said.

*Perhaps it was for the best.*

Later, I heard a faint knock at the parlor door. Before I could answer, Rosa opened it and motioned the young man in. As I rose to greet him, she closed the door a little harder than was necessary, emitting a loud bang. Our visitor jumped a little and reflexively turned back to the now shut door, before spinning back to me with eyebrows raised.

"Not to worry, sir, we don't permit her to carry iron." The man, J.K. Livingston, laughed as we shook hands. It was Zio's responsibility as immigration commissioner to entice settlers to Dona Ana County. One such effort was the leasing of fruit and vegetable railroad cars that toured middle western cities. Zio had hired Livingston to accompany the cars, and the *Republican* hired him as a correspondent. When we had settled in our chairs, he said, "I arrived on the Saturday afternoon train. I swear, that storm was right on our tail. Colonel Fountain had told me to report as soon as I arrived back in Las Cruces." I could see why Zio had hired this young man. Livingston looked around for Zio and then at me before his shoulders slumped. "Ah, yes, he's on the court circuit, isn't he?"

I concurred and let him know we were afraid the storm had caught the Colonel somewhere between Lincoln and Hillsboro. There was another quick tap on the door and Rosa entered, again without my invitation. She carried a silver tray with the family's fine china cups, saucers, and teapot.

Livingston had brought one of the side chairs to face my desk. Rosa turned her back to me and held the tray before him. "Would you like a fresh cup of coffee, Mr. Livingston?"

He replied he did and as Rosa poured, I placed my now empty cup at the front of my desk for her to refill. Instead, after she handed him the steaming cup and saucer, she left the room without so much as a glance toward me.

I restrained my sigh of disappointment. Between sips, Mr. Livingston said, "What a lovely girl. Is she a Fountain?"

"Who? Her? Oh no, she's just the maid." I regretted saying it right away.

Livingston continued to sip his coffee, then paused with his pinky finger extended. "Ah, just what a body needs on a morning like this. We had cold weather in Chicago, but I never expected to see it here, and especially not with snow."

My smile hid my angst about Rosa.

"Well, I'm just dying to tell someone about my trip, although I'm sure you read the columns that I wired to Metcalfe?"

I nodded, but before I could suggest he wait until Zio returned, he charged ahead like a joyous boy that had run home to brag that he had put the school bully in his place.

"What an experience, uh, uh Juan, is it? No, no, it's Jesús. What an experience, Jesús. And I just could not believe how everyone here sent fresh produce replacements. We have quite a community. And the visitors? Oh, my Juan, we had over 60,000 visitors over the five weeks in Colorado, Kansas, Missouri, Iowa, and Illinois. I don't think we can appreciate the vast amount of good that will accrue to New Mexico and the Mesilla Valley from this advertising scheme." He stopped for a sip, but before the cup met his lips, he continued. "And our greatest promoters were people that had lived or visited here." He tipped the cup again but thought of something more and placed the cup back on the saucer. "And, and there were many. Juan, I hardly had to lift a finger. I just sat back ... oh, uh, don't tell the Colonel that ... but honestly, I just had to let those people talk to the other visitors about our beautiful and bountiful valley. What could be better than that?"

At last, he paused for a breath and another sip of coffee. I considered reminding him my name was Jesús, but decided that in his state, he wouldn't remember.

"The scene was simply incredible. We had arranged over one hundred and twenty feet of aisles amongst the fruits and vegetables. People lined up throughout the day to walk through the exhibit."

I guess I didn't seem impressed. "Is something wrong, Juan?"

"No. Mr. Livingston, it's just that you'll have to repeat all this when the Colonel returns."

"Oh. Oh no, no matter. It's a joy to talk about my experience. I'll gladly tell anyone that seems the least bit interested."

He droned on for another fifteen minutes until his cup was empty and since I made no offer to refill it, he stood to leave, and I showed him out.

Over several days, I would touch the scarves in my desk drawer. Then I realized they still smelled of her. I became engrossed with the effect of placing one of them over my face while I rubbed the other between two fingers. My arousal was shameful, I knew, but irresistible.

One day, as I sat in the office with the yellow scarf over my face, the parlor door opened. I snatched the scarf away, just in time … at least, I hoped I did because Rosa stood in the parlor doorway with a man behind her. I might have imagined the hint of a smile before she coldly said, "A Mr. Dimitri Diamandis is here to see you." She left, again with a louder than necessary slam of the door.

*At least she wasn't scornful.*

I invited the man in. He sat in one of the two chairs I had moved from Zio's desk. He smelled of beer and something else that I didn't want to think about. I started toward the door to show him out, but he stopped me and said, "I have something you will want."

That sparked my curiosity, and I showed him into our office. Dimitri had an odd accent, and I had to ask him to repeat what he said several times. He took a newspaper clipping from his breast pocket and slapped it on my desk with just the headline exposed. It read, "Blood on the Moon". His hand couldn't cover all the clipping and, at the bottom, someone had scrawled "*Saint John's Herald*, Saint John, Arizona, November 7, 1889".

"How am I to determine if it's of interest if I can't read it?"

He scowled as though he hadn't considered that and withdrew his hand as I tugged at the other end.

As I scanned the article, he had second thoughts and snapped it back. "You pay first." Anyway, that's what I thought he said. His accent was worse than Gruff's. Dimitri wore filthy clothes faded with age and rubbed thin in the elbows and knees. The stench of his weeks without bathing filled the room.

"I won't pay for something when I cannot examine it." Dimitri again repeated that he wanted money. I reached into my pocket and put a Liberty half-dime on my desk. "I'll give you this now and if it is of value to us, I'll add to it."

He grimaced, looked at the clipping, and then deposited it next to the half-dime while he scooped it up in a single motion. I scanned the clipping and right away noticed that the Good and Lee names were mentioned. I took another half-dime from my pocket and gave it to Dimitri. He smiled, and I carefully reread the article. It wasn't well written, but the reporter mentioned Oliver, Cooper, and a man named Cornett, along with a Las Cruces lawyer named Paul. It would take some time to decipher the inadequate reporter's phraseology. So, I gave Diamandis a dime and ushered him out.

Rosa appeared at the entrance to the hall with her hands on her hips. "That man scared me. Is everything alright? He wasn't uh …"

"No, he didn't threaten me or Zio. He had some information for me — a clipping from an out-of-town newspaper. If he comes around again, I'll notify the sheriff, but I think he's just down on his luck."

As Rosa opened her mouth to reply, Katie and Little Henry broke into screaming fits. Rosa frowned, dismissed me with a wave, and turned back down the hall to resolve the sibling feud.

The man's noisome presence filled the office. The office windows were high above the bookcases, and I didn't want to get a ladder to open them. I reached into my desk drawer for one of Rosa's scarves and put it over my nose while I held the article with my other hand. The writing was so bad that I had to study it several times and sometimes re-read sentences over and over.

As it turned out, Zio and the other circuit riders had made it to Hillsboro, although it was with considerable difficulty and frostbitten digits. Word came when the trains resumed, and Rosa heard about it at Lohman's store. When Rosa told Mia Tia, she said, *"Es como el gato de nueve vidas."*

# 50: Bill McNew

The article Mr. Diamandis brought told the story of a conflict between a Mr. More and a Mr. Bruton. Mr. More and Mr. Bruton were brothers-in-law. The two made a deal. More gave Bruton eight hundred head of cattle for five years. To conclude the deal, Bruton was to return double that amount. The trouble began when, after five years, Bruton refused to return any cattle and wouldn't tell More where they were.

Bruton fled the territory, despite an outstanding bail bond, for another matter. More found out Bruton had jumped bail before in Texas. Anyway, the reporter wrote Bruton fled to the Rincon Mountains west of Rincon, New Mexico, where he joined the notorious Good and Williams Gang. It seemed to me I would have known about a gang with the Good name attached to it.

Besides, word was, John Good and his family had departed for Arizona. Perhaps one of John's sons had stayed in New Mexico, and I had heard of the outlaw Williams before. I wished Zio was home, for he knew everyone in Southern New Mexico. But then, in the next paragraph, I read More enlisted Oliver Lee and Jim Cooper's help. I didn't believe Oliver would get involved unless it would enable him to make things 'right' with the Tularosa Good clan.

A third man by the name of Cornett was also involved. He had two sisters named Betty and Bonnie. Betty was married to Bruton, but Cornett found out that while married to Betty, Bruton had 'ruined' his other sister, Bonnie. Somehow word reached him that More wanted to gather an impromptu posse manhunt because

Bruton and Cornett joined with the More side to get revenge against Bruton. The similar names and poor writing made it hard to follow, and I had to create a diagram to keep it all straight.

The article alluded to the feud between the Goods and Oliver Lee in the Tularosa and that confirmed my suspicions. There was another person, an attorney named Paul. So, the More group included Cornett, Oliver, Cooper and Attorney Paul. I knew of no attorney in Las Cruces by the name of Paul. As inept as the reporter was, I wondered if perhaps the reporter had mistaken "Fall" for "Paul".

I put the clipping on my desk and replaced Rosa's scarf in my drawer. Then it hit me. More was the Fitzgerald Moore and Williams was C.T. Williams. The *Republican* had reported Fall represented Williams in court a month before; and so the lawyer Paul *was* in fact Fall. The only Moore I knew was Charles (Oliver called him Charley), who had tried to help Oliver and Cooper surrender to the sheriff.

I knew C.T. Williams was the gang leader in the Rincon area, but why would Fall represent Williams when the Arizona paper had published that "Paul" was involved with the More band? It made perfect sense that "Paul", whom I was certain was Fall, would represent More because Fall and Oliver had become good friends and Good had joined the opposition Williams gang. Perhaps the *Republican* had reported the court case incorrectly.

A client interrupted any further consideration, and I wished I hadn't spent the few cents for the article. I slid the clipping under some papers on my desk and met with my client.

At the end of November, Jack, a couple of his cowboy friends, and I rode over to the Sacramentos to hunt for a few Thanksgiving turkeys. I knew the area the best and so I decided we would head toward Escondido Canyon, where I thought I might find Virgil on the range. When we got there, I stopped one of the cowboys that I knew and asked for Virgil.

"Why if it ain't Ol' Nasty?" The cowboy reached over and patted him on the neck, and we shook hands. "Virgil?" The man chuckled and shook his head, "He done flewed the coop, Hey-you. I don't think we got as much snow as you from that storm the beginnin' of the month, but it was enough for Virgil to pack up and skedaddle. Said he was goin' to San Antone."

I laughed. "Well, he said that's what he'd do. I'm not surprised at all."

I wanted to kill a nice turkey and drop it off at Lee Well. Riding into the Sacramento highlands brought some pleasant and exciting memories. Little had changed. When a location reminded of an event, I pointed it out to the others and told them what had happened there. Oliver's men had dug a new watering hole or ditch here and there, and the snowstorm runoff had sparked some tender late season greens for our camp pot. I enjoyed handling a rifle again and the six-gun felt comfortable on my hip. We roamed into the Sacramento River valley for a couple of days but didn't have much luck. Still, I enjoyed being outside in familiar terrain. At sunrise, on the third day, a flock of mature turkeys moseyed right into camp looking for water. In about five minutes, we had a dozen nice ones.

When we dropped in at Lee Well, Mary responded to my "hallo the house". I had told Jack not to reveal his real last name. She wasn't toting a shotgun and for a moment, I wondered when I had last seen her greet a visitor without one.

"Jesús. Oh. You've brought us visitors. Nettie! Nettie! Come on out here," she winked at me. "Hey-you is here."

Nettie rushed out with a strange man trailing her. We dismounted to introductions, handshakes, and hugs. Nettie, all fidgety with excitement, introduced us to her new husband, Bill McNew. I sized up Mr. McNew as we chatted about the prospects for rain, and the general catching up folks do when they haven't seen each other for a while.

He was so unlike Oliver, and yet they were a perfect match. Bill had brilliant blue eyes, whereas Oliver's were dark brown — almost black — and while Oliver was lithe and willowy, Bill was taller with a powerfully solid build. Later, I learned that, unlike Oliver, Bill would move like the wind to right a situation and never worry his actions might have been wrong.

As I expected, he had a firm shake and a natural smile. "Hey-you, I've heard an awful lot of good things about you. I know Oliver would love to have you come back to join us."

That caught me off guard, and I glanced at Jack to see his reaction. "Well, thank you. Oliver, Mary, and Nettie treated me like family, and I owe them a lot."

Bill said nothing, but the simple nod and his eye contact made it clear the family still expected loyalty from me.

"Well, we can't stay long, but I wanted to drop off a turkey for you folks and maybe a couple for the bunkhouse."

Nettie smiled and took my hands. "That is so thoughtful of you, Jesús. I'll be certain to see that Chuck, who's doin' all the cookin' there now, gets 'em. You heard about Virgil movin' on?"

I nodded. "Well, he was true to his word. It was snow that brought him to us from up around Datil and it was snow that drove him further south. Hard tellin' where he might end up, I suppose."

Bill nodded and said, "Yes sir, men like Virgil are plentiful out here. They roam in search of something they may never find, but they can always get work."

I turned to Nettie. "So, have the two of you made a land claim yet?"

Bill scanned the ranch yard. "Nah, Oliver's fixin' to build a new headquarters at the mouth of Dog Canyon. We'll stay here and take over when he's got enough built for him and his Ma."

There were final handshakes and hugs. The goodbyes weren't tearful, but they were full of memories relived and wonders of what was to come.

On the way home, Jack told me he thought the folks he met were very nice, and it was clear they thought well of me. So far as I can remember, Jack said nothing to anyone but me about our visit to Lee Well.

<hr>

When we arrived home, I discovered Larlo had surprised the Fountains with a visit. He had recovered from his accident the previous summer at Lake Valley and was about to return to his original job in Pinos Altos. He had let us know he had gone to Pinos Altos to arrange for living quarters and attend to some business. We didn't know that Luciana Shaw, who he called Lucy, was still in his life.

Lucy shut down her boarding house, and the two appeared at our doorstep arm in arm. Whenever I saw her, it reminded me of the Bronco Sue trial when Zio and I visited the rooming house her mother ran. Lucy was cute then, but she had matured to a handsome young woman.

It was another nice Thanksgiving meal with the two turkeys I provided. As we ate, Larlo asked if my accident the previous spring worried me during the hunting trip. I hadn't even considered it, but his question made me wonder if I should have.

Between the cautionary speech Zio gave me and the cold shoulder Rosa offered, I felt a certain freedom to look elsewhere. Besides, Rosa had the day off as the Fountain women cooked and the men cleaned up. Perhaps my yearning for Rosa made me vulnerable, but for whatever reason, I thought Lucy wanted to flirt with me. After she and I made eye contact a couple of times, Larlo thought I enjoyed it a little too much. The second time, his harsh glare made it clear that Lucy was spoken for. Still, Lucy's mestizo features were alluring, and I was constantly tempted to stare.

As I fought off the image and sensation of Lucy in my arms, I could see that the relationship between her and Larlo had advanced. The first time she came — for the fourth of July, I believe it was — he didn't seem that amorous toward her and she spent a lot of her time with Marianita and Maggie. This time, throughout the holidays, he was attentive, and he only played cards with his old buddies twice. The first time she went with him, but the second she refused. When the next poker night came, Larlo showed no interest. Instead, he and Lucy went to a party with Marianita and Carl.

The family loved Lucy. She wasn't only beautiful; she was quick-witted, funny, and a social princess. When they returned to Pinos Altos, we expected an engagement within the next year.

The family got together often throughout the holidays, and Mia Tia and Zio beamed the entire month. Katie was at the age where she began to enjoy our various celebrations. That Christmas I had gotten her a rag doll. As she ripped open some of Maggie's beautiful wrapping paper, Katie ripped the rag doll's arm off. Stuffing popped out of the doll, and Katie screamed as she flew into her mother's arms. Little Henry sat on my lap and smiled at the wondrous row of Christmas stockings that were hung from the story-hearth.

As was customary, Zio attended Christmas Mass with the family. Everything was fine until Father Lassaigne made political remarks in his homily. He suggested that the proposed statehood constitution would cause the closure of all Catholic schools and their children would have to attend heathen taught schools. Zio rose to walk out, but Mia Tia grabbed his jacket sleeve, and he sat back down. He never talked about it again, but I felt certain that he returned the next week to set the Father right. Not that it did any good. Before long, the Catholic priests throughout the territory mimicked the Democrat's propaganda about the proposed constitution's public-school language.

# 51: Here Be Dragons

Since the fall court sessions, Zio had often complained about the number of alleged Edmonds-Tucker Act violations. The docket was flush with them, and he feared the spring session would have more.

I looked up the law, but even after I read the summary a few times, it puzzled me. It focused on the behavior of a certain religious group I wasn't aware of.

In mid-January, Zio wrote yet another letter to New Mexico District Attorney Thomas Smith about the payment he was due for the multitude of cases he had handled for the fall session. When he wrote anything, he would often become nearly catatonic in his focus. When I first came to the Fountains, I quickly realized it was a mistake to interrupt him.

He paused and stood to stretch, then looked in my general direction, which gave me the chance to ask for his help.

"Zio, I can't understand this Edmonds-Tucker Act. I don't think I know anyone it would apply to."

Zio frowned. "Yes, well, it results from many years of the federal government's attempts to deal with Mormonism. It's complicated. And, yes, you're right because few people that practice polygamy live here. Although, come to think of it, I have wondered what goes on at the Shalom Colony."

"If they aren't here, where are they?"

"Utah. It's a territory northwest of New Mexico. A religious sect called the Mormons settled there. They are Protestant, but they have some odd beliefs about marriage. The primary issue is cohabitation, or what they sometimes refer to as polygamy. They believe that a man can have as many wives as he can support. They eschew cohabitation without marriage, but the law does not recognize their polygamous marriages."

I nodded. "And so, the rest of the law prevents them from teaching and legally allowing the practice?"

"Mostly, yes. Utah has wanted to become a state for some time now, and the federal government has been at odds with them over their 'religious freedoms' for over twenty years. Mr. Edmonds wrote a previous law that was enacted in '82. But it had some problems — I don't recall what they were just this moment — but anyway, Mr. Tucker joined with Edmonds to amend his previous law. The law passed the senate nearly unanimously and then simply on a voice vote in the House. President Cleveland refused to sign it, but he didn't veto it. As a result, it became law because Congress was still in session." Zio gazed out the window toward the sky, put his hand to his chin and said, "Cleveland didn't sign it, but he knew it would become law, and I think that speaks volumes about the man." Then he removed his hand and grumbled, "Cleveland was a vetoing fool."

"So, we don't have Mormons in New Mexico, do we?"

"Not enough that you would know."

"So, why are these allegations happening?"

"Exactly, Jesús. That is precisely what I have puzzled over. It seems like there is an ulterior motive at work — nothing at all to do with Mormonism."

"So, what happens to someone if they are convicted?"

He waved his hand dismissively. "So far, the court has only assigned bail, and it has mostly been two-hundred-and-fifty-dollars for women and five hundred for men. I don't believe our court has sentenced anyone yet. We were unprepared for these types of cases."

"I think I read in the law that the fine could be as much as five hundred dollars and males could lose their voting rights."

Zio's eyes got as big as yucca pods. "I wonder ..." Zio rushed out the door without his overcoat as he said, "Holy smoke Jesús, I think you've got it."

I went for another cup of coffee. The pot was empty, and when I off-handedly asked if anyone planned to make some, Rosa shrugged. She didn't even make eye contact.

Each time she ignored me, it reminded me of the street fight, which I would dismiss immediately because I believed I couldn't have done anything. This time, I decided that before I could formally court Rosa, I would have to know how to manage a similar situation if it arose. At length, I realized we should have continued down the boardwalk and not looked back.

*There, now I need to get her to forgive me.*

When Zio returned, he told me he had gone to the courthouse to check the voters' roll. He said almost every man accused of cohabitation outside of their marriage was a registered Republican.

Zio threw up his arms. "The Democrats want to have Republicans removed from the voter rolls."

That seemed incredible to me. After all, how many could they remove? So far, the numbers were small, and the district courts could handle just so many cases before the November elections. Until then, Zio had regarded it as an irritation because they clogged the docket.

After the constitutional convention, the Republicans pushed hard to convince their fellow citizens it was time for statehood. But they weren't specific about the benefits and often led with the vague claim statehood would lead to many of the things that New Mexicans wanted.

With the cooler weather and holidays, the Democrats' enthusiasm waned a bit. However, their plan had taken root and dissatisfaction with the Republicans spread through the saloons and Catholic churches. By spring, the Democrats had a good head of steam.

The Mexican population had grown weary of the Republicans' long tenure. In the north, many Spanish descendants saw their land grants challenged by men like Republican Thomas Catron, the reputed Santa Fe Ringleader. He used his political prowess to place corrupt land agents. In turn, they looked the other way as Anglos claimed vast amounts of land, while the GOP turned a blind eye. In doing so, Catron had quietly become the largest landowner in New Mexico.

Sometimes the Spanish and Mexican land grants were difficult to prove, but often, the families had cultivated and grazed those lands for centuries. For some time in the north, the 'White Caps', or *Las Gorras Blancas*, had raided what they considered Anglo squatters, intending to push them off their ancestral lands. Their cause spread and sentiments against the Republican party followed. Zio had made progress to protect the Spanish and Mexican land grantees in the south, but that seemed to get lost in the Democratic Party's propaganda onslaught.

In Dona Ana County, Albert Fall's newspaper published his constant criticism of what he referred to as failed Republican efforts. He often published in Spanish and English, and he always hammered home the Republican's so-called attacks on the Catholic schools. Their misrepresentation of the proposed constitution confused those few Mexicans that could read, and as a result, many believed Republicans threatened their religious freedoms.

One day in early February I went to the small library the Sisters of Loretto maintained at The Academy of the Visitation School they operated for girls. As I thumbed through a reference, I noticed Albert Fall was there as well, and he motioned for me to meet him outside. I asked if he had seen Oliver recently.

"Oh yes, he asked me to say hello to you. What an industrious young man Oliver is. He's learning Greek and Latin, you know. His ranch building skills will eventually get him a ranching empire in the southern Tularosa; you just watch him."

I nodded. "I hope so. He deserves it."

"He will, and that McNew boy that married Nettie is the perfect brother-in-law for him. Oliver and Nettie are as much like brother and sister as any I've known."

We stood silent for a moment and then Fall said, "Your uncle and I will represent a young man in an appeal of his conviction under the Edmonds-Tucker cohabitation statutes. The court sentenced him to a one-year jail term and forfeiture of his voting rights."

I thought that was curious. "Was the convicted man a Republican?"

"I wouldn't know. Some lawyers ask their client's political leanings, but I do not."

I didn't believe him, but I nodded in apparent approval. "How is the Moore - Williams case proceeding?"

"That Republican rag has it all wrong, like usual," he began. Fall turned to look down the street. "I represented Moore, not Williams, and that Arizona paper wrote that my name was Paul. It's one reason I started the *Independent Democrat*. I'm tired of all the errors and lies."

"So, in fact, you represented Oliver's side. I thought that must be the case, but you're right, newspapers err and fabricate things sometimes — all newspapers."

Fall smirked at my lightly veiled accusation and turned back toward the temporary library. I had completed my research, and I stood and watched him.

Noise from the construction site of the new Academy at the south end of the Main Street drew my attention. The two-story building went up fast. Colonel Van Patten had taken a strong interest in the project and bank-rolled much of the construction. He paid the labor costs for the many native Indians employed on the project. The nuns projected the new school would open later that year.

I glanced back at the temporary library to see if Fall had reentered it. Instead, he surprised me, as he stood three feet away with his eyes trained on the new structure. "It will be a beautiful edifice when it's completed," he said. "This territory owes a lot to the Catholic faith."

I expected he wanted to bait me into some political statement and so I just nodded and turned toward home. Before I had taken two steps, Fall spoke again.

"Say, is the Colonel paid for his work as the special assistant district attorney?"

Few people knew that was Zio's correct title. It threw me off, and I answered with a hint of anger in my content and manner. "Of course. He does the work of the Territory, although it's a pittance compared to the value of his practice."

Fall smirked.

---

The following week, an article in Fall's *Independent Democrat* suggested that Special Assistant District Attorney

Fountain was flimflamming the territory. With twisted logic, Fall wrote, "Furthermore, he is using these Democratic dollars to fund his Republican campaign." While his statement was technically true. Zio had been hired by the Democratic administration, but he could have financed his campaign far more effectively if he had devoted more time to his much more lucrative private practice. Nonetheless, Fall's arrow found its target, and the damage was done.

Early in the year, his fellow members reelected Zio Commander of the Grand Army of the Republic and then in early February, the Masons voted him deputy grand master of the local Lodge. His status as the current Speaker of the House and his oratorical prowess put him in demand as an orator all over the territory. But he was selective. He often begged-off because of his court obligations.

The spring court circuit took Zio to Silver City. He had to fill in for District Attorney E.C. Wade, who was ill. He also took advantage of his travel to speak about the importance of statehood for the territory and how the proposed constitution could deliver for its citizens.

As was his custom, he sent a telegram that let us know he had arrived safe and sound, and with the date he expected to return. He concluded his telegram with "Here be dragons". We weren't sure what he meant, but it put Rosa and Mia Tia on edge again.

When at last he was home, Mia Tia and Rosa stopped him in the parlor. Mia Tia asked if the dragons were vicious. I stood in the doorway between the office and parlor. Zio laughed. "No, no. I'm sorry I alarmed you. It was an attempt at humor, which is always precarious in a telegram. But no, I remembered Wade's illness and that the ague had stricken me down there last fall as well. It just seems like disaster always befalls us in Grant County despite all the cases I've won there. Remember when Albert's horse died from the cholla attack?"

Rosa still had a concerned expression. "But what does illness have to do with dragons?"

Zio snickered, "Nothing, I suppose. I'm sorry if I've alarmed you. It's just that my ship captain's father collected old maps and he had — I don't know — at least one that had a 'here be dragons' notation. I supposed the mapmaker intended to warn seafarers away from a dangerous area. When I was young, my brothers and I would apply that phrase to some places in New York City."

The weekend before the Las Cruces district court session, Zio prepared for his cases and I had a contract or two to finish. At one point, he looked up at me and said, "You know Jesús, I don't pity District Attorney Wade. It wouldn't surprise me if the man was sick last week from the turmoil Governor Ross foisted on him. And now it's gotten worse as Ashenfelter has threatened to contest his position. If I was Wade, I'd just walk away."

Zio looked this way and that, then back at the papers on his desk. Before he could refocus, I asked, "Well, why can they do that?"

"That's just the problem. No one knows what the limitations are, and the politics muck it up. I believe Republican Governor Sheldon commissioned him in '84. Then, after the election that November when Democrat Ross became governor, Ross removed Wade and appointed Ashenfelter, but Wade contested his removal and won his case."

Zio raised his arms in frustration. "It seems Ashenfelter may file an appeal. It comes down to whether a governor can remove someone that was appointed by a legislative body. A court has never tested it. It could end up before the Supreme Court."

"Yes, that sounds like it could tie you up in knots."

"I've got plenty of other problems to deal with without putting my career in someone else's hands. That's why I'm content to serve as an assistant district attorney."

The next week, I accompanied Zio to the Las Cruces District Court. The docket was long, and the Edmunds Act cases added work that many court officials felt was outside the law's purpose. Undeterred, Judge McFie and his staff, which included Albert Jr. as court crier and bailiff, whisked through the cases as they and the lawyers performed like a fine-tuned instrument. Still, the court ran into problems as the session progressed. Minor offenses had flooded the courts. We had a good idea why the Edmunds cases mounted. We weren't sure why minor offenses had increased. Zio suspected the Democrats had 'encouraged' court complaints so the public would believe crime was on the rise.

On Tuesday, a jury convicted Dona Ana Democratic Party leader Charles Bull for 'insulting while armed' and fined him one hundred dollars. Charles Bruton, whom Mr. Diamandis 'introduced' to me, appeared in court on a charge of carrying a deadly weapon, but the court deferred his hearing until the following Tuesday when he was convicted and fined.

Zio had said nothing about the San Marcial land fraud cases for some time. I thought they had all resolved, but I was wrong. They ended at long last that session. The court dismissed conspiracy and perjury cases against the original Ring members, but they convicted Terrence Mullen, and he served time in the penitentiary.

After we returned to our office, I asked Zio why the United States dropped the cases. He shrugged. "Sometimes it is hard to know. Often, I'm not consulted. The accused had excellent attorneys, and they often filed for continuances. The government may have determined we had spent enough time and money. People fear they cannot win against the government because their coffers are limitless, but that isn't so.

"If nothing else, their attorney fees probably cost these men whatever they might have made on their illegal land deal ... and in the case of the surveyor Lampton, his life. It may look like they 'got off', but I would give odds that anyone of them in confidence would tell you otherwise." He gazed through the high window at the puffy clouds as they drifted across the sky. "Sometimes we just don't have enough evidence to convict."

Never one to neglect his obligations and promises, Zio did as he promised in April and used Fall's supporting evidence to get their client's conviction overturned on the cohabitation, which amounted to adultery under the Edmunds Act charge. However, despite smooth progress with the case, it was the last straw for Zio's efforts to work with the Democrats and with Albert Bacon Fall in particular. Zio never said why. Perhaps it had to do with their joint representation on the case or the Democrats' political shenanigans about the constitution question. Whatever it was, I never found out for sure. Regardless, the Democrats were not interested in a cooperative or even a civil relationship.

The Edmunds cases continued to grow and after the April session, it somehow spilled over into the Democrats' attacks on the proposed constitution. Father Lassaigne and even the *Rio Grande Republican* took the Democrats' bait in their quest to defeat the constitution measure. Their confusing rhetoric led many citizens to believe that the Republican's proposed constitution would diminish or outright remove the importance of the catholic religion in Mexican voters' lives.

Although John Good had left the territory, the court still had business with him. It found him in violation of his rental lease and in default on a mortgage note to Sheriff Mariano Barela. They awarded the sheriff with a judgement of $1,324.00. I doubt the sheriff ever collected on that debt. However, the story that Dimitri Diamandis presented to me, along with the recent court cases against Bruton and Williams, left me suspicious about John Good's supposed exodus. Fall had said he represented the side Oliver had joined. Still, I couldn't confirm the involvement of John Good or his allies. It shouldn't have mattered, but I couldn't explain it and so it distracted me. I needed to discover the truth.

# 52: The Truth Isn't Freeing

**May 26, 1890**

As was often the case, a multitude of events occupied Zio. Among them was the opening of the Agriculture College; the award of the contract to build the first building there; a party to honor the one-year anniversary of Judge McFie's placement on the Territorial Supreme Court; Zio's appointment by the Grand Army of the Republic to locate and maintain military records of Union soldiers in the Civil War and the ongoing lobbying for the proposed constitution. I have never known a man before or since that could do so many things well and still have time for his family.

As he refined his speech to support the proposed constitution, he stopped at one point and asked if I would listen to what he had written.

Before I could reply, he said, "I think this is very good, but I'd like your opinion." That, of course, signaled he expected I would remark that it was brilliant. What he read was good. It focused on how his constitution edits countered the Democrats' recent religious, racial, and cultural accusations about the GOP's public-school proposal.

Whether he was in front of a thousand voters or just me, Zio couldn't speak without his entire body being involved. I nodded my approval each time he glanced my way. I can't recall him writing anything I could find fault with. Rather, this exercise was about him gaining confidence.

Zio wasn't one to threaten consequences to convince someone, but at the end of his speech, this caught my ear. "A favorable vote on the constitution will assure prompt statehood; rejection means a ten, twenty, or possibly even thirty-year delay of this cherished goal."

When he finished, he looked at me for approval. "Sounds right to me, but do you think statehood will take so long if this one fails?"

"I do, Jesús. The congress barely approved the authorization to proceed with the tasks required for statehood this time. If we fail, it will take considerably more effort the next time to convince the congress and our citizens." He frowned. "And there's a good chance I'll be gone by then." He grimaced at the thought that he might never see New Mexico in the Union. As he sat back at his desk and picked up his pen, I saw my chance.

"Would you mind if I took a few days to visit a friend?" He was already engrossed in an edit. He hardly looked up, but nodded and gave a half-hearted wave.

As an afterthought, he said, "Just be back in time for the Memorial Day reception here."

When I arrived at Lee Well, Oliver stood in the late afternoon shade at the front of the porch. He had a stick in his hand and had scratched something in the dirt. When he saw me, he dropped the stick and started my way as I dismounted next to the watering trough where Ol' Nasty plunged his snout into the warm but clear water. I hadn't noticed that Oliver had approached me, and I took my canteen from the saddlehorn. When I turned toward the well, I almost ran into him.

He stuck out his hand. "Jesús. I'm so glad you are here." I looked past him, and Nettie and Mary appeared on the porch. As we walked to the well, they joined us. Nettie said hello, brought up the bucket from the well, and filled my canteen while Mary gave me a hug and greeted me.

"I'm glad to see y'all, as well." It was easy for me to fall into some of the cowboys' speech patterns. "What were you drawin' over there, Oliver?"

"Oh, that? I've been thinkin' on the layout for the ranch house I plan to build at the foot of Dog Canyon. Come here," he motioned with a wave, "let me show you what I'm figurin' on."

He picked up the yucca stalk he had used and pointed as he spoke.

"This here will be the front door facin' east. I like comin' out in the mornin' to face the risin' sun and there will be a porch, just like here, only bigger. I also like havin' the shade in the evenin' and it will help keep the house cool."

The lines formed squarish rooms in the dirt. "Only four rooms? I thought this was to be your grand ranch headquarters."

"Just to start. Someday, there might be a Missus," I thought he blushed a little, "and maybe some children, and then I can add rooms here and here." He motioned to either side of the proposed four rooms. "And we'll have windows, lots of windows, and the porch will be on all sides."

"That's impressive Oliver. Did you consider a design like the wealthy Spanish homes that have *placitas* in the center?"

He smiled. "That sounds interestin', Jesús. I might see if I can find a home like that, so I can consider it fully."

"Mesilla has a few of those style homes."

He shrugged. "You know I don't care to go west of the Organs. There must be other places I could find them, but this layout reminds me of the house Ma's second husband built, where I was born, in Taylor County. I dare say I wouldn't be comfortable in a Spanish home."

He took his booted foot and wiped it all away. "But you ain't come here to talk about my dreams. Come sit with me so we can catch up." He walked toward the house where the front door was open, and said, "Nettie, bring us a piece of that meat pie you made this mornin' and a cup of coffee. Tell Bill he can join us if he likes."

Nettie leaned out from the doorway and told Oliver. "He's up in the bunkhouse playin' cards with the 'boys."

Oliver waved as if to say, 'not a problem.'

He sat to the right of the doorway, and I sat on the left in my old broken-down Windsor chair. "This won't do," he said. "Move on over here and put your chair there." He pointed to a place about three feet in front of him.

I did as he asked. "Now," he said, "I know you were addled in the head — been over a year now, eh?" he winked and smiled. I didn't remember him as someone to joke around. Perhaps he felt relaxed now that the Walter Good case was all but resolved. "Surely, you ain't ridden seventy miles just to hear my voice. Out with it. What's on your mind?"

I took a deep breath. "I guess I'm confused about somethin'."

"Yes."

"Well, it doesn't seem important now that I've ridden all this way."

"A long ride clears the mind. Your horse is watered and fed," he motioned to one of the hands that had put a feed bag on Ol' Nasty. "You can turn right around and head back if you like, but you know, or maybe you don't, when you lie in your bed tonight, it'll still be in the back of your mind."

I knew he was right. "Alright then. Now don't be angry with me."

Nettie appeared at the door with two slices of pie, and Mary followed with two cups in one hand and a steaming pot of coffee in the other. Oliver moved a barrel between us for the women to set our vitals.

Mary took two forks from her apron pocket and handed them to us. "Good thing y'all ain't enemies and this ain't steak. I wouldn't want to hand y'all knives." She smiled, and we laughed, which broke our slight tension.

We took a few bites and sips, and then Oliver eyed me.

"I just can't get this Bruton and Williams case out of my mind. Now, I know it's not my business … ." That was when I realized I shouldn't have come. It wasn't any of my business.

Oliver picked at the last bite of pie. "You mean Fitzgerald Moore?" He scooped up the last bit of pie and put it in his mouth. Oliver washed it down with a swallow of the coffee. "He's a cousin of Charlie's."

I should have suspected that. "Alright."

"Charlie came to me with Moore's story about how Bruton had swindled him. As I think you know, Charlie was a big help to me and mine. We stick together over here and when someone comes to me and says they need help, well, they'll be there for me when *I* need it someday."

I finished my pie and poured another cup of coffee for the two of us. We sat in silence. Oliver knew the reason I came made me uncomfortable. He would say that if you had tough questions to ask him, your distress was the price you paid for putting him on the defensive.

"Why did you hire Fall to represent you?"

"You're all confused there Hey-you — I mean Jesús. You must have read the papers. Moore hired Fall. I had no need for him. But, yes, I recommended Mr. Fall to him."

"Why didn't you suggest Colonel Fountain?"

"He's a prosecutor."

"But that was a civil case, and he could have taken it, and I could have helped you ... I mean, Mr. Moore."

Oliver bent over in frustration. "Jesús, Fountain has been on the prosecutin' end of every situation that's involved me." He turned back to face me. "Why would I hire someone that has always been tryin' to see me jailed?"

I pursed my lips in frustration. Before I could reply, Oliver continued. "Albert Fall understands us folk over here. He knows that Fountain and his ilk don't understand that we have our own ways of keepin' the peace and it don't haveta be in nobody else's hands. This business of paperwork and waitin' for grand juries and trials takes too long. A crime punished right away will deter bad men faster than gittin' hung two years after the fact."

"But Fall only became a lawyer a year ago, and the Colonel has been one most of his life. He's gotten lots of people off ... I mean to say, he's gotten innocent verdicts for lots of people as a defense lawyer."

"You're not listenin'." Oliver pounded his fist on his knee and his voice got louder. "Fall knows how to keep us folks over here out of jail and the courts so we can make a livin' for ourselves and protect our families. You wait and see. The man's a genius when it comes to protectin' us. What he's done for me, Jim, and Perry against the Goods and Fountain is just a hint of what he can do. Fountain might be good at swayin' a jury, but Fall will keep us out of court entirely. You and I know the Goods brought on all the trouble over here. John didn't leave because of anything that happened in the courts. He left because we wore him out. He could see he couldn't intimidate us. Didn't have a thing to do with losin' in the courts ... which I hear he continues to do."

I was stunned into silence. I took a drink of coffee and Nettie came for our plates and to leave a fresh pot of coffee.

"You boys havin' a friendly visit?" I looked at her and smiled. Her cheeks were rosy, and her eyes were bright with joy.

*Marriage must agree with her.*

I could see the tension in Oliver's shoulders relax and I felt my grip on my knees loosen.

"Sure are," said Oliver. I smiled.

Nettie poured us a fresh cup from the hot coffee pot. "I was afraid you might be talkin' about the proposed constitution."

"You mean the one that wants to take the Mexican's religion away from 'em?" asked Oliver. "I can't say I care much about the Catholics one way or t'other, but when politicians start tellin' you who's Bible to read, well, I can't see how that's right."

I scrunched up my face and closed my eyes. "That's not what it says."

Nettie picked up the empty plates and cold coffee pot and went back inside. This time, she closed the door.

When it was clear she was out of earshot, Oliver said, "I've read it and that's what it says to me."

"You've read it wrong, then. That isn't what it intends or says."

"Jesús, you're a smart young man and you've had lots more book learnin' than me, but you gotta understand that the way I read and see things ain't gonna always be the same way ... well, how I guess you and Fountain does. I had hoped livin' with us had rubbed off on you. I guess it ain't. The folks over here are of a mind that the politicians in control have no concern for us." He paused, sipped his coffee, and wiped his mouth. "When it comes right down to it, it seems clear to Tularosans that if Republicans had their druthers, they'd druther see us pushed aside. We won't stand for it and when somethin' like your constitution borders on styfulin' folks you don't like, well then, we figure borderin' is just a small step from doin'."

His face was red, and the blood vessels stood out in his neck. He glared at the mountains. "I know you understand us, but ...."

I stood and walked out to Ol' Nasty. The cowboy had unsaddled him. Oliver followed for a bit and stopped halfway from the house. I gathered the reins in my hand and glanced at the stars. A half-moon had risen over the Sacramentos. I felt exhausted. "Think I'll just bunk with the 'boys tonight. I'll head back in the morning." More than anything, I had hoped for a path forward for the two sides that would allow me to feel comfortable.

Oliver sounded tired. "I've said too much — more than I meant to. You won't come back to us ... I know that. We want you to know that we will always have you in our hearts and that you are welcome at our doorstep anytime." He walked to the house, and I heard the door latch.

After I saw to Ol' Nasty's needs, I went to the bunkhouse. The familiar smells of hard-worked leather, sweaty stockings, tobacco and stale beer made me smile.

The card game was still on. I watched for an hour or so. Bill McNew wasn't the poker player that Oliver was, but then few were. He left after Stumpy busted him. After McNew left, Shorty asked if I wanted to join them.

"You fellas know I'm not a card player."

Stumpy said, "Well, ya look a little down in the mouth. I thought playin' cards might pull you out of your gopher hole." Just then, Eliseo strummed his guitar and Darkie, the black cowboy, sang along. It was a ditty I hadn't heard before. That lightened my mood, and I later retired with thoughts of rising early to make further amends with Oliver and do my Tai Chi.

The next morning, the clip-clop of horses' hooves awakened me. I wasn't accustomed to the ranchers' early hours, and I rushed out in my drawers to catch Oliver as he turned his white stallion to the south. He saw me and stopped.

"Headin' to El Paso," he said. "You goin' that uh-way?"

"No, I just didn't want to leave things as we did last night."

Oliver shifted in his saddle and looked ahead toward El Paso. He spoke before he looked back at me. "Well, Jesús, if anyone was to be apologizin' it was probably me, but words ain't fists or bullets and most of the time I don't worry too much about hurtin' somebody's feelins … 'specially when we know each other like you and I do."

"I suppose I'm too soft-hearted, Oliver, but I didn't like how I felt about our discussion."

He shifted in his saddle and gazed off to the south again. I was still in my drawers. We knew it wasn't possible, but the desert appeared so flat that a person might expect to see a hint of El Paso eighty miles away. "I know you want Fountain and me to see eye to eye, and for your sake I wish it could happen, but that would mean I had forsaken all that my pa and them that came before him believed in." He turned back to me. "Now, you can continue to try to match us up, if you like. It won't affect our friendship unless you help him come after us for somethin'."

With that, he slapped his reins on his horse's flanks, and they darted south. My ride back to Las Cruces, as always, was filled with competing thoughts and few answers. I looked forward to my morning Tai Chi ritual and stopped at the White Sands to do it.

# 53: Fishy Story

June passed like many other Junes. The weather was sunny and hot. Siestas resumed and yuccas bloomed as children ran barefoot through the dusty streets. Zio's evening Memorial Day celebration for past California Column comrades had become stale, but the parade was exquisite. Zio donated a handsome flag embroidered by Marianita which preceded his forty Grand Army of the Republic members of the Sheridan Post as they marched in perfect union down Main Street.

An injunction case needed to be heard the second week in June. Interested parties packed the sweltry courtroom as Zio and Wil Rynerson represented a Lincoln County rancher in a water diversion suit. Zio's client accused a neighbor of diverting his water. Both ranchers contended they had first right to the flowing stream. Albert Fall and Attorney Young represented the accused.

In mid-June, the Republican Central Committee called a special meeting in Santa Fe. Zio and J.H. Riley attended on behalf of Dona Ana County while Wil Rynerson served as Mariano Barela's proxy.

When Zio returned, he reported it was an enthusiastic meeting buoyed by the likelihood that they would still accomplish statehood. He said they acted on resolutions regarding statehood, land court problems, and the repeal of the McKinley Act. That legislation had removed ore tariffs, and the result was a flood of lower priced ores from Mexico. That crippled our mining industry. Their resolutions had no legal effect, but they carried considerable weight with the Territorial representatives in Washington and gave them the ammunition they needed to lobby for legislation.

A few days before Zio journeyed north for the Republican Central Committee meeting, he was honored by a group of boys that had assembled a junior militia. They had applied to the governor for recognition and commissions for their officers under the name of "The Fountain Rifles."

About that time, Tommy asked if I wanted to come with him and Jack on a fishing trip with some younger boys to the Ruidoso. Any fishing expedition with Tommy and Jack was sure to be fun, and I needed a distraction from my predicament. We cleared it with Zio, with the assurance that one of the boy's parents would accompany us.

We spent three glorious weeks on the trip and caught fish almost every day on the Rio Ruidoso. The cooler air refreshed us and when we weren't fishing, we swam or played games. Tommy was in his glory as he pulled practical joke after practical joke. I reminded him he had pledged to give up on his pranks. He just smiled and said, "There's no harm in it. Just a bit of fun, that's all."

Granted, there were lots of laughs, but when a late-night prank earned him everyone's anger, Tommy stopped. Or did he?

We lost count of how many fish we caught, but we didn't lose count of how many horse thieves we captured.

One night, about halfway through our stay, something awakened me. The campfire had died to embers and the waxing crescent moon flickered in and out of puffy clouds. I lay still as I wondered if Tommy had resumed his pranks.

It was quiet for a short time, and I had nearly fallen asleep again when one of our horses made an unfamiliar noise.

"What was that?" whispered one of the younger boys that lay on my left.

"Never mind, it's only Tommy up to his old tricks," I said.

"It's not me," murmured Tommy on my right.

I then heard the other horses shuffle and snort.

Tommy jumped up, followed by Jack and me. We drew on our breeches, and Tommy and Jack grabbed their pistols. Tommy told us to flank the string where we had tethered the horses while he went toward the sounds.

I could see, even in the dim light, that Ol' Nasty was gone. There was thick undergrowth in places, but I walked as fast as I could down the valley as I stumbled over exposed roots and scattered stones. I could hear Tommy and Jack to my right as they also picked up their pace. We continued down the river for several hundred yards as the crescent moon ducked in and out of the clouds. Suddenly, I found myself face to face with my horse. As the man threw a saddle on Ol' Nasty, he nickered at the scent of me. The man stooped over as he reached under the horse's belly to grab the cinch. I think I surprised him as much as he surprised me. He must have seen my feet through Ol' Nasty's front legs, for he made a quick move and I assumed he went for his six-gun. Just then, Tommy appeared behind him and pushed his pistol into the man's back. The man surrendered, and we marched him back up the valley to our camp.

When we reached camp, the others had stoked the coals into an agreeable fire. A pot of coffee gurgled on a well-positioned rock as the fire's smoke rose, randomly shifting direction with the rise and fall of the night breeze.

In the glow of the flames, I could see the man was skinny and short, perhaps as short as I had been when I arrived in Las Cruces. His hair was matted, and his beard was a gray tangled mess. I imagined he was younger than he looked. He struggled to keep his arms stretched to the sky.

As I examined him, his hand went to his gun-belt, and I realized no one had taken the man's gun from him. The wind shifted and with a brief gust; the smoke went into the man's eyes as he pulled his six-gun. Everyone ducked for cover while the man emptied all six shots before scrambling back down the valley. When he stopped shooting, Tommy and Jack fired back into the darkness, but the man was gone.

Jack stood guard for the rest of the night, but with the excitement of the event and the discussion that ensued, no one slept a wink. When we gathered around the campfire the next morning, Tommy said to me, "I thought you took his six-gun when we surprised him."

"And I thought you had when you stuck your own gun into his back. I turned back to get Ol' Nasty, and it was so dark I couldn't see it in his holster, so I thought you took it from him while I had my back turned."

"I guess I couldn't see it either. Darn, this would have made a good story for the *Republican*, don't you think?" We laughed, but Tommy's face revealed mischievous machinations.

We returned home on July third in time for the fourth celebrations. After Tommy's militia company finished their parade duties, I couldn't hear what they said, but I watched as Tommy and the *Republican* editor, Charles Metcalfe, gestured back and forth. Charles had heard so many stories from Tommy. I wondered what he would print this time — if anything.

Memorial Day and the Fourth had become mandatory reception events at the Fountain adobe. Zio always put a lot into the parties with his fellow veterans. This fourth was no exception. Besides many of his old California Column buddies, he invited the officers and men of his 1st Cavalry Regiment. I couldn't put my finger on why, but something was different about that celebration. Perhaps it was the sheer number of people or that Father Lassaigne entertained us with Bible stories that a soldier could embrace. Or perhaps it was the events that followed.

**July 5**

The next morning, having Tommy and Jack at the breakfast table reminded me of the Saturday breakfasts we had when I first arrived at the Fountains. I reflected on how complete things would have been if Larlo and Marianita could have joined us. But Larlo couldn't get away from his job in Pinos Altos and Marianita and Carl had their own Saturday morning breakfasts. Katie could now sit on the catalogs and handle silverware pretty well on her own. Big sister Maggie sat to her right and helped as needed. Mia Tia tried to keep tabs on Little Henry, who put his tiny hands into his mashed food and smeared it all over his face. It did no good to wipe it off each time, so it stayed there until he had finished his meal. He seemed to smile all through the meal and often erupted into a hiccuppy laughs. For a while, the little man had tried to throw food, but thankfully, Mia Tia had broken that habit. Zio ate his *mollete*, then sipped on his coffee as he scanned the *Rio Grande Republican* for interesting articles to share

He glanced at the front page. "Ah, yes, another federal lands timber cutting land court case. I'm not sure why this seems to bother our government, but as their appointed attorney, it is mine and others' responsibility to enforce the laws of the land."

As he turned to page two and folded the paper in his special way, Jack asked, "Papa, some *vaqueros* at Rynerson's Ranch have told me about the *Gorras Blancas*. Some of my friends say they want to join them in Las Vegas. They say over a thousand men are there to protect the land rights of Hispanic people whose families have been there for centuries."

Zio sipped at his coffee as he listened to Jack. Before he could answer, Tommy said, "Anglos call them 'White Hats'. The things they do remind me of the Robin Hood stories."

Zio chuckled. "Well, yes, I can see how you might think that. I shouldn't laugh though because it's a grave situation. It's one reason that we have pushed the Congress to pass legislation to clarify how we should handle land grants. The possibility that the papers that granted land to an ancestor centuries ago could still exist is next to nil. And some courts won't recognize claims even when the citizens have the required paperwork. Our Spanish and Mexican friends have seen hordes of Anglos flood into the territory. They stake claims faster than the Latina and Hispanic families can make counterclaims. Even when they can make counter claims, some Anglo-controlled courts up north turn a blind eye." He flipped to the front page and pointed to a first column article. "We need the Congress to adopt our proposed bill, but here on the front page I see that the Texas and Alabama Senators are against it. If it fails, I'm not sure how we can resolve these cases fairly."

He turned back to page two and refolded the paper. "Ah, as I suspected, The President signed the bills that admit Idaho and Wyoming yesterday ... and it says further down the column that they both elected state officers and adopted their constitutions before the congress signed their admission bills." He raised his finger. "Just as we have proposed." He scanned our faces. "Another Democratic misrepresentation." We had become so accustomed to Zio's political railing that we didn't notice the anger that came with this remark.

"How about this?" He pointed to a brief article and showed us where it was. "This local note tells us, 'The highest that the fine thermometer, which hangs in Moreno's drugstore, has reached this summer is 92 degrees.' Hmm, I'm not so certain I trust it."

It seems Metcalfe had reported on our fishing trip and Zio noticed. "Oh, and here's an untitled article about you boys' trip to the Ruidoso." He read the account to himself, for we had told the story on the story-hearth the night we returned — with some slight embellishments. "Says here you caught 'hundreds of trout'."

Jack and I looked at Tommy. "Well, Papa," Tommy began, "you know everyone tells whoppers about how many fish they caught. I couldn't very well tell Mr. Metcalfe I didn't know how many we caught, now, could I?"

Zio stared at him over the top of the newspaper. "It also doesn't explain how this supposed horse thief got the drop on you.

You told Metcalfe that, didn't you?" Jack and Tommy couldn't see from their seats, but from where I sat, I saw Zio had a smile on his face.

Tommy's face tensed. "Why, of course I did. Perhaps the typesetters didn't have room in that column and had to remove some type."

"Or perhaps he just didn't believe you?" Again, Zio smirked out of his son's view.

Tommy fiddled with his fork. "He believed me about the fish." Tommy believed Zio had scolded him.

Zio lowered the paper and roared. When he had composed himself, he said, "Tommy, I do believe that if you ever tire of soldiering, you would be a fine fiction author."

Everyone at the table laughed and nodded. Little Henry threw up his hands as bits of rice flew, and we all laughed again.

After our pleasant breakfast, I endeavored to regain Rosa's good graces when I swept up the rice grains and collected the dirty dishes. She barely looked at me as I deposited them into the washbasin. I turned to leave, but then she poured the heated water from the stove into the basin and handed me a wash rag, soap, and brush. She had gotten the best of me in our little spat. I completed my implied task without complaint and went back to the office hoping I had gotten a little closer to restoring our ... I wasn't sure what to call it, but I knew it was something I wanted ... a lot.

Late in the afternoon, we received a telegram from Larlo that he and Lucy would arrive by train on Monday the seventh. He concluded his message with 'I have some exciting news'.

# 54: When You Least Expect It

**July 6, 1890**

Jack returned to the Rynerson Ranch and Tommy went back to his duty near the Van Patten skating rink where the 1$^{st}$ Cavalry Regiment had encamped. Carl Clausen and Marianita joined us in the Fountain pew at the front of the nave. It was one of those odd occasions when Zio attended church with the family. I secretly thought Zio wanted to see if Father Lassaigne still extolled the Democrat's nonsense about the proposed constitution.

With the recent surge of Edmunds-Tucker Act indictments, Father Lassaigne's homily preached the sins of coveting another's wife and relations out of wedlock. After the mass, I saw Zio and the good Father talking. Zio's fists were clenched, and Father Lassaigne's face was red, but they didn't raise their voices. I knew that Zio, while not devoted to Catholicism, believed in the sanctity of marriage and that the defilement of God's gift of sex was a sin. However, Zio wanted the church to stop fanning the flames the Democrats had ignited with their illegitimate use of the Edmunds-Tucker Act. By then he was convinced that Democrats had targeted registered Republican voters. After a few moments, the two calmed. They shook hands and walked together to the church entrance. Many of the parishioners had gathered on the steps and in the plaza.

Sheriff Mariano Barela, who had not attended church that day, stood at the bottom of the steps, away from the gathered parishioners. When Father Lassaigne and Zio appeared at the church's double doors, the sheriff motioned for them to join him. Maggie caught my arm as I walked past her. "The sheriff says he needs to talk with Papa. That scared Mama. Something bad has happened, but he wouldn't tell us."

Carl and Marianita joined us at the top of the steps. The sheriff took Zio out of earshot of the family and the others on the plaza. Barela said something and Zio half-bent over with his hands over his eyes.

Rosa's mother retrieved Little Henry and Katie, while Rosa ran to me with terror in her eyes. "What has happened?"

"I don't know, but something has. Something bad." Maggie escorted Mia Tia to us as the sheriff shook his head and patted Zio on the shoulder. Zio turned his back to us and wiped his face with his handkerchief.

Mia Tia put her hands to her cheeks. "*Madre de Dios.*" Maggie put her arm around her mother, who buried her head against Maggie's chest. Rosa and I reached to comfort her as well, and the four of us stood huddled as we watched Zio walked toward us with his head bowed.

Zio took a ragged breath. "It's Larlo. He's been shot in the stomach at Pinos Altos. He is still alive." The sheriff must have also told Father Lassaigne because he and many of the parishioners gathered to comfort us. Zio remembered something and stepped back as he checked his watch, "Nine fifty-five. The southbound train leaves at ten o'clock. We might still have time to make it and get the connection in Deming to Silver City. We could be in Pinos Altos late today."

Carl ran to his buggy and Zio and Mia Tia got in as he snapped the reins, and they sped off toward the depot. The rest of us stared after them in disbelief while Father Lassaigne continued to do his best to comfort us.

Everyone stood spellbound by what we had witnessed. After a moment or two, Rosa's parents suggested we go back to the

Fountain's adobe. While Rosa clung to my arm, her father borrowed a horse to get word to Tommy and Jack.

We had no sooner reached home when Zio, Mia Tia, and Carl came in the front door. We all rushed to the parlor to see why they had returned so quickly.

"Today of all days, the train was early. It pulled out as we approached. We'll have to wait for the evening one to Silver City."

Mia Tia's friends ushered her, Maggie, Marianita, and the children to the kitchen while the men discussed the quickest way to get to Pinos Altos. They could wait a couple of hours for the stage's scheduled Silver City departure, or they could drive their own carriage. The last option was to wait for the evening train, which would leave Las Cruces at eight forty-five.

Soon, the parlor, hallway, and kitchen filled with Zio's and Mia Tia's friends, who came to offer whatever comfort and help they could. Among them were the Rynersons, Van Pattens, Judges McFie and Henderson, the Branigans, Martin Lohman, the Hadleys, and Carl and Rosa's parents. W.H.H Llewelyn, Numa Reymond and others chatted in respectful tones. The women brought food and kind words for the Fountains and Rosa.

No one could imagine why anyone would want to shoot Larlo. As I walked around the parlor, I heard people say, "He's such a sweet boy" and "What a generous young man."

When Tommy and Jack arrived together, the family gathered again as sobs suffused the room and tears trickled down cheeks. Tommy repeated several times, "But he's alive and they will get him to a good doctor. He will come home to us. Just wait and see."

There was no consensus, but the majority felt it would be a mistake for Zio and Mia Tia to drive the distance or take the stagecoach since axles break and horses go lame. You could never tell when someone would happen by if you needed help. The tension of the dilemma showed in Zio's face as he and several others talked about the alternatives. Although his mind and body demanded action, in the end, he agreed it would be best to wait for the evening train.

Albert Jr., Teresita, and Albert III arrived from Mesilla as Tommy brought in some planks so the women could fashion a makeshift counter out of the game table for the baked goods and covered dishes people brought. Albert Jr. and Teresita immediately went to Zio and Mia Tia to hear what had happened.

About noon, a boy appeared at the front door with several telegrams from around the territory. Whomever answered the door invited the boy in and gave him a drink and sent him to the baked goods table. The telegrams were from the many friends Zio and the family had throughout the territory. Their brief notes offered their hope that all would turn out well.

As the boy opened the door to leave, Miles Wilson stood ready to knock. He spun the boy around and said, "Go get Colonel Fountain."

Zio had overheard Miles. He stood with the boy between them as Miles nervously creased and re-creased the folded telegram.

"Colonel sir," began Miles. "Right after I sent little Davey here away with those telegrams," he pointed to the papers in Zio's hand, "another message came over the wire."

By now, the rest of the family sensed a turn of events and gathered behind Zio.

Zio reached out. Mile's hand shook with emotion as he handed Zio the sheet of paper. The room hushed, but whispers persisted. Zio stood tall, took a deep breath, and unfolded the telegram. He read it to himself, then looked at Mia Tia with a deep sadness I never thought I would see from him.

"He is dead." That was all he said. A deafening pall fell onto the room; the groans were unanimous and dark.

Zio handed me the telegram. It read, "Edward passed at 9 a.m. stop His dying words were 'Father - Mother' stop more soon." I passed it to Maggie, who stood next to me.

As Miles said something about closing the telegraph office and leaving his son for other messages, Zio slipped past him and I followed onto the *porche*.

Zio walked to the end of the *porche* and gazed west as though he hoped it would bring him closer to his number two son. When he turned back, I was there, and he said, "It was a certainty he would die of such a wound." His voice softened. "I just hoped I was wrong." He grimaced and then threw back his shoulders. "I didn't want Mariana to go through this. I guess there's no reason to hurry off to Pinos Altos now."

Miles came out, and I shook his hand and thanked him. "I better get back to the office. I'm sure there will be other telegrams. If I get something more, I'll send it with little Davey here right away." He put a hand on my shoulder and the other on Zio's. "I'm so, so, sorry Colonel. This is the part of my job that I truly despise."

Zio nodded as a tear escaped from the corner of his eye near his nose. He tried to talk, but his emotions were raw, and a muted squeak was all that came out.

I handed him my handkerchief. After he wiped his reddened cheeks, he said, "I think we should go back inside."

Zio composed himself and appeared to remember something. He turned and called to Miles, who had walked toward the street. "Miles, could you please send a telegram to District Attorney Anchetta in Silver City? Please ask him to see that the undertaker properly embalms Larlo's body."

"Of course, Colonel. I'll see to it right away." Miles departed on the run with little Davey on his heels.

The entire family met us as we pulled together in another giant hug. The women wailed, and the men hoped the commotion drowned out their own whimpers and sobs. I had shed a tear or two and stressed over the situation before, but now the dam burst, and although tears flowed, I tried to maintain a strong demeanor. Rosa stood with her parents as they tended to Little Albert and Katie. She saw my distress, left the children with her parents and came to me.

The family gathered near the front door as we greeted new arrivals and thanked those that had decided there was nothing more to be done. But most hoped additional information would arrive and stayed. Despite the presence of so many of Zio's influential and personal friends, he didn't leave Mia Tia's side the entire day.

Rosa put her hand on mine, and I clasped it. She didn't resist and instead moved closer. "I'm sorry," she whispered in my ear. I tried to smile, but it triggered tears again, and my mouth scrunched as I suppressed a sob. Through my blurry, reddened eyes, I saw an expression from Rosa that was probably for Larlo, but I thought it might have been for me. My selfish thought flashed guilt over me, and I turned away from her.

When I regained control, I looked at her and said, "I didn't know him as well as Tommy and Jack, but he still felt like a brother to me."

"Yes, he was always good to me, as well. But when I said I was sorry, I meant that I'm sorry for how nasty I have been to you all these months over what happened on Main Street. I guess you know what violence does to me."

Rosa surprised me when she leaned into me and squeezed my hand; I melted. "Well, it was my fault. Now I know how I should handle it."

"You would pull the man off the other man and tie him up?"

"No, we just should have walked on past them."

Despite the somber occasion, Rosa laughed, but she hid her mouth with her free hand and made a quiet huffing noise, which made me laugh, too, and we ducked into the corner to compose ourselves.

When we had recovered, the two of us strolled between groups of people in the parlor and thanked them for their condolences. Everyone had a story about Larlo, and they wanted every family member to know it. Eugene Van Patten and Captain Branigan had ridden with Larlo when he was part of the militia company that fought Indians. Branigan reminded us, "He's still," the captain winced, "or at least he was the color guard for our company."

Several people remarked on several baseball plays that they had seen him make on the diamond and a couple of his close poker playing friends reminded us that Larlo loved poker. "He loved to win, but he would never cheat."

When we came to Marianita and Carl, he said, "Marianita may be the socialite of Las Cruces, but if you needed to liven up your gathering, you best invite Larlo. I've seen the dullest parties become rousing successes when he walked in the door."

The room loosened up as everyone shifted to memories of good times with Larlo. Tommy came to me with the memory of the Harry Snatch telegram practical joke that Miles and I played on him. Tommy said, "I'm still not sure if I know what it meant." The fact he said it in front of Rosa proved he still didn't understand. Fortunately, Rosa didn't either.

Jack's memories were of Larlo as his protector from boys that tried to tease him about his splotchy scarred face. "He was angry with Tommy about that, but brothers stick together." Tommy and Jack reminisced about their first trips to a saloon with Larlo for a beer. Jack put his arm around Tommy. "I'd like to hoist one in tribute to him with you, brother." They went off to see if there was beer in the adobe.

It hit me that Larlo and Lucy were supposed to arrive with some big news, and we all expected they would announce their engagement.

As the afternoon warmed, the front door remained open, and the women shielded flies from the food with tea towels. As Rosa and I looked for something to eat, little Davey appeared on the doorstep again. He handed his message to Carl, who had been on the *porche*. Davey followed Carl inside as he looked for Zio, who came to read it. I could see it was a longer message addressed to Editor Metcalfe of the *Rio Grande Republican*. When Zio finished, he frowned and asked Carl to read it to the crowd.

It helped that Carl was taller than most people in the room. He began as Zio stood next to him. "From Mr. Robert Nash, editor of the *Pinos Altos Miner*, who was at Pinos Altos at the time of the shooting of Edward Fountain." I heard Larlo called by his given name so infrequently that at first, I thought he was talking about someone else. Carl read that Mr. Nash reported he had spoken with Edward an hour before his death and learned of the circumstances of the incident. Carl glanced at Zio for confirmation that he wanted him to continue, and Zio nodded.

"'Young Fountain was the successful competitor of the baseball match among the miners of Pinos Altos on the Fourth of July and received several money prizes which he expended on the evening of the fifth, as he entertained his many friends. They were at his boarding house and Lucy had cooked for them. The party went on into the night and everyone, including Lucy, became intoxicated. As will happen in those situations, there was a disagreement, and she and Edward argued. Edward thought that Lucy was too close to one of his friends. Lucy swore at Edward, and he replied he would not quarrel with a prostitute.'"

The crowd gasped and Carl stopped, but Zio said, "Please continue Carl, we must reveal the truth because the lies would be far worse."

"Edward was walking away and had got about fifteen steps from the house when the woman — Lucy, fired the fatal shot."

The gathered friends gasped again, and Carl read ahead to decide whether to continue. "But it says here that she only intended to scare Edward and the other boys away. She didn't try to hit him." Carl resumed reading.

"She said she had no intention of shooting anyone. Young Fountain lived about seven hours after being wounded; and an hour before his death, he was conscious and sent a verbal message to his father, Colonel Fountain. He said, 'Lucy was not to blame, as she did not know what she was doing.'"

Many people in the room knew Larlo and Lucy had courted. The reaction to this last sentence sent a prolonged mournful groan through the room followed by remarks like "That is so much like Larlo," and "He would take responsibility if he could, and he did."

Late that evening, everyone returned to their respective homes. Zio had said he bring the body home alone, but Tommy suggested he and his father should wear their military uniforms, which befit his brother's status as the 1st Cavalry Regiment's color sergeant.

When everyone had left, we gathered at the supper table. Rosa asked if she could stay and clean up. Mia Tia felt it was too much to ask and told her to go home, but Rosa insisted. As she poured the kettle of boiling water onto some of the soiled dishes, she said, "You know, I once hoped that Larlo and I would ..." she stopped and covered her mouth, then faced us with her hands on her hips. "But he was a gentleman. He told me, 'I love you like a sister, Rosa, we all do.'"

With that, Mia Tia motioned for her to come and sit between her and Maggie. I don't think anyone slept that night.

# 55: Pomp and Circumstance

**July 7, 1890**

Tommy and Zio got into their dress uniforms several hours before they needed to get to the station for the seven thirty-six train. Jack and I went along to the depot, where the stationmaster and other staff extended their condolences. The train was late, and the sight of the two of them on the platform has stayed with me for all these years. Tommy had Larlo's uniform draped over his arm and Zio stared to the west, deep in thought. Jack and I waited with the wagon until the train arrived.

While Zio and Tommy were gone, several other people came by the adobe to extend their condolences and apologize for their late arrival. They said they had learned what happened late the previous night or that morning.

Just past noon, a middle-aged man arrived and asked Rosa if he could speak with the Colonel. I was in the parlor and told him he and Tommy had gone to Silver City.

He removed his hat and stepped inside. "I have something to tell the family regarding Edward." Rosa and I escorted the man to the supper table and Rosa offered him something to drink or eat from the previous day's food.

"No, thank you. My name is Jack Younger, and I am the general manager at the old Stephenson Mine. I just thought you would want to know that Edward was eager to return to Las Cruces to become my primary assistant. We didn't get to know each other well, but he came highly recommended. I'm so sorry I'll not have a chance to work with him and get to know him better. Please pass my condolences on to the Colonel and the rest of the family." He shifted between his feet and fingered his hat. "I don't want to impose on you. I will be at the funeral. When is it?"

Mia Tia, still somber, said, "We appreciate you letting us know about Edward's plans. The funeral will be at St. Genevieve's tomorrow morning at ten and the burial will follow at the Catholic Cemetery."

"I'll be there, ma'am. And please, if I can do anything, all that is required is that you ask."

Mia Tia attempted a smile, and the man said, "No need to bother further with me; I can show myself out."

---

Zio and Tommy rode in the baggage car with Larlo's body on the way back to Las Cruces. By the time they arrived, Zio had gotten Larlo into his dress uniform. They brought the casket home and placed it on top of the game table in the parlor. Zio, now dog-tired from lack of sleep and stress, struggled to place a flag in the coffin and to drape the regimental colors at the coffin's foot.

The next morning, Mia Tia and her daughters arranged flowers over the bottom half of the split topped coffin. The top would remain open during the funeral mass with Larlo exposed from the chest up. The militia's field staff officers were pallbearers, and there was quite a procession from the Fountain home to St. Genevieve's. The Sheridan Post of the Grand Army of the Republic followed an armed escort of the Sons of Veterans. Behind them came companies A and B of the 1st Cavalry Regiment of militia, with a lengthy string of friends in carriages from Las Cruces and Mesilla trailing behind. Father Lassaigne began the service. "Young Edward, whom we all lovingly called Larlo, was just twenty-two years, nine months and eight days old. He was taken before he could fully impress us in his prime. But impress us he did, with such promise that it is a tremendous loss for all of us here today, and indeed, for all humanity that might have had even a short time with him had he lived a full life."

The *Rio Grande Republican* reported a full column on Larlo's death and the services that followed. Next to the article were notices by The Grand Army of the Republic and the 1st Cavalry Regiment honoring Larlo with resolutions and tributes. The 1st Cavalry Regiment tribute to Larlo closed with an order that the regiment colors remain draped over his grave for eighty days, during which commissioned and non-commissioned officers would wear the usual badge of mourning. Eugene Van Patten, Lieutenant Colonel signed the order.

# 56: Rosa II

On the evening of the seventh, after the funeral, people gathered again at the Fountain adobe. Rosa and I had just seen someone out. "I feel numb, Rosa."

She turned and reached for my hand on the street side, where no one nearby could see. She looked up at me. "Yes, it's like we are living a dream … a frightful dream." She scanned the rugged Organ peaks. "Jesús, I am so tired. Do you think it's the lack of sleep or the dreadful news?"

"I think it's both, and the stress made it worse." We gazed at the majestic Organs, resolute regardless of what happened at their feet. "The weather is clear and there is a pleasant breeze from the east. I think we will get rain tomorrow. Come walk with me, will you?"

She smiled that memorable smile that I saw after I bought her the last scarf - the one that was still in my desk.

"Someone needs to go to my parents to get Little Henry and Katie. You can walk with me there and then bring them home. Wait for me while I tell Mariana that I'm leaving."

While she went to the kitchen, I slipped into the office and put the scarves into my pocket. I met her at the back door, and we walked a block to the edge of the desert before we turned south toward her parents' adobe. At first, we walked without a word as we listened to mournful melodies from the critters that skittered about as they prepared for dusk. The wind whistled through the yucca blooms and gobernadora. At any other time, it would have refreshed us, but in that moment, it struck a woeful chord.

As we walked through the night, I said, "I can show you how a ... well, I guess you'd call it an exercise ... no, or maybe ... a dance that could help you deal with your stress over Zio's safety. Or any stress, for that matter."

I could tell by the look on her face that she was about to mock me light-heartedly. "Oh, and how do you know how to do it if you don't know what it's called?"

"My friend Frank Rochas demonstrated it for me. He said a celestial showed him." I stopped and posed. "This is called the Prepare Form." She snickered. I continued and executed the moves just as Frenchy had taught me. "I don't do them every morning, but when things become unbearable, I sometimes do them in the evening as well."

Rosa was no longer smirking, and her eyes widened as I finished them moves. "It is so beautiful. I would love to try it."

"Meet me in the stable tomorrow morning before you come to work, and I will show you how."

We turned back toward her house as I reached for Rosa. She gave me her hand with an affectionate squeeze.

With my other hand, I pulled one of the scarves from my pocket. It was the yellow one — the first one I had bought for her. The airy fabric floated in the breeze, and she grinned. She stopped and pulled up her hair. I slipped behind her and tried to position it the way I had remembered. I was all thumbs, but she waited until I had finished and then deftly repositioned it with one hand. At first, I was afraid I had spoiled the mood, but her expression didn't change, and she pushed her shoulder against my arm as we continued toward her adobe.

After a few steps, she said, "When will I get my other scarf?"

It was an opportunity to tease her in a playful retaliation over her treatment of me during the last several months, but I couldn't do it. I pulled the plum colored one from my pocket, smelled it one last time, and handed it to her. "You must promise me you won't wear any other scarves."

"You won't buy me another?" she asked with a wink.

I laughed, and we glided onward. When we were within fifty feet of her family's adobe, I half turned to her and asked, "What are we to do, Rosa?"

She didn't answer right away, but as we neared her front door, she stopped and turned to face me. "I'm going to bed, and you are going to ask my father if you can court me."

# Acknowledgments

Once again, as I wrote the first draft, my mother heard me read every word during our 4:15 p.m. daily phone calls. Husband, Norman "Skip" Bailey Jr., was a valuable sounding board for thoughts, questions, 'what's that word' queries and as a partner for read-throughs.

The first two books have sold very well locally and those readers that wanted to know more about Jesús have enjoyed the prequel novelette, *When the Doves Coo*.

My undying appreciation goes to our local booksellers. Mike Beckett and the staff at Coas Bookstore; Paul and Cheryll Blevins at Mesilla Book Center; Alice Davenport at the Moonbow Book Nook, and Kellie Guthrie and the staff at the Barnes and Noble in the Mesilla Valley Mall deserve my sincerest thanks. Through them and Amazon sales, the word has gradually spilled out to the thousands upon thousands of former Las Crucens who long for stories about their old hometown or college haunts.

While the book reviews on Amazon are wonderful, they don't reflect the love I got from my readers. Please, please, please leave a review. Short and sweet is fine. There's no need to portray yourself as a critic. This is important because Amazon's algorithms drive potential readers to books with the most reviews and reviews also keep me plugging away at *The Two Valleys Saga*.

My sincere thanks go to Keith Bird, curator of the Gadsden Museum and descendant of the Fountain family, for his general support and encouragement.

Leah Tookey of the Farm and Ranch Museum went above and beyond to help me understand Tularosa ranching practices of the late 1800s. We had a memorable afternoon in her office at the 'Farm and Ranch'. By the way, if you ever have a chance to visit the New Mexico Farm and Ranch Heritage Museum in Las Cruces, don't miss it!

While I'm mentioning museums, I want to thank the Alamogordo Museum of History for their information and support regarding family histories in the Tularosa Basin.

My beta readers deserve credit for trudging through a draft that needed a lot of editing. Thanks to Peggy Hawbacker, Larry Murley, and my sister Susan Armstrong. To all that have helped, I'm not just noting your efforts. I want you to know I valued and appreciated every minute you spent. Special thanks to my sister who has read the first two books multiple times. I should be paying my mom and sister for the way they promote my books. (Don't tell them I said that.)

My biweekly coffee klatches with author friend Susan Findlay have been insightful and energizing. Her self-publishing and method experience has been worth at least as much as the seven bucks for a bagel with cream cheese, and coffee at Milagros every two weeks. *wink*

While I wasn't able to incorporate the information she provided, I want to thank Kathy McAllister for finding an audio recording of "Lizard in the Sun". In Frank Dobie's book *Cowboy People,* he suggested it was the basis for many night herd songs.

Karl Lambauch, a local Archaeologist/Historian, was always there to answer my questions and especially regarding historical information about his archaeological dig at Frenchy Rochas place. He has also relayed insights from Oliver Lee's ancestors.

The staff at Oliver Lee State Park helped me with questions I had about the guns that Oliver used and how he might have 'personalized' them for his own expert marksmanship.

Las Cruces own Branigan Memorial Library was a valuable resource. Library Assistant Charlotte Zimmerman also hosted me for a Mesilla Valley Book Club interview.

I have done more book signings and interviews than I can name, but I want to give a shout out to two. Old friend back home in Ottumwa, Greg Cloyd, offered his Pallister's Brothers Brewing Company bar for a book signing during the summer of 2022. His tasteful selection of beers were nearly as wonderful as the book lovers he attracted to my event. Second, Alice Davenport's organization of the "Celebrate Authors" book signings each September at the Branigan Library is unmatched in the crowds and camaraderie.

The Facebook group "Las Cruces Memories & Photos" continued to step up for local historic and cultural information.

The Basilica of San Albino staff in Mesilla provided the information for Colonel Fountain's visit to their cemetery.

And last, but certainly not least, I can't imagine being without the vast resources of The Library of Congress. Their staff has always been efficient and helpful. My research through The Library of Congress and NewspaperArchive.com enabled me to tie Jesús' life to the actual events and mood of the era as chronicled in the newspapers of the day.

# Character Refresher

**Jesús 'Chuy' Perez Contreras Verazzi Messi is our Protagonist (Fictional character) (Born: December 25, 1871)**

Jesús fictionally writes this and all the books in *The Two Valleys Saga* as a memoir some thirty years after the murders of Colonel Albert J. Fountain and his eight-year-old son, Henry. *The Two Valleys Saga* is his attempt to find closure and understanding by writing about the years leading to that fateful day.

**Colonel Albert Jennings Fountain 'Colonel', 'A.J.', nickname 'Zio' is fictional (Historic character) (Born: October 23, 1838)**

World Traveler, Civil War Veteran, Indian Wars Veteran, Texas Legislator, Lawyer, Special Assistant District Attorney, noted Politician, former Speaker of the New Mexico Territorial House, Actor, Newspaper Editor/Publisher, Cherished Citizen of Mesilla and Las Cruces.

Jesús and the Colonel decided on 'Zio' as the name Jesús would call him in book one. Zio is the Italian translation of uncle. Jesús and the Colonel arrived at the nickname by combining Spanish and Italian. Jesús' fictional father is Italian and his mother, Mariana's sister, is Mexican.

**Mariana Perez Fountain 'Mia Tia' nickname is fictional) (Historic character) (Born: 1 March 1850)**

Mia Tia's nickname comes from Jesús's family and their occasional mix of Italian and Spanish. Mariana was Jesús' mother's sister. Mia Tia was content with her prominent place in the administration of St. Genevieve's Church. She was a devoted wife and mother. While she went with the Colonel to parties and functions, she was content to be in the background.

### Albert Fountain, Jr. (Historic character) (Born: 6 December 1863)

The firstborn, Albert, was an overachiever. He was well-spoken and well educated and he becomes an accomplished lawyer, businessman, and respected citizen of Mesilla. He was the most responsible of all the children and the least rambunctious as a child.

### Teresita García Fountain (Historic character)

Albert Jr.'s wife and daughter of a Mesilla businessman.

### Marianita Fountain Clausen (Historic character) (Born: 23 May 1865)

Marianita was beautiful and a very talented writer, artist, and in-demand socialite. Of all the Fountain children, she was the most loved and respected by the community. She and Maggie attended the expensive Convent Academy of the Sisters of Mercy in Las Cruces.

### Edward 'Larlo' Fountain (Historic character) (Born: 30 September 1867)

Nearly everyone called him Larlo. Larlo was the party animal of the Fountains. He loves baseball and fishing. He enjoys his beer and has a standing poker night on Wednesdays when he is at home. Larlo seems destined to follow in his older brother's footsteps with a career but is not quite so committed.

### Maggie Fountain (Historic character) (Born: 30 May 1870)

Maggie didn't have the beauty of Marianita and was more reserved, studious, and creative than her older sister. She eventually became very active politically.

### Thomas Fountain 'Tommy', 'Tomás (Historic character) (Born: 2 February 1873)

Called Tomás by the girls in the family, the men and most of the rest of the town know him as Tommy. He was raucous, wild, and not very respectful of authority in his youth. Tommy was even more fun-loving than his brother Larlo. He was the closest in age to Jesús, and so they chummed around together often. As a youngster, Tommy was constantly in trouble. He was responsible for a gunpowder accident that scarred Jack for life. Although he was well educated, he never fit into the lawyering crowd.

### John A Fountain, 'Jack', 'Jacky' (Historic character) (Born: 31 August 1876)

In a misguided childhood experiment, Tommy scarred Jack for life when gunpowder exploded near Jacky's face, leaving him with splotchy scars. Not much has been written about him, so I have concluded that he was the shy child of the family. So far as I can determine, he did not attend St. Michael's in Santa Fe and so its inclusion is fictional.

### Catherine J. Fountain 'Katie' (Historic character) (Born: 4 September 1884)

In book three, Katie grows out of the toddler phase. She shows some of the Fountain spunk and mischief as the story progresses.

### Rosa (Fictional character)

Rosa is a fictional housekeeper and cook for the Fountains. She is slender and attractive. She looks upon the Fountains as her family, although she lives with her parents and brothers.

### Mateo (Fictional character)

Mateo is a fictional stableman for the Fountains. He is paunchy and jovial. He is extremely good at his job and, like Rosa, looks upon the Fountains as his family.

### Miles Wilson (Fictional character)

Telegraph Operator. Cheery and friendly, he took a more important role as a mentor to Jesús in book two.

# Cast of Characters

(Alphabetical order by last name or only name)

Altman, Emma (Historic)
Altman, Perry (Historic)
Altman, Rena (Historic)
Anchetta, District Attorney (Historic)
Ascarate, Santiago 'James' (Historic)
Ashenfelter, S.M. (Historic)
Baca, Pablo (Historic)
Barela, Saturnino (Historic)
Barela, Sheriff Mariano (Historic)
Baylor, John (Historic)
Benito (Fictional)
Bennetts, Mr. (Historic)
Bergère, Alfred (Historic)
Bergère, Eloisa Luna Otero (Historic)
Bob (Fictional)
Bowman, George (Historic)
Bracegirdle, Mrs. (Fictional)
Brazel, W.W. (Historic)
Bruton, Charles (Historic)
Buchanan, Mr.(Historic)
Bull, Thomas "T.J." (Historic)
Carlton, General (Historic)

Carr, Bill 'Good eye' 'Tuerto' (Historic)
Chuck (Fictional)
Coghlan, Patrick (Historic)
Cooney, Michael (Historic)
Cooper, Ira (Historic)
Cooper, Jim (Historic)
Cox, W.W. (Historic)
Dankworth, Mr. (Fictional)
Davey, (Fictional)
Davis, Governor (Historic)
Diamandis, Dimitri (Fictional)
Earhart, Bill (Historic)
Edmonds, Mr. (Historic)
Eliseo (Fictional)
Elizabeth (Fictional)
Fall, Albert Bacon (Historic)
Felipe (Fictional)
Field, Attorney Neill B. (Historic)
Fletcher, Thomas (Historic)
Foster, Mr. (Historic)
Fountain, Albert J. III (Historic)
Fountain, Albert Jr. (Historic)

# Selected References

## Printed References:

Bronson, Edgar Beecher *Red-Blooded Heroes of the Frontier*, George H. Doran Company, 1910

Cook, Mary J. Straw, *Loretto: The Seven Sisters and Their Mysterious Chapel*, 2002

Cleaveland, Agnes Morley, *No Life for a Lady,* University of Nebraska Press, Lincoln and London, 4th reprint.

Dobie, J. Frank, *Cow People*, Little, Brown and Co., Boston and Toronto, First edition, 1964

Eidenback and Morgan, *Homes on the Range*, A DOD Legacy Project

Eidenbach, Peter L. and Morgan, Beth, *Homes on the Range, Oral Recollections of Early Ranch Life on the U.S. Army White Sands Missile Range, New Mexico*

Gibson, A.M., *The Life and Death of Albert Jennings Fountain*, U. of Oklahoma Press, Norman 2nd printing 1975

Harris, Linda G., *Las Cruces, an Illustrated History*, Arroyo Press, Las Cruces, 1993

Heitzler, Gretchen, *Meanwhile, Back at the Ranch*, Hidden Valley Press, Albuquerque, New Mexico, March 1984

Keleher, William A., *The Fabulous Frontier*, University of New Mexico Press, Revised edition 1962

Kelly, Florence Finch, *With Hoops of Steel*, 1900.

Larsen, *New Mexico's Quest for Statehood*, 1846-1912

McNew, George, *Last Frontier West for the Altman, Graham, Lee and McNew Families in the Tularosa basin of South-Central New Mexico*, self published, May 1, 1983

Metz, Leon, *Pat Garrett*, U. of Oklahoma Press, Second Printing 1975

Owen, Gordon R. *Two Alberts*, second printing 2006

Owen, Gordon, *Las Cruces, New Mexico MultiCultural Crossroads*, Cultural Society of Mesilla Valley, Third Printing 2005

Parsons, Jack and Earney, Michael, *Land and Cattle – Conversations with Joe Pankey, a New Mexico Rancher*, University of New Mexico Press, Albuquerque, 1978

Poe, Sophie A., *Buckboard Days*, University of New Mexico Press – Albuquerque, Reprint

Prince, Le Baron Bradford, "New Mexico's Struggle for Statehood, Sixty Years of Effort to Obtain Self Government"

Recko, Corey, *Murder on the White Sands*, U. of North Texas Press, 2007

Rhodes, Eugene Manlove, *The Best Novels and Stories of Eugene Manlove Rhodes*, University of Nebraska Press, Lincoln and London.

Sonnichsen, C.L., *Tularosa*, U. of New Mexico Press, 1980.

Wheeler, David L. "The Blizzard of 1886 and Its Effect on the Range Cattle Industry in the Southern Plains." *The Southwestern Historical Quarterly* 94, no. 3 (1991): 415–34. http://www.jstor.org/stable/30238759.

Wimberly, Eidenbach, and Betancourt, "Cañon del Perro – A History of Dog Canyon"

## Historical Newspapers:

Deming Headlight
Las Vegas Daily Optic
Lincoln County Golden Leader
Pinos Altos Miner
Rio Grande Republican
Santa Fe Daily New Mexican
Santa Fe Herald
Socorro Chieftain
Southwest Sentinel

# Online References

(see ebook version for url links)

# What's next for Jesús?

# In Book Four

## Rosa, Rosa, Rosa

Can Jesús extricate himself from his dilemma?

Does New Mexico become a state?

Coming in 2024!

Scan this QR code to get my newsletter for updates and fun!

# About the Author

Mary, a retiree from a diverse career spanning various fields of land planning and design, found a new passion in writing when she landed a gig as a weekly columnist for the *Las Cruces Sun-News*. Her articles quickly gained popularity, leading her to explore more creative outlets. Her historical fiction play, *It is Blood*, got rave reviews after a well-received theater performance, inspiring Mary to embark on *The Two Valleys Saga*.

Drawing on her love for fiction and deep respect for history, Mary's meticulous research and attention to detail bring historical settings to life. The way she masterfully weaves historical figures with engaging fictional characters brings out compelling narratives that explore complex themes, which prompts reflection on the human condition.

In 2021, Mary's exceptional work was recognized when *The Mesilla*, a part of *The Two Valleys Saga*, won an award from The Historical Fiction Company.

Java, their beloved Cavachon, leads Mary and her husband Norman "Skip" Bailey on daily jaunts around their Las Cruces neighborhood.

---

Email Mary at mary@maryarmstrongauthor.com
Webpage/blog: https://maryarmstrongauthor.com/
Facebook page: https://www.facebook.com/maryarmstrongauthor
Instagram handle: https://www.instagram.com/contrarymaryauthor/

www.ingramcontent.com/pod-product-compliance
Lightning Source LLC
Chambersburg PA
CBHW030847030726
47495CB00005B/1413